"Katharine Britton's debut novel, *Her Sister's Shadow*, about time, memory, family, love, and death is a book for the ages. Because of the skill in the plot, the complex characterization, and the lyricism of the prose, the book is a deeply satisfying read. It's also very wise. Britton tells us that 'It's best to share secrets, but only if they're yours.' Words that ring true for all of us, but especially for the protagonist of *Her Sister's Shadow*."

—Ernest Hebert, award-winning author of *The Dogs of March*

"Anyone with sisters, secrets, or a family house where memories are stored will be held captive by this haunting story of love, loss, loneliness, and the healing light of truth. *Her Sister's Shadow* by Katharine Britton is the quintessential summer holiday book. It invites you to linger in the garden, breathe the salt air, listen to the hiss of the tide. And best of all, it is a story that will not let you go." —Sally Ryder Brady, author of *A Box of Darkness*

"Anyone who has lived with long-held family secrets will relate to this story of two aging sisters who can't escape their tragic past, or their abiding sense of, what—duty? nostalgia? love?— that reluctantly brings them together. Evocative, compelling, and exquisitely written, *Her Sister's Shadow* will make readers reconsider the resentments within their own family relationships, and how time is too short to let past events shadow the future." —Joni B. Cole, coeditor of *Water Cooler Diaries*

"In prose both evocative and precise, Katharine Britton creates the fictional town of White Head, Massachusetts, and the house in which the Niles sisters grew up, with such assurance that readers will feel certain they should find both on a map. *Her Sister's Shadow* is a story of loss, grievance, and the permutations of time, rendered with disarming honesty."

—Catherine Tudish, author of *Tenney's Landing* and *American Cream*

Her Sister's Shadow

KATHARINE BRITTON

BERKLEY BOOKS, NEW YORK

THE BERKLEY PUBLISHING GROUP
Published by the Penguin Group
Penguin Group (USA) Inc.
375 Hudson Street, New York, New York 10014, USA
Penguin Group (Canada), 90 Eglinton Avenue East, Suite 700, Toronto, Ontario M4P 2Y3, Canada
(a division of Pearson Penguin Canada Inc.)
Penguin Books Ltd., 80 Strand, London WC2R 0RL, England
Penguin Group Ireland, 25 St. Stephen's Green, Dublin 2, Ireland
(a division of Penguin Books Ltd.)
Penguin Group (Australia), 250 Camberwell Road, Camberwell, Victoria 3124, Australia
(a division of Pearson Australia Group Pty. Ltd.)
Penguin Books India Pvt. Ltd., 11 Community Centre, Panchsheel Park, New Delhi—110 017, India
Penguin Group (NZ), 67 Apollo Drive, Rosedale, Auckland 0632, New Zealand
(a division of Pearson New Zealand Ltd.)
Penguin Books (South Africa) (Pty.) Ltd., 24 Sturdee Avenue, Rosebank, Johannesburg 2196,
South Africa

Penguin Books Ltd., Registered Offices: 80 Strand, London WC2R 0RL, England

This book is an original publication of The Berkley Publishing Group.

This is a work of fiction. Names, characters, places, and incidents either are the product of the author's imagination or are used fictitiously, and any resemblance to actual persons, living or dead, business establishments, events, or locales is entirely coincidental. The publisher does not have any control over and does not assume any responsibility for author or third-party websites or their content.

PRINTING HISTORY
Berkley trade paperback edition / June 2011

Library of Congress Cataloging-in-Publication Data

Britton, Katharine (Katharine Fisher)
  Her sister's shadow / Katharine Britton. — Berkley trade pbk. ed.
      p.   cm.
  ISBN 978-0-425-24174-5 (trade pbk.)
  1. Women artists—Fiction. 2. Sisters—Fiction. 3. Massachusetts—Fiction. 4. Psychological fiction. 5. Domestic fiction. I. Title.
  PS3602.R5345H47   2011
  813'.6—dc22   2010054211

PRINTED IN THE UNITED STATES OF AMERICA

10   9   8   7   6   5   4

For Katy

Acknowledgments

With thanks to my early readers and supporters: Polly Medlicott, Nancy Lagomarsino, Margo Nutt, Cynthia Barton, Margot Lewin, Charles and Genevra Higginson, Dorothy Gannon, Chris Ivanyi, and the gang at the Writer's Table; and to my husband, Doug Britton, for making this journey possible; my agent, Jennifer Unter, for unlocking the door; and my editor, Jackie Cantor, for turning on the lights.

One

LILLI Niles planted her handbag on the ceramic elephant in the front hall of her Hampstead flat, hung her mac on the peg above it, and locked the door. Exhausted after a long day at her Whitechapel gallery, she changed into silk lounging pajamas, put on *La Traviata*, poured herself a large glass of a crisp Pinot Grigio, and began ladling chicken stock into a risotto on the AGA. So mesmerized was she by the fat bubbles rising and popping beneath her wooden spoon that, when the telephone rang, she actually jumped, then cursed silently, and, keeping one eye on the risotto, checked to see who was calling her. She would answer only if it was her assistant, Geoffrey, who knew never to bother her at home except in an emergency—defined as the gallery, or someone in it, being on fire. She had no intention of speaking with chatty Cybil Winslow from the London Association of Art and Design Education, or the depressive Minnie Mortimer from the Kensington Science Museum board, but she would happily have spoken at length with either when she saw the familiar overseas telephone number of her sister, Bea.

Lilli hadn't been back to her childhood home in White Head, Massachusetts, where Bea lived still, or seen her eldest sister since 1969, and always preferred to keep their conversations as brief as possible. They talked on holidays, birthdays, and when a friend or relative died. Bea, self-appointed archivist of the Niles family, not only knew all their cousins, first, second, and once removed, but kept in touch with most of them and would place them reverently on the family tree, much as she would the Christmas ornaments each year, each in its assigned spot, regardless of the size or shape of the tree. For Lilli, the names of those whom Bea would call and report as having passed on—Cousin Eugenia, Uncle Parker, and former neighbors in distant White Head, Massachusetts— were like characters from a barely remembered Victorian novel. She'd moved away from all of that, and from all of them—first to Chicago for most of a year, and then to New York City for art school, and finally, in 1978, to London.

Lilli considered not answering Bea's summons. She'd had a long day, and doubted that whatever news Bea had to impart would affect her much. Besides, they had just spoken the week before, on Bea's birthday. But, as Lilli was held hostage by her risotto, she would have been forced to stand there and listen to Bea deliver her news through the answering machine. Bea would begin, as she always did, "Lilli, you know how I hate talking into these things," and then, intuiting that Lilli was standing beside the phone, would add, "Lilli, I know you're right there. Pick up."

Lilli reached with her free hand for the receiver and said, "Hello, Bea."

"Lilli? It's Bea."

"Yes. Hello, Bea," Lilli repeated, and then waited. When Bea offered nothing further, Lilli asked, in an offhand way, just to move things along, "Who died?" and drizzled another ladleful of stock into the risotto. She scraped stuck rice from the bottom of the pan as she waited again for a response from her sister. Conversations with Bea were always awkward. There was too much between them: too many years, too many miles, and much too much history. Glancing up, she caught her reflection in the bottom of a stainless steel pot above the AGA. She looked tired and every minute of her fifty-eight years. Lilli gave her reflection a sympathetic smile.

"Randall," said Bea.

Lilli dropped the ladle.

"Brain aneurysm. It was very . . . sudden. Very, very . . . fast. Here one minute, gone the next."

Lilli heard amazement in Bea's voice. Whether it was due to Randall's sudden and wholly unexpected death, or the fact that he'd taken this momentous step without Bea's say-so, Lilli wasn't sure. Probably some of both.

Perhaps realizing that the situation called for a greater degree of delicacy and tact, neither of which had ever been her long suit, Bea then added, "I suppose I should be thankful. Not that he's gone," she quickly amended. "I didn't mean that. But that he didn't suffer. How could he? There simply wasn't time . . ." As she trailed off, Lilli stared at the broth and bits of rice now splattered across the stovetop, as though they might hold a clue about how to respond to this startling news. She looked up at her reflection. It offered no help. Lilli wished for the foghorn that bellowed through the soot-colored mist that would settle over White Head. When she was a girl, after the accident, she would go down onto the rocks, pick her way carefully along their slick surface, and shout her grief and guilt into the deep bass notes of that foghorn. Her kitchen, all stillness in pools of white light, offered no such camouflage.

She reached a tentative hand out to her reflection above the AGA, both seeking and offering comfort, thinking, as she did so: *Randall's dead.* And then: *Will his death change anything?* The tiniest tendril of hope began to unfurl inside Lilli then, like the morning glories that her mother used to plant beside the back door in White Head. The vines began as impossibly slender shoots, like silken threads, blindly seeking something on which to haul themselves up toward the sunlight. Where did they find the strength, the reserves to do this? By August, the whole shingled wall would be covered in blue trumpet-shaped blossoms and shiny green leaves. All from those tiny, tender shoots.

Randall Marsh had spent summers in White Head when Lilli was growing up. He'd stayed next door with his aunt and uncle and would appear at the Niles house just as the beach roses at the edge of the cliff began to bloom, string the hammock between two birch trees at the foot of the yard, and spend hours swinging Lilli and her younger sister Dori higher and higher, until they squealed with delight and terror, begged him to stop, and then pleaded with him to begin again. He would set up their badminton net and play all four sisters left-handed. Charlotte, five years older than Lilli, a terrific tennis player—good enough to turn pro, some said—was the only one who could get the shuttlecock past him. After their father died, it was Randall, although then only fifteen, to whom their mother turned for advice about how much to inflate the tires on the Country Squire and when to change the oil. Each September, as the roses began to fade, he would take down the hammock and the net and return to Maryland, a place then as unknown and exotic to Lilli as Marseilles. Lilli stood in the sterile stillness of her London flat, clutching the receiver to her ear, afraid if she loosened her grip she would drift away.

"Lilli?" Bea's voice jolted Lilli back to the present, where she smelled scorched risotto. She turned off the heat, crossed her kitchen, and sat down, straightening the knife, fork, and small salad at her place. A large blue-glass vase filled with yellow sunflowers stood at the center of her table. Lilli shifted it and reached up to a small shelf where a dried starfish leaned against several photographs and a small silver cup, tarnished and bristling with paintbrushes. The starfish, still, after so many years, smelled faintly of the sea. She pressed it to her cheek and stared around her compact kitchen at the gleaming cappuccino machine, pasta maker, and food processor, each in its place; at the pans and whisks dangling by size from polished chrome hooks, and the knives nestled into slots in their wooden holder. She compared it with the kitchen of her childhood, with its red Formica-topped counters rimmed with metal strips that snagged your sweater if you weren't careful, and with its towering glass-fronted cupboards, which held the best china, with its sprays of pink rosebuds. The windows were always filmed with salt spray and were hung with yellow café curtains patterned with green ivy that matched the stenciling on the walls, a project their mother had started and never completed. Blythe had mixed her paints on a little white enameled table that stood under a north-facing window. Lilli wondered where that table had gone and how the room looked now, pictured granite counters and Mexican tile, or perhaps highly polished hardwood, replacing the old linoleum—

"Hello?" Bea's voice, querulous and tentative, crackled across the miles. "Lilli, are you there?"

"Randall's dead." Lilli wondered if saying it aloud might make it seem more real. The full impact of Randall's passing was beginning to settle over her, subtly changing the landscape of her life, the way a snowstorm used to fill the yard and gardens in White Head, until the bench and sundial became transformed into soft white mounds. "I'm so sorry, Bea," Lilli said. He was her husband, after all.

There followed another long silence, and Lilli, having nothing else to say and wanting to be alone to examine the possible implications of Randall's death, was about to ring off, when Bea said, "I thought you might come for the service."

Lilli clutched the starfish so tightly that a tiny piece broke off one of the legs. "Oh, no," she whispered, staring down.

"No?" Bea sounded surprised and a little hurt.

"No, I . . . I didn't say no." Lilli cleared her throat. "I didn't say anything."

"Charlotte tells me that you're selling the gallery."

Lilli put the starfish on the table and fit the broken piece precisely back in place. She would need to navigate this next bit of water carefully. "When did you talk with Charlotte?" Lilli kept her tone casual and checked the time: six P.M. Which would make it what in Santa Barbara? She couldn't think. Numbers flew from her mind like spindrift in a stiff breeze.

"I should think, with so much time on your hands, you'd be bored silly. I know a number of working people and they all say the same thing. I thought you might . . . stay a few days."

"I didn't sell it. I took on a partner. In fact . . ." Lilli paused. Did she want to tell Bea that her new partnership with Felicity Grummage included a second gallery in Boston? Not really. Not at all. Lilli wanted to end the conversation. She needed time to think.

"Didn't sell it?"

"And I'm still painting. More now, that was why I—" She stopped. *Why am I telling her this? She never listens to me. She doesn't care.*

"I see. But you'll have some spare time. Won't have to paint every minute. Come for the service. At least."

Come for the service. Lilli regarded this invitation as she might an unusual piece of art she was considering for her gallery, studying it from various angles, holding it up to the light, trying to picture how, and if, it would fit. She had been back in the United States many times since moving to Europe, many more times, certainly, than Bea was aware of. There'd been art shows and installations, vacations and residencies, but she had never gone back to that small coastal town on its rocky promontory south of Boston, or to the house in which she'd grown up. With Randall gone, was now the time? She fingered the broken starfish. Was there anything to gain?

"I don't know what kind to have," Bea was saying. "Randall would never talk about death. Thought it would bring it on. Fat lot of good that did."

"Maybe he didn't think it mattered what he wanted," Lilli said.

"Perhaps not," Bea said, missing, or ignoring, Lilli's sarcasm. "After all, it's not as though he'll have to sit through it. I don't suppose you have any thoughts on that."

"On what?"

"What kind of service we should have."

"Obviously, Bea, I haven't given it much thought."

"Point to you. But could you give it some thought now? Perhaps you could come on a Sunday, and then we could have the service on Monday. That would give us time to get settled. Or we could have the service on Tuesday, if that worked better for you."

"Who said I was coming?" Lilli glanced at the red file folder on her desk in the alcove off the kitchen. It held the itinerary and travel documents for her trip from London to Boston the following month for the celebration of the gallery merger. Felicity had mailed invitations to Grummage Gallery's best customers, who would sip champagne, nibble fancy hors d'oeuvres, and admire Lilli's watercolors of English gardens. She hadn't intended for Bea to know about this trip or the gallery merger; Lilli's half-interest in the Grummage Gallery offered her a reason to spend more time in the United States. "When did you talk with Charlotte?" Lilli repeated.

"Just now. I called to tell her about Randall."

Lilli stared at the red folder, which seemed to intensify in color. She shifted her gaze back to the shelf and to the photograph that had been hidden behind the starfish. A Kodachrome print: Lilli and her three sisters, arranged by age and seated together on the bottom of an overturned rowboat on the beach below their house. Little Dori—her blond hair uncharacteristically curly that day from the Spoolies Bea had set it in the night before—holding up the starfish she'd just found; then Lilli, dark and serious ("Gypsies," her mother would tease when Blythe and Lilli, with their dark hair and eyes and their firm features, gazed together into a mirror); Charlotte, next, sturdy and grinning in her tennis whites; and finally Bea, the eldest, straight-backed, chin lifted, as though facing off with the future. Behind them, up on the rocky bluff, stood their large, shingled house with its multiple gables and octagonal sunporch wreathed with wisteria.

Next to that photograph stood Charlotte's wedding portrait: She and Graham Bottomley, with their arms linked beneath a rose-covered arch, were flanked by Lilli, Bea, Randall, and several bridesmaids and groomsmen. To the casual viewer of the photo, Lilli would seem to have an odd, glassy-eyed expression and forced smile. Randall, she remembered, had grabbed her hand and held it, hidden, behind the folds of her dress. There were a dozen tables scattered about the lawn behind them, all draped with white cloths that the sisters had anchored with rocks that afternoon.

She studied the photograph of herself and her sisters, wishing she could see more of the detail hidden within the snapshot—its colors had intensified but the details had faded, giving it a garish, surreal appearance—wishing she could see the beautiful gardens her mother used to tend from morning to night. In Lilli's earliest memories, her mother was always laughing, organizing games, and holding tea parties for her two youngest girls and their dolls. And she was full of pranks, like raising the small-craft warning flags whenever her mother-in-law came to visit. It was understood by those in White Head, and enunciated by the girls' grandmother, Lydia Niles, who lived in Charles River Square, that her son, George Osborne Niles III, had stepped outside his prescribed social circle when he'd married Blythe Giardino. She was clever, artistic, and eccentric. All the things George wished he were. And then George died young, leaving Blythe to raise four daughters, when all she really wanted was to make her odd sculptures of driftwood and flotsam, and to garden.

Lilli sagged back in her chair. She should go see Bea, who'd just turned sixty-seven, because, who knew? Here was Randall dead at sixty-two, and Lilli hadn't said good-bye, hadn't said . . . so much. Perhaps, if they had a little time together, she and Bea could set things right. Lilli doubted it. A visit might bring some closure, but she knew it would take more than one quick visit to close all the doors ajar in her past. Still, she would like to see the house—it held so many memories—and the cove and her mother's gardens. "I could see about . . . driving down for a day."

"You must spend a night at least. I've got your room all ready."

Lilli immediately wished that life had a rewind button, much as she had the previous week when she'd locked her car door with her keys inside. She wanted to see the house, it was true, but she did not want to spend a night there. It would be too much. "Is that motel by the harbor still there?" she asked, all she could think of in the moment. *Stupid.* She didn't want to spend a night anywhere in White Head.

"You'll be much more comfortable here."

"Harbor View, wasn't it?" Lilli asked, feeling as though she were standing in a queue and being drawn forward, not sure how she'd gotten there, what she was in line for, or how to break free.

"Still is. But—"

"Is Charlotte coming?" Lilli demanded more than asked,

her voice rising. Then, more quietly, she added, in what she hoped was a casual and offhand way, "Or Izzy?"

Lilli's imaginary queue suddenly seemed to stop. There was silence on the other end of the line. Lilli waited. Then Bea said, "All the way from Santa Barbara? I doubt it. Charlotte's having trouble with her hips, or knees, or something. Anyway, she doesn't like to fly. And Izzy . . . Well, Izzy wasn't really all that close to her uncle Randall, was she? I mean, she visited from time to time as a child, but she hadn't seen him for ages. I don't see why she'd come."

Lilli would have pointed out that England was at least as far as California, but Bea was saying, "So it's settled then? That's wonderful. I'll see you next month. Good-bye, Lillianne." And, before Lilli could either deny or confirm her plans, Bea had hung up.

"Good-bye," Lilli said to her silent kitchen with its gleaming appliances and ruined risotto.

AFTER SHE HUNG up, Bea sat for a moment at the wooden table set against the ivy-stenciled wall in her kitchen, smiling. She stood, using the table for support, stepped over to the counter, took a glass from the cupboard, and filled it with water from the faucet. She reached for one of a half dozen pill bottles lined up in front of the battered aluminum canisters stamped with the words *Flour* and *Sugar*, and squinted at the label. She replaced it and selected another, popped open the lid, and peered inside. She tried the label again and, still unable to make out the words printed there, scanned the room for her reading glasses. Where had she left them this time? Honestly, she was getting more forgetful by the day.

She set the pill bottle down and spied a pair of men's glasses on the windowsill. She put them on and peered again at the label, moved it varying distances from her face, and then held it to the light filtering in through the window and tried closing one eye. Seemingly satisfied, she pried open the lid, grimacing a bit as she did, tipped one of the white tablets into her palm, and considered it for a moment before popping two into her mouth and swallowing them with a long draft of the tepid water.

She stood awhile, gazing out the salt-filmed window toward the greenhouse, picturing Lilli running up the driveway in tears all those years earlier. Poor child. Bea had thought so often of saying something. But how could she? What was there to say? She turned and considered the dirty dishes stacked beside the sink. "They won't get any dirtier," she muttered. "Maybe my fairy godmother will stop by and wash them for me." She chuckled softly, then sighed and headed out of the room, massaging her hip with one hand.

LILLI PHONED CHARLOTTE as soon as Bea hung up. Graham answered and, after exchanging brief pleasantries about the weather in Santa Barbara and London, gave the phone to his wife. "Lilli! Hi! I'm putting you on speakerphone." There was a click on the line, followed by the sound of running water, the clatter of pots and pans, and finally Charlotte's voice again. "Are you there?"

"Yes, still here," Lilli said.

"Has Bea called you?"

Lilli could now hear chopping. "Yes."

"What's that?"

"Yes, Bea called," Lilli said, louder.

"I'm sorry, Lilli," said Charlotte, her voice distant, as though she'd moved away from the phone, then louder, "Quite a shock, wasn't it? Did she invite you to the service? I told her not to bother." *Chop, chop, chop.* "I said you'd never go back, so not to—"

"I'm going."

The chopping stopped. "Lilli. You're not." Her tone was half astonishment, half command. Lilli could hear Charlotte telling Graham, "Lilli's going to White Head," and Graham telling Charlotte that he could hear Lilli every bit as well as Charlotte.

"Are you coming, too?" Lilli asked, already knowing the answer.

"To Randall's service? Hardly. My knees have been getting steadily worse. Too much tennis as a girl, Bea always said. Probably looking at one, maybe two replacements this summer. But Lilli, why are you going?"

"I want to see the house again," Lilli said. It wasn't an outright lie; that certainly was part of the reason. She pressed the broken piece back onto the brittle leg of the starfish, wondering if the glue would hold. "And, I was thinking, with Randall gone . . . maybe now is the time . . ." Lilli wished Charlotte would take her off speakerphone so they could talk privately. Lilli wanted to ask Charlotte what, if anything, Randall's death might change. What, if anything, she could say to Bea.

"The time for what, Lilli? No, now is not the time. Now will never be the time. We agreed. Hand me that jicama, will you?" Charlotte said. "No, let's use the plastic plates and eat by the pool. Over the microwave. Cloth napkins."

"How's Izzy?"

"Sorry, Lilli, what did you say?"

"Nothing. Sounds like you're busy. I'll call you next week. Let you know how it goes."

"Yes. Please do. And, Lilli, promise me you won't say anything. Take it all out on one of those trays. It'll be much easier. Bye-bye!"

A MONTH LATER, Lilli stood in the doorway of the Harbor View Motel in White Head, Massachusetts, hugging her jacket against a sharp east wind. It was past eight o'clock and the sun, settling toward the horizon, was burnishing the landscape so it resembled an old photograph or, thought Lilli, a half-forgotten memory. Had she arrived earlier, she and Bea could have had dinner together, maybe shared a bottle of wine, something to help bridge the breach between them. She was anxious about this first meeting with her sister after so many years, unsure of what to say and how to say it. As it was, Lilli had called from the airport and told Bea not to wait. It had been a challenging day, arriving at Heathrow early, the inevitable delays, the long flight, a harrowing drive down from Logan Airport, with cars speeding past her in the breakdown lane. She stepped out onto a paved pathway that divided the lawn from the white-clapboard motel and stared toward the parking lot, past the Adirondack chairs, painted in bold primary colors, facing the harbor.

Below the motel was a stony beach, where two girls were playing. One had dark hair, the other blond. She and Dori had often played past sunset on the beach at Sandy Cove, and then raced up the steps that their grandfather had carved into the boulders beneath their house, plunged into a hot bath, and pretended they were captured explorers, being boiled alive. They'd shriek as the scalding water enveloped their cold feet, hands, and bottoms. Bea would rush in to make sure they were all right, and the girls' faces, already red, would turn even redder from trying not to laugh. Bea would sprinkle some of her prized Jean Naté bath salts into the water and tell them not to soak too long or their skin would prune, which was precisely what the girls wanted. They would then pretend they were two old ladies taking the cure at a hot spring in Arkansas, something Lilli had read about in *Life* magazine. Lilli's stomach tightened as she remembered the vivid, sweet scent of Jean Naté. Her muscles clenched further as she thought that soon she would be walking up those very rock-steps, be in that very house. The sensible thing, the safe thing, would be to climb right back into her rental car and drive back to Boston, she told herself. Lilli didn't think she had it in her. But she could call Bea, say she was too tired to come by this evening, and suggest they meet somewhere for breakfast before the service . . .

Lilli considered this as she watched the dark-haired girl on the beach below gather stones and hand them to her friend, indicating where to place them in the trench they'd dug. The fair-haired girl was smaller, as Dori had been. But Lilli wasn't convinced that these two were sisters; their interactions were too careful, too intentional. Not like girls who share a bedroom—many nights a bed—and drift off to sleep whispering to one another, until the whispers become dreams and, in the morning, it is unclear who dreamed what and who whispered what to whom.

But then, that was not true of all sisters, Lilli was reminded, as the dark-haired girl abruptly marched off up the beach, the blond girl calling after her. "Jessie," it sounded like. But Jessie—if that was her name—kept right on walking, trudging through the soft sand above the high-tide mark. She hoisted herself onto the retaining wall and hurried down the street toward the center of town. The one left behind simply watched her go, and then resumed her project, selecting more stones, laying them carefully in place, digging here, reinforcing there, before standing back to assess her efforts, seemingly unmoved by Jessie's abrupt departure. Lilli thought of Bea. She'd never once pressed Lilli to visit. Not that Lilli would have come.

Lilli struck out across the parking lot of the motel, not intentionally following the dark-haired girl, but curious. She decided that her jacket would be warm enough if she walked briskly. She wanted to get this initial meeting over—no need to stay long, a quick visit to assess the situation—and be back before dark. She glanced over at the beach, where the fair-haired girl sat, hugging her knees, chin on arms, surveying her handiwork, waiting, Lilli knew, to see if her channel would hold with the incoming tide.

Lilli quickly lost sight of the girl and became disoriented in the streets of White Head, which seemed to have grown much narrower over the forty years she'd been away. Some streets seemed even to have disappeared. Gone was the lane she expected to find behind the old florist, now a dog spa. Gone was Finch's Market, where their mother had "traded" for groceries, replaced now by an unattractive steel-and-glass restaurant. Gone was the Simmons Block, a large brick building that once housed a Woolworth's, where Bea used to buy Slinkies and yo-yos for Lilli and Dori, and small metal watercolor sets, and where she outfitted them each September with five new pairs of kneesocks and seven new pairs of Carter's underpants each. There'd been a hardware store, too, with smooth wooden floors, where Lilli's father had taken her on Saturdays in the winter. They would rummage through bins of different-sized nails—Lilli could still recall the chalky, solid feel of them—and come home with dozens in small sacks for projects that George intended but never quite managed to undertake the following summer.

She walked past the large, mostly Victorian houses that still lined the street leading down to the harbor. Some of the changes in this town were subtle: the shrubs bracketing the front doors of the houses a little larger, the shutters painted a different shade. Others were more blatant. The Wakeman place, for instance, had been converted into a retirement community called Beacon House, which also offered "progressive care." Lilli pondered this adjective as she studied the massive white structure, the one building in town that was easily as big as she remembered. Progressing toward what, exactly? Then she realized that it didn't only seem larger, but was. They'd added a whole new wing out back. She and Nancy Wakeman used to play jacks and pick-up sticks on the house's wide front porch, and later smoked cigarettes that Lilli had pinched from Bea's secret stash, beneath the very same porch. She could see several women chatting at a table in front of the bay window in the living room, where the Wakemans' Christmas tree once stood.

She continued toward the weathered-shingled yacht club, which seemed unchanged, except for a rusting gas grill at the edge of the parking lot. Lilli considered asking one of the young people on the front porch if she might look around inside, but she wasn't quite ready to confront the memories that might linger there, nor quite willing to discover that they'd moved on.

Beyond the clubhouse she found the shortcut that she and Dori used to take through the woods. The feathery branches of the tall cedars strummed a familiar melody in the wind. Halfway in, Lilli closed her eyes.

"What about skunks, Lilli? I'm afraid. Let's take the road."

"No time. We're already late. Just make a lot of noise. Skunks hate surprises. They won't bother us if they know we're coming."

"Promise?"

"Promise. . . ."

"Ready, Lilli?"

"All skunks go to Hell," Lilli whispered and smiled, hearing Dori's laughter in the call of gulls as she continued through the glade to Sandy Cove, thinking about the tensile nature of promises.

Several children were playing in the soft sand high up on the beach, their nannies on blankets, plastic coolers at their side. A large contemporary house occupied what used to be an empty field where her father, uncles, and male cousins—strangers when they arrived each year, inches taller than they'd been at the last visit—played football on Thanksgiving. The Niles house would fill with laughter and with Uncle Parker's sweet, earthy pipe tobacco, his tweed coat infusing the closet for weeks with the scent. Lilli scanned the bluff of pink granite at the far end of the cove for her old house: the rambling, comforting presence that once anchored her world, worried that it would be so greatly changed she wouldn't recognize it, or it wouldn't recognize her. But it was hidden behind a wall of vegetation, which struck Lilli as odd. Why block the million-dollar view?

Big-big, the name given to the immense rock formation at the center of the cove by those who lived around it, appeared less grand but still imposing, and so familiar that Lilli half-expected to see Dori waving to her from its top. The tide was out, and Lilli was tempted to walk across the narrow stretch of sand and climb up onto it. But when the tide came in, Big-big would become an island—or an ocean liner or battleship if you were young and had a very good imagination—and the water was very cold here, even in summer. She made her way across the cove, the smell of low tide stirring memories buried deep and sealed tight, like the clams they used to dig from the mud. Lilli had always admired clams' ability to dig themselves in so quickly. You don't expect much of a clam; they do only a very few things, but they do them surprisingly well. She spotted, at her feet, a lucky stone, which was what the girls called rocks with white bands of quartz running through them. The luckiest, they'd maintained, were those bisected with the widest swaths precisely at their centers. This one was blue-gray with just a sliver of quartz cutting diagonally across one end. She picked it up— she could use some luck, she thought, even if minimal and off-center—and pocketed it, palming its smooth surface as she continued along the sand at the water's edge, her pale footprints trailing behind.

As she walked along the beach, she occasionally glanced up, hoping for a glimpse of the house. At one point she caught the glint of sun on glass, the window in her mother's room. She pictured Blythe leaning out and calling to the girls, "Time for tea!" The girls would race each other up their grandfather's steps, the smooth, pinkish boulders warm beneath their bare feet, to find—standing on the wide lawn—a table, draped with a linen cloth and set with their grandmother's rosebud china. Several of the girls' dolls would be seated on chairs brought out from the dining room. Their mother, wearing a big floppy hat, a gown, and long gloves would billow out of the house, bearing a tray of lace cookies, baked by Charlotte, and a teapot—one of her colorful scarves trailing behind.

Lilli climbed the granite steps slowly. At the top, her way was barred by bittersweet, blackberry bushes, and spindly maple saplings. She pushed through, thorns on the rugosa roses snagging her jacket. Her mother and Mr. Sylvia, the family's gardener, had kept all this cut back; there'd always been a wide path open to the steps. She couldn't imagine why Bea and Randall had let it grow. Until she saw the house. Perhaps the idea was not to block the occupants' view out, but to block anyone else's view in.

In Lilli's youth, the Niles house had stood on a lawn large enough for tea parties and games of tag, badminton, and cro-quet; large enough to have easily accommodated tables for the more than seventy guests at Charlotte and Graham's wed-ding. It had been edged with gardens filled with foxglove, roses, iris, daisies, lilies, and peonies, with pansies, begonias, phlox, lantana, nicotiana, columbine, and feverfew. The peonies, Lilli remembered, harbored ants that she and Dori would grow faint trying to blow off before Bea allowed them into the house. The lawn was now reduced to a narrow band of mostly crabgrass trapped between the house and the tan-gled morass she'd just struggled through. Peering back into it, Lilli spotted a few pale irises, stunted and fighting a losing battle, all that was left of the garden. To her right, a wall of honeysuckle, birch saplings, and overgrown cedars blocked what was once a clear view to the opposite point, where the Chapins' house had stood, probably still did, although Lilli doubted any Chapins lived there now. Lilli could see the remains of the wooden arch that had once been covered with red roses. Something was growing up over it still, threatening to take it down.

Of the big house itself, the only part clearly visible was the many-chimneyed and many-gabled roof. Wisteria shrouded the octagonal sunporch (Lilli couldn't imagine it got much sun these days), and junipers the size of lorries blocked the dining room and living room windows. Lilli passed through the narrow opening in the lilac hedge and up to the kitchen door, partially obstructed now by forsythia. She knocked. Silence. She knocked again, louder, and listened. She could hear the sound of a television or radio coming from the rear of the house. The door was unlocked, so she let herself in.

Her shock at the change outside was nothing compared to her shock at the lack of change within. Certainly several of the pairs of shoes jumbled under the layers of coats in the back hall were hers, and the dog collar and leash dangling from the doorknob belonged, if she wasn't mistaken, to Patter, Charlotte's brown-and-white springer spaniel, who died in 1960. She remembered how Charlotte had begged Mother to leave the collar there. They'd all found great comfort in its rattle whenever the door was opened or shut.

In the kitchen, the ivy vines that their mother had painted still snaked their unfinished way up now-yellowed walls. The big wooden table was there as well, its top covered with mail. The refrigerator was new, at least since Lilli had last been there, purchased, most likely, in the 1970s, judging from the coppertone finish that matched the one on the dishwasher and electric stove. A few dirty dishes stood on the Formica counter beside the sink. The tall, glass-fronted cupboards looked the same, filled with their familiar towers of china. In some places, the linoleum floor, while clean, was worn down to the wood.

As Lilli stood there, trying to make sense of it all, she heard muffled footsteps approaching from the den. Soon a tiny woman appeared in the doorway. "Hello, Bea," she said. It was obviously she.

Bea looked up, startled. "Who's there?" Her once-blond hair had gone as white as milkweed, but her eyes, magnified by oversized glasses, were as sharp and blue as ever.

"It's Lilli. I knocked, but . . . I guess you didn't hear me, so I let myself in."

"Yes, I can see that. Well, you gave me quite a start. Try calling next time."

Lilli found to her surprise that she wanted to give her sister a hug. She was deeply moved at the sight of her, here, in this kitchen, so like the room she'd left forty years earlier. Bea took a step closer, and Lilli had started to reach out to her, when Bea stopped abruptly and said, "Let me look at you." She peered at Lilli through the oversized glasses, then seemed to collapse slightly, like a soufflé just out of the oven. "I can't find my damned glasses. Everything is blurry." She moved over to the table and glanced ineffectually around the piles of mail. "I'm useless without them."

Lilli gestured to indicate that Bea was wearing her glasses.

"These are Randall's," Bea said, removing them. "Worse than nothing." She tossed them on the table. Lilli watched as they landed on a pile of catalogs and slid off to one side but stopped herself from reaching out for them, although she was curious. Randall hadn't worn glasses when Lilli knew him.

Bea began hunting around the kitchen, peering beneath a gathering of plastic shopping bags on the counter, behind a bunch of green bananas in a bowl. "Aha!" She snagged another pair with silver metal rims from behind the dirty dishes. "There you are. You see? If you'd done the dishes as you ought," she scolded herself, "you'd have found them." She slid them on and turned to study Lilli. "How long has it been?"

"Forty years. Give or take."

Bea continued to gaze at Lilli's face. Lilli knew she'd changed much in that time, but perhaps not so much as Bea. Charlotte had told her that Bea had osteoporosis and was taking medication for it. She'd always been petite, but she seemed even smaller than usual. Perhaps the osteoporosis was more advanced than Charlotte knew. Lilli, still a commanding five foot ten, towered over her. She instantly felt, as she always had around Bea, oversized and ungainly, and was already starting to experience the familiar sense of being eclipsed by her older sister. It was a subtle transformation, the way clouds—nothing but vapor—can effortlessly slide across and completely darken the moon. How did she do it? My God, she barely cleared five feet!

Although people still remarked on Lilli's looks—a handsome woman, they called her now, rather than beautiful—she didn't always see it. She wondered what Bea saw now.

"Lilli," Bea said. "Beautiful as ever." And then she added, "That color looks very natural. It isn't, I assume?" She was staring at Lilli's carefully darkened hair, which she generally wore pulled back tight from her face but today had left in loose curls around her face due to a headache, which was slowly worsening.

"It's nice to see you, too, Bea," Lilli said.

"Where's your suitcase?" Bea asked.

"I'm staying at the Harbor View, remember? My suitcase is at the motel." She glanced away from her sister, her glance landing on an overfull wastebasket in the corner.

Bea followed her gaze. "I've been meaning to empty that. Randall always takes out—" Bea cut herself off, and the two women gazed in silence at this most mundane of unfinished tasks, hardly a stirring memoriam to a life cut short.

For the briefest moment, Lilli considered taking the wastebasket out to the trash cans, which she'd have bet good money were the same metal barrels they'd always kept alongside the one-car garage. But she resisted. She needed to keep her distance from this house. Although, like a strong current, the house seemed to be trying to pull her back in.

"Nonsense. That place is frightfully expensive. You're staying right here. Plenty of beds. You'll sleep in your old room."

"You look well," Lilli countered.

Bea sniffed. "Well, that's a damned lie. Vision's going. Cataracts, or so they tell me. So's my hearing lately . . ." She trailed off, as though listening to something, perhaps for a clue to the whereabouts of her lost hearing. "My bones are brittle, and I've got a bit of rheumatoid arthritis, apparently. To top it all off, some days, I can't remember my own name." She laughed. Lilli didn't. She could see that Bea's knuckles were swollen and somewhat disfigured. She probably couldn't do much knitting, once a favorite pastime. *Life ages us each so differently.* It seemed to have been particularly unkind to Bea.

"But I'm upright and taking nourishment, so I can't

complain." Bea shifted a few pieces of mail on the table from one pile to another. "More than I can say for Randall."

"Bea."

Bea waved a hand as though shooing away a fly. "No sense going on and on about it."

They stood a moment in awkward silence until Lilli said, "Well, it's late. I just thought I'd stop by and say that I'd made it. Take a look at the old place. It's . . ." She paused, glancing around the kitchen, hoping for inspiration. "Very much as I remembered." In truth, only somewhat as she remembered. The house had always seemed so *alive* to Lilli. Even after all that happened, the house had remained vital and forceful, almost like a member of the family. It was, she realized, the one constant in her youth. She had wanted to see it all. But she didn't now. Now she wanted only the sanctuary of her motel room with its generic seascapes and faux-wood furniture. There were few signs of Randall in the kitchen, but she could sense him, and Dori, and her mother. She needed air.

"Yes, I expect it is," Bea said, settling herself into one of the chairs at the table and gazing at the faded ivy vines creeping up the wall beside her. "You must be tired after your long trip. Why don't you bring your suitcase in and take it up to your room?"

Lilli took another step backward. "I think I'll just head back to the motel," she said, suddenly feeling a bit uneasy about Bea's mental state, then dismissing it; Lilli herself forgot things all the time.

"Randall said the rooms are quite nice." At this Bea slumped in her chair and gazed into the middle distance beyond the filmy glass of the kitchen window.

Lilli wondered if she was being dismissed. The notion of

unburdening herself to Bea, of clearing the air, setting things right, all now seemed much less appealing. Whatever it was that Lilli had hoped she might gain, or rid herself of, by settling the accounts seemed impossible and unimportant. But maybe . . . tomorrow after the service. "Randall's service is tomorrow at ten, you said?"

Bea sat up. "Ten o'clock at the Winston Funeral Parlor. You should write these things down, Lilli." This instruction delivered by an older sister, reasserting her dominance. Bea reached for an envelope apparently addressed to Randall. "It's funny, when he was here, I was always hoping he'd go out somewhere. Now that he's really gone, I keep . . . hoping he'll come home." She said this as though she'd forgotten to whom she was speaking. Bea suddenly tossed the envelope on the table and added, "At least then he could open his own mail."

Lilli took the opportunity to move into the back hall. "Yes, well. I'll see you tomorrow, then."

"Come for lunch. We'll have sandwiches out on the sunporch."

"That sounds very nice," Lilli lied, thinking she could always fabricate some excuse the next day, if necessary.

Bea had begun sorting through the mail. "Ten o'clock, Lillianne," she called. "Don't be late."

As Lilli retreated through the back hall, she noticed a dozen pairs of men's socks, neatly rolled, nesting in the bottom of a laundry hamper. Glancing back to make sure Bea wasn't looking, she reached down and took one, bunching the soft fabric in her fist. "I won't," Lilli said. "I'll see you tomorrow."

"Want to go for a walk, boy?" she whispered as she let herself out the door, giving Patter's dog leash a playful tug to set the tags jingling. He could hear that sound from anywhere in the house and would come bounding to the back hall, quivering in anticipation. Lilli listened for the scrabble of nails on linoleum, saddened, a little, by the ensuing silence. Patter had particularly enjoyed going with the girls to the train station to meet their father coming home from his office in Boston. They'd all enjoyed that. Their father had died of cancer, far too young and perhaps unnecessarily, on January 1, 1962. He'd refused any treatment. Lilli didn't know why. Blythe had held and rocked her husband through the long night, which they all knew was his last and through which no one slept and at the apex of which no one marked the arrival of the New Year. Bea had put the girls to bed at midnight, telling them not to worry, that everything would look better in the morning. "Sweet dreams and roses on your pillows," she'd said.

"Don't let the bedbugs bite," they'd chorused in unison, as they did every night.

"But if they do, hit 'em with a shoe," Bea would say, before softly closing the door.

Lilli and Dori had lain awake for hours, first one, and then the other, whispering, "Are you asleep?" Until Dori finally padded across the narrow divide and climbed in with Lilli, and they'd held one another, sharing secret prayers. By morning their father was gone. It took hours of pleading by Bea before their mother, barricaded behind the bedroom door, would allow their father's body to be taken away.

Lilli walked past the overgrown lilac hedge and down the narrow drive, deciding that the longer route to the path behind the Hammonds' would be easier than fighting her way back through the brambly weeds to the steps leading to the beach. Halfway down the drive, she paused by the old greenhouse, now nearly hidden beneath grapevines, its panes—those that weren't broken or missing—still opaque with milky whitewash.

She would come back tomorrow. Everything would be clearer tomorrow.

L ILLI could feel Dori's face above hers, her breath like a whisper on her cheek. Lilli waited a second, then two, and then opened her eyes—not fluttery and unfocused like a person rising from a deep sleep (or pretending to, as the girls often did when Bea came in to wake them for school) but wide open all at once—and shouted, "Happy birthday!"

Dori shrieked and fell back, complaining, "Lilli!" Although she should have known Lilli would do this. She did it every year. But Dori rose each day with her mind clear and untroubled, like the still water of a tidal pool, revealing all that lies within.

"Thirteen years old. Do you feel different?" Lilli asked when they'd both recovered.

Dori patted her arms and legs—a brief inventory to ensure a completely truthful answer. "No. Do I look different?" Her voice was hopeful.

Katharine Britton

Lilli pretended to study her little sister's face, beginning with her dimpled chin and working her way up to her lightly freckled pug nose. She stopped, stared, and exclaimed, "Your eyes!" Dori was so easy so tease.

Dori scrambled off the bed and ran to the mirror above the shared dressing table, which Blythe had painted the morning-glory blue of her youngest daughter's eyes. "Really? Are they finally brown like yours and Mom's?"

So easy to tease it almost wasn't fun. "Today's the big day," Lilli said to cheer Dori, who was looking at Lilli with reproach in the mirror. In an instant the look was gone, and Dori wheeled around, buoyed onto her tiptoes by enthusiasm. "Racing with the seniors will be so cool!"

"You and Bea will probably win," Lilli said, encouraging her, as though winning were what mattered most to Lilli. Winning mattered, but what mattered most to Lilli was that, with Dori crewing for Bea, Lilli would crew for Randall Marsh. This was enough to propel her from bed to dressing table, where she sat beside Dori on the cane-seated bench and looked cautiously into the glass, wondering who would look back. Each morning the face in the mirror appeared just a little different, and Lilli, uncomfortable around strangers, found this unsettling. Her hair—already a mane of dark curls that she could scarcely get a brush through and that refused to stay in place no matter how many barrettes she used—seemed to have increased in both volume and bounce. Bea had tried to straighten it once, at Lilli's request, first applying some foul-smelling cream that made their eyes water, which did nothing, and then slathering on Dippity-Do and ironing it between two of their grandmother's linen towels. The results resembled the hair on one of Dori's older dolls:

spiking out in all directions. Lilli had sobbed, and Bea'd had to shampoo her hair three times before it returned to close to normal and Lilli would stop crying.

LILLI'S EYES THAT day were clear and seemed deeper set, her nose more pronounced, and her eyebrows heavier than they had been just the day before. She didn't dislike the young woman she saw, she simply didn't know her. Lilli had always been a tomboy, more interested in climbing trees than sitting under them, in digging clams than cooking them, and not the least interested in boys. Until this summer. She smiled at the semistranger, who was not only interested in boys, but who seemed to interest them back. Dori thought Lilli was smiling at her and grinned back. Then she lifted her nose in the air and said, "Do I smell . . . ?"

Lilli recognized at once the buttery fragrance wafting up from the kitchen, but couldn't quite believe it. Charlotte had spent the night at a friend's, so who was cooking in the kitchen on a Saturday morning? The girls rushed around, searching for clothes. Lilli might have grown up quickly that summer, but she wasn't so grown up that she didn't still adore pancakes.

"We smell pancakes," they chorused as they clattered down the back stairs and into the kitchen, heavy with the fragrance of burned butter.

Their mother stood with her back to the girls, stirring a small pot on the stove. A light dusting of flour covered the floor, the counter, and Blythe's paint-splotched smock. Three cast-iron skillets stood upended in the sink. Mrs. Foley, the housekeeper, who did most of the cooking for the Niles family, did not work on weekends. It was a strange sight for the girls to see their mother in the kitchen. "My birthday girl!" Blythe said, turning to face them. "At last."

Dori ran over, wrapped her mother in a tight embrace, and came away dusted with flour, which her mother patted off, laughing, before shooing her youngest daughter to her seat at the large wooden table. Blythe sashayed across the kitchen, plucked a construction-paper crown—she made one for each of her daughters on their birthdays—from a small white-enamel table mottled with various shades of green paint. Their mother used this table to mix the paints for the ivy she was painting on the kitchen wall. She would instruct the girls which tubes to open, and they would unscrew the caps and press green, and yellow, and blue squiggles out onto the table, where their mother would mash them together with her rounded knife.

Dori's crown, covered with glitter and sequins, was topped with colorful tissue-paper roses on pipe-cleaner stems. Blythe walked back across the kitchen, holding the crown in front, and placed it with great ceremony on Dori's head, as Lilli trumpeted a quiet fanfare. Their mother curtsied. "The pancakes are not quite ready, Your Majesty. It's a new recipe and . . ." She trailed off, a half smile tugging at the corners of her mouth, and returned to the stove, saying, "One minute, and I'll bring you each a slice."

The girls glanced at one another as they took their seats. A *slice* of pancake? Their mother, who did little in moderation, had cooked ten easily, plenty for each to have two. Dori turned to the painted ivy snaking its way up the wall, selected a single vine, and ran her finger along its stem, carefully following where it twined around the others. "When are we going to finish?" she asked, having reached the vine's abrupt end. "I've traced every single one."

Blythe, busy at the stove, said, "This week."

"School starts Wednesday," Lilli reminded her, and not for the first time.

"Does it? Well then, next weekend."

"Or tomorrow?" Dori offered, just as Blythe turned around, her face beaming, holding in front of her a towering and listing stack of pancakes, thirteen brightly burning candles rising from a sea of gooey, purplish-black jam that ran down the sides and puddled on the plate.

"Oh," was all Lilli could say to this unexpected sight.

But Dori bugled, "A pancake cake!" clapped her hands, shot from her chair, and danced across the kitchen for a closer look. "With blackberry roses!" She bobbed up and down, the flowers on her crown dancing wildly, plucked a berry from the sticky jam, and popped it into her mouth.

Blythe placed her creation in front of Dori, stepped back, and curtsied deeply. "Your Ladyship." She set a delicate china plate from the set with the sprays of pink rosebuds in front of each girl, sending Dori right over the moon. "The good china!" she shouted, unable as usual to contain her enthusiasm.

"Shhh, you'll wake Bea," Lilli warned.

Dori, fixated on the brightly burning candles, glinting like stars in her guileless blue eyes, seemed not to hear her.

"Bea is already up and gone to the yacht club." Blythe attempted to shore up the pancakes with a spatula. "She and Randall had something to do before the race."

"What something?" Lilli asked. She didn't like one bit hearing Bea and Randall's names linked. Lilli had waited all summer for her name to be coupled with his.

Blythe merely winked at Lilli, which increased her agitation, and then said enigmatically, "Oh, just something, nothing important," before turning her attention to Dori. "Hurry and make a wish, dear, before the wax gets all over."

Dori squeezed shut her eyes. "I wish—"

"Don't tell, Dori," Lilli said, cutting her off. "Wishes are meant to be a secret. If you tell, they won't come true. Remember?" She had a pretty good idea that Dori had wished for Randall to ask Lilli to the dance at the yacht club that night, and she didn't want to take any chances.

"Are you sure, Lilli? I thought wishes made on your birthday always came true. Mine do." She squinched shut her eyes for a silent moment, and then exhaled dramatically in the direction of the candles, extinguishing all but one.

Blythe attempted to cut wedges from the stack, but the soft layers collapsed in on one another under the still-warm jam and slid off to one side. Blythe doubled over laughing. "Oh, my. Oh, heavens. I guess I should have thought this through a bit more. Let the jam cool longer. That's what I should have done. I used honey, you see."

Dori and Lilli looked at one another. *Honey?* "We've got plenty of sugar," Lilli said.

"Honey is supposed to be much better for our . . . skin, I think. I found a recipe in *Ladies' Home Journal*. Besides, we needed the sugar for something else," Blythe said, cutting her off and giving her a mock-stern look and a wink that meant nothing to Lilli. She stared at her mother, hoping for an explanation, but Blythe had returned her focus to the mounds of pancake and gooey jam that she was now spooning onto the little china plates. "I guess I should have used the cream soup bowls . . ." She laughed again and pushed her hair from her face with a wrist, leaving a sticky red streak.

"I made my birthday wish for you, Lilli. I wished—"

"Don't tell," Lilli said. "I can guess." Dori knew about Lilli's crush, although that seemed a childish word now to Lilli, not nearly expansive enough to cover all she felt in Randall's presence. But appropriate, in a way. The potent mix of emotions, at times both suffocating and deafening, were crushing in their way, leaving her breathless.

Blythe delivered pancakes to the girls, and they each took a bite, chewed, and studied their plates to avoid eye contact. The jam was so tart that it transformed the dense pancakes into a puckering paste.

"Whipped cream would have been just the thing," Blythe mused, gazing with regret at her creation, which had lost all structural integrity and turned an angry purple. Then she shrugged, the experiment and her disappointment past, and turned to Dori. "You'll be careful today. Do whatever Bea tells you. Keep your head down. And always keep—"

"One hand for the boat," Dori recited dutifully but with some difficulty, as she was having trouble swallowing. This rule had been drummed into them, first by their father, and then by Bea, since infancy.

"We've sailed the Herreshoffs together loads of times," Lilli reminded her.

"Sailing's one thing. Racing quite another."

"And she's raced Rookies for years—"

"Could I eat just a little of this now?" Dori interrupted, motioning to her plate. "And save the rest for later?" She disliked and avoided arguments of any kind, whereas they seemed drawn to Lilli like flies to the attic window at the end of summer. Lilli pushed back her chair and hurried to the sink. "Good idea, Dor. If Bea's already at the club we better get going.

"Just leave your plates, girls. I'll wash them."

"Are you coming down to watch?" Dori asked, wrapping her arms around her mother.

Blythe removed the paper crown, which Dori almost certainly would have worn to the yacht club, and tried to comb her hair with her fingers. "I've got a little something to do myself before your party tomorrow." Lilli glanced at her mother. There was that tone again. "I'll watch from the point."

The girls scraped the remains of their breakfast into the trash can in the corner, gathered their shoes from the big basket in the back hall, pawed through the layers of jackets hanging six deep from hooks, and headed out the back door, setting Patter's dog leash jangling. "Wear a life jacket," their mother called as the two locked arms and skipped past the lilac hedge, its leaves dusted gray with mildew. They ran down the driveway and collapsed in a giggling heap outside the greenhouse. Giuseppe Sylvia's fat-tired bicycle leaned against one wall. "God, those were awful," said Lilli.

"*Buon giorno*, Isadora." Giuseppe Sylvia, barrel-chested, his broad face wreathed with dark hair, emerged from the greenhouse, grinning and wiping dirt-covered hands on his pants. The sleeves of his collarless shirt were rolled up on thick, hairy forearms.

"*Bon jee-or-no*, Giuseppe. *Come va?*"

"Dori," Lilli whispered, mortified. "You address him as Mr. Sylvia." *If you were to address him at all*, she thought, always a bit timid around this bear of a man, who seemed to spring from the dark loamy soil in which he worked. The girls' father had been slight and fair, and Mr. Sylvia seemed to Lilli like a different species altogether.

He stood beside a half dozen large, terra-cotta flowerpots in which he was planting mums that Blythe had bought earlier in the week. The plants were still small, and Lilli thought they looked lonely and uncertain in their new, oversized homes. Each fall, Mr. Sylvia placed these heavy pots of yellow, white, and rust-colored flowers, which smelled, to Lilli, like mildew, around the yard to extend the season as, in the surrounding gardens, summer blossoms turned to seed and plants yellowed, then browned, and then collapsed with the first frost. "No, no, Miss Lillianne. Here, in America I am liking very much to be called Giuseppe. Joe, even, if you please."

"Joe," Dori said, "is teaching me Italian."

"That's nice. Now come on. We'll be late."

"And I'm teaching him to read English." Dori turned to Mr. Sylvia. "How are you coming with the new book?" she asked, her words loud and careful.

He ducked into the greenhouse, and they watched his shadow through the whitewashed glass reach into the pocket of the coat that always hung from the hook inside the door. He returned with a battered paperback and showed with obvious pride where he'd marked his place, halfway through, with a dried seed pod.

"*Little Women?*" Lilli said, embarrassed. "Don't you think he might like something, I don't know, more for grown-ups?"

"But I am like a child with my English. There will be time for me to . . . to . . ." He struggled to find words. "Meet grown-up books later. Now, Miss Isadora, today is a special day for you, no?"

"Yes!" Dori said. "I'm racing with Bea today. With the seniors."

"I think Mr. Sylvia means that today's your birthday." But the mere mention of the race was enough to make Lilli grab Dori's arm and try to tug her away.

"Yes, *tuo compleanno*. I have something for you. *Un regalo di compleanno. Un momento*."

Dori held her ground, and they watched him once again enter the greenhouse, going this time to the potting bench, a rickety affair constructed by their father with much care and devotion and many nails hammered in at odd angles and, even to their inexperienced eyes, odd places. He had presented the bench to Blythe on their first anniversary more than twenty years earlier. Against all logic it had persevered through the years. Mr. Sylvia was grabbing something off the bench, they couldn't make out what, and soon he reappeared, holding a basket brimming with blackberries, which he handed to Dori. *"Mora."*

"Mora," Dori repeated. "They're my favorite. Mother made me a birthday cake out of pancakes this morning and had *mora* on top. They looked like roses."

"Sì, sì, decorazione di frutta. Molto bene."

"Gratzy, Giuseppe," Dori said, giving a little curtsy.

"Grazie, Isadora," he replied, holding the tattered copy of *Little Women* to his chest and bowing deeply from the waist. *"In bocca al lupo!* Good luck today."

Lilli carried their jackets, and Dori the basket of berries, both girls shoving fistfuls of the fat fruit into their mouths as they ran the rest of the way down the drive beneath yellowing birch and russet oaks, whose leaves would hang on longer than all the others until they finally dropped, covering the

driveway with a slick brown goo. At the bottom of the drive
the girls turned onto the grassy path behind the Hammonds'
and walked single file through the cedars and out onto the
rocks. The tide was low, lower than normal because of the
full moon, and the water had shrunk almost to Big-big's far
side. Dori jumped down, spilling a few berries, which hit the
beach and scattered like pool balls. She chased after them—
despite Lilli's pleas to leave them, come on, hurry up—and
walked out across the muddy sand to swish them in the shallow water. She popped them into her mouth, wrinkling her
nose at the taste. "Salty."

"What did you think?" Lilli snapped, losing her patience.
Here was another change in Lilli this summer: mood swings.
They roared in savagely, like nor'easters, drenching and
upending things, and generally wreaking havoc. Holding
both jackets in one arm, Lilli now took charge of the basket as well, and Dori began a sort of jig, flirting with the
water, twirling this way and that, dodging what few waves
there were in the light breeze. Lilli warned Dori not to get
her shoes wet, and then, eager to see Randall, she set off at a
trot down the beach. Dori, Lilli knew, would become lost in
the moment, but she wasn't Lilli's responsibility. When Lilli
finally did glance back, Dori had climbed to a level spot on
Big-big about five feet above the ground. She had her arms
lifted to the sky, her head tilted back, her eyes closed.

"Dori! NO!" Lilli called. Too late. Dori jumped and was
falling. She hit the sand, and her knees buckled so she crumpled into a heap and rolled a few times before coming to a
stop. Lilli rushed back as Dori sat up, shaking her head. "I've
been working on touching the sky this summer, Lilli. I've
only got a little more time."

Touching the sky? Lilli couldn't imagine where Dori came up with these notions. "Well, that's fine, Dori, but right now you're sitting on wet sand. Look at you. Get up." Lilli tried to ignore the small, but irritating, burr of resentment working its way beneath her skin. She'd been frightened. The sand here, ridged from the recently receded tide, was hard as cement. Dori could have easily broken an ankle. And what would *that* have done to Lilli's day? She extended a hand, which Dori grabbed, and for a moment it seemed that Lilli might end up beside Dori on the beach, before she managed to lever her up. By then both girls were helpless with laughter, and Lilli's anger had vanished. She patted the wet sand from Dori's damp bottom and tugged her down the beach and onto the path through the woods to the yacht club.

"What about skunks, Lilli? I'm afraid. Let's take the road." Lilli was expecting this. Dori brought it up every time they passed this way. "No time. We're already late. Just make a lot of noise. Skunks hate surprises. They won't bother us if they know we're coming."

"Promise?"

"Promise. Have you ever seen a skunk in here?"

"Ready, Lilli?"

"All skunks go to Hell!" they shouted as they raced down the path.

When they emerged, Lilli could see John Bradley, Susie Pierce, Ellen Sibley, and Janey Hallowell, chatting in front of the yacht club. They looked up as Dori came shouting out of the glade and waved greetings. Dori and Lilli waved back, and Lilli scanned the group for Randall, trying not to be obvious.

"He's probably inside," Dori said.

"Who?" Lilli asked, embarrassed and feigning innocence, and annoyed with herself for both.

Dori rolled her eyes. "Rock Hudson. Wait, no, there he is."

Randall was walking down the gangway, sail bag on his shoulder, khaki skipper's cap set at an angle on his head. "Randall!" Dori called, racing across the road. Lilli cringed inwardly, worried what Dori might say, but also envious. Only last summer she'd had that same careless confidence with this boy who'd been like a brother to her most of her life. But she'd shed that along with her child's body, and now every interaction seemed fraught with both potential and peril. One wrong word or move . . . This was not the entrance she'd planned to make.

He turned, spotted Dori, and shouted, "Ahoy!" tossing the sail bag to John Bradley, now on the float below. "Hey!" John barked as he caught the bag and staggered back, braking just short of falling in the drink.

Randall grinned. "Sorry. Toss it into the *Whisper*, will you?" He bounded back up the gangway, greeting the downward stream of people. Lilli straightened her shoulders, lifted her chin, and smiled as she strolled across the road. Dori was talking to Randall, gesturing toward Lilli. Randall looked up at her and smiled.

"Morning, Lilli," he said, tipping his hat, a mannerism he'd picked up from George Niles, who had always worn a hat and always tipped it to ladies. Lilli found it irresistibly gallant. Dori misunderstood and saluted.

"Good morning, Randall. Whose boat are we sailing on?" Lilli didn't care, but it was all she could think of to say. She scanned the fleet at their moorings, as though they had their choice of boats. In truth, her face had flushed and she wanted to conceal it. "We could borrow the Batchelders'. I don't think Batch is racing today. I'm pretty sure she said she was going into Boston with her mother to shop for school clothes. Yes, I'm certain she did." Lilli took a breath and glanced around at the gathered sailors, looking for her school chum, which made no sense since she'd just said she wouldn't be there. *Stupid.* At least she'd stopped chattering. "Oh, wait, is that her? No—"

Randall put a hand on Lilli's chin, bringing an instant stop to her babbling. And thinking. And breathing. "My, my, Lilypad," he said. "You're looking particularly fetching this morning. Do I detect a little lipstick?" Lilli opened her mouth, stood there, unable to think what to say. She was not wearing lipstick, much as she might have liked to. Bea would have been on her for it in an instant.

Dori wiped her own berry-stained mouth, and offered, "*Mora,*" in a loud stage whisper. Randall looked puzzled. "Blackberries," translated Dori. "We ate a whole basketful this morning." She pointed to the now-empty basket that Lilli still held, and then, frowning, put a hand to her stomach. "In fact . . ."

Lilli swiped at her mouth and shot Dori an angry look. Dori should have said something to her.

"I thought it looked good," Dori said, sounding indignant, in response to Lilli's look.

Randall winked. "It does. You should eat *mora* more often. A little color on your lips suits you." Lilli felt herself blushing again and assumed that her whole face now resembled a blackberry. This day was going all wrong.

"And how are you this fine morning, Miss A-Dori-ble?"

Randall asked, hoisting Dori in his arms and planting a loud, wet kiss on her cheek.

Dori hugged him tight around the neck and began to warble, "I'm in the mood for love, simply because you're near meeeeee."

Randall threw back his head and whooped with laughter. Then, with Dori in his arms, he swept her around the crowded dock, both of them singing, "Funny, but when you're near meeee, I'm in the mooooood for looove." Passersby dodged out of their way, smiling. Lilli watched, jealous and frowning, as Randall and Dori twirled and dipped, narrowly missing Bea as she walked out of the clubhouse, carrying life jackets and oars.

While Lilli was changing daily—one day a child, the next nearly all grown up—Bea seemed to become ever more of who she'd always been. Today, her starched white shorts were cinched at the waist with a navy belt, and she wore a red boat-neck sweater she'd finished knitting the previous week. Her blond hair was swept back from her face and anchored with two slim barrettes. Lilli could feel her curls already escaping from the caisson of clips and pins she'd mobilized for the task. Bea never faltered when she spoke, never paused, searching for just the right thing to say. She never looked embarrassed. When she walked into a room, people and conversations organized themselves around her. At only five foot two and a mere 105 pounds, she seemed to Lilli to have a gravitational pull second only to the sun.

Lilli, at fifteen—nine years younger than Bea—was now her same height and weighed more. And the weight was distributed all differently. Just that morning Lilli's blouse had stretched so tightly across her blossoming chest that she'd had to try on three others before finding one that fit, and her shorts were so snug around her hips and behind that she'd had trouble buttoning them. So she'd worn a skirt. Their father had always insisted that Bea and Charlotte wear skirts when sailing, so, although impractical and unusual, it wasn't unprecedented. Or unflattering.

"What on earth . . . ?" Bea halted as Dori and Randall sashayed across her path, and an oar clattered onto the decking. She gave the two an indulgent smile. "Happy birthday, little one." Spotting Lilli, she said, "Here you are. I thought I'd have to find someone else to crew for me."

"What do you mean? I'm racing with Randall," Lilli said.

"Change in plans. You'll be with me in the *Loon*." Bea started across the porch to the gangway, paused, turned back, and added, "Looks like I need to take you shopping." She glanced at Lilli's outfit. "Although *my* skirt does look very nice on you." Lilli felt her face grow hot. "Better on you, in fact. You might as well have it. It never really fit me."

Bea started down the ramp.

"But why can't I sail with Randall?" Lilli managed to say.

"The wind's too strong. I'd rather Dori sail with him. It will be safer."

Lilli looked at the water in the harbor, flat as a millpond, the drooping burgee on the flagpole. "There isn't a bit of wind."

"Not now, no. But it will pick up later. I don't want to take the chance, this being Dori's first senior race. Do you?" The question settled around them for an uncomfortable moment as Lilli considered this. To break the silence, Dori piped up with, "I want to sail with you, Bea. I want to win!" She wiggled out of Randall's arms and went to stand beside Lilli.

Randall hooted. "I'll try not to take that personally, Dori baby."

Lilli felt Dori's hand reaching for hers, and knew she should take it and squeeze thanks for the effort. But her anger was back and going every which way, like those berries shooting across the sand. *It wasn't fair!*

"That's very sweet. You're a good girl, Dori," Bea said. "Next year you can sail with me. Lilli, take this stuff down to the *Whisper*. I'll row us out." Bea offloaded the gear she was holding and reached for the dropped oar.

"But—" There was much Lilli wanted to say, but Bea had turned and was marching down the gangway, nodding to people on their way up, who parted like the Red Sea.

Lilli felt betrayed by the weather, by Bea, by her mother and her stupid pancake cake, by Dori. If they'd gotten here earlier, perhaps . . . She felt helpless. It was not a feeling she liked.

"Better get down there," Randall said, putting a comforting hand on Lilli's shoulder, which made her knees turn to jelly and her disappointment spike. "Having crewed for Bea the past four summers, I can tell you she hates to be crossed on race day. When she gives an order, she means it."

Lilli felt defeated, humiliated, and angry. Bea had ruined everything! After their father died, Bea had become the girls' self-appointed guardian, getting them off to school in the morning, making sure they took baths and did their homework. Lilli supposed she should be grateful, but Bea used to do more fun things, like cooking them Jiffy Pop at night, teaching them to knit, and taking them to the Pleasure Island amusement park and allowing them to drive the little electric cars, even though they were too young. As Blythe had become more and more . . . distant, Bea had begun to bring to her unofficial motherhood role the same close-hauled vigor that made her the club sailing champion year after year. Lilli wished that her mother hadn't quite so readily abdicated her duties, happy simply to putter in her garden, create her sculptures—odd assemblages of driftwood and flotsam that she fashioned into whimsical shapes resembling, she insisted, animals—and organize tea parties and picnics.

Randall was grinning at Lilli, the corners of his eyes crinkling in such a way that made her heart gallop, and then seem to stop altogether, leaving her breathless and, once again, speechless. She'd known Randall for years and had never experienced such emotional upheavals. She would have enjoyed the physical changes if she'd known that these mental lapses were normal and would pass. She'd mentioned it to her mother, asked how she could reclaim the ease she'd always had around him. Blythe had hugged Lilli and said, "Life is like a garden, Lilli. You must enjoy it at every stage. Don't be so eager for the blossoms yet to come. Before you know it, it will be fall, and the flowers will die and leave you forever. You can't rely on another person for your happiness, Lilli. You must learn to be self-reliant." If her mother had meant to convey a message, it was completely lost on Lilli.

Charlotte, whom Lilli had asked next, clearly had never experienced what Lilli was undergoing. Charlotte was not moody. She couldn't have brooded on a bet. She'd listened, her eyes steady and probing, as Lilli described the tempest brewing inside her. Then she'd put a comforting hand on Lilli's shoulder, smiled, and said with gravitas and certainty, "You need a toasted cheese sandwich." It was the same tone she would use to say, years later, about one of her tiny patients, "This baby needs a striped hat."

"Cheer up," Randall was saying to Lilli. "You're bound to win. Bea always does."

Lilli nodded, noting that his eyes matched perfectly the color of the Atlantic after a storm when the sky begins to clear and the sun peeks through—

"Lilli?"

He'd asked her something. She had no idea what.

"See you after the race?"

Lilli nodded, blushing again, knowing there was some simple reply she could give to that question but unable to think what. She pictured them standing close together by the railing after the race, nearly touching, awaiting the results.

Randall seemed puzzled and slightly amused by Lilli's silence and, after touching her lightly on the end of her nose, turned to take Dori's hand. "C'mon, Dori my lass, let's see if we can beat the pants off those two. Whadya say?"

Lilli watched them walk off together, Dori looking back as she trailed Randall down the gangway. Lilli knew that Dori wanted a smile from her, wanted to know that Lilli didn't blame her for how things had turned out. But Lilli didn't feel like smiling. She was still trying to formulate a response to Randall's simple question, and so her expression conveyed little, not nearly enough for Dori, who needed things clearly spelled out. "But Lilli's not wearing pants," Dori said, sounding worried and confused, clinging to this one solid bit of truth. At this Randall laughed, which did make Lilli smile, and at that Dori's expression brightened. She waved to Lilli, and Lilli waved back before she turned and went into the club-house for the rest of the gear.

AN HOUR LATER, the fleet of Herreshoffs was heading out the channel past Brant Point to await the start of the race. The wind, as Bea had predicted, and as much as Lilli hated to admit it, had strengthened. The boats tacked back and forth, and, when the horn sounded, Bea and Lilli were first across the line. Randall and Dori, in the Batchelders' boat, the *Heron*, crossed second, but fell behind approaching the first mark. Lilli could hear them singing an old sea chanty, and when she glanced back she saw that they were laughing. She resolved to lose the race for Bea and sat with her arms folded, gazing backward, imagining herself in the boat with Randall. "Eyes forward, Lilli," Bea said. "Boating is serious business. Anything can happen if your mind wanders for even an instant. Trim the jib. It's luffing."

Lilli glared, but Bea was staring up at the mainsail. The jib was so taut and the sheet so tight that, even braced, Lilli could not pull it in farther. "Could you fall off a bit?" The boat was heeled at an angle Lilli found alarming. Although Lilli didn't talk about it, she didn't care for racing.

"Falling off is not how you win races."

They increased their lead as they rounded the second mark until they were ten lengths ahead of the second boat. Lilli searched for the *Heron*, but it was buried in the middle of a dozen Herreshoffs, their hulls mere slashes of white above the dark water, their sails a slowly shifting forest of white. That was how Lilli pictured painting it, first sketching with charcoal, then rubbing the lines to soften them. She could almost feel the grain of the paper and the grit of the charcoal beneath her thumb, the lines growing fainter and fainter until they were mere suggestions of lines, gradually disappearing the way real boats do when they sail into the horizon.

"Lilli!" Bea was glowering at her. "Eyes forward. Look at the mainsail. Get your head in the race."

Getting through the race was all Lilli cared about. It wasn't that she was afraid of boats, exactly, but there was something unnatural about buoyancy, about being so weightless in water, that unnerved her. And although from a distance a boat under sail looks silent and peaceful, on board the wind shrieks through the rigging and the sails snap. The boat rises up the fronts of waves, as if pulled by a chain, and then careens down the backsides, smacking into the next wave, sending cold spray over the bow. Water churns into white foam as it races beneath the hull.

"Lilli!"

Lilli looked up, surprised to note that they were nearing the final, downwind leg.

"I said ready the spinnaker."

"There's too much wind." Lilli hated setting spinnakers. They didn't use them generally in the Herreshoffs, but, in this final race of the season, the Chowder Cup, anything went.

"Oh, now there's too much wind? Ready the spinnaker."

Lilli wormed her way onto the bow, set the spinnaker pole, and began preparing the filmy sail. She kept one hand for the boat, making it all but impossible—even without the stiff wind and heavy chop that seemed determined to dislodge her from the deck—for her to manage the bulky sail bag, lead the sheets outside the side stays, attach the spinnaker pole, and pray that the stops all ripped open after Bea jibed around the buoy. To make matters worse, her skirt kept billowing up in the breeze. She tucked it between her knees and had nearly finished attaching the spinnaker halyard, but had not yet freed the jib sheet or raised the spinnaker, when Bea shouted, "Ready to jibe—jibe ho." She was rounding the final mark.

"Wait!" Lilli shouted. Too late. Bea had pushed the tiller starboard, the bow slid to port, and the tip of the spinnaker pole submarined into the water, taking the spinnaker with it. The nose of the *Loon* started to follow. "Head off, Bea. Pull up," Lilli screamed.

"Get that sail out of the water!" Bea shouted with genuine alarm.

Lilli grabbed lines and began frantically pulling, but the weight of the sail was too much. She needed to get hold of the sail itself. She reached forward, bracing her leg, grabbed the sail with both hands, and hauled, putting all of her weight into the effort. Her heel slipped on the slick deck, and she pitched forward, releasing the sail and grabbing the coaming just before she would have followed the spinnaker into the foaming water sliding beneath the bow. Bea headed the *Loon* into the wind; the mainsail luffed crazily, cracking like gunshot, and the halyards slapped against the mast. Loose sheets flew as the boom swung wildly side to side. Bea grabbed Lilli's waist and wrestled her upright. Together they hauled the soaking spinnaker back onto the deck.

"What were you thinking?" Bea yelled. "You very nearly went overboard. What did Daddy always say about keeping one hand for the boat?"

Lilli felt humiliated as six or seven Herreshoffs, the *Heron* among them, glided past, heading for the finish line, their crews looking over with concern and frank astonishment to see Bea Niles in such a predicament. Randall shouted something, but his words were swallowed by the wind and waves.

Lilli turned to Bea, "It wasn't my fault. I told you to wait, to head off. I wasn't ready," she volleyed, venting all of the morning's pent-up frustration. "All you ever think about is winning. Well, guess what? You're not going to win this one."

Bea sat silent a moment and then said softly. "I might not win this race, but I'm sure as hell going to finish. Take the helm. I'll set the spinnaker."

Lilli squeezed past Bea and moved to the stern, waited for Bea to give the thumbs-up, and then allowed the *Loon* to fall off and the wind to fill the sail. She let out the mainsheet until the boom was at almost a right angle to the hull, the sail like a big, white wing. The boat surged forward, surfing across the finish line well behind the other boats. Lilli, sorry now for both what she'd done and what she'd said, wished that she could glide away so smoothly.

Three

MAY 2009

LILLI wandered back along the beach from Bea's house to the Harbor View Motel. It was nearly nine, which meant nearly two in the morning for her, still on London time. The sun had set, but the sky was still light, a dove gray mottled with puffy apricot clouds. A young woman was sitting on the beach, pad in lap, painting Pequot Light—rising straight out of the Atlantic, marking a ledge at the entrance to White Head Harbor—and Big-big, now surrounded by shallow water streaked with orange. Lilli recalled how she and Dori used to climb up onto the big rock and pretend it was the *Titanic*. They would be dowagers making the return crossing after an audience with the king. Each would claim a section of the rock for a stateroom and invite the other over for tea, using clamshells as cups and round stones for crumpets. Neither of them knew what a crumpet was—both guessed it was something between a cracker and a dumpling, although the word mysteriously suggested trumpets and crumpling—but they loved the word. Eventually the *Titanic* would hit the iceberg, Lilli always decided when, and they would cling together in mock terror before leaping overboard into the icy water and paddling bravely back to shore as the big ship went down. Dori, who had a great fondness for war movies like *Twelve O'Clock High, Thirty Seconds Over Tokyo,* and *The Sullivans,* also liked to pretend that Big-big was a destroyer, and they were sailors on a dangerous mission, gliding silently into enemy waters. At night, the beam from Pequot was the enemy's searchlight, and the girls would flatten themselves on the rock, often still warm from the sun, each time it swept by.

These memories startled Lilli. They were so perfectly formed in her mind that she could feel the scrape of the stony crumpets on the rock, hear the dull clunk as the girls toasted "Long live the king" with their clamshell teacups, recall exactly the weightless free fall as they abandoned ship, and the icy grip of the water. She shivered. Where had the memories been hiding all these years? What other memories might be tucked into the tight crevices of these rocks or buried in the sand, waiting to be revealed as if by an outgoing tide? To those girls, who had stood on that very rock, in this very cove, gazing out at that very light, the world could be anything they wanted. Their futures were as distant and unknown as the horizon, as untrammeled as the beach after the tide has swept it clean.

She shivered again and hurried on, searching her pocket for a tissue to blot unexpected tears, finding instead Randall's balled-up socks, which did the trick nicely, and the lucky stone that she'd picked up earlier. This she fingered for a moment before making a wish and skipping it out across the cove. It bounced three times before disappearing. *Not bad.* She hadn't skipped a stone for decades. Her eyes followed the ever-widening rings of the stone's passage across the water to the Chapin house on the point, wondering who lived there now and whether people in White Head thought of her old house as the Nileses' or the Marshes'. She searched for another stone and sent it out across the water, where it hit a wave and sank.

She took the rest of the beach in long strides and hurried along the path through the woods, whispering loudly, "All skunks go to Hell." The front porch of the yacht club stood empty—the sailors no doubt having gone to someone's house for an after-race party—and Lilli decided to see what time and memory had done to her old haunt. The clubhouse, recently shingled and painted, looked tidier than when she was a girl. Buckets of blue and yellow pansies flanked the top of the gangway, and more pansies smiled from boxes under the club's windows. She rarely painted pansies, finding their colors either too intense or too washed-out. These weren't bad, though, she thought—creating a frame with her index fingers and thumbs—set against the gray shingles. She stepped onto the porch and gazed down at the fleet of Herreshoffs, more numerous than in her youth. A few appeared to be restored wooden originals, but most, she could tell even from that distance and in the now rapidly fading light, were fiberglass. As were the sailing dinghies, stacked like loaves of bread in racks on the float. They bore no resemblance to the fat Rookies she'd sailed in her childhood. The once-open area below the clubhouse, where they used to hold swim races, was now crisscrossed with docks, each fringed with dozens of small boats. Out in the harbor, schooners and yawls, brightwork shining, sails furled beneath trim blue sail covers, rode quietly at their moorings. She was surprised at how peaceful she felt.

"It's lovely this time of day, isn't it?"

Startled, because she'd thought she'd been alone, Lilli turned to see a wiry, middle-aged man with the creased and ruddy complexion of one who spends a great deal of time on the water, sitting in one of the rockers, with a small picnic basket beside him. His khaki pants and wrinkled white shirt perfectly matched the bleached wood and white trim of the clubhouse. His collar was carelessly tucked under on one side, and his thick salt-and-cayenne hair was rumpled, suggesting that he'd recently worn a hat. He gave her a pleasing, warm smile.

"It's my favorite time of day," she said. "The light." She offered no further explanation. That she was a painter would take the conversation in a direction she did not wish to travel.

He nodded, seeming to understand. "I come down here every evening. Usually have the place to myself."

"I'm sorry," Lilli said, a bit flustered, thinking both that he was telling her to move on and that he was a bit rude for doing so. "I'm visiting and was just passing by . . ." She turned to leave.

"Oh, please. Don't go. I meant it was nice to have someone to share it with. The kids are in such a hurry to clear out once the race is over. Not like the old days." He shook his head and laughed. "Listen to me. Neddie, you old coot."

"I saw a bit of the race earlier. Were you on the committee boat?" She guessed he could be the commodore of the yacht club.

He looked at her in mock offense. "Committee boat? I was racing." When Lilli did not respond, he said, "Do you sail?"

"Used to. Sort of. Haven't been out on a boat since . . ." Lilli paused, then decided it wasn't worth going into detail. "Not for many years."

"Once it's in your blood it's there for good. When I round my last mark, it's going to be in a boat. Wouldn't have it any other way. I'm Ned Chapin, by the way." He stood and stepped forward, hand extended. "Sorry I didn't introduce myself sooner. Bit tired . . ."

Lilli stared, too shocked at first to speak. "Ned Chapin?" She studied the pale blue eyes; the slightly upturned nose, which in his youth was always pasted with zinc oxide; and could see a glimmer of the young Ned. His face had been weathered and somewhat lengthened by gravity and life, but he was there. *Good Lord*, she thought, *we really are getting old*.

He was staring back, caught off guard by her reaction, alerted to the fact that he should know her and clearly having no idea from where. But then, before Lilli could introduce herself, he said, "Lilli Niles. Good heavens. You're back. Randall's service." He produced these bits of information in the manner of someone attempting to decipher a code and not quite finding the full meaning. Then he added, "I'm so sorry. He was much too young." They started to shake hands, both independently switched to a hug, and then changed their minds midhug. They ended up tangling arms and laughing at their own awkwardness. They started over with one of those half embraces, where shoulders touch and light pats are delivered to backs. Lilli wished she'd stuck with the handshake. "Bea told me about your wife. I'm so sorry."

Ned stepped back and acknowledged her comment with a nod and a sad smile. "You've been gone . . . many, many years. You left so suddenly. We all wondered—" He stopped, aware that some censoring might be in order and not sure what or why. They looked at one another, smiling, trying to think how, or whether, to fill the forty intervening years. "Bea said you're living in London."

Lilli nodded.

"An artist."

She nodded again.

"When did you arrive?"

"This afternoon."

There followed another awkward pause, during which Lilli knew she must either say *It was so nice to see you again* and leave, or start giving more than one- and two-word answers.

"Did you see much of Randall . . . or Bea?" She was curious to know how others viewed her sister and the house. Wondering if, as was the case with Sandy Cove and the town of White Head, their conditions seemed altered to Lilli only because she'd been away for so many years. She didn't think so, but it was worth checking.

"No, not much. Used to see her at garden club meetings, occasionally. Randall was still a fixture around the club. Didn't race, but liked to . . . be a part of things, I guess."

"I just saw her. She seems . . ." Lilli paused, unsure how best to describe Bea. Her sister seemed diminished, and not just physically. Lilli couldn't quite put her finger on it. Maybe Bea's lapse in memory had been nothing more than nerves. Why shouldn't Bea be jittery at seeing a sister gone for so many years and with so much unresolved between them? But Lilli could hear Bea's voice—*Family matters are private matters*—and left her sentence unfinished.

"She must have been delighted to see you," Ned said, seeming not to notice. "Delighted that you decided to come back."

Delighted. Lilli considered this a moment. "I'm not sure I'd use that word, but pleased, perhaps." *Victorious* fit better, Lilli thought. She had definitely detected a note of what she could only describe as self-satisfaction in Bea. And why not? Here was Lilli, not only back in the town to which she swore she'd never return, but spending the night—and having lunch with Bea the next day. She felt slightly dizzy thinking about this, as though she were back in one of the little electric cars at Pleasure Island. The ride would hum to life, and you'd depress the accelerator, which sometimes did nothing at all and other times shot you clear across the enclosure. The car seemed completely unresponsive to the steering wheel, and you were constantly being bumped off course by other drivers. To change the subject, she said, "One of those is yours, I assume?" and gestured out to the Herreshoffs.

Ned pointed to one at the dock below. "The *Sea Gull.*" And then to one out at a mooring. "And the *Spindrift.*"

"Two," she said, impressed.

He shook his head, looking uncomfortable for a moment. "Three. The other's . . . moored over by my house." He wore an odd expression, which Lilli took as embarrassment at owning three Herreshoffs. It was not unlike owning three Jaguars, except perhaps with more maintenance. And Herreshoffs were much slower. And less useful.

"Do you have children who race? Three boats is practically a fleet."

"Used to. Well, still have the children, of course, but they're all married and busy with their own children, careers, life. Life seems to have grown so much more important than it used to be, don't you think?"

"More time-consuming, certainly."

"Yes. That's better. Not more important, just people take it more seriously and spend more time on it."

They lapsed into another silence, and Lilli was about to excuse herself when Ned asked in a gentle voice, "Would you like to see inside?"

Lilli hesitated. Although exhausted, she wasn't sleepy and was not quite ready for the solitude of her motel room. "That would be lovely."

They walked across the narrow porch, Ned drawing from his pocket a ring of keys attached to a long piece of stiff, braided twine, its other end hooked to his belt loop. He selected a shiny brass key, fit it into the lock, and opened the door.

The worn wooden floor, the big flagstone fireplace, the masts lying in even rows above the rafters were all just as Lilli remembered her yacht club. Life preservers and foul-weather gear still dangled from pegs, and charts and photographs still hung between the windows that lined three walls. Exposed studs still served as makeshift shelves, holding shackles and cotter pins, signal horns, and lost sunglasses. At the same time, Lilli had to acknowledge that it was no longer her yacht club. The room belonged to others now, and she was a stranger, an outsider.

The smell of creosote and brass polish pulled her back to the day when, as a girl of fifteen she'd stood here after the race—her last race, although she hadn't known it then—still a bit scared and angry, but also humbled. The room was packed with people, awaiting the race results. They'd brought in a cake for Dori. Charlotte had made it and used up all the sugar; that was why their mother had used honey in those god-awful pancakes. She mentally scanned the crowd. Ned must have been there, but she had no memory of him.

"Would you like a glass of water? Or . . . a cup of tea?"

"Water. Thank you."

"I'll just pop into the galley," Ned said, gesturing, and headed out through the door at the back. Lilli smiled at his use of the nautical term and began a tour of the photographs of past commodores and yellowed newspaper clippings pressed behind dusty glass.

July 12, 1960

By virtue of winning their respective sectional elimination championships, the lady skippers and crews of the Manchester and White Head Yacht Clubs will travel to Greenwich, Connecticut, the opening week of September to represent Massachusetts Bay in the sailing for the Mrs. Charles Francis Adams trophy. The White Head captain, Elizabeth "Bea" Niles, who is also president of the South Shore Ladies' Yacht Racing Association, with her crew Ellen Sibley and Priscilla Sears won the Charles Lee Memorial trophy from a field of four competitor clubs in their district, while the Manchester crew, captained by Mrs. William P. McCallister and her two daughters, Frances and Mary, serving as crew, defeated three rival North Shore clubs to win the George E. Hills trophy.

Lilli stared at the beaming faces of the three young women in the photo above the caption, blouses tucked neatly into shorts, hair windblown and sun-streaked. They looked jubilant and carefree: so very young and innocent. And why shouldn't they? There were more clippings and photos, announcing the victories of Elizabeth "Bea" Niles, always with the confident, debutante smile and coquettish tilt of the head. Lilli spotted a small framed clipping, resting on one of the exposed wall studs, slightly hidden behind a tarnished silver trophy. Moving the trophy to one side she read:

September 3 1966

Isadora Niles, who turned thirteen years old today, claims the Rookie championship. Her Widgeon scored a close win in Wednesday's race to finish the junior season undefeated.

There was more to the story that Lilli didn't care to read. She knew all too well how the day had ended. Above the text was a photo of Dori. She was smiling, not at the camera, but at someone to the photographer's left: Lilli, who had stood beside the photographer, mugging to get Dori to smile. Now, as Lilli gazed into the grainy black-and-white image, she had the uneasy feeling that her younger self—the girl who'd gotten Dori to smile—was there beside her, in another dimension. She moved, reflexively, a step or two away, bringing her smack into Ned, who'd quietly returned bearing two plastic cups of water, which sloshed over his hands and onto the floor.

He shrugged off her embarrassed apology and held out one of the two cups. "I think they say time for cocktails."

"Yes, that's it precisely," Lilli agreed, staring at the little appliquéd flags sandwiched between layers of plastic. "The Halls used to fly those from the back stay of the *Off Call* whenever they were out from Boston for the weekend."

Ned laughed. "Preston Hall the Third lives here year round now." He pointed out the window to a large Concordia in the harbor. "There's the new *Off Call*. Although Preston's permanently off call now. Retired. He named their dinghy *Off Calling*."

"Preston Hall the Third?"

"There's a Preston the Fourth, too. They keep having Prestons, and, thankfully, they keep improving." Ned glanced at the clipping of Dori that Lilli had been reading. "That deserves a place of greater distinction."

Lilli ran a finger over the glass, wiping away the dust. "People always look so happy in photographs. Why is that?" She asked, without expecting an answer. "Why do we always feel compelled to make people smile?"

"Never thought about it. Good manners?"

"Good manners. That was our reason for everything, wasn't it?"

They touched glasses with a hollow clunk.

"What are we toasting?" Lilli asked.

"Your return, of course."

"Good thing we're having a short one then. I'm leaving after lunch tomorrow."

He raised his eyebrows and seemed about to ask a question but said only, "Well then, here's to the past."

CHARLOTTE WASN'T HOME when Lilli called from the motel. She still wanted to ask Charlotte what, if anything, she could say to Bea and to describe the condition of the house, the grounds, and Bea. She didn't want to leave a message on her home phone—no telling who might hear it—and Charlotte rarely checked her cell phone, which she referred to as a fashion accessory. So Lilli simply said that she'd arrived in White Head, had seen Bea, and wanted to talk, and asked Charlotte to please call her back soon. When they spoke, Lilli would detail the overgrown path to the beach, the wisteria running riot over the house, the dirty dishes left on the counter.

She thought back to when they were young. Lilli and Dori used to plop their plates on the counter and start to scamper off after a meal, and Bea would ask whether they thought perhaps their fairy godmother was going to do the dishes. "Rinse and stack, girls," she'd commanded back then. Lilli had walked past Beacon House again on her way back to the motel, and it occurred to her that Bea might move somewhere like that now that Randall was gone. She had no idea what Bea's plans were, and it was certainly none of her business, but the house seemed too much for her. The house, frankly, deserved better.

Lilli would suggest that Charlotte call Bea and propose such a move. Lilli could assure Charlotte that the place looked very well run and attractive. She would even offer to contact a real estate agent to handle the sale of the house. Lilli preferred such solid, tangible tasks to the shifting sands of interpersonal relations, especially with her eldest sister.

Charlotte would know just what to say and how to say it, and Bea would listen. Everyone listened to their sister Charlotte. And trusted her. No reason not to. Competent, accomplished, effervescent, and friendly, she was the person Lilli called when deciding whom to invite to a dinner party, what to wear to a bar mitzvah, or where to spend her summer vacation. Charlotte always had an answer. She had become a neonatologist, one of only a handful of women in her class at the University of Chicago. When asked why she'd chosen to study neonatology, she would smile and say with typical self-effacement, "Because it's so simple. You just gotta keep 'em pink."

As Lilli navigated through dozens of channels on her television set, trying to fall asleep, wondering what it was about American shows that she found so off-putting, she continued to think about this plan, mentally listing all the benefits of such a move: convenience and companionship chief among them. Bea, she convinced herself, would love the idea. Who wouldn't? Lilli pictured them looking over a brochure together, perhaps even stopping by Beacon House for a visit after the service, and then returning to the house and discussing which pieces of furniture Bea would take with her when she moved. Like sisters. Who knew where such an afternoon might take them? Lilli was so convinced of Bea's enthusiasm that she resolved that she would raise the subject herself, should Charlotte not call before lunch the next day.

At nine forty-five the following morning Lilli arrived, bleary-eyed, at the Winston Funeral Parlor, a large Victorian that she recognized as the old McGrady place, where she used to pick up bottles of paregoric, cough syrup, and mercurochrome, which Bea would paint on the girls' scrapes. It stung horribly; Bea used to tell them to blow on it, which, miraculously, took the sting away.

Gone, now, were the high counter, the antiseptic smell, and rows of mysterious brown bottles. The walls were now painted in such muted colors that they seemed to recede in the soft lighting. Thick moss-colored carpeting muffled guests' footsteps, and brass buckets held potted plants with leaves so perfect Lilli wondered if they'd been embalmed. Invisible speakers delivered soothing music.

Lilli stepped forward to sign the guest book and paused. Was she merely a guest? A family member wouldn't sign the guest book. But then, a family member would have helped plan the service and would be secreted away somewhere in a back room, comforting others. Was she a close friend? Hardly. Close friends made casseroles and delivered them on the day of the service. Close friends also saw each other more than once every forty years or so. In the end, aware that others were waiting, she wrote her name and address as other guests had done and then stepped into a room to her left, where some sixty folding chairs had been set up. Lilli was glad she'd arrived early, as nearly half the seats were already occupied, most by women. She saw Ned Chapin sitting near the front, his hair now combed into place, his sunburned neck encased in a crisp collar. There was an empty chair beside him, but Lilli took a seat in the back. She saw no sign of an urn and wondered what Bea had done with Randall's ashes.

A tall woman with a thin nose took the seat next to her, and Lilli shifted slightly to make room. "Big crowd," the woman murmured. Her hair was brownish-gray, short and unstyled, and her face was tanned, deeply lined, and devoid of makeup. She wore a tailored gray tweed suit and a string of graduated pearls. Others around Lilli were similarly dressed. In her flowing, hand-painted, gray silk pantsuit, accessorized with a thick silver necklace, bracelet, and earrings—made for her by a friend in London in exchange for one of her paintings—Lilli felt, with a mixture of pride and embarrassment, like an abalone among oysters.

A plump woman with lacquered curls, penciled-in

eyebrows, and a perfume that was slowly giving Lilli a headache turned around and whispered to the thin, tweedy
woman, "Jane, did you get my message about the luncheon?"
Lilli tried not to listen, but the perfumed woman's bright pink
lipstick reminded her of Charlotte, and Lilli couldn't help
staring, wishing Charlotte were there with her. Grounded
and steady, Charlotte had been both anchor and compass
for Lilli in her youth. She'd listened without judgment the
day Lilli had fled White Head and arrived in Charles River
Square, sobbing. Charlotte had cradled Lilli's head in her lap
as Lilli ranted about how deceitful Bea was, how uncaring,
how selfish and mean. Charlotte's strong, gentle hands—
practiced from years of bread-making—had kneaded Lilli's
back, her sweet voice reassuring Lilli that everything would
be fine. And then, later, she had done far more than most to
make certain that was the case. Lilli sat in the funeral parlor
and pictured Charlotte and Izzy seated there with her, the
three of them holding hands and passing around tissues.

The organ music in the funeral parlor swelled with the
sound of Pachelbel's *Canon*, and Bea entered, holding the
arm of a young man wearing an ill-fitting dark suit and a
pious expression. He seated Bea and stepped to the front of
the room. "Welcome," he said. "We gather today to celebrate
the life of Randall Marsh."

Forty-five minutes later, after several brief tributes, some
familiar hymns, a period of meditative silence, and a reci-
tation of the Twenty-third Psalm, those who'd gathered to
celebrate the life of Randall Marsh filed out into the May
sunshine. Lilli moved to one side of the even flagstone walkway to wait for Bea. Nearby, the two women who'd been sitting near her resumed their discussion of the luncheon. This

turned out to be a monthly garden club affair, with a theme or guest speaker, and was to be held the following week. The tall woman with the thin nose glanced over and caught Lilli's eye. Embarrassed, Lilli moved farther out onto the brilliant, blemish-free green lawn, wondering again if they mixed embalming fluid with their plant fertilizer. Off in the distance, between the rooftops and trees, the water in the harbor sparkled. Lilli remembered, as a young girl, leaving the drugstore with a package of medicine in hand and change jingling in her pocket. She would stop at the ice cream parlor for a root beer barrel, a fireball, or a strip of licorice, Bea having told her she could buy something for herself with the money left over. She felt a hand on her arm and turned, expecting Bea, but instead, finding herself face-to-face with the tall woman, who said, "I'm sorry, but I've just now realized who you are."

Lilli stared, hoping for an insight, got none. The plump, perfumed woman was beside her, smiling broadly.

"It's Jane Hunsicker. You knew me as Janey Hallowell. I was a friend—"

"Of Dori's," Lilli finished. "I thought you looked familiar, but I couldn't quite place you."

"Well, I imagine I've changed some." She laughed, and Lilli could see more clearly the young girl who'd sailed with Dori in the Rookies.

The plump woman extended her hand. "I'm Susan Bradley. Pierce. Susie Pierce Bradley. I was in your sister Charlotte's class at Winsor."

Lilli shook her hand, unable to locate the trim, athletic young woman anywhere in this woman's round face and coiffed hair.

"Welcome back!" Janey said. "When did you arrive?"

"Just last night." Barely twelve hours! Lilli had lost track of time. She scanned the crowd for Bea and found her chatting with a long line of well-wishers.

"Oh, well, then I guess we can forgive Bea for not letting us know."

"We're having our monthly garden club luncheon next week," Susan said. "This is presumptuous, but we were wondering . . . We know what beautiful paintings you do. Your gardens, flowers . . . magnificent. Of course you might have plans already, but Bea did mention . . ."

Lilli stared. She seemed to—but couldn't possibly—be inviting Lilli to attend their luncheon.

"To come and talk to us about your painting," Janey finished. "Join us for lunch, and then speak for fifteen or twenty minutes on what inspires you, who's influenced you, what you're saying to the world through your art, and so forth."

"Excuse me?" Lilli, trying not to look or sound incredulous, wondered whether there was anything she might want to do less. Realizing that her tone might have seemed rude, she added, "When did you say the luncheon was?"

"Next Wednesday."

"That's a lovely invitation. Quite flattering, really." Lilli attempted to conceal her relief. "But I'm leaving for Boston quite soon and back to London Saturday. But thank you."

The two women looked perplexed.

"I came just for the service," Lilli explained. "Well, I'm staying for lunch." She chuckled. The two women did not join her. "Then I'm driving back to Boston." She kept her voice even, as she felt her spirits soar. Being here was harder than she'd imagined. She hadn't fully realized how hard until she thought about leaving. Every house, every turn in the road, every vista, it seemed, wanted to whisper of some long-hidden memory best left unremembered, to shine a light on some long-lost image best left in shadow.

The two women exchanged a concerned glance, and then Janey put her hand on Lilli's arm. "I am so sorry about Randall. I should have said that right off."

"We all miss him," said Susan.

"I understand he was still active at the club," Lilli said, trying to sound agreeable to make up for any earlier bluntness.

"Very. You know, Jane, we could ask Ned Chapin to come speak again about his roses."

"Well, it was good of you to come back and . . . see her," Janey said.

Lilli smiled and shook their hands. "Isn't that what sisters are for?"

The emerald sweep of front lawn had cleared, and Bea was nowhere in sight. Lilli wondered if she'd forgotten their lunch. It wouldn't surprise her; Bea had twice asked Lilli about her luggage the night before, having completely forgotten that Lilli was not staying at the house. If she had forgotten the lunch, that would be fine, Lilli decided. What business was it of hers, really, she now wondered in the stark light of day, standing on this unblemished lawn in this town that seemed determined to draw her back, where Bea lived? She could just head back to Boston now. She'd been doing well enough all these years, hadn't she? What was to be gained by raising such difficult subjects with such uncertain outcomes—

"Ah, here you are. I didn't see you inside." Ned Chapin came up beside her.

Lilli smiled, happy to see him. "I was sitting in the back.

Next to Janey Hallowell. Hunsicker, sorry. Jane Hunsicker. Bea and I were supposed to have lunch, but I think she may have forgotten."

He shook his head. "She's inside, wondering where you are. Thinks *you* forgot."

"Yoo-hoo." A familiar voice hailed from the doorway. "Lilli, where on earth have you been? I've been waiting and waiting in here."

"It was good to see you, Lilli," Ned said, giving her arm a squeeze. "And please accept my condolences."

"Right here, Bea," Lilli called, thinking that she could as easily apply Ned's well-wishes to her upcoming lunch with Bea as to Randall's death.

Bea made her uneven way down the steps, holding tight to the railing, and onto the flagstone walkway. "How would I know to find you out here? Well, never mind, I've found you now. I could use something restorative after all that. A drink and a bite to eat?"

"Is there somewhere close by?"

"Nowhere I care to go. All overpriced places that serve three sprigs of watercress and one raspberry and call it a salad." Bea straightened her shoulders. "I don't trust a restaurant that feels it needs to tell you every single ingredient in a dish. I call that trying too hard. False pride. Half of them shouldn't be anywhere except, maybe, in the centerpiece. Hibiscus soup? Fennel pollen? I ask you. No, let's go to S.S. Pierce and buy sandwiches and take them back and eat on the porch."

"S.S. Pierce? Didn't that go out of business some years ago?"

Bea waved her free hand. "Yes, yes, but there's a store there now that sells exactly the same things. New name, same store.

driving lesson. It had been one of those defining moments for the two of them, nothing ever quite the same after. She shut the door and walked around to the passenger side, checking her watch again, wanting to hasten the time when she would be away from these people she once knew, who seemed to think she wanted to know them again. Their lives had been running parallel for the past four decades, like two very different movies playing in adjacent theaters at the multiplex. Lilli felt as though she'd gone out for popcorn and wandered back into the wrong theater.

She slid into the passenger seat and glanced over at Bea, who was taking items out of her small blue clutch—a tube of lipstick, an embroidered eyeglass case, a wad of crumpled tissue, a bottle of Motrin—shaking and examining each one. Lilli remained silent as Bea upended the purse and gave it a good shake.

"Let me guess. You've lost the keys."

"Not lost, misplaced. Temporarily misplaced."

Two hours, thought Lilli, reexamining her decision to come to White Head, to stay for lunch. *Eyes forward*, she told herself. *Keep your eyes on the road ahead.* "Did you by any chance wear a coat this morning?"

"What's that?"

"DID YOU WEAR A COAT THIS MORNING?"

Bea considered this. "I may have." She massaged her ear and gazed back toward the funeral parlor, as though the rummage through her bag had exhausted her reserves.

"I'll go," Lilli offered, wanting to avoid further delays.

"Would you? My hips . . ."

Lilli got out, crossed the lawn to the front door, and returned a few moments later with a tan trench coat over one arm. She placed it in the back and dangled the keys in Bea's direction, contemplating using them as ransom and demanding that Bea allow her to drive. But she simply handed them to Bea through the open window and returned to the passenger seat.

Five minutes later, Bea pulled up in front of the convenience store that occupied the former home of S.S. Pierce.

"I'll run in," Lilli offered, climbing out before Bea could protest. Bea lowered the window and called out, "Be sure to get the real turkey, not that processed kind. And white bread. And Swiss cheese." As Lilli prepared to enter the store, she turned and waved acknowledgment, but Bea was chatting with someone on the sidewalk through the open car window.

Lilli emerged a short while later with a shopping bag in one hand and a brilliant pink azalea in the other. She thought it would brighten up the house, and Bea could take it with her to Beacon House. Lilli had called them while she was inside and learned that they would have a unit in the new independent-living wing available next month. Their grandmother had left each of them a sizable inheritance, so Lilli was not too concerned about the finances. Besides, she was sure there would be plenty of money from the sale of the house.

"What's that?" Bea asked, as Lilli opened the rear door.

"An azalea."

"Yes, I can see that. What's it for?"

"For you. I thought it might cheer you up."

"I wasn't aware I needed cheering up. And why an azalea?"

"It's what they had," Lilli said, already regretting this impulse purchase.

"We always get our plants at Emerson's, Lillianne. They

have a much better selection. And better stock." Bea was assessing the plant, which, Lilli now noticed, had a bare spot on one side, which she rotated away from Bea as she secured the plant on the floor of the backseat.

"I'm sure you do. But this one was here, and I thought it was rather nice." Lilli climbed in and put on her seat belt, noting that Bea was not wearing hers. "I suppose if you don't want it, I could put it on Randall's grave," Lilli prompted, hoping to elicit some information.

"What's that?" Bea asked, pulling away from the curb. A car horn sounded as a Volvo SUV swerved to avoid the Mercedes's front end. The young blond woman behind the wheel, with a cell phone pressed to her ear, barely gave them a glance.

"Nothing," Lilli said. "I didn't say anything."

Four

BEA and Lilli settled into a stony silence after the business with the spinnaker. The wind had dropped, but the dark clouds convoying across the horizon signaled rain later. Lilli prayed that she would sail close enough to the mooring for Bea to grab it on her first try. When her prayers were answered, she rowed them back to the float, where Bea clambered out, saying that she had something to do, with a wink and the same mysterious intonation that Blythe had used that morning. She told Lilli to bring in the gear before dashing off up the gangway.

Racers were milling about the main room of the clubhouse, awaiting their results, when Lilli—windblown and loaded down with life preservers, sail bag, and foul-weather gear—struggled in. Randall spotted her and headed over to help, but before he'd made it halfway across the room, Bea, her hair tidied and an apron knotted around her middle, hailed him from the kitchen. He sent Lilli an apologetic smile and a big wink, which lightened her load a little, before spinning on one heel and setting off at a trot toward Bea. Ned Chapin—who'd recently removed his hat, leaving his red hair flat on top and wind-whipped on the sides, giving him a somewhat clownish appearance—was leaning against the door frame. Ned Chapin was that boy in the middle of class photographs, overshadowed by those in front and behind. Lilli thought of him much the way she thought of the tables in her house: familiar, useful, and always where needed. He'd had a crush on her since she was in fourth grade. He'd been in seventh at the time, which she would have found flattering if she'd been interested, and annoying if he'd pressed. But she wasn't, and he never had. He'd apparently noticed Randall's abrupt about-face and stepped in to offer Lilli a hand. With a grateful smile, she deposited the entire load into his eager arms.

The commodore had made his way through the crush and stood, shuffling papers, by the big fireplace at one end of the room. "Quiet! May I have your attention!" he called out. The crowd moved forward, bearing Lilli along, and the din rose. Someone finally rang a bell, and everyone quieted. "As you know, this was the last race of the season," the commodore said, and cleared his throat. "Of course we'll continue sailing until the ice in the harbor gets too thick." He paused here, waiting for the laugh he expected every year.

"So, I'm announcing today's winners, as well as giving prizes for the club championships." He shuffled through his papers. "Today's best time was Randall Marsh, our favorite summer resident, ably assisted by Miss Isadora Niles. This was Dori's first senior race—"

His speech was interrupted by applause and cheers. Lilli hadn't realized that Randall and Dori had won and she tried to get Dori's attention, but Dori was immediately swarmed by friends, hugging her and thumping her on the back.

"Because she is celebrating another very special occasion today—" the commodore said, raising his voice. With that the kitchen door banged open, and Bea proceeded in with four friends, one of them Randall, who bore an enormous birthday cake topped with thirteen brightly burning candles. All of them were singing "Happy Birthday" loudly and slightly off-key. All eyes shifted from the commodore to this unexpected sight, before the crowd joined the singing. Lilli threaded her way closer to Dori, who was clapping her hands and bouncing up and down as Randall placed the cake on a table beside her.

"Another cake!" Dori squealed. "A real one."

"Make a wish, Dori!" someone shouted.

Dori closed her eyes, and the room grew quiet. After a long moment, she opened them and seemed genuinely startled to see so many faces staring expectantly at her. She turned a delighted gaze to the blazing candles anchored in their glistening field of white, as though she hadn't the least idea how or when this dazzling sight had arrived beside her. Lilli knew that in those few moments Dori had drifted off to some private place, far from the White Head Yacht Club. She whispered, "Blow out the candles."

"What did you wish for?" called someone, as Dori inhaled.

"Lilli says I can't tell or my wish won't come true," she said on the exhale. The crowd laughed. Dori took another breath and blew, extinguishing all thirteen flames. People cheered and surged forward, eager hands extended, as Bea began to slice.

"Oh, Lilli. Isn't this wonderful?" Dori said. "I can hardly remember a better birthday. And I didn't think I'd have one at all." Dori and Lilli forked large pieces of the spongy spice cake into their mouths, pressed the sugar-crusted frosting against the roofs of their mouths, and rolled their eyes in delight.

Lilli thought she might faint. When she could speak, she said, "Not have a birthday? Why not?"

"I don't know. I just didn't think I would this year." Dori's expression grew serious. She lowered her plate. "I'm so sorry, Lilli. About the race. I know you wanted to sail with Randall. It wasn't me. I didn't say anything. Honest."

"I know. And Bea was right, the wind did pick up." She wiped a bit of frosting from Dori's upper lip. "I hate it when she's right. Which is almost always. She's so annoying." Dori giggled.

Finally the commodore regained the group's attention and continued the awards. "Now for the championship of the junior division. The trophy for the Rookies goes to captain Isadora Niles and her crew, Janey Hallowell, for the best times, good seamanship, and for keeping their boat shipshape all summer."

The crowd gave a sugar-enhanced cheer as Janey and Dori, another bit of frosting clinging to her upper lip, accepted their small silver cups. Lilli knew that she did not want to be in the room, or anywhere near it, when the club championship was announced, and she began to make her way to the back, hoping to slip out, unnoticed. If Bea didn't win, Lilli would never hear the end of it; it would be all Lilli's fault. If she did, Bea wouldn't give Lilli a mention. Not that Lilli deserved any mention, but still . . . She had already endured enough humiliation for one day. She squeezed behind a row of people in front of the fireplace. Just a few more steps and she'd be out the door.

"Our club champion is a sailor of extreme skill and talent. While she did not win today's race due to a bit of bad luck on the course, she still has the best record—" People began to clap in anticipation of his announcement. The commodore raised his voice and said in a rush, "For the sixth year running, the trophy goes to Miss Elizabeth Niles."

The crowd cheered as Bea left her station by the empty cake tray and stepped forward to accept the large silver bowl. So she'd won. Lilli watched from the door as Bea held the trophy over her head, and someone snapped a photograph.

At this Lilli stepped outside and hurried along the porch, determined not to let the tears, unexpectedly rimming her eyes, fall until she was well out of sight of the yacht club. She had some pride. A hand grabbed her arm, spinning her around.

"Just where do you think you're sneaking off to?" Randall stopped when he saw Lilli's damp cheeks. "Hey," he said, cupping her face in one hand, pulling a handkerchief from a back pocket, and dabbing at the tears. "Hey, let's have none of that."

Summer after summer, she and Randall had played tag on the lawn, swung together in the hammock, lain side by side on the rocks sunning themselves. His body near hers had never raised so much as a goose bump on her arm. Now, his light touch on her face sent an electric current racing up and down her spine and radiating through her limbs. She could practically feel the blood rushing from her brain to her face, flushing her cheeks. But she was determined neither to babble incoherently nor to stand silent as a stone, so she pulled away and swiped at her cheeks with the back of her hand. "I hate her." She sounded childish, but that was the truth of things. She mostly meant Bea, but her loathing applied equally well to the dopey Lilli impersonator that had invaded her body and brain that summer.

"Oh, now. You don't mean that. Bea is . . . Bea. I know exactly what happened out there. Your boat was on its ear, and Bea wouldn't let off one degree while you were trying to set the spinnaker. I could see you plain as day. I'm a lot bigger than you and I'd have had trouble. The wind really picked up out there for a while."

He understood her so well. She'd known he would and adored him all the more.

Randall shrugged. "And what difference does it make? She got her trophy and"—he paused, leaned close, and wrapped one of Lilli's loose curls around his index finger—"I've got you." He tightened his grip on her curl. He needn't have; Lilli wasn't going anywhere.

Lilli could sense his gaze on her, feel the warmth of his hand near her cheek, smell the salt on his skin. She looked up. A fine layer of it dusted his forehead.

"She knows whose fault it was out there. She won't admit it, but she knows. She's a tough competitor. She doesn't back down and she'll do whatever it takes to win. Remember that. Meanwhile—" He put his other hand on Lilli's shoulder and gave it a squeeze. "About tonight."

"Tonight?" she repeated, her entire consciousness now directed to the area of her collarbone beneath Randall's thumb.

"The dance. You're coming, right?"

"I . . . I'm not sure."

"Well, you better because I want a dance with you. Maybe two." He tucked the curl behind her ear. "What do you say?"

At that moment, not one single thing. She stood, thrilling at the feel of his hand now grazing the side of her neck, the intimacy of being connected to him in this way. She dared a glance into his eyes and found him gazing at her with a look that made her insides melt. She didn't know what that look meant, but its effect was incendiary.

"Randall." Bea's voice came from the other side of the clubhouse. "It's time for photographs. Are you out here?" She rounded the corner and stopped when she saw the two of them. Her glance went from one to the other, and her expression was much like the one she'd worn out on the race course as she'd assessed the speed and direction of the wind, the placement of the other boats, the distance to the next mark. *Goodness*, thought Lilli, *could Bea be jealous?*

"Later," Randall said softly, untwining his finger from Lilli's curl.

Lilli nodded, still unable to speak, and watched as he walked toward Bea. "You come, too, Lilli," Bea commanded. "We're taking photographs and Dori's asking for you."

Dori had never liked having her picture taken. She said she didn't see the point in capturing one moment so you could enjoy it in another. *"Why not just enjoy now, now?"* she would ask. Lilli had explained how some people like to keep photographs so they can remember events later and share them with people who weren't there. Lilli knew Dori would pose for her, so she followed Bea and Randall back inside and stood beside the photographer and made faces. Dori had laughed and made faces back, so the photographer had to take several before he got one of Dori smiling—not at the camera, but at Lilli.

As soon as the photographer finished, Lilli grabbed Dori's hand and pulled her homeward, wanting to beat Bea, who was next up for photos.

"Why are we running, Lilli? Wait, I forgot my basket."

"Hurry. I need to ask Mom something right away."

They dashed through the glade, Dori shouting, "All skunks go to Hell," as Lilli pulled her along, then clambered over the boulders rimming the cove, and onto the beach. Lilli could see her mother, across the cove, in her garden, weeding or perhaps installing another of her sculptures. Blythe worked in the garden from early morning until long after dusk, weeding and feeding the flower beds a weak fertilizer tea that Mr. Sylvia brewed up by sun-steeping a big bucket of the Hammonds' horse manure in water. Dori stopped to catch her breath in front of Big-big, lapped on all sides now by the incoming tide. "Let's wade out and look for enemy subs." She had seen the movie *The Russians Are Coming, The Russians Are Coming* the week before and ever since had looked with suspicion at every new face in town and wanted to keep a nearly constant vigil for "enemy subs" in the surrounding waters.

Lilli had neither the time nor the interest. "Two dances," Randall had said. She could still feel the spot on her neck where his thumb had rested as he'd toyed with her curl. "We can come back tonight," Lilli said. "When the tide's out."

"Promise?"

"Promise. Race you up the steps," Lilli said to urge her on.

"Let's play school." This was a game their father had

invented to get the girls up the steps when they were little. He'd hide a pebble in one hand and, if you guessed correctly which, you could advance one step. Certainly not the fastest way up. Dori was holding her hands out, both fists clenched.

"Not today. I told you. I'm in a hurry." Lilli was already at the bottom step, then climbing, and then at the top, sighting her mother in a flowered halter top and shorts, kneeling beside a large mound of cut flowers. Mr. Sylvia had placed the oversized pots with little mums around the lawn, one right beside the old sundial and the wrought-iron bench, where their father used to sit, gazing out across the cove at sailboats sliding silently past. Now Bea sat there, snapping green beans into a bowl.

Lilli cursed silently. *How had she gotten home so fast?* As Lilli hesitated, taking in this disappointing sight, Dori raced past her and across the lawn, brandishing the little silver cup above her head. "Mama, look!" She pranced around the pile of cut blossoms. "I won."

Blythe rocked back on her heels. "Oh, that's beautiful! Perfect. A goblet from which you shall sip your wine at supper." Dori's "wine" would be grape juice, but no matter, it would still be a festive occasion with her at the head of the table, wearing her paper crown.

"No, I think I'll use it as a vase," Dori said, picking up a pair of clippers and looking for likely blooms.

"I'm sorry your race didn't go well, dear," Blythe called to Lilli, who lingered in the shadows of the cedars, willing Bea into the house.

Lilli crossed the lawn and plopped herself down beside her mother. "When did Bea get home?" she whispered, thoroughly vexed. Lilli wanted to tell her mother how unfair Bea had been, making her change places with Dori, the unnecessary risks she'd taken, the danger she'd put them both in.

"When? Oh . . . just a few minutes ago. Randall dropped her off," Blythe said, without looking up or catching Lilli's aggrieved tone. "I asked him to come for supper."

Lilli's face flushed at the mere mention of his name, and she started to wonder if she was coming down with something. "Randall?" Lilli glanced over at Bea, who snapped the head off a green bean.

Dori had clipped zinnias, stocks, and sweet peas, and stuffed them into her small cup. "They gave me a great big birthday cake. Did Bea tell you?" She was bending over a clump of asters, dotted with monarch butterflies, trying to coax one onto her bouquet. "Oh—" Dori stood and wheeled around to face her mother. "That's why you didn't have sugar for the pancakes. And I didn't even bring you a piece." She dropped the bouquet, cup, and clippers, and dropped into her mother's lap. "And I hardly ate any of your lovely pancake cake, because it really did taste very peculiar, and now I feel so-o-o bad." She buried her face in her mother's shoulder.

"Nonsense," Blythe said, holding her tight. "We can eat whatever we want on our birthdays. And as much. Or eat nothing at all. I think I'll take a little nibble off your ear." She leaned down and gave Dori's ear a little nip. Dori started to giggle.

"Mom, can I go to the dance tonight?" Lilli said softly, taking advantage of this diversion, so Bea wouldn't hear.

"You won't have a cake for your party tomorrow, though," Blythe said, rubbing Dori's back, ignoring Lilli.

"All my friends are going," Lilli lied. She spoke a little louder, thinking that perhaps her mother hadn't heard.

"I don't care," Dori said, her face still buried, her words muffled.

"Bea said you'd rather have your cake today. Although, now that I think about it, I'm not at all sure why . . ." Blythe looked over at Bea with the innocent, open gaze of a child. "But I do have a nice surprise for you," she said to Dori, still cradled in her lap.

Dori peeked up. "You do?"

Blythe threaded a few blossoms into Dori's hair and nodded.

"Mother!" Lilli exploded, frustrated by her mother's inattention. It was all just too much. Randall driving Bea home, the mutiny of her own body and mind, and now her own mother ignoring her.

Blythe, startled, stared at Lilli, sensing that she'd done something wrong and having no idea what. "What, dear?"

"May I go to the dance tonight?" Lilli said, punching out each word.

"You know the rules," Bea said from the bench. "Daddy was very clear: No dances until you're sixteen."

"But that's a silly old rule," Lilli said, furious at herself for losing her temper and raising her voice. Her mother would almost certainly have said yes. "Daddy's dead. Things are different now."

An uncomfortable silence settled over the gathering in the garden then, as Blythe, looking as though she'd been struck, turned her back and began methodically cutting stems of flowers. Dori was biting her lip trying not to cry, and Bea had narrowed her eyes and was looking daggers at Lilli, who knew she shouldn't have said what she said and most sincerely wished she hadn't.

"Some things are different," Bea said quietly. "And some things are the same. For instance, the table still needs to be set for dinner. Go inside, girls, and wash up and see what else Charlotte needs."

Lilli turned to plead her case with her mother, but she was cutting blossom after blossom, adding them to her enormous pile, and softly humming a tune Lilli couldn't quite make out. Lilli helped Dori collect her scattered flowers, and they crossed the wide lawn to the house, as Dori whistled snatches of Blythe's odd tune and arranged the stems in her trophy cup. Lilli tried to reduce the rolling boil of her anger to a simmer.

"Stay out of the den, you two," Bea called. Lilli pretended she hadn't heard.

They approached the sunporch. Lilli lagged behind Dori, certain her life was over at fifteen. She had watched her father give Bea dancing lessons years before in the living room—tables and chairs pushed back, the hi-fi warbling out a scratchy version of "The Dipsy Doodle"—giggling, certain she would never want to do anything as silly as dance with boys. And here she was, so heartsick at the thought of missing the opportunity to dance with Randall that she could barely breathe. Another victim of the dipsy doodle. *". . . if it gets you, it couldn't be worse. The things you say will come out in reverse."* She'd even lied to her mother; few, if any, of her friends would attend the dance. But the age rule seemed arbitrary and senseless. Lilli felt far older than fifteen. That should count for something. She closed her eyes and imagined Randall's cheek close to hers, his arms around her. This made her prickly hot in unaccustomed places, strange, but not at all unpleasant.

"Lilli, what are you doing?"

Lilli opened her eyes to see Dori standing inches away, staring at her, much as she had done to Dori that morning. "You looked silly." Dori imitated Lilli's pose: eyes shut, head tilted up, mouth slightly open, like someone awaiting a kiss. "Like that. What were you doing?"

"You don't know anything. You're too young," Lilli snapped. She was surprised by her tone of voice, but she needed to punish someone for the disappointing way this day, once so full of promise, had unfolded.

If Lilli's tone surprised Dori, she didn't show it. "Well, I know I'm hungry. And I know I want to show Charlotte my trophy." Charlotte would carry the small, lopsided nosegay into the dining room and place it with great ceremony at the center of the big table. She'd tip her head, pretend to study it, and say, "What do you think? Too big?" Dori would laugh and tilt her head, as Charlotte had done, pretending to consider, but not quite understand the joke. "*I* think it looks splendid," Charlotte would finally say. And Dori would nod, although the flowers would look ridiculously small.

If only I had left it at that, Lilli would often think later, as she tried to unravel the strands of that terrible day to determine how far back she would have had to go to secure a different outcome. If she had eaten more of Blythe's awful pancakes and arrived so late that Bea would have found someone else to crew for her? Kept her mind in the race so she wouldn't have fouled up setting the spinnaker? Made it home before Bea? Not lost her temper? Any one of these would have had its effect, the way a single wrong stroke can alter an entire drawing, changing the perspective, destroying the composition. But those were not the decisions Lilli had made earlier, and Lilli didn't leave it at that. Instead, she said, for reasons she didn't understand then and couldn't adequately explain later, "Let's peek in the den."

Dori, who would follow Lilli anywhere, frowned. "Bea said not to." She knew black from white and could navigate neatly between them, but she had difficulty distinguishing among gray tones, and this suggestion seemed to lie squarely in their shadowy midst. She struck out for the safety of the familiar. "I want to show Charlotte my trophy and put my flowers on the table," she said, as if reciting instructions.

"The dipsy doodle will get you someday. And when it does, the things you will say."

"She said not to *go* in. She didn't say anything about not *looking* in." Lilli made her tone conspiratorial, normally irresistible for Dori. But still Dori hesitated, and so Lilli grabbed her hand and pulled her around to the back of the house, ducking under the kitchen window—through which she could hear the clatter of plates and silverware and Charlotte singing as she set the table—past the front door that was used only on formal occasions or by strangers, to squeeze behind the lilac bushes that in May filled the den with their dizzying perfume. They stood on tiptoes and peered in over the sill.

Lilli knew right away that she'd made a mistake. The "something" that Blythe had mentioned at breakfast, the "something" that she "had to do," that had kept her from watching the race, was to unwind a dozen balls of yarn in blue, yellow, red, green, white, pink, and brown to create in the den a giant spiderweb. She'd woven the yarn between slatted chair backs and around the handles of sailing trophies. She'd sent it over the top of their grandmother's stern countenance above the fireplace, and around the brass poker, tongs, and shovel beside it. She'd wound it around the spindled legs of tables and the stout bases of lamps, under footstools and seat cushions, and around the doorstop shaped like a spaniel, in a chaotic intertwining of color that ended at their father's rolltop desk, where a dollhouse stood—a miniature replica of their own house, right down to the ivy-stenciled kitchen walls, which, in this case, were finished. Who had made such a marvel, Lilli wondered? On a lawn of green felt Blythe had placed flowerpots the size of thimbles, inside each a brightly wrapped candy, one for each of the girls who would attend Dori's party the next day and unravel this web.

"Oh, Lilli," Dori said, falling back against the lilac bush and giving her sister an accusing look. "This was wrong. We shouldn't have even peeked. Mama's so sad already, and this will make her even sadder. It was meant to be a surprise. I knew I wouldn't have a birthday this year." She ran off toward the front door, scattering blossoms along the way.

CHARLOTTE WAS IN the kitchen, apron tied around her broad midsection, breaking off bits of dough and planting them on a baking sheet when Dori burst through the door. "Whoa there. How did it go today?" Charlotte called, as her youngest sister shot past and clattered up the kitchen stairs. Bea had already told Charlotte that Dori had won, but she would pretend she knew nothing and let Dori tell. Dori's tales were enchanting, if hard to follow: long on detail, short on context, often focused on some quite minor event that few others even noticed, and she rarely put herself at the center, as though she saw the world entirely in the third person.

Lilli tried to slip through the door unnoticed, but

Charlotte spotted her and called out, "Lilli, what's wrong with Dori?" Getting no response, she sighed, rolled a bit of dough between her thumb and index finger, and popped it into her mouth. Obviously dinner was going to be delayed. She'd been looking forward to the special birthday meal she'd prepared: leg of lamb and roasted potatoes, with mint and green beans from the garden. Charlotte chewed the gummy dough, wondering what Lilli had done this time. She knew Lilli was struggling that summer, but she also knew that she was doing nothing to help herself, lying around all day on the sunporch glider, dreaming about Randall Marsh. Everyone thought he was so charming, so helpful, so handy to have around. Handy if what you wanted to do was play games all day! He struck Charlotte as one of those people for whom things seem to come too easily. Then again, he almost entirely lacked ambition. When you don't want much, it's likely to come with very little effort. He was handsome, certainly. Maybe too good-looking. Something about him didn't ring true. Charlotte didn't trust him, although she couldn't exactly say why.

And he was nineteen, far too mature for Lilli right now, despite her insistence that she felt older than fifteen. If Lilli's crush puzzled Charlotte, Bea's attraction to him positively mystified her. Bea hadn't spoken of it, but Charlotte could tell. Bea, who worried herself sleepless over their mother's increasing carelessness and fretted incessantly about the weather, the condition of the house, whether their meals were balanced. What could someone like Randall offer her but one more thing to worry about? Bea felt so responsible for everything and everyone. She'd worry herself sick, Charlotte was sure of that. She was equally sure that Bea would stay on in this house until Dori had left home—at least.

Their mother was growing increasingly childlike and . . . peculiar every day.

Just the week before, she'd arrived at the dinner table in an evening gown, lavender elbow-length kid gloves, a necklace she'd made of shells, and one of George's old hats into which she'd stuck a seagull feather! Dori thought it enchanting and raced upstairs to put on a dress. Charlotte had exchanged concerned looks across the table with Bea, who had pursed her lips and shaken her head ever so slightly. Charlotte wasn't sure if Bea was shaking her head in condemnation (she looked very like their grandmother and was beginning to take on some of her mannerisms) or warning Charlotte not to say anything. As if she would! Poor Lilli simply looked pained.

Charlotte ate a spoonful of mint jelly and sighed.

Bea remained in the garden after sending the girls inside to set the table. She watched her mother, humming, cutting flowers—far too many—for a centerpiece for the table. She added coreopsis, coneflowers, phlox, stocks, and fairy roses to her bouquet, and then wandered off to a patch of wildflowers growing by the side of the yard and began to cut Queen Anne's lace, cornflower, and bittersweet. Last night Bea had come home around eleven and found her mother out in the garden. Under the nearly full moon, Blythe had looked positively spectral in her nightgown, sunbonnet, and oversized gardening gloves, poking at the soil with her trowel. Bea had sat with her for a while. It was clear that Blythe thought it was still midday, so Bea finally suggested they go in for tea. "Lovely idea," her mother had said. "Let's take it in the garden."

Now Bea sighed and stared down at the bowl of green beans in her lap. "Blast," she said. "Blast and damn." Cradling the beans, she headed into the house.

LILLI IGNORED CHARLOTTE and made for the front hall, intending to flee, she knew not where, but it seemed that everything she touched that day had turned out wrong, and she wanted to be away from those she cared about most lest she do more damage. If she could have climbed out of her skin, like the black and orange caterpillars, and bound herself inside a chrysalis to hang, undisturbed, for the next few hours, days, or even months, she would have. Gladly.

Bea entered through the sunporch, just in time to see Dori clatter up the stairs, her cheeks wet and her eyes red. Lilli was close behind, so Bea planted herself in Lilli's path as she came down the hall and asked why Dori was crying.

Lilli told her to mind her own business and pushed past her up the stairs, when Blythe breezed in through the sunporch. Her bouquet was so large it required both arms; her cheeks were flushed the color of the pink fairy roses. "Who's crying?" She buried her face in her bouquet.

Bea was staring hard at Lilli. She knew what Lilli had done. She had a gift for unearthing Lilli's misdeeds, much the way certain pigs Lilli had read about in *National Geographic* could roust out truffles buried deep beneath the litter of leaves on a forest floor.

"Dori is crying," Bea said to Blythe. "I've no idea why. Do you, Lilli?" She kept her gaze on Lilli.

Lilli stared back. Clearly a challenge had been made. A gauntlet thrust to the ground. Lilli's face glove-smacked. She knew what she had to do. "We peeked in the den," she said. "It was Dori's idea. Mostly."

Her mother turned a startled gaze on Lilli, now frozen on the bottom step and said, "Oh, she wouldn't do that."

They were now both staring at Lilli, trapped in her lie on the stairs, her face flushing, not the pale pink of the fairy roses, but blood red like the roses climbing up the arbor. "We didn't go in," Lilli said defensively, inching farther up the stairs, knowing that what she'd done was wrong, that her lie was wrong, and unable to confess or explain why she'd done it, either to herself or to her mother—or to Bea, who stood there, always so perfect, judging her. Charlotte, who might have understood, had remained in the kitchen. Lilli felt very alone and small.

Blythe put out a hand and caught Lilli's where it rested on the banister. Their eyes met, and Lilli sensed that her mother could see inside her, into the dark, tight space deep within her that she didn't dare explore, like the closet, coated with cobwebs and containing who knew what, tucked behind the furnace in the far section of the cellar. Then her mother smiled at Lilli. "Just peeked in? You didn't mean to hurt Dori." Lilli, buoyed by her mother's empathy and understanding, felt at once comforted, excused, and forgiven. She smiled back at her mother and started down the steps, intending to take the flowers and get a hug from her mother. But Blythe's eyebrows knit together as she withdrew her hand from Lilli's, and her gaze seemed to turn inward. "Did you?" she added.

Blythe usually assumed good intentions of everyone. But with those two stout, sturdy words, Lilli got the clear impression that her mother wasn't quite so sure about her. Of course she hadn't meant to hurt Dori! Had she? Suddenly, in the presence of another's suspicion, Lilli began to doubt herself. She wished Blythe would get angry so she could meet that anger with her own, now boiling up inside her. This measure-less mistrust offered her nothing to push against, like when she would swim out from the beach too far and reach with a toe for the ridged sandy bottom, only to find that there was nothing below her but water. Unaware that her daughter was floundering, Blythe's eyes remained on Lilli, her gaze still as distant as that ocean floor. "You were so sure it was the right thing," she said, "so sure he'd get better."

Bea and Lilli froze. They exchanged looks, Lilli's of aston-ished puzzlement, Bea's of frank concern. Was Blythe talking about their father?

Just then Charlotte poked her head out from the kitchen and said, "Dinner's ready. Could someone finish setting the table?" And the moment passed. Blythe thrust the fragrant bouquet at Lilli as though nothing had happened. "I picked these for you. To paint. Why don't you go find a vase and make a nice centerpiece? Bea, you and I will finish the table. We'll use the good china and have a lovely party." Bea and Lilli stood a moment in a stunned tableau: Lilli on the stairs hugging the blowsy bouquet, Bea below her. Both of them were gazing at Blythe, now radiant at the prospect of a party, the incident with the den and her recent comment quite forgotten.

Lilli grabbed one of Charlotte's plump dinner rolls, now browned and fragrant, as she passed through the kitchen. She climbed up on the counter in the pantry to get the heavy green glass vase—the only one large enough to hold all those flowers. As she hopped down, she snagged the hem of her skirt on the metal edging and swore. She took a bite of the roll, located a pair of scissors in the top drawer, and began snipping off stems. Through the wall she could hear her mother and Bea talking as they set the table.

"Worried about Lilli?" their mother was saying. "Why? Remember when you were that age—"

"I was never that age," Bea shot back.

A small gray spider rappelled from the lip of an orange lily, landed on the counter, and scurried under the toaster.

"She wants so much to go to the dance tonight. Don't you think we could let her?"

"I really don't think we should. Rules are rules," Bea said. "Besides, we can't leave Dori alone on her birthday."

Blythe would be home, Lilli mused; how much company did Dori need?

"Dori thirteen!" Blythe exclaimed. "I wish she could stay my little girl forever." Lilli heard the sound of drawers sliding open as her mother spoke. "Why do children want so badly to grow up when childhood is so lovely? No one should wish their life away."

The clatter of silverware drowned out Bea's response, but Lilli, jabbing flowers into the vase, wondered what it was that made grown-ups forget the truth about childhood. Adults could stay up past midnight, drinking and singing at clambakes on the beach. Adults could take the train into Boston whenever they wished and spend the day chatting in smoke-filled rooms and riding on trolley cars. Ladies could wear gowns, lipstick, and high heels, put their hair up, and waltz at the yacht club with Randall Marsh. Adults could make their own decisions. How could anyone think childhood was idyllic with all this waiting? Lilli wished her childhood well past.

She paused, scissors aimed at a phlox stem, as she heard

Bea and Blythe begin again. "I think she has a crush on our Randall," Blythe said, and Lilli snipped off a good two inches more than she'd intended.

"Oh, really?" Bea said, sounding mildly surprised and entirely disinterested.

Liar. But how did her mother know? Lilli held her breath and pressed her ear to the wall.

"Wouldn't that be lovely? He's been like a son to me, especially since your father died. And he's so handsome. Your father was very handsome." Lilli sat back and plucked the petals from a daisy. Was it that obvious? Did Randall know? Was that a good thing? Bea murmured something. Lilli couldn't hear what.

"I wondered," Blythe was now saying, "whether there might be something between the two of you."

Lilli strained to hear Bea's response, but both voices faded as the two left the room. He wouldn't. Couldn't! Bea was five whole years older than him and acted even older. Lilli consoled herself with the mathematical impossibility of such a union as she carried the vase of flowers into the dining room, placed it in the center of the table, shifted a few stems, and stood back. The arrangement was much too large—she should take out half of the flowers—but at least it would give her something to hide behind. Blythe would say it looked enchanting; Charlotte would smile and ask Dori if she thought it wasn't just a bit too small. Dori would laugh and say, *Yes, perhaps a bit too small,* not quite understanding the joke. The earlier episode with the spiderweb would be forgotten and forgiven. And Bea . . . what would Bea say? Lilli didn't know anymore.

Five

Bea parked the Mercedes in the sagging garage, with its moss-covered roof, and the two sisters crossed the leaf-littered drive to the house. Lilli carried both their lunch and the azalea, so she wouldn't have to take Bea's arm again. It had felt so fragile Lilli feared that if she squeezed too hard it would snap, like the starfish. Bea had always been tiny, but resilient. She'd never before struck Lilli as fragile.

The air inside the house smelled stale, and Lilli wished she could open a window and let in some astringent salt air. She put their lunch on the counter next to the dirty glasses still waiting beside the sink.

"Gin and tonic?" Bea suggested. "I could use one."

A little early for Lilli, but the situation seemed to call for it. "Sure." Eager to escape the stale air and unpleasant odor, and seeing no possibility of eating at the mail-cluttered kitchen table, Lilli suggested they eat on the porch. She carried the azalea through the dining room, noting that the walls had faded to a listless blue that now clashed with Grandmother's Wedgwood, still stored in the corner cabinet. She recognized the large dining table, all its panels, inexplicably, in place, the wood at the near end still puckered where the stain had lifted. She started to cross the front hall to peek into the living room, but veered off, startled by the sight of Randall's docksiders beside the front door. They looked so natural there that, for an instant, she imagined he might have just slipped them off, was here somewhere inside the house, and would be back for them soon. She collected herself and stepped out onto the glassed-in sunporch, where she found frayed wicker furniture with worn cushions, once perhaps red, now faded to beige, and several geraniums, shriveled and brown. She decided the azalea would fare better outside for the few weeks until Bea moved to Beacon House. In her mind Lilli had not only already installed Bea there, but decorated her room and planned her schedule: up by eight, breakfast, walk into town, monthly garden club luncheons, bridge in the afternoons, occasional trips to Boston for the flower show, a play, or a visit to the Museum of Fine Arts . . . She moved toward the door leading outside.

Charlotte hadn't returned Lilli's call, nor had she answered when Lilli called again from the convenience store. She'd left another message, wondering if Charlotte might have gone away for a few days. Had she mentioned something about a conference? It wasn't like her not to call back. Whereas Lilli preferred to focus on one task at a time, Charlotte was a multitasker, known for breezing into the preemie ICU, kicking off her trademark high heels, snatching the spectacles off the nearest person to use herself, congratulating a nearby nurse on her upcoming wedding or child's graduation, cracking a joke to ease any tension, and still somehow managing to give the tiny patient her full attention.

The door to the garden opened with mild protest, and Lilli ducked beneath the awning of wisteria and crossed to the rusty wrought-iron bench and old sundial. The piece that cast the shadow was gone, so all that remained was a cement pedestal and a corroded dial. She set the azalea down. It looked small and ridiculous. Lilli wondered whether Bea would even notice it out here—she certainly didn't seem to do much gardening—and so neglect to water it, but, as Bea hadn't seemed to want it anyway, she left it there. In the nearby undergrowth was a section of newspaper, which she retrieved, crumpled, and rubbed over the bench. Bits of rust flaked off and sifted to the ground, and the paper came away coated with powdery residue. Perhaps, Lilli thought, the new owners of the house would restore the bench and reclaim the gardens. Maybe they would have children who would play tag and badminton, and have tea parties on the lawn. Lilli hoped so. The house deserved it.

"Lilli?" Bea called from the porch.

Lilli adjusted the azalea so the side with the blossoms faced the house. "Coming."

Bea was holding a tray, bearing two gin and tonics and the bag with their lunch. "What were you doing out there?" Her hands were shaking.

Lilli removed the two glasses and then glanced around to see which of the cushions looked the least dust-covered and which of the fraying wicker chairs the least likely to snag her silk slacks. Bea, who had changed into pants and a pilled cable-knit cardigan, sat down on the love seat. Lilli handed her a glass and took a seat in one of the matching chairs. After an awkward pause, she said, "Lovely service. I think Randall would have been pleased."

Bea didn't respond at first, and they sat in silence, save for the sound of settling ice cubes. Lilli gazed out between cords of wisteria, through the salt-filmed windows of the porch to the shadowy outline of the trees and gardens, the lighter tones of the sky, and the blurry pink blaze of the azalea. It was a bit like looking into dense fog, Lilli thought, and then she realized, with a start, that this was what she'd been painting for the past thirty years: landscapes and gardens viewed through the filmy veil of memory and salt-encrusted glass.

"Yes, I suppose he would," Bea said finally. "Although, at this point that doesn't much matter, does it?"

Lilli sipped her gin and tonic, noting that Bea had a heavy hand with the gin. She wanted to keep a positive tone to this lunch. Charlotte could call anytime, and Lilli did have things she wanted to tell Bea, although she had no idea how to start. "The reading from *Gift from the Sea* was a good idea. Yours?"

Bea took a large swallow. "The funeral director's. Seemed appropriate."

They lapsed again into silence. Outside, the shadowy tops of the cedars swayed, and Lilli pictured the surface of the cove below, furling into white caps, the waves breaking against Big-big and the rocks rimming the cove.

"Did I mention that I talked with Dori the other day?"

Lilli shot her sister a startled look, but Bea was gazing down into her drink as though the ice cubes might hold the long-sought answer to a pressing question. "With who?" Lilli asked.

Bea looked up, her eyes the innocent clear blue of a summer

morning. "Isadora. Charlotte's daughter. Our niece?" She parsed this information out as though she were speaking to someone who was a bit slow.

"Ah," Lilli murmured, relieved. "Izzy."

"What's that?" Bea rubbed her right ear with her index finger.

"IZZY. YOU TALKED WITH IZZY."

"Oh, so I did tell you."

"No, you just said you talked with *Dori*," she said. Then, remembering that she wanted to keep things positive, she amended, more gently, "I thought you said Dori."

"Well, now that would be something. No, *Izzy*. She's getting married. She and a fellow . . . It's a strange name."

"Matumbé."

"Yes. So you know about that?" Bea sounded surprised.

"I didn't know they were getting married. I met him in . . ." Lilli hesitated, not wanting to reveal that she'd been in Chicago last year; it would only prompt questions, perhaps begin the conversation she still wasn't quite ready to have. "London," Lilli lied. "They came over," and then, quickly, to change the subject, "When's the wedding?"

"July."

"I'm surprised she didn't tell me." Lilli was more than surprised. She was hurt. She and Izzy had always had a special relationship. Or so she believed.

"They only just decided," Bea said, reaching for the lunch bag and peering in. "Knowing that she can have it here convinced her." She pulled out Lilli's salad in its plastic tub and handed it to Lilli. "That looks healthy."

"Here!" Lilli thunked her drink on the glass coffee table, hoping she hadn't heard right. "Here, here? *This* July?"

Bea nodded and smiled.

"That's two months away!"

"Right out there in Mother's garden." Bea looked past her, out the cloudy and shrouded windows as though she were seeing the ceremony right then and there. "We'll have zinnias and all the flowers in full bloom. Rows of chairs. Tables with white cloths. We'll string those little lanterns in all the trees, and fill the arch with red roses . . . Just like at Charlotte's wedding." She shifted her gaze to Lilli, who was attempting to stab her salad with a plastic fork. "Are you listening?"

"That was in 1969, Bea. The garden is . . ." Lilli took a bite of salad to stop herself from saying, *a morass*. She chewed, counting, swallowed, and said, as evenly as she could, "Not quite right for a wedding, do you think?"

"And why is that?" Bea's tone sounding challenging, as though she were prepared to be offended.

Lilli spoke toward the bleary window. "Well, for one, there's no lawn for those chairs. For another, no beds for those flowers. Third, the arch is about to collapse . . ." She could hear her voice growing shrill. Wanting an excuse to step away, she said, "I'd like a real fork. Why don't I get you a plate and us both some napkins."

Without waiting for a reply, she went to the kitchen, where she considered what to do about Bea's news, which had arrived on her doorstep like an uninvited guest. If Bea sincerely believed that she could get the place ready for a wedding in two months, then Bea's mental condition could be worse than Lilli had realized. Could it be early dementia? If so, who knew what the house and grounds looked like inside Bea's head? Lilli, in that case, should not wait for Charlotte, but broach the subject of moving to Beacon House herself.

She could then get hold of Izzy and suggest that she book her wedding elsewhere. Izzy hadn't been here for years, would have no idea how the place looked. Lilli found a plate and fork and began searching for napkins.

What if, however, Izzy wasn't getting married, and Bea only *imagined* that she'd spoken with her? She scraped pieces of congealed egg and tiny bullets of rice off several plates into the trash, lifted the overflowing bag, and tied it off. Lilli pondered this question, along with what to do with the bag of trash. That certainly meant Bea was in worse shape than Lilli had thought, but it was more appealing because it meant that Izzy hadn't shared this important news with Bea before Lilli. She redeposited the bag in the trash can and moved to the sink, loaded the plates in the dishwasher, found some detergent under the sink, filled the dispenser, and shut the door. Then she turned the dial and pushed start. Silence. She pressed a few more buttons, opened and reclosed the dishwasher door. Still no satisfying gurgle and swish of incoming water. *When Izzy gets married,* Lilli fumed, *it will most certainly be in a place with a working dishwasher!*

Option two was also more likely, Lilli decided, as she continued to search through drawers for napkins. After all, Bea had referred to Izzy as "Dori," and to the gardens as "Mother's." Looking at the ivy-stenciled walls, peeling linoleum floor, and outdated appliances, Lilli could easily imagine Bea's mind cruising quietly along in the wrong decade. What that meant for Bea's immediate future—did Beacon House even have a memory unit?—she wasn't certain. But she was more certain than ever that Bea couldn't stay here alone. *Charlotte, please call!* Lilli leaned against the sink, mentally exhausted, wishing she were in her gallery in London, going over invoices and shipping orders with Geoffrey. She would head home through the busy streets of London to her tidy flat, stopping at the grocer on the corner for cheese and wine, and into the used-book shop next door to browse. She pictured her studio with its tall windows and blank canvases, all those gardens waiting for her to bring them to life.

Through the kitchen window, she could see the narrow driveway edged with a glistening russet veneer of last fall's oak leaves. Only a bit of the greenhouse roof was visible through the overgrown honeysuckle and grapevine. At one time you could see the whole of it. When the sun was shining, the whitewashed windows were opaque, but on cloudy days you could see Mr. Sylvia or her mother, moving around inside like shadows. She thought of Charlotte's wedding and sighed. Izzy getting married. Was it possible? She took the clean plate and fork and two paper towels that would have to serve as napkins, and headed back to the porch.

She paused in the dining room and watched Bea as she sat on the porch, staring out the salt-filmed glass at the wreckage that was once her yard. *What did she see?* She must miss the view down to the cove, miss being able to sit on the bench and watch the boats glide by. Why do nothing as, every year, her world shrank a little more, the weeds and brambles creeping closer and closer to the house? *"You make your bed, you lie in it."* Wasn't that what their grandmother used to say? *Yes,* Lilli thought, *but didn't she also say, "God helps those who help themselves"?*

Bea looked up as Lilli entered. "Oh, there you are. Thought I'd lost you. I think I'll just freshen my drink. You?"

"Mine's fine, but I would have—"

Bea waved her off and headed out to the kitchen.

Lilli put Bea's food on the plate she'd brought out, took a fortifying sip of her drink, checked her watch, and sat down. Lilli had now convinced herself that Izzy's wedding was a fabrication, knitted together with strands of who knows what from the confused contents of Bea's jumbled mind. Bea's mental condition wasn't likely to improve, and the sooner Bea moved over to Beacon House, the better. She'd have a spacious unit on the first floor, someone to do the cooking and cleaning, an easy walk to the shops in town, companionship, activities, outings . . . Bolstered by these arguments, Lilli smiled warmly when Bea returned with her drink. But Bea ignored her and walked to the window, squinting slightly as she peered through it. "Right out there in Mother's garden. Just like Charlotte."

A friend of Lilli's, whose husband suffered from dementia, once told her that it was important to join the afflicted person in their reality rather than challenging them, and then gently lead them back to the present. "So you think the garden is right for a wedding at this point?"

"Of course not. It's April. What do you expect? You never did care much for gardening, did you? Always more interested in the results than the process."

Lilli wondered if she should mention that it was May. "No, not much."

"You never had a feel for it."

"I have a *feel* for how much work it would be to get this place ready for a wedding." She tried to keep her voice even, but she could feel her patience fraying, unraveling strand by strand like one of the sagging wicker chairs. "And I'm just talking about the garden. There's also the house." How many strands could break, she wondered, before the unwary passenger plunged straight through to the floor?

Bea shrugged, her back still to Lilli.

Lilli swallowed the last of her gin and tonic, regretting that she hadn't asked for another, and softened her tone. "Don't you think it would be simpler having it somewhere else? There's the White Head Inn. It has a big lawn out back with lots of flower beds. I walked past it this morning. Their irises and peonies and clematis are almost ready to bloom." She felt ridiculous having this conversation because she was certain Izzy was not getting married, certain she would have told Lilli.

"Izzy has her heart set on having it here." Bea turned, walked across the porch, and lowered herself onto the love seat. "I'd hate to disappoint her, wouldn't you?" She picked up half a sandwich, lifted the top slice of bread, "Mayonnaise?"

Lilli smiled. "When, exactly, did you speak with Izzy? And what did she say, you know, about her wedding? Does she want a large one? Formal?" Lilli's tone sounded patronizing even to her.

"What's that?"

Lilli remained silent, certain that Bea had heard.

"You can ask her yourself. She's coming tomorrow."

"What?" Lilli sputtered. Izzy would have told Lilli if she'd planned to visit. Wouldn't she?

Bea took another bite of sandwich, chewed stoically. "Loaded with empty fat calories."

"Izzy is coming tomorrow? Here? From Chicago? Why didn't you tell me?" Much as Lilli wanted to believe that this was another of Bea's mental misfires, it was impossible to ignore, like one more entirely unexpected guest at the door.

"Didn't I? I thought for sure I had. Honestly, I'm so forgetful these days. She couldn't come for the service. She's arriving around lunchtime and spending the night."

"Here?" Lilli repeated in disbelief. She took a few more bites of salad, found she'd lost her appetite, and decided not to wait for Charlotte to call before raising the notion of Bea moving. Joining Bea in her murky reality wasn't working. "I passed the old Wakeman place yesterday. Remember it?"

"Remember it? Why wouldn't I 'remember' it? I'm not the one who's been gone for forty years. It's a nursing home now. People rocking themselves into senility on the front porch for all to see. Shameless putting it right there in the middle of town."

Not an auspicious beginning. "It's not a nursing home. It's a retirement community, with independent-living units. Not everyone there is senile."

"You seem to know a good deal about it. Why is that?" Bea, having finished off the first half of her sandwich, started in on the second and turned a steely gaze on Lilli as she chewed. Gone was the innocent blue of a spring morning.

Lilli took a large bite of salad to buy time. "I just wondered what you were planning to do . . . now that Randall is gone."

The high-pitched whine of a teakettle issued from the kitchen. "Sounds like the train whistle, doesn't it, Lilli? Remember when we used to walk to the station to meet Daddy? Dori would ride home on his shoulders wearing his hat, and Patter would run alongside peeing on everything."

Lilli nodded, and the two sat a moment lost in their own thoughts as the kettle shrilled.

"Coffee?" Bea asked finally.

Lilli checked her watch: one thirty. Suppose Izzy really

was coming? Lilli would dearly love to see her. She could easily stay an extra day—this was only Monday and the gallery reception wasn't until Wednesday. In truth, she could drive up Wednesday afternoon and be there in plenty of time. Felicity and her assistant were handling everything. She hated to admit it, but arriving now, Lilli would probably be more in the way than helpful. If she stayed, she could see Izzy. Maybe they could work on Bea together. Charlotte would surely have called by then. They could have a sort of family intervention. "Yes, coffee would be nice," she said, not yet ready to commit to staying. She might be able to use it as leverage to get Bea over to see Beacon House. She checked her watch again.

"You sure you have time?" Bea's tone was heavily mulched with sarcasm.

Lilli nodded.

"Then let's move inside." Bea put her empty plate and glass on the tray, rose, and looked again out the filmy windows. "What is that pink out there?"

Lilli added her half-eaten salad and empty glass to the tray. "The azalea."

"Azalea? I don't have any azaleas. Much too fussy."

Lilli picked up the tray, resisted hurling it through the hazy windows, and headed into the dining room. She paused halfway when, behind her, Bea said, "You know, Lilli, looking at it through these filmy windows reminds me of your paintings."

"I DIDN'T REALIZE you'd seen my work," Lilli said, plucking the screeching kettle from the burner.

"Your work? Oh, yes. I've seen it, many times. I remember

thinking that your paintings looked very like gardens viewed through fog. Not a great surprise given where we grew up." She chuckled. "Although, Lilli, you know it was sunny here occasionally. Did you ever think about painting one that was a bit . . . lighter?"

"Coffee filters?" Lilli asked.

"I'm out. Use a paper towel."

Lilli tore off a square decorated with red and blue flowers, tried not to think about what the ink would do to them, and tucked it into the filter basket.

"We might as well use the good china," Bea said, gazing at an upper shelf of a nearby, glass-fronted cupboard.

"Coffee?" Lilli asked.

"In the bread box." Bea had opened the cupboard and was on tiptoe stretching to reach a teacup on a high shelf.

Lilli turned. "Here, let me help," she said, striding across the kitchen. Too late. The teacup tumbled off the shelf and landed on the counter. The sisters looked at the delicate, rose-patterned cup, now broken neatly in two.

"A little glue's all it needs," Bea said.

Lilli picked up the cup and held one half to the light. She could see the shadows of her fingers through the thin porcelain. "It's too delicate," she said, pressing the two halves together. "The break will show."

"Only a little. It'll hold."

"I remember this china," Lilli said. "It was Grandmother's, wasn't it?"

Bea nodded.

"There were bowls, too, flat ones, for cream soup. You used to serve me oatmeal in them. It was awful."

"You would remember that." Bea was smiling.

"You must admit, Bea, you weren't much of a cook. And you'd make me sit until I ate it all."

"Which you never did. I kept telling you to add milk."

"That only made it get bigger!" Lilli took two cups from the shelf and placed the broken one on the windowsill. She found the can of coffee in the bread box, scooped some into the makeshift filter, and drizzled in water. Bea sat down at the table and ran her finger along one of the painted ivy vines. "Remember how you and Dori used to trace these up the wall?"

Lilli fed in more water, watching the grounds wash down from the sides and puddle at the bottom, fragrant brown liquid dripping into the glass coffeepot.

"Hard to believe she would be fifty-five this year."

"Fifty-six," Lilli said.

"Pity you can't stay another day. I'm sure Izzy would love to see you."

"Yes," Lilli said, noncommittal, considering how to use her decision to stay to her best advantage. She was now determined not to leave White Head until Bea had not only visited Beacon House but put down a deposit. She poured two cups of coffee and delivered them to the table, pushing aside a stack of mail, much of which was addressed to Randall. Then she went to the refrigerator for milk. She found very little of anything, and no milk, but something had spoiled; she could smell it. "When did you last go shopping, Bea?"

"What's that?"

"YOU DON'T HAVE MUCH FOOD HERE."

"She's going to spend the night here. With me. You could share a room just like old times." Bea was tracing the ivy vine up the wall.

Lilli stared at her sister over the refrigerator door. She had never stayed in this house with Izzy. Bea's mind had drifted again, back to the days when the ivy stenciling was new. She had, once again, confused Izzy with their sister, Dori. Lilli shut the refrigerator and sat down across from Bea. "If I do stay, and I'm not saying I will—I want to swing by Beacon House."

"I think you'd be much more comfortable here," Bea said.

"I meant for you."

"I know I'd be more comfortable here." She started to sip her coffee but set it down at once, frowning. "I like mine light."

"You don't have any milk."

"There's powdered creamer in the bread box right next to the coffee."

Lilli pushed herself up from the table, crossed the kitchen, and located an unlabeled plastic container of a white powder that could as easily have been baking soda, detergent, or even rat poison as nondairy creamer. She held it up. "Is this it?" There were numerous brown pill bottles with white caps lined up beside the bread box. Lilli could make out Bea's name on several of the labels, and Randall's name on at least one. She wondered what it was for.

Bea squinted at the container and nodded. "So you'll stay?"

Lilli handed the powder to Bea, who shook a large quantity into her coffee and stirred vigorously.

"If you'll go see the old Wakeman place. I think you'd be . . . better off there. You'd have your own room with a nice view. Lots of people to—"

"Hand me the sugar, will you?" Bea pointed to a battered

aluminum canister on the counter. Lilli delivered it. Bea tapped on the hardened sugar to loosen it, and then stirred a large chunk into her coffee.

Lilli sat down, sipped her own coffee, and half-listened as Bea detailed the lives of those in White Head, some of whom Lilli remembered, most of whom she did not, none of whom she cared about, aware of each passing moment, waiting for an opportunity to seal the deal. She became aware that Bea had stopped talking. Lilli took their empty cups to the sink, washed them with the lavender soap, and placed them in the drainer.

"So you'll stay?" Bea asked again.

"Will you go look at Beacon House?"

Bea didn't respond, simply followed an ivy vine up the wall with her eyes. Lilli was about to add that she herself had considered at least putting her name in at such an establishment in London, when Bea said, "Fine."

"Fine?" Lilli was too startled for anything more.

"Good," Bea said, picking up a gardening catalog and thumbing through it. "Since you're staying, you can help me sprinkle Randall's ashes."

"Sprinkle . . ." Lilli, astonished, looked at Bea, who was busy folding down page corners. "Where are they?"

"What's that? Oh, in the . . ." Bea paused, tapped a fore-finger against her chin for a long moment. Too long. "Den. I think."

"You think?" Lilli shifted her gaze to the unlabeled plastic container of white powder now sitting on the counter, thankful that she took her coffee black. "You think!"

"In the den. In the den," Bea's tone was impatient, her nose back in the catalog.

"In the den. In the den," Lilli muttered, as she headed out of the kitchen.

LOCATED AT THE back of the house, its windows shaded by lilacs, the den had never been sunny. Now, with the lilac bush overgrown and overrun with honeysuckle and maple saplings, the room was nearly dark. Lilli flicked on a light switch, which didn't help much. On the bottom shelf of the bookcase several layers of folded cardboard supported the front edge of a television. Two armchairs were positioned for optimum viewing, and a metal table alongside one bore a collection of dirty glasses. Magazines and catalogs stood in teetering towers on the shelves and floor. Their father's old desk still occupied one wall, its rolltop raised and the surface piled with mail, like a gaping mouth preparing to ingest a papery meal. The room offered Lilli a depressing and unwanted glimpse into Bea and Randall's married life—and harbored painful memories. She remained in the doorway and visually swept the room for something urnlike. Near one armchair was a cardboard box surrounded by packing material. She inched forward and peered at the side: *Footlights*, it said, and bore a skeletal illustration of a foot. Lilli realized that she'd been holding her breath and exhaled loudly. Having found no urns or other likely containers, she returned empty-handed to the kitchen. "The ashes aren't there," Lilli announced.

"What?" Bea was still sitting at the table. She looked up, startled, and stared at Lilli. She'd been looking at something, which she slipped, facedown, under a stack of mail. Her expression and tone suggested to Lilli that Bea might have forgotten she was there.

"I didn't find Randall's ashes in the den."

"Randall's ashes? In the den? Whatever for? They're in the car."

"You said den."

"Did I? Yes, well, I *meant* to take them in there but left them in the car."

"Are you sure?" Lilli didn't recall seeing them that morning. "Shall I go bring them in?"

"Don't bother. We're going to sprinkle them, remember?"

"Now?" Lilli thought longingly of the Adirondack chair outside her motel room, where, after a nap, she'd planned to spend a quiet afternoon, sketching the boats in the harbor.

Bea stood and moved to the sink, and Lilli glanced down at the pile of mail, shifted a few pieces, and saw that Bea had been looking at the program from Randall's service. Gazing out the window in the direction of the greenhouse, Bea said, "Good a time as any to put it behind us."

AFTER Dori's birthday dinner, the girls lay on their narrow beds. Dori was reading *The Clue in the Jewel Box*, softly murmuring the words, and Lilli, alternating between reading *Wuthering Heights* and staring up at the cracks and stains on the ceiling, was thinking about Randall and the dance she was missing, picturing couples arriving at the yacht club, boys with slicked-back hair, and girls in fancy dresses and high heels.

Lilli had apologized over and over for showing Dori the spiderweb and spoiling her birthday surprise, but still she felt a deep sense of shame. She was older and supposed to set a good example. Then again, Lilli had reasoned, if anyone had bothered to let *her* in on the surprise, she wouldn't have needed to peek. Besides, she acknowledged, Dori'd had two celebrations already, three if you counted the pancake cake. And would have a party the next day, which Lilli would be expected to attend. She felt too old for birthday parties now and resolved only to watch the girls attempt to untangle the colorful strands of yarn. It would not be easy, Lilli noted. Their mother had made these webs for the girls before, but had gone a bit bonkers with this one. Too many strands, too many colors, woven too tightly. Lilli put her book down and sighed.

Dori looked over. "What's wrong?"

"Nothing." *Everything.*

Dori got up, walked to the window, and raised the shade. "The moon is so bright, Lilli, it's almost bright as day out."

Lilli glanced in the direction of the window. "Very nice." She lacked the energy to rise and concluded that she was definitely coming down with something, hoped it was fatal. Then Bea would be sorry.

"No, come look. You can't see it properly from there. Let's go down on the rocks and look for Russian subs. Remember you said we could. It's the perfect night."

Lilli checked the clock on the wall. Only eight o'clock! Had she forgotten to wind it? She pictured couples dancing, the girls wearing bright pink lipstick and bouffant hairdos, and the boys in crisp blue blazers and creased pants. Lilli pictured Randall, his dark hair, usually windblown, neatly combed back; imagined a hint of Old Spice, although she wasn't sure he shaved yet.

"Are you mad at me?" Dori had left the window and sat cross-legged at the foot of Lilli's bed.

"Me mad at you? *You're* the one who's supposed to be mad. I'm really sorry I . . . You know."

"But I'm not mad, Lilli. The spiderweb will still be there tomorrow, and we'll have such fun unwinding it. Let's do one together." She plucked at a loose thread in the pink chenille spread. "So, can we go look for subs now?"

Dori asked so little. Why did life suddenly seem so difficult for Lilli? "I am truly sorry," she whispered, her voice cracking, her cheeks wet with fresh tears.

"Are you crying, Lilli?" Dori asked, her confusion and alarm evident. "Why?"

"I don't know," Lilli fumed, furious that tears often leaked out now for no good reason. Her feelings had become as undependable as the wind, shifting direction without warning. Dori looked so mystified that Lilli started giggling, which made Dori laugh, and soon they were both holding their stomachs and groaning, until Dori got the hiccups and finally rolled right off the bed, which made them laugh all the harder. If Bea had been home, Lilli was sure she would have come in to see "what on earth was going on." But *she* had gone to the dance. Her mother was . . . who knew where? Perhaps in the garden—Lilli had sometimes seen her down there at night—or in the greenhouse. Lilli often went there to be alone, a rarity in this household, and several times she had found her mother sitting on one of the narrow steps across from the potting bench, staring up through the dark glass, softly humming. Lilli liked the greenhouse. It was quiet and smelled of paper-dry tulip bulbs and damp earth: things past and things to come. She would watch her mother's shape through the glass, and then go in and sit beside her, and stare up through the glass panes, wondering what she saw.

"It's Randall, isn't it?" Dori said, climbing back onto Lilli's bed.

Lilli wiped her cheeks. For someone who drifted through

life not thinking too deeply about things, Dori was, at times, surprisingly perceptive. Lilli's mood darkened, and she nodded.

"Bea said you couldn't go to the dance." Dori said.

Lilli looked away, angry. *Stupid girl, why bring that back up?* But Dori drew herself close, her face just inches away, her blue eyes wide, and whispered, "Bea said you couldn't go to the dance."

Lilli's anger ebbed. She was weary of this day, weary of whatever game Dori was playing, wanted only to return to Cathy and Heathcliff's thwarted love, and then to sleep so she could wake the next day, a little older, a little more changed, perhaps this time for the better. She picked up her book.

"She didn't say you couldn't go . . . to the *yacht club*."

Lilli slowly lowered her book and stared at Dori, whose words hung between them glittering with ambiguity. The corners of Lilli's mouth curved into a smile.

"We could take the *Whisper* out and look for Russian subs in the harbor," Dori said.

Lilli blinked once, twice, and then tossed her book aside, leaned forward, and gave Dori a wet kiss, before scrambling off the bed and rushing to her closet. Dori pulled a tan sweater over her short-sleeved white camp shirt and green shorts, and then watched Lilli try on first a cream-colored silk blouse and skirt that was much too small in the waist, and then a navy blue sleeveless dress that it took two of them to zip and was so tight Lilli could barely move. Lilli went to Charlotte's room and returned wearing a flowered sundress, not Lilli's taste, and more appropriate for a garden party than an evening dance, but that fit perfectly. It was too small for

Charlotte and, anyway, she wouldn't mind. Charlotte would only smile and say, "Smashing dress, Lilli. Wherever did you find it?" And give Lilli a big wink.

"Lilli," Dori gasped. "You look so grown up. You've got bosoms!"

Finally, someone had noticed.

Lilli sat down at the dressing table and fussed with her hair, trying first a headband so her curls wreathed her face. She recalled how Randall had admired those curls, wrapping one around his finger, how his thumb had grazed her neck—this memory enough to bring color to her cheeks. Gads, what had come over her? But the mass of curls seemed overwhelming, and the night was very hot. Besides, she wanted to expose her neck in case Randall's thumb should happen that way again. She swept one side back and secured it with several clips and combs. Bea would have said she looked like a vamp and, for once, Lilli would have agreed with her. Dori came up behind her, gathered Lilli's curls like a bouquet, and held them up behind her head. They stared. Lilli looked more like twenty than fifteen.

"I love you, Dori," Lilli said, and handed her a box of hairpins.

Charlotte's feet were larger than Lilli's, as were her mother's. But Lilli knew of a pair of red high heels with open toes, hidden in a box in Bea's closet. They pinched a bit but would do. She slipped into her mother's room, sat at her dressing table, and—remembering Randall's earlier comment—rummaged through her lipsticks until she found one called Sunset Blush, which she applied, rubbing her lips together as she'd seen Blythe do. Then, for good measure, she dotted her cheeks. The blue eye shadow was tempting, but she resisted. She did dab a bit of Tabu behind her ears, clipped on a pair of gold love-knot earrings, and then tried to blot off most of the lipstick and "rouge." At eight thirty, shoes in hand, the girls headed down the stairs.

THE NIGHT WAS still as they crossed the beach to the yacht club, the waves so slight they made no more sound sliding onto the sand than the exhalation of a sleeping child. The moon shone on the surface of the water like a lighthouse beacon frozen in time. They could hear the music from the party as they passed through the small grove, and Dori wanted to stop and dance, and so they did for a minute. The leaves on the trees above them dangled limply as though exhausted from their frenzied activity of the breezy afternoon. Then Lilli, anxious to arrive, reminded Dori about skunks, and they hurried on.

They stood in the parking lot just beyond a narrow strip of light slipping through the curtained kitchen window. Couples were still arriving, although it was now eight forty-five, and Lilli was worried that someone would spot them and tell Bea, so they tiptoed along the narrow porch at the back of the clubhouse and stood on sail lockers to peer into a room that looked little like it had just hours earlier, when they'd gathered to hear race results and to sing "Happy Birthday" to Dori. Couples danced or stood in small groups, drinks in hand, laughing and talking. Lilli wondered again why anyone would prefer the silly games of childhood to this. She didn't see Bea, which worried her a little. The first rule of espionage was to keep the enemy in sight. Nor did she see Randall, which worried her more. Were they together? The night was warm, uncomfortably so, and they could hear voices, amplified in the stillness, coming from the front porch. They inched forward, toe-heel, toe-heel, "like Indian scouts," Dori said, a great fan of James Fenimore Cooper. Lilli, unused to walking in high heels, warmly welcomed this suggestion. A Tony Bennett song started up, and Lilli whispered, "Let's dance." After fumbling arms, and arguing about who would lead, they began an awkward box step in the narrow space between the sail lockers and the railing, stifling giggles. A slight breeze rose, cool against Lilli's neck. She closed her eyes, imagining herself in Randall's arms, moving to the music, the unhappy events of the day receding. She felt a tap on her shoulder. Startled, she broke free of Dori's embrace and spun around, expecting Bea, prepared to defend herself.

"May I?" Randall stood, grinning, with his arm extended and his hair falling across his forehead, looking—in the flesh—far better even than Lilli had imagined. He exuded an air of sophistication, Lilli thought, well beyond his nineteen years.

She stood, mute and blinking, trying only to breathe.

"Go on," Dori said, and gave her a little shove. "I'll keep an eye out."

"An eye out?" Randall asked, folding Lilli in his arms as though they'd done it a thousand times. "For who?"

"Um," was all Lilli could manage.

"Russian subs," Dori said, and Lilli loved her little sister even more.

Randall drew Lilli close and they swayed slowly to the strains of "Hold Me, Thrill Me, Kiss Me," and Lilli was convinced for one mortifying moment that she was going to faint, certain that he could feel, and even hear, her heart thudding through the scant layers of fabric between them—this thought enough to make her knees grow slack, at which Randall tightened his grip. Lilli took a shaky breath and wondered if one could burst from happiness. In her heels Lilli was nearly as tall as Randall, her face almost even with his, her cheek mere inches away, and she could smell his Old Spice—so he was old enough to shave, after all—and something else, a clean smell, like the beach after a rain. She concentrated on keeping her breathing even—to keep breathing at all! She felt each finger of his right hand press into the small of her back; the crook of his elbow lightly cradling her side; and the smooth surface of his left palm, in which her right hand rested. His hold was strong and practiced, and she felt protected within this safe circle of his arms. Wanted never to leave it.

They fit together perfectly, and she believed, with all the wisdom of her fifteen years, that this meant they were destined for one another. She believed that no one had ever loved another precisely this way, and she believed equally that all women in love had felt exactly this way. That this was love, Lilli had no doubt. Her mother had told her that summer, when she'd found Lilli sitting, misty-eyed, on the wrought-iron bench one day, that love was God's greatest, and most challenging, gift. It had the power to create lives and to end them. "True love always comes with the potential for heartbreak," she'd said, sitting down beside Lilli. Then she'd sighed, put an arm around her daughter, and said, "The great challenge is to be in love and not give in to the ever-present fear of losing it." They'd sat in silence, staring out at the sailboats gliding past. "A life without one's true love," Blythe added after a moment, more to herself than to her daughter, "is no life at all."

Lilli had not understood then what her mother meant, but thought she understood it now as Randall pulled her closer still and whispered in her ear, "You look sensational, Lilli. Why didn't you come earlier?" She shook her head, not trusting herself to speak, nor wanting to tell the truth—that she was too young and her older sister had forbidden it. Her silence seemed to satisfy him. "And why are you hiding out here?" His breath on her ear made her dizzy. "I . . ." Her mind swirled, a dense wall of fog. She glanced toward Dori for help. But Dori, with the practiced ease of one used to counterintelligence work, was peering around the side of the yacht club for signs of the enemy.

"I get it," he said, tightening his embrace so their bodies pressed together, igniting something deep inside her that she found slightly terrifying. What might she be capable of if it got loose? She wanted to pull away, but he was holding her tight. "You didn't want to leave Dori alone on her birthday. You're a good sister, Lilypad."

Lilli didn't much like lies and thought she'd woven enough of them for one day, but she figured at least part of what he'd said was true and let it pass.

"I like your hair this way. You should wear it up more often."

"Lilli!" Dori said from her station. "The Russians are coming."

Bea called from the other side of the clubhouse. "Randall?"

Lilli pulled away and backed into shadow. Randall looked at her quizzically and with—*was she imagining it?*—disappointment. "Don't tell her we were here." Lilli gave him a look that she hoped made her seem, not like a child misbehaving, but like a mysterious and alluring adult, like Ingrid

Bergman in *Casablanca*. Lilli had practiced that look often in her dressing table mirror. He shrugged and nodded, and Lilli tugged Dori back along the porch into the shadows just as she heard Bea asking, "What on earth were you doing back there?" There was a pause, and then he said, "Just checking something in my sail locker, Cap'n." Lilli smiled. She and Randall had a secret. A secret from Bea. Bea had won the race tonight, but Lilli had the feeling that the championship was hers if she wanted it.

Dori grabbed Lilli's arm and pulled her back along the porch. The breeze had freshened and the moon slid behind clouds as the girls crossed the parking lot. They lowered their heads as they passed several couples at the top of the gangway, but the couples were too taken with one another to notice them. Lilli had the nagging feeling that she'd forgotten something, had left something important undone, but she was too lost in the memory of Randall's hand on her back, his breath on her neck, the secret they now shared, to think or care what. She'd tried to maintain a modest distance when they danced, as she'd seen her father instruct Bea and Charlotte, having no idea, then, why he'd done so. When Randall had drawn her close, and the space between them had become charged in a way both disturbing and strangely pleasing, Lilli had begun to understand. Again she had to wonder about adults and their misplaced nostalgia for childhood.

"There it is, Lilli." Dori pointed to the *Whisper*, jouncing among the boats at the float. "Oh, gosh, I hope the oars are in it!"

Was this what she'd forgotten? Maybe. But Lilli didn't recall pulling them out after the race; she'd had too much other gear to haul up to the clubhouse. Dori tugged on the painter, nudging other boats out of the way. Lilli no longer wanted to row out into the harbor—now so dark that the white hulls of boats were barely visible—to look for Russian subs, of which she knew there were none. And what if there were? She wanted only to return to the house, kick off her shoes and tug off her earrings, as she'd seen her mother and older sisters do, and then recline on the sofa, sip brandy, and recall the evening. Lilli would sip Ovaltine rather than brandy, and she'd have to return Charlotte's dress to her closet and Bea's shoes to their hiding place, like Cinderella, but she would not have to give back the memory of her dance with Randall. That she could keep forever, securely knotted, so it could never drift away.

Dori announced, "They're here!" and commanded Lilli to row, while she watched for subs. Lilli knew she should say no, that it was too late to go out and too dark to see anything. She could tell Dori that they were far more likely to see enemy subs from Big-big and, once they were that close to home, persuade Dori to go inside instead for a game of Don't Touch the Floor. The rules of this silly game that they'd invented years before were simple: Make your way around the house, climbing on tables and chairs, clinging to shelves and banisters, and tiptoeing along baseboards. A single tour of the house could consume hours of a rainy day—what Dori called "runny" days. She knew she could persuade Dori to do this, but then she remembered Dori's tears at seeing the spiderweb in the den, and how she'd said she didn't think she'd have a birthday this year, and how it had been Dori's idea to come to the yacht club. So Lilli removed Bea's shoes and carefully placed them on the float, climbed into the *Whisper*, and took the middle seat, hoping it was dry and wouldn't ruin

Charlotte's dress, because Lilli didn't like to break promises and she'd disappointed enough people that day.

Dori hopped into the stern and shoved off, as Lilli set oars in oarlocks and began to row out into the darkness. Though the night had grown gusty, it was still oddly mild for early September, and Lilli was soon damp with sweat and wishing she'd brought a change of clothes. Then the moon broke through, and Dori exclaimed, "Look at the water!" and turned to drag her hand behind the boat, creating a shimmering trail. "It's starfish!"

"That's not starfish, silly. They don't make the water sparkle. It's phosphorescence."

"It should be called starfish. Let's make a wish."

"You wish on stars, Dori, not starfish."

"And on birthdays. I'm going to make a wish."

The wind dropped then, as though someone had turned off a fan. The chop in the harbor relaxed, and the little boat shot across the now-glassy surface, heading out toward Brant Point, where Dori—half out of the boat, playing with the phosphorescence and peering down into the inky water for signs of Russian subs—said they were most likely to see something. The oars in the oarlocks complained and the water whispered beneath them, as Lilli sent the little boat skimming across the water, rowing somewhat in time to the music drifting across the harbor from the yacht club, and dreamily reliving her dance with Randall. When they nearly collided with the Halls' boat, Lilli snapped out of her reverie and ordered Dori to face front and keep better watch. "You'll see the periscope," Lilli said, "long before you see the sub." But Dori was soon turned around again, trailing her hand to make "starfish," and Lilli returned to her daydreams, of traveling the world with Randall. Mrs. Randall Marsh. Lilli Marsh. She liked the sound of it. Neither girl took much notice of how far they'd gone.

The night was not just still, Lilli would later recall, but had an *absence* of air, as though a vacuum had formed over the harbor. When Lilli snapped out of her daydreams she got an uneasy feeling in all that vacancy and suggested to Dori that they head in. Then black clouds rolled in, drawing against the moon like curtains, and the wind rose and continued to rise. And rise. Increasing until it whistled through the rigging of unseen sailboats and roiled the water, turning it within seconds from glassy to frenzied, the whitecaps, in the darkness, the one bit of bright. Not a comforting sight. When Lilli heard waves washing against rocks she knew they must be very near Brant Point—too near—knew she must have been rowing harder than she thought, because Brant Point was a good distance from where they started, which meant a good long row back, not easy in those conditions. And the wind was still rising, shrieking now as it tore through the trees on the shore.

"Lilli?" Dori's voice was uncertain, coming through the darkness from the stern, which heightened Lilli's fear. Lilli could see only the white collar of Dori's shirt.

The *Whisper* was pitching in the waves by now. Rowing was pointless, impossible really, and so Lilli used the oars as outriggers for stability. She wanted to bring them in so she could hold on to something solid, but didn't dare. Seawater was washing into the boat and sloshing around her ankles, eddying into its own tiny tempest that sent the painter and bailing cup rushing first in one direction and then another. "Hold my hand, Lilli," Dori called. Lilli wanted, more than anything, to take Dori's hand, but she couldn't let go.

Over the roaring wind, Lilli heard a loud POP, followed by what sounded like a series of tiny explosions. She thought at once of Russian subs—did they have guns? Did they sound like that?—and turned instinctively to look, as one does, even though she knew she'd be unable to see anything in the darkness, knew there were no subs. She would learn later that a tall cedar had snapped and crashed down onto the roof of the McCallisters' garage, only moments after Peg McCallister returned home from the dance, worried, when the wind came up and it looked like rain, about windows she'd left open. But Lilli didn't know that then, and she turned, thinking Russian subs, because it sounded like gunshot, and as she turned, the right oar came out of the water, and the wind grabbed it, just as a wave hit, throwing Dori and Lilli against the leeward side of the boat. The right oar lifted even higher, not a stabilizer now but a sail, carrying the *Whisper* down the side of the wave, and the left oar became a keel, digging deep into the trough. The boat began to fill, and then to roll. It was at that moment that Lilli realized what was missing, what she'd left undone, what she'd forgotten. Life jackets. The girls, Dori particularly, who had never been a strong swimmer, were not allowed out on boats without them.

GOOD TO HIS word, Randall said nothing to Bea about seeing the girls at the dance. It wouldn't have done much good, because even he didn't know that they'd slipped down to the dinghies and taken the *Whisper* for a moonlight row. No one did.

When the wind came up, people at the dance raced around bringing in chairs and glasses, running after napkins that filled the air like confetti. John Bradley offered to check on the boats, and Randall said he'd go, too. They went down the bucking gangway to make sure painters were secure. When they came back, dripping water onto the floor of the club-house, because by then the rain had started, slanting sideways in the wind, Randall reported that the only boat missing was the *Whisper*. Said it probably broke loose and drifted away. And then he held up a pair of red shoes. "Do these belong to someone? They were down on the float."

Bea stared. "They're mine. How the devil did they get down there?" she asked, genuinely perplexed.

He handed her the shoes, confessing only then that Lilli and Dori had been to the dance and sworn him to secrecy. "You don't suppose . . ." He glanced out the black, rain-spattered window.

Bea said, "Lilli was here?" And then she snapped, "Why are you standing there? Go out and find them."

THE MOMENT LILLI knew they were going over, she dropped both oars and shouted, "Hold on!" She felt icy water rushing over her bare feet and half-dived, half-jumped, her skirt act-ing first as a sort of parachute, buoying her up, and then, like the bulky spinnaker earlier that day, dragging her down. The icy water seemed to flow right into her heart, filling her with horror and a guilt that threatened to drown her then and there. As her head went under she thought of Dori, how frightened she must be, uncomprehending, unable to reason what to do. What had Lilli done? Why had she come out here? Why could this day not have ended with her fairy-tale dance in the moonlight? Punishment. That was what it was. For disobeying. And she deserved it, she thought, as she struggled to the surface, gasping for air. Another wave washed over her, her mouth filled, and she went under again. She'd never known such fear, never wanted to feel such fear again. She fought harder, but she was tiring, couldn't do this for long. She surfaced once more, struck out with one arm, seeking anything solid and stationary, found an oar. "One hand for the boat," indeed. In the moments, or hours, that followed—Lilli lost all sense of time and orientation—she called and called Dori's name as she clung to that narrow strip of wood, her arms and legs growing numb. She wanted to remove her waterlogged dress but didn't have the strength to try. Once she thought she heard Dori call for her and she tried to shout back, but her teeth chattered so much she couldn't form the words, could only wail softly, her warm salty tears stinging her eyes.

The wind and rain slowed, and then stopped. The clouds parted, allowing enough moonlight to shine through that Lilli could see that she was no longer in the harbor. That she had rowed, or drifted, beyond Brant Point, to the outer channel. She was tired and cold, content to let the current take her out to the race course and even beyond. For a panicky moment she wondered if there *were* any subs in the area, watching her drift past. She could not see the *Whisper*, tried to call again for Dori, but her jaw was so tightly clenched she couldn't open it.

She could see the outline of the shore, not so very far away, the shapes of houses and trees darker against the sky. She thought she might be able to make it if she could just get a little rest. So she laid her head down on the oar and drifted off, and when the bright light fell across her face, she thought

Bea had come into the girls' room and turned it on, the way she did when she heard one of them crying from a bad dream. Lilli was certainly having one of those. Her eyes burned terribly when she tried to open them, and she was so cold she felt transparent, as if she were made of ice. She could hear a thrumming. The light hurt her eyes. It was full on her now, piercing, and she wished Bea would turn it off. The thrumming slowed, and something landed near her with a splash. *Splash? What a peculiar dream she was having.* She couldn't turn her head to see what it was but soon felt a strong arm around her, smelled, faintly, Old Spice. She was moving, being pulled along, the oar dragging sluggishly behind, as she couldn't open her fist to let it go. When they reached the idling launch, someone leaned over the side and pried open her fingers, and then arms grabbed her and pulled her aboard. "Is she breathing?" someone asked. She heard other voices, too. "Check her pulse!" "Wrap her in that blanket." "Is she alone?" "Shine the light. She must be nearby." Lilli felt herself being swaddled in blankets; someone was rubbing her arms and legs. Randall said, "Let's get her in and come back out and look." That was when Lilli knew that Dori was still missing. Still out there. Lilli wanted to tell them to look now, but still she couldn't unclench her jaw, could manage only another raspy whisper. Randall put a hand on her shoulder and said, "Shhhhh."

Lilli hoped Dori had remembered to keep one hand for the boat.

LATER, LILLI LAY in her bed, staring up at the familiar cracks and stains in her ceiling: the yellowish one above Dori's bed that was shaped like a chick; an uneven spot in the plaster over the dressing table in the shape of an elephant; and the crack, running down the middle of the room, which Lilli had told Dori looked like the Nile. Ever after, Dori had referred to it as "the Niles." Lilli marveled that they appeared just as they had earlier that evening, before they'd gone out in the *Whisper*. She certainly didn't feel the same. The shade was still open, and the moon cast shadows of wildly waving branches, which looked vaguely tribal and made the elephant blink in and out of darkness.

Dr. Bartlett had been among those who'd met the launch at the dock. There had been a confusion of voices as Lilli was handed over the side to someone on shore, excited instructions shouted back and forth as people jumped off the launch and others climbed on. Dr. Bartlett had done a quick examination and ordered Lilli home to a warm bath, hot liquids, and to bed with plenty of extra blankets. She remembered being carried up the gangway, and then someone driving her home. She wasn't sure who. The launch, with Dr. Bartlett and Randall aboard, had headed back out to rejoin the search for Dori. Charlotte had been the one to sit on the edge of the tub, adding hot water and rinsing Lilli's hair with a measuring cup she'd brought up from the kitchen, along with a mug of hot, milky, sweet tea for Lilli to drink. Lilli tried to tell Charlotte the story, to explain about the dress, but her throat hurt, and everything—her frustration about the race, her resentment toward Bea, her despair at missing the dance, and the mysterious feeling she'd had when Randall held her—sounded rather silly and childish in the stark bathroom light. Charlotte told her to hush, that she'd put honey in the tea that would soon soothe Lilli's sore throat. But Lilli had questions. Well, one question, really.

"Where's Dori?" she asked, when Charlotte tucked her into bed and piled on comforters wreathed in clouds of camphor that she'd unearthed from a trunk in the attic. "Will she be home soon?" Charlotte smoothed the top counterpane and asked if she'd like more tea.

Lilli shook her head. "Bea?"

"Downstairs. Waiting."

"Waiting for Dori?"

"Yes, for Dori. Are you warm enough? Are you feeling sleepy?"

"Is she—"

"The doctor gave you something to help you sleep. Do you feel sleepy?" Her voice was so hopeful, almost insistent, that Lilli guessed she wanted to go downstairs and join the others.

Lilli did feel sleepy but was fighting it. She wanted to go downstairs, too. No, she wanted her mother to come up and wait with her here, because she felt sure that she would recognize and understand the fly-away feeling Lilli had had when Randall danced with her, understand perfectly how she'd been unable to think of anything as sensible as life jackets. Lilli knew she should not have gone out in the *Whisper*, and she made a promise to the yellow chick and the plaster elephant-shape above her that if Dori was safe, she'd never tell a soul that it was Dori's idea. She'd make Dori promise as well. Lilli was two years older. She should have known better, should have said no, should have taken responsibility. She felt grown up now, having decided to shoulder this burden and so vowed to apologize for going to the dance, too, which she'd also claim was her idea, and for borrowing—and ruining—Charlotte's dress, and for taking Bea's shoes without permission—which never would have been granted. Oh!

Bea's shoes. Lilli startled fully awake for a moment. She'd left them on the dock! Those were probably ruined as well, she realized as she slipped back down into the warm world of comforters and sedatives. One more thing to atone for. Lilli was not sure she felt quite that grown up.

But when they'd brought Lilli into the house, her mother had only hovered around the edge of the circle of men, like the butterflies in the late summer garden that flit from blossom to blossom, barely lighting before moving on, as though seeking something elusive, and only recognized when found. Blythe's eyebrows were pinched and her fingers nervously wound and unwound one of her colorful scarves. Lilli had reached out for her, wanting her mother's assurance that everything would be fine, all would be forgiven. But Blythe had looked right past her. Her mother was there, Lilli realized, but like the tree shadows on her bedroom wall, in form only, not substance.

"They must have taken Dori to the hospital," Lilli murmured to Charlotte. That was why she wasn't home yet. Lilli clung to consciousness and to the belief that Dori was fine, as tightly as she had clung to the narrow oar, so tightly she could almost hear the knock at the back door, the creak of heavy footsteps as Dori was carried up the stairs, could picture herself perched on the rim of the tub, streaming in more hot water, rinsing Dori's hair, tucking her into Lilli's own bed beneath the layers of quilts, and then climbing in beside her. Their mother would hover nearby and kiss them both good night, and Lilli would promise never, ever again to misbehave. And she would mean it. Wind-whipped branches tapped against her windowpane, and her mother's earlier words of doubt drummed in Lilli's head, didyoudidyoudidyoudidyoudid . . .

Charlotte slipped a towel under Lilli's wet head and told her to sleep.

Lilli closed her eyes so she wouldn't have to see the shadow branches on the wall and to hasten morning, when she would look over at Dori's familiar shape beneath the covers of her narrow bed, perhaps smell the delicious fragrance of bacon frying downstairs, and hear the flutter of the lawn mower, the snip, snip of hedge clippers trimming the boxwood, the scratch of a shovel plunging into dirt: the comforting sounds of Mr. Sylvia going about his chores. She and Dori would whisper to one another about their adventure—it would become that, an adventure, in the sparkling-clean morning light, not the nightmare it was now, in the dappled moon-glow with rain pattering against the window—and plan how they would spend their day, one of the few remaining that summer. First, they would search for specimens in the little tidal pools. Dori had wanted to bring some in to show her classmates and new teacher. She'd mentioned it several times, but Lilli had put her off. She wouldn't do that again. Ever. Then there was the party. Lilli would help Dori untangle a strand of yarn—ten of them!—and make it extra fun for her, make her laugh—Lilli loved Dori's laugh—and help her set up the dollhouse after the other girls went home.

This vision was so beguiling that Lilli made her breaths deep and even, pretending to be asleep, and soon she heard Charlotte move over to Dori's bed and fuss with the bedcovers. Turning it down, Lilli guessed. She then listened to Charlotte's footsteps cross the room and recede down the hall. Lilli opened her eyes and looked over at Dori's bed. Charlotte had not turned it down, but rather, had neatly made it, tucking the covers in tight, and setting the stuffed animals in a neat row on the pillow, in a way Dori never would have. The spread was no longer dented where Dori had lain earlier, reading her Nancy Drew mystery. Lilli wanted to get up and fix it, but she was drifting, drifting, rising and falling, in and out as memories sailed past: Dori and she dancing in the glade; Dori jumping off Big-big, shouting, "I'm going to touch the sky"; the bow of the *Loon*, plowing into the wave, the wave, sliding down the side of the wave, the cold water pouring over the gunwale, this can't be happening, this must be a dream—

Something thuds against the windowpane. A bird blown by the wind. Lilli can't see what kind, something light. It beats its wings against the glass, once, twice, three times before flying off. A figure appears beside the bed.

"Dori?" Lilli says, her heart lifting.

The figure stands very still, and Lilli can smell lemon drops. Daddy always carries a tin in his pocket. If I can guess which pocket, he'll give me one. Lilli sees his wire-rimmed glasses sparkle in the moonlight. "Daddy?" she whispers, knowing it can't be.

"No, not this one," he says. "The other one."

Who is he talking to? "Take me, Daddy. Take me." Other shadowy shapes gather in the room. "Bea?" Lilli whispers. There's an insistent tap, tap, tapping at the window. Grandmother rapping her thimble on the glass? The bird beating its beak against the pane? No, just branches blowing in the wind, didyoudidyoudidyoudid . . .

LILLI AWOKE TO the sound of car doors slamming, voices below her still-dark window, footsteps on the drive. *She's here!* She pulled herself to a sitting position, tried to clear her head, and listened as the back door opened and shut. More voices rose from the hallway below. She untangled herself from the layers of quilts that Charlotte had tucked around her and lurched across the room, grabbing the doorjamb for support. Hugging the wall, she made her unsteady way to the top of the stairs, where she was stopped cold by a wail like a siren from below. Her mother. Beneath the keening, Bea's voice murmuring.

Lilli crept down a few steps and saw her mother clutching one of Dori's old dolls. Dori hadn't played with dolls in years, but Lilli remembered that this one's name was Annabelle. She didn't know where her mother had even found it. Probably Charlotte had unearthed it when she'd retrieved the comforters from the attic. The town constable was there, in the front hall, and Pel Hardaway, the harbormaster, their slick black raincoats dripping.

Seven

L ILLI clung to the boat with both hands, feeling like one of the gray moths that used to land on the webs of the fat black and yellow spiders in her mother's garden, as Bea steered the aluminum dinghy away from the dock, between the boats in the harbor, and out into the channel. Lilli was showered with cold salt spray as they hit the wake of a passing motor yacht and gave up her silk suit for lost. That didn't bother her. What bothered her, as she sat facing aft, avoiding eye contact with her sister, was that Bea had managed to get her into this unseaworthy vessel and to motor across the one body of water Lilli wished never to venture into again. Lilli had not been on a boat smaller than a ferry since the night she'd capsized with Dori. The spiders, she remembered, would dance forward along their spun-silk snares, inject their victims with venom, and then scuttle back and wait, leaving their helpless prey not dead, but paralyzed, precisely how Lilli now felt, certain that if she moved one inch to either side she'd be done for.

All this to sprinkle Randall's ashes, which Lilli had finally located in a black plastic box in the trunk of Bea's car. They had set off, Bea, once again insisting on driving, being rather vague about where they were heading. Lilli's suspicion had mounted as they'd neared the yacht club—although, she had to admit, the harbor did seem an appropriate final resting place for Randall. Lilli pictured them, standing on the porch, or more likely on the float, since the tide was low, saying a few words before committing his ashes to the sea. After which they would go to Beacon House to obtain the appropriate paperwork, and Lilli could go back to her room for a nap.

But Bea had parked in front of the yacht club, where she was greeted by the club steward, a wiry man in khakis, who seemed to be expecting her, and the two walked off together. Lilli stayed in the car and glanced around. The scene looked much as it had the previous day, with young people carrying sail bags down the gangway. Much, in fact, as it had in Lilli's youth, although these young sailors exuded an air of confidence that could easily have been mistaken for boredom, as though they were completing what they believed to be a nuisance assignment, marking time while waiting for their real lives to begin. Lilli understood this. She'd felt the same way when she left White Head after Charlotte's wedding that August of 1969, and through that long winter in Chicago, living in a rented room near Charlotte and Graham, going through the motions of living, but without real thought or intention, believing that she was taking a sabbatical from her real life, not understanding, then, that life does not offer sabbaticals. And then, after she'd left Chicago for New York and art school and the life she'd dreamed of: living, studying, and painting in Paris, Italy, and London, opening the gallery, she kept thinking that someday her *real* life would begin, when all the while her real life was humming by like cars on a busy freeway. Standing here, gazing down at these young sailors, she wanted to shout down to them, "There is no starting gun. The race, your life, has already begun. Stop marking time."

That was when it dawned on her that she and Bea would not simply be able to walk down onto the float and upturn the box that held Randall's ashes. For one thing, there were too many boats and people. In addition, a fairly brisk onshore breeze would blow the ashes right back onto the dock and those standing on it. Lilli guessed that Bea was asking the steward to take them out in the launch, to the race course, which would be an even more fitting final resting place for Randall. Although Bea had changed out of her suit into slacks and a sweater and had added a battered canvas hat and bright blue running shoes—no doubt recently received from Footlights—Lilli still wore her silk suit and leather pumps, hardly a suitable outfit for boating, which, she noted with satisfaction, would provide a perfect excuse for her to wait on the dock.

Bea was starting down the shifting gangway to the lower float. The steward had disappeared into the clubhouse. Lilli got out of the car. Below her, dinghies bobbed in the light chop, some with oars neatly stowed, some with masts, others with outboard motors. The gangway rolled with the surge, adjusting to the motion of the float below, and Bea, with the black box cradled in one arm, was having a hard go of it. Lilli knew she should offer to help, but the dancing dinghies and waving masts were making her queasy. Bea, clutching the railing, continued down the gangway. A redheaded boy of about ten—add a patch of zinc oxide and it could have been Ned Chapin fifty years ago—was attaching a sail to one of the Knockabouts. He glanced up, saw Bea struggling, clambered onto the dock, and scampered up the gangway. He offered Bea a hand and escorted her down the final few feet. As Bea chatted with the boy, the steward reemerged and bounded down to meet them. Bea's young escort climbed back into his little boat and continued attaching the blue-and-white sail. Bea and the steward talked, each in turn gesturing first toward the mouth of the harbor, and then at various dinghies tied to the float. Lilli's unease rose like the spring flood tides. She could see her motel room across the harbor, the Adirondack chair in front. She could be there in ten minutes. Why was she still standing here? The steward had taken Bea's elbow and was leading her to an aluminum dinghy with a small outboard motor. She glanced up at Lilli and called, "I thought you were going to help me with this."

"Where's the launch?" Lilli shouted back.

Bea signaled for Lilli to come down. With a last, longing glance across the harbor to the empty Adirondack chair outside her room, Lilli made her way down the gangway. She felt like she was going to an execution. She would help get Bea settled, and then wait inside the clubhouse while Bea and the steward motored out to sprinkle the ashes.

Bea introduced Lilli to Dexter Parmenter, who could only nod, since he was holding Randall's ashes in one arm and Bea's hand with the other, and was attempting to steady the aluminum dinghy with one foot.

"Lilli, you get in first."

"First?" Lilli's chest felt as though it were seizing up. She no longer cared a hoot about Beacon House, Randall's ashes, unburdening herself to Bea, or anything beyond escape. What difference did it make where Bea lived or what unidentified white powders she accidentally ingested? "I'm not going out in that"—she pointed first to the dinghy and then to her outfit—"in this."

Dexter looked from one to the other. "May I?" He indicated that he'd like to put Randall's ashes on the float.

"No worse than the trunk of Bea's car," Lilli muttered.

Dexter placed the box reverently on the dock, hopped into the dinghy, and helped Bea get in and seated in the stern. He started the motor and set it in neutral before stepping back onto the dock.

"Is the launch not available?" Lilli asked.

"Mrs. Marsh said you'd prefer to do it yourselves."

They stood there for an awkward moment as Lilli examined her options and found few. Finally she slipped off her shoes. With help from Dexter, she half-fell, half-climbed into the idling dinghy. He handed her a seat cushion. "At least sit on this. I'd hate to see you ruin that outfit. It's gorgeous. Looks like silk." Bea was gazing intently out toward the entrance to the harbor.

Ned Chapin had recently arrived and joined the red-headed boy, obviously his grandson. Ned glanced over and asked if they needed a hand. Lilli would gladly have given him her seat, but Bea waved him off. Dexter gave the black box to Lilli, who was seated as close as possible to the middle of the dinghy, gripping thwarts with both hands. Reluctantly, she released one, took the box, and tucked it between her feet. Bea told Lilli to hold it, but Lilli insisted that it was safer wedged there. In truth, she wanted not one hand free for the boat, as they'd always been instructed, but two. Bea argued that the box would get wet in the inch or so of oily water at their feet. Only after Lilli pointed out that the ashes would soon be entirely submerged did Bea relent. Dexter, who looked somewhat pained during this exchange, untied the painter, tossed it into the bow, and gave them a push.

"Where are we going?" Lilli asked as they bumped through the chop.

"Brant Point," Bea said. She slipped the motor into gear and they roared off, narrowly avoiding the Knockabout with Ned Chapin, smiling broadly, and his grandson, and setting them bobbing in their wake. Lilli closed her eyes. She felt like the trapped moth in the spiderweb. She tried to concentrate on Beacon House; on Izzy, whom she would see the next day; on Randall, whose entire life had been reduced to ash; on anything except the very few inches of freeboard beneath her white knuckles and the churning green water.

When Bea cut the engine, the silence was profound. Lilli opened her eyes, and they drifted a bit, listening to the slap of the water on the hull, the whine of an outboard, the distant buzz of a lawn mower. As Lilli was slowly relaxing her grip, Bea jerked forward and reached for the box of ashes stowed between Lilli's feet. The boat pitched and rocked.

"What are you doing?" Lilli cried, reengaging her grip. Her mouth was dry, her throat tight. Lilli had never known precisely where the *Whisper* had capsized, remembered only passing the dark shapes of boats and hearing the wash of surf on rocks. She couldn't see the rocks but knew they sounded close, knew that they would be on them before they ever saw them. She wondered about Bea's motives in choosing this spot to commit Randall's ashes, in choosing a boat that so resembled the *Whisper*. Lilli began to wonder about other things, such as Izzy's surprise wedding and unanticipated visit.

"I'm just trying to get the ashes, Lilli. Relax."

"Here." Lilli nudged the box forward with her foot.

Bea grabbed it, and Lilli watched as Bea attempted, unsuccessfully, to pry open the lid.

"As intractable in death as he was in life. Here, see if you can open it." Bea leaned forward to hand Lilli the box and, as she did, her foot slipped out from under her. She slid off her seat and ended up in a heap in what was now several inches of oily salt water sloshing around the bottom of the boat. This set the vessel rocking again, and every muscle in Lilli's body constricted. Bea grimaced and rolled to one side. The dinghy dipped, sending a shot of adrenaline through Lilli. She inhaled through gritted teeth.

"Ugh. Give me a hand," Bea said, struggling to regain her seat. "And don't you dare laugh! I suppose you think it's funny that I'm now completely soaked."

Lilli had to admit that there was something faintly comical about the sight of her sister struggling, like the spider being jounced on its own web. She overcame her fear enough to release one hand and offer it to Bea, who grabbed hold and hoisted herself back onto the seat. "Thank you," she said with an attempt at dignity, a challenge under the circumstances: her canvas hat askew, her pants soaked.

Lilli took inventory: The boat was still upright, she was no wetter than before, and Bea had a damp bottom but otherwise was fine. She slowly released her other hand, took the box of ashes from Bea, examined it, and quickly determined that they would need a knife to pry it open.

They considered the box for a moment.

"I suppose we could toss the whole thing over," Bea said.

Lilli set the box in her lap. "I rather think it will float, don't you? End up on shore?"

Bea pursed her lips, as though calculating the distance, the prevailing winds, the effects of the tides and currents, and nodded. "Without a doubt. That would be just our luck." Still, she studied the box and seemed to be weighing her relief at ridding herself of it against her embarrassment of having someone locate it wedged into the rocks, or banging against a piling, and somehow trace it back to her. Lilli felt a giggle rising. She cleared her throat and swallowed, then frowned. But Bea had seen the smile tugging at the corners of her mouth, and she arched her eyebrows in mock offense. Lilli contracted every one of her facial muscles in an effort to keep from smiling. She bit her cheeks, but a laugh, somewhat disguised as a cough, escaped. She clamped her mouth shut. And then she viewed the scene as it must look to Ned and his grandson, whose blue-and-white sail she could see a short distance away: two middle-aged ladies, one in a battered canvas hat and bright blue shoes, the other in a soggy and wrinkled silk suit, hunkered in a small aluminum boat, bobbing in the afternoon sun, arguing over a black plastic box containing a quart or so of ash that Lilli earlier feared Bea had used for nondairy creamer. At this Lilli gave in and started to whoop. Once she started she couldn't stop. Waves of laughter rolled through her, one after another.

Bea watched her, smiling, and then she began to join in. She bent down and wrung out the hem of her pants, and the two sisters started howling. Bea pointed at Lilli's wet suit, which was plastered, somewhat revealingly, to her front.

"Oh," Lilli moaned through gales of laughter, thinking of her ruined outfit.

Bea assumed the tone and manner of their grandmother. "Shameful, Lillianne. Turn around, young lady, and let me see your backside."

Lilli screeched, and Ned and his grandson glanced over. Even from a distance she could see that Ned was smiling.

"Now, if Mother were here, she'd be jumping overboard at this point," Bea said.

At this, Lilli instantly sobered up and stared uncertainly at Bea. "What?"

The two women sat silent, the little boat patting the water with wet slapping sounds as it jounced in the waves. The lawn mower's distant whine now sounded like the buzzing of an insect. The sun burned hot on Lilli's shoulders. Nearby, a gull, perched on the railing of a yacht, opened its beak and tilted its head skyward.

"Nothing," Bea said. "I'm . . . Lilli . . . I didn't—"

"Let's head in, shall we?" Lilli said softly, looking toward shore. "You can always come back and do this another day."

"Yes, all right. Let's go back in. We can try again later." Bea started the motor. "Nice afternoon for a boat ride though, wasn't it?" she said, pointing the bow toward the yacht club, the whine of the outboard making a reply impossible.

BEA DOCKED THE boat, and the two climbed back onto the float with the help of several young sailors—who eyed, but did not question aloud, the black box—and then retreated to the Mercedes, placing Randall's ashes on the floor of the backseat.

"I'd like to change before we go to Beacon House."

Bea steered the Mercedes out of the lot and onto Harbor Drive into a steady stream of traffic. "Since you're staying the night, and Dori—"

"Izzy."

"—Izzy won't be here until around lunchtime tomorrow," Bea continued. "Why don't we put off our visit to Beacon House until the morning? There's no great hurry, is there? We're both soaked, and I'm"—she stifled a yawn—"quite tired. I should think you'd be exhausted, too. I'll drop you off, wait while you change, and we can go back to the house for a nap before dinner."

Lilli stared out the window at Beacon House, which they were then passing, feeling the sticky spiderweb snaring her once again. In truth, she was exhausted. She could call Beacon House from her room and arrange a time in the morning. "What time?"

"Nearly four, I should think."

"I mean, what time tomorrow?"

"Ten-ish?"

Bea was navigating down a series of side roads, past the Simmons Block and the new glass-and-steel restaurant.

"Fine. But I've got some calls I need to make. I'll come over around six thirty, and we can go somewhere nice for dinner. My treat."

"My dear, we old folks don't have the energy—"

"Bea, you're only sixty-seven."

Bea put on her blinker and pulled into the motel lot. "Let's just have a quiet dinner at home. Tomorrow night, when Izzy's here, we can all go out somewhere."

Lilli nodded. She could think of little she'd rather do less than eat dinner in that dark dining room or cluttered, depressing kitchen. But she lacked the energy to argue. After a long hot shower, and calls to Beacon House, Charlotte, Felicity, and Geoffrey, she'd nap. Then she would call Izzy and verify that she was indeed coming the next day and was planning to get married in two months—something she should have done, she realized, before she'd agreed to stay. "Why don't I pick us up something on my way over?" Lilli offered, thinking of the bare refrigerator.

"Suit yourself. Nothing too rich, mind you. My *Art of French Cooking* days are well behind me." Lilli smiled slightly, remembering the imitations of Julia Child that Randall had done one summer, providing a running commentary as Lilli struggled to learn to master the art.

Lilli climbed out and headed to her room, stopping by the front desk to ask if they could recommend a dry cleaner. The young man took in her bedraggled appearance and promised to send her suit out with the motel's linen that very night.

As she went to her room, she glanced down at the stony beach. It was empty, now, except for a flock of gulls, awaiting sundown.

LILLI SHOWERED, NAPPED, and then bundled herself into a terrycloth robe from the closet for the long-awaited sit in the Adirondack chair, where she sipped a cup of coffee and made her calls, doodling on a note pad. She called Geoffrey. The gallery in London was fine, he told her, and he'd watered the plants in her apartment. Lilli drew a philodendron. Next she phoned Felicity, who assured her that she was not needed before Wednesday and ran down the finalized menu for the reception. Lilli half-listened, jotted down *lamb, chicken, mushrooms,* then drew one of each as Felicity listed several top clients whom Lilli would want to meet. She wrote down their names and rang off. Then she called Charlotte, wondering why her calls hadn't been returned. R. J., one of Charlotte and Graham's twins, answered. He was house-sitting, he told Lilli, and taking care of Charlotte and Graham's Norfolk terrier. They were both at a conference up in San Francisco. "Is there a message, Aunt Lilli?" he asked. "They'll be home Wednesday. You could call her cell, but if it's important, I'd phone the hotel. Do you want the number?"

Lilli wrote it down, then rang off and gave the lamb on her notepad a thick fleece and allowed it to munch one of the leaves on the philodendron.

She punched in Izzy's number and sketched her face from memory, using as a model an old school photo Charlotte had sent years earlier.

"Hi, it's Izzy. I'm *so* happy you called and *really* sorry I missed you! *Please* leave a message. I promise I'll call back soon. Bye!" Beep.

"Hi, Izzy. It's Aunt Lilli." Lilli drew a self-portrait beside Izzy's. "I'm in White Head with your Auntie E." This was the name that a very young Izzy had given to Bea. "The house looks almost the same as it did when I was here last, which was . . . well, when I was much younger." Lilli rounded her face and softened her features, lifted the eyes, tightened the chin and neck—took off forty years. "She tells me that you're coming for a quick visit tomorrow. Is that true? It will be terrific to see you, if it is." Lilli drew a frame around the two portraits. "Ah, okay, I guess that's it. So, take care, and I'll hope to see you soon. Tomorrow!"

Only after she hung up did Lilli realize that she hadn't asked how Izzy was, about her sculptures, or her job, or Matumbé, all the questions that hung, straight and level, on the walls of Lilli's mind like portraits in a gallery that she visited almost daily. Nor had she asked about the wedding. *Well, Lillianne*, she scolded herself, *you are certainly a piece of work*. She drew another leaf on the philodendron to replace the one the lamb ate.

Feeling refreshed after her shower and her short nap, Lilli delivered her suit to the desk clerk, who assured her he'd have it back—one way or another—by Wednesday, and set off in her rental car for Bea's. Lilli would have been happy with takeout sushi, consumed while sitting in her robe in the Adirondack chair, but there it was.

She stopped at Beacon House. The office was closed, but a young man in a blue polo shirt with a Beacon House logo gave her a glossy brochure that described the various levels of care, the meal plans, and available activities, making it sound rather like a resort. He showed Lilli around the nicely furnished common areas, the dining room with its dozen tables and its windows facing onto the back lawn where she and Nancy Wakeman used to play croquet. Aside from an occasional walker and portable oxygen tank, and a few more wheelchair ramps, it even *looked* rather resortlike. The unit that would be available in June was in front and had a door leading onto the wide porch, where wooden rockers offered a fine view of the harbor. Fifteen minutes later she was on her way, wondering, as she passed the yacht club, whether Ned Chapin was there watching the sunset, just now beginning to color.

A bit before six, Lilli arrived at the house, which looked,

if possible, even more forlorn than it had the day before. She opened the kitchen door, setting the old dog leash rattling, half-expecting Patter to rush out begging for a walk, and called out. Silence. She crossed the kitchen and went into the dining room, taking a closer look than she had earlier. The Oriental carpet was nearly threadbare and the brass light fixtures in need of a good polishing. When all six of them were alive, they'd eaten dinner together here almost every night, as well as Sunday lunch, a three-course affair after the service at the Unitarian church, sometimes with the minister as a guest. Blythe loved parties. The mahogany table with all panels in place could comfortably seat ten, but it wasn't uncommon to see twelve adults, wreathed in cigarette smoke, squeezed around the table at one of her dinner parties, which went late into the night and usually ended with the guests, laughing and singing loudly, gathered around a fire on the rocks below the house, after a late-night swim. But Blythe had never entertained after George died, and the panels had disappeared, one by one, as the family had grown smaller.

Lilli crossed the front hall, this time picking up one of Randall's docksiders, the leather faded and salt-stained, and the toes upturned, wondering why Bea had left them there. She replaced the shoe and went into the living room. When Dori and she were small, they loved to play Don't Touch the Floor, crawling, climbing, and scaling their way around the big house. The living room, Lilli recalled now, was by far the least challenging with its many overstuffed chairs, side tables, and footstools, and the wide mantel, which they would cling to and inch along, fingers aching.

The mantel was now crowded with photographs. In the front was one she remembered well, as it used to stand on her dressing table. Randall, grinning, very handsome in a varsity letter jacket, arms around the shoulders of two teammates, all wearing funny hats. Beside it was Bea and Randall's wedding portrait. Randall stood ramrod straight, hair combed back, looking directly into the camera, but Bea's focus was elsewhere. She looked distracted, as though recalling an errand she'd forgotten to run. Dozens of small, tarnished silver frames encased grainy snapshots of friends in front of the yacht club or on the rocks below the house. There was a framed photo of three couples entering the Copley Hotel for a dance. Lilli recognized them, but could not recall their names. Several glossy holiday cards were tucked into its frame, presumably those same people, years later, with their families: one lined up on the deck of a yacht, another clustered on a ski slope, the third gathered around a richly decorated Christmas tree. All smiling.

In the back row of this mantel gallery was a portrait of the Niles family on the front lawn, the gardens behind them in full bloom. It was a Sunday, and they'd been to church. Dori sat on her parents' right. It was taken the day after Bea had set her hair in all those Spoolies, so it was quite curly. Their mother had her head tilted slightly, as though she were about to rest it on their father's shoulder. To their left, Charlotte held a young Patter in her lap. Beside them, Bea's hand rested lightly on Patter's head, her gaze and smile open and— uncharacteristically, Lilli noted—almost childlike. Lilli stood behind them with a hand on each of her parents' shoulders, her head turned, her expression hidden. She remembered that she'd been looking at sprays of lavender beside some puffy pink phlox and pale yellow coreopsis, whose delicate blossoms were bobbing in the breeze on stems as thin as silk, thinking what a nice subject they would make for a painting. A bumblebee, coated with bright orange pollen, was buzzing drunkenly among the foxgloves. Lilli studied the portrait, and her heart ached. Each of them had been so blissfully unaware of what lay ahead.

Beside the photo was another of Charlotte and Graham; their twins, R. J. and David, then twelve, both plump and bespectacled like their father; and Izzy, sixteen, her steady gaze holding the viewer's. Lilli had the same portrait back home, matted, framed, and hanging above her desk in the living room. And here was Izzy's baby picture—with booties, kittens, and rattles dancing around its pink cardboard frame—lying on its back. As Lilli snaked her arm through the forest of frames to right it—certain if one fell it would take down all the rest—she saw, sandwiched in Plexiglas, a postcard-size reproduction of one of her paintings: an English garden in muted pinks, lavenders, and pale yellow. A recent work. The one she'd used for the invitation to her upcoming gallery opening in Boston. Lilli was struck by its location beside the old Niles family portrait. It looked as though Lilli were staring out of the one toward the other.

Lilli stepped back, trying to imagine ever having been small enough to wiggle, legs dangling, along this mantel. Then she walked on to the den, where Bea, ensconced in the sagging armchair, head tilted back, mouth open, was snoring lightly, her feet propped up on the ottoman in front of a silent but glowing television. The Weather Channel was broadcasting Local on the 8s. The skies, it seemed, would be clear for the next few days. Lilli returned to the kitchen with several of the dirty glasses clustered on the metal television table, turned the oven on low, and put in the roasted chicken she'd bought, along with the container of mashed sweet potatoes. Wanting to refrigerate the Waldorf salad, she held her breath and opened the door, recalling the pungent odor that morning. She located a partially liquefied onion covered in green fuzz in a plastic bag in the crisper and added it to the full trash bag, which she took out to the cans that were, as she'd suspected, still alongside the garage. She checked her watch—six thirty.

SHE HAD TO push through a tangle of grapevines, poplar saplings, and bittersweet to reach the greenhouse door, which was slightly ajar. She tugged it open, flattening the surrounding weeds with her foot to make space, and was rewarded, as she stepped inside, with the scent of sun-baked wood and dried foliage. On her right, three narrow stepped shelves stood against the wall. In Lilli's memory, they had the stature of stadium bleachers. In fact, the topmost, where she and Dori used to sit and watch their mother and Mr. Sylvia tuck seedlings into flats at the potting bench, was only about three feet high. Mr. Sylvia was always warning the girls to watch out for splinters and not to cut themselves on the sharp metal brackets. When they finished planting, he would shoo the girls off and place the flats of seedlings on the shelves, turning them daily so they would grow straight and tall for the garden.

The potting bench, built by their father, looked comically spindly-legged and wholly insufficient to support all that now burdened it: three big terra-cotta pots full of dirt and the dusty remains of last year's mums; several large bags of soil, one open, its contents spilling out; rakes, shovels, several trowels, a pair of red-handled pruning shears, loppers, hedge clippers, and a basket of papery bulbs that crumbled in Lilli's hand as she touched them. She did so warily, as the bench looked top-heavy and unstable. She stepped across the dirt floor, dry as chalk, took a seat on the lowest step, and gazed up through the milky panes of glass veined with grapevines, to the dark treetops bending in the breeze.

She knew little of Bea's life with Randall, and the house, so far, had revealed almost nothing more. Bea had never talked much of their life together. Understandable, given the circumstances. Lilli certainly had never asked. She had seen Randall only once after leaving White Head on the night of Charlotte's wedding. He'd come to New York City in 1990, when Lilli had her first exhibit in the United States. She hadn't known he was coming. Izzy, then nineteen and in her sophomore year at Columbia, was there, too. Lilli had been shocked speechless when she saw Randall, standing under a light in the gallery, talking with Izzy. He looked older, heavier, still handsome, but like a stranger who resembled someone she'd once known. She'd fled the gallery, caught a cab, and told the driver to head uptown. After twenty blocks she got out and walked back. The gallery owner was frantic. Where had she been? People had been asking for her! Was she all right?

Lilli had sold several paintings that evening.

Now she returned to the house to find Bea peering into the oven. "Randall?"

"No, it's Lilli."

Bea considered her for a moment. "Where the devil have you been all this time?"

Lilli considered the question, not sure whether Bea was referring to the forty years since she'd left White Head or the roughly two hours since their unsuccessful attempt to sprinkle Randall's ashes. "I came earlier. You were sleeping, so I took a little walk."

Bea gazed around at the stovetop and the kitchen table before moving to the sink and peering out the window. "Where did you go?"

"To the greenhouse."

"The greenhouse. I see. And?"

"And then I came back."

Bea crossed to the oven and opened the door. "The chicken looks like it's ready."

"Yes."

"Do we have time for a quick drink?"

"Don't see why not. I'll make them."

Bea hesitated before giving Lilli a half smile. "Thank you. Let's sit in the den," she said and started out of the kitchen.

"Here." Lilli scooped up a pile of mail from the table and handed it to her.

Bea waved it away. "Nothing but ads. Maybe a few bills. Randall opens and sorts it—" They stared at the pile of mail for an uncomfortable moment. "Yes, all right," Bea muttered, accepting the armload and heading to the den.

Lilli mixed two vodka tonics and followed her sister, picking up fallen circulars and bills along the way. She found Bea, once again, sunk deep in the armchair, the television now blaring. Lilli handed her a drink along with the dropped mail.

"Where are my glasses?" Bea asked.

"What?" Lilli could barely hear over the din of the evening news.

"My glasses."

"I've no idea."

"I called and asked you to bring them from the kitchen. Didn't you hear?"

"Mind if I turn this down a bit?" Lilli didn't wait for an answer but located the remote control on the arm of Bea's chair and hit mute.

"They're right beside the stove."

Lilli was certain they were not and shook her head.

"No? I was sure . . . Then they must be in my bedroom." She looked at Lilli, expectant.

"Fine." As Lilli headed toward the front stairs, she heard Bea call, "I'm in Mother's old room."

Lilli turned left at the top of the stairs, walked down the hall, past Charlotte's room and the door to the attic, which stood slightly ajar. She shut it firmly and continued on to her mother's old bedroom. She flicked on a light, illuminating the familiar canopy bed, the dressing table, the tall bureau with its once-shiny brass pulls, now so tarnished they were as dark as the mahogany. She checked the bedside table, which was littered with crumpled tissues, a half-full tumbler of water, and an empty eyeglass case. The bed was unmade. She shifted the covers: no glasses. On the dressing table were several over-due library books, a bit of yarn, and several cardboard jewelry boxes containing a jumble of orphaned earrings, beads, and buttons. Dori gazed solemnly up from inside a silver frame. No eyeglasses. There was also no sign of Randall, and Lilli guessed they had slept in separate rooms. She glanced at her reflection, not surprised to see that her eyes were puffy and ringed with dark circles. She'd aged ten years in twenty-four hours. She returned empty-handed to the den, where Bea was glancing through a seed catalog, with her glasses perched on the end of her nose. "They were in my pocket all along."

"Imagine that."

FIFTEEN MINUTES LATER, they were sitting across from each other at the dining room table. They ate in silence for several minutes. Finally Bea said, "The potatoes are quite sweet."

"I think it's maple syrup." Lilli watched her sister, busily separating the raisins out of her Waldorf salad with her fork. Lilli felt uneasy in this room, at this table, with all the carefully avoided memories waiting within the Wedgwood sugar bowl, the tarnished brass candlesticks, and the dust-covered glass globes of the chandelier. Who knew when they might burst forth?

Bea didn't respond or even look up for a long moment. Finally she said, "So, what shall we serve at Izzy's wedding?"

"Nothing with raisins, obviously."

Bea glanced up. "You sound offended."

Lilli took a large mouthful of potato, which was much too sweet and had an odd undertaste. *Anise?* "No, not offended. Just tired." She took a fortifying sip of the Sauvignon Blanc she'd bought. A bad choice. It was puckeringly dry with the potato. "I've been thinking about Izzy's wedding . . ."

"Oh?"

"I'm sure, once Izzy sees this place, she'll see . . . And if we tell her—"

"Tell her what?"

"That your plans have changed and that you're thinking of moving—"

"We'll do nothing of the sort. She has her heart set on

having it here, and have it here she shall. We can all plan it together."

"I stayed an extra day, Bea . . ." Lilli paused. "Have you thought about what you're going to do now that Randall is gone?"

Bea, working her way through the sweet potatoes, remained silent.

Lilli assumed a more conversational tone. "We have an appointment at Beacon House tomorrow at ten." She took another sip of wine. Celery, she realized, would be just the thing to counter the cloying flavor of the anise. She watched Bea spear a bit from her salad, crunch, and search for another. Lilli decided to try humor. "Just think how many fewer places you'll have to look for your glasses. Plus, they have paid staff there to help you find them." Lilli's tone was caustic rather than cajoling, perhaps from the astringent effect of the wine. Perhaps from something that had been fermenting far longer.

"Are you through?" Bea was dabbing the sides of her mouth with her napkin. All that remained on her plate was a small pile of raisins.

"No, I'm not through." Lilli hadn't intended to pursue the discussion about moving Bea to Beacon House without Charlotte's skillful salesmanship, but she hadn't been able to reach Charlotte. "There is no way you can maintain this house by yourself, let alone have it ready for a wedding in two months, and you know it. The weeds have all but taken over the garden, and the wisteria is going to pull this house right down on top of you one of these days." She took a breath.

Bea carefully folded her napkin and placed it beside her plate. "I meant with your supper. I'd like my dessert."

Eight

PEL Hardaway stood in the Nileses' hallway holding Dori's body, before placing it gently on the dining room table and retreating to the living room. When Blythe draped herself over the body and keened as though channeling all the sadness in the universe, Bea and Charlotte stood on either side, holding her. Their backs were to the stairs, so they didn't notice Lilli creep down and stand at the end of the long table. Only when she reached out a tentative hand to touch Dori's foot—finding it as wet, cold, and smooth as the inside of a clamshell—did Charlotte see her. She released Blythe and grabbed Lilli just as she emitted a small gasp, snatched back her hand, and started to collapse. Randall, standing in the hallway, wrapped in a wool blanket, tried to catch her eye as Charlotte ushered her back to bed. But Lilli had pulled tight within herself, like a periwinkle, all folded up and tucked inside, tighter than seemed possible, and didn't notice.

For three days, Blythe sequestered herself in her room. Bea cajoled and pleaded with her through the keyhole. Charlotte left meals on a tray outside her door, only to pick them up later, untouched. Lilli might have eaten, might have slept, she couldn't say. She was as unconscious of her actions during those days as the shadow is of its navigation around the sundial.

It was hot and bright at the cemetery the day they buried Dori. The grave looked dark and cool and almost inviting, thought Lilli, in her too-tight navy blue dress, standing beside her mother and sisters. The branches of a huge beech tree spread overhead, providing some shade, but not enough to counteract the steady, hot breeze that stirred the leaves, twirling them this way and that, as though getting them ready for their fall flight. Lilli wished she could open her arms and sail away. In the distance a dove cooed, and a lawn mower issued a muted flutter. Across the grave stood a softly weeping Janey Hallowell with her parents, and Randall, who should have gone home and back to college, but had stayed in White Head an extra week. He had been at the house every day: bringing casseroles and Bundt cakes from his aunt; helping to hang the storm windows; and sitting with Blythe, who had finally opened her bedroom door to him but still had not spoken to anyone else. No one spoke of Dori's death to Lilli, just as no one had spoken of George's death. Death was a private matter in this family, and grief not for public display.

She looked at the pale wood coffin with its mantle of pink carnations, suspended over the dark, chiseled hole. It disturbed her to think that Dori lay right there, just a few feet away, inside that box. She wanted to flip back the latches and see her one last time, to offer her a hand, help her out. Say,

Let's go dig a trench on the beach and wait for the tide to fill it.
Or suggest a game of hide-and-seek among the gravestones,
or look for Russian subs in the cove. But they were going
to lower Dori down into that hole, down with the worms
and beetles. Dori liked bugs, so she wouldn't mind that. But
then they would pile dirt over the top, and there wouldn't be
any sunshine or moonlight, and Dori loved those. This, then,
was death: losing the things you love. Lilli stared up into the
branches of the beech tree overhead, because she could feel
tears welling and didn't want them to spill. "The Lord is my
shepherd," the minister invited them to recite.

"I shall not want," murmured Lilli.

THAT FALL, WHEN it was warm, Blythe would sit on the
sunporch. When it was cool, she would be in the living room.
She was always holding a book, or some sewing, but she never
made any progress on either. She reminded Lilli of the crab
shells she and Dori used to find on the beach: beady eyes
staring up, claws ready to pinch. But when they turned them
over, the insides were completely gone, eaten away by gulls.

Charlotte returned to her dorm at Radcliffe, and Lilli
crept around the house alone, sometimes not touching the
floor, other times walking toe-heel-toe-heel, always trying to
be very quiet, as Bea had instructed. She was careful not to
muss anything, or leave any of her books or clothes where
they might be in the way. Bea had not told her to do this,
but she did it anyway, always feeling that she needed to pull
even further into herself, to make herself as invisible as possible. She slept, cocooned beneath her covers, in the bedroom
she'd shared with Dori, although she didn't sleep well. When

it rained and the wind blew hard enough to set the branches of the maple tree tapping against her window, she didn't sleep at all.

One rainy night, very late, Blythe came into Lilli's room. Lilli lay motionless, pretending to sleep, listening as her mother's footsteps crossed to Dori's bed. Even through the layers of blankets, Lilli could smell the sweet scent of Tabu and sense the warmth of her mother's body. The bedsprings creaked as Blythe sat down. Someone had propped Dori's doll Annabelle against the bedspread, her brown doll hair all frizzled against the chenille. Lilli didn't like sharing her bedroom with this glassy-eyed stranger, but she hadn't dared move her, even though Annabelle, Lilli knew, had never been Dori's favorite. From deep inside her nest, Lilli heard rustling, and guessed that her mother had picked Annabelle up. Soon the bedsprings creaked again, and then Blythe's warmth and light footstep left the room, leaving behind only her familiar fragrance.

She came again the next night, and the next, her visits becoming a nightly ritual. Sometimes Lilli lay awake, waiting. Other times she'd have fallen asleep but would wake when she sensed her mother at the door. She began to leave a peephole in her cocoon of bedcovers, so she could watch, and then she left her cocoon altogether and waited, eyes half closed, feigning sleep, and finally she abandoned the pretense and watched her openly. Her mother would sometimes smile but she never spoke, and Lilli began to believe that they had such a secret, special connection that words weren't needed.

Then, one night, a few months after Dori's death, as Lilli lay awake, listening to the steady patter of the rain on her window—thinking about that other rainy night, and of the bird that had flown into her window and tapped its beak, no longer certain she'd seen a bird, though; more likely she'd dreamed it, along with the visit from her father—her mother came to the doorway, but instead of going to Dori's bed, she stood and merely said, "Get up, Lilli. We're going out."

Lilli was so startled to hear her mother speak that she bolted upright, threw back the covers, and scrambled to her feet. Her mother spoke so little these days. Lilli couldn't recall the last time she'd heard her issue a command of any sort, or even offer a suggestion. She would reply when someone asked her a question, would murmur some sort of vaguely appropriate response, but she never initiated a conversation. So, wanting to encourage this new turn of events, Lilli followed her mother, who was now holding a finger to her mouth to indicate that Lilli must be very quiet. They went down the back stairs to the kitchen. Lilli wasn't frightened, but wondered if she should be, as her mother headed out the door into the rainy night without putting on a coat. Lilli grabbed her own coat, and one for her mother, as she ran after her, already halfway to the garage. By the time Lilli got there, Blythe was behind the wheel of the old Ford. Her mother hadn't driven for months, and Lilli hardly dared think what sort of emergency could be so secretive and take place in the middle of the night. Who was ill? Had something happened to Charlotte? Never mind, her mother was taking action. She climbed, shivering, into the front seat, hugging their coats, and Blythe, who seemed not to notice the damp shoulders of her dress, backed out of the garage, and then followed the familiar route to the cemetery. Bea drove them over there most Sundays, so Lilli knew the way well.

They slid between the big pillars supporting the iron arch,

past the neat granite office building, and up the rise to Dori's grave with its carved marble stone—just like her father's, only smaller. Dori's had mud splattered onto it, because the grass hadn't yet grown over the top of her grave. Lilli waited in the car for her mother, who got out and stood beside the two graves, her head bowed, her shoulders shaking. Lilli finally breathed onto the window, fogging it, so she couldn't see.

They made frequent late-night visits to the cemetery that winter. Lilli would sit huddled in the car, staring up at the million pinpricks of light so distant and safe between the now-bare branches of the beech tree. The tree itself seemed to be reaching skyward as though in supplication, sending up a prayer for the leaves' return.

In early March the weather turned unexpectedly warm, and the snowdrops and crocuses bloomed. Lilli's spirits soared. A week later, a storm buried the tiny plants beneath six inches of wet snow. The night of the storm Blythe didn't come to Lilli's room, nor did she come the next night, or the next, or the three after that. Lilli knew then that the night-time visits were over. The six inches of snow soon melted, and Lilli believed that, this time, spring had truly come.

On Easter Sunday, Lilli woke early. She slept with the shades up, not minding the early-morning sun slipping between the branches of the maple outside her window and threading its way across the room to her bed. She preferred it to the claustrophobic feel of waking in a shade-blackened room that offered no clue as to what lay outside. Being sealed in darkness that way reminded her of that cold, dark water slowly swallowing her the night that Dori drowned, her dress tugging her down with a fervor that matched her own desire to reach the surface. Heart racing, she would rush to the window and raise the blinds, gulping in light like air, her chest tight, thinking of Dori buried deep in the earth.

Blythe, Bea, and Charlotte—home for the holiday—were still sleeping as Lilli made her stealthy way down the back stairs—toe-heel-toe-heel—through the kitchen and out the door, holding the dog leash so it wouldn't rattle. The morning felt cool, and mist hung over the landscape like gauze. But Lilli believed the day held promise. Something in the way the daffodils held their tightly wrapped buds atop their sturdy green stems. They'd wisely waited, unlike the battered and broken crocuses and snowdrops nearby. Lilli felt certain they would pop open today.

She scuffed across the dew-covered lawn, her sneakers soon soaked through, between garden beds still asleep beneath their blankets of leaves, although she could see a few pale green shoots rising through the sodden mass. Mr. Sylvia had not yet raked the leaves away, or cleared the tree limbs that had fallen onto the lawn during the winter, or cut back the brush that topped the rocky ledge and attempted its assault on the yard every year. The hammock was still in the basement, alongside the badminton net. Lilli wondered if Randall would put them up this year. She was ready for spring and summer, ready for Randall to come back to White Head. She wanted her mother to come back, as well, from whatever remote place she'd drifted off to and start gardening again, and organizing picnics on the rocks and tea parties on the lawn, to make her sculptures and silly birthday crowns. Lilli's sixteenth birthday had come and gone that winter, all but unnoticed by her mother. Charlotte, home on break, had baked a cake for Lilli and made her favorite dish, chicken à la king. They'd eaten by candlelight at the dining room table. Bea had knit Lilli a pale blue Fair Isle sweater to go with her new Villager skirt, and Charlotte gave her a watercolor set twice the size of the one she had. But there'd been neither a gift from her mother nor a paper crown. Perhaps she thought Lilli was now too old for paper crowns. Most days Lilli felt too old, too; she longed for a return to childhood.

Lilli picked her way down the stone steps to the beach, avoiding a few spots still slick with frost. She liked to come down here when fog cloaked the cove and the foghorn issued its mournful wail. Lilli would sometimes match its low tone with cries of her own. The tide was now low, as she knew it would be, the perfect time to look for specimens in the tidal pools. It was here that she felt Dori's presence most strongly and so she came, if she could, when the tide was right. The others would be getting up soon, but it would take some coaxing to get their mother ready for church. She moved now as though every motion pained her. After church they would have some sort of meal—not a full-blown Sunday dinner like they used to—but Charlotte would do something. Lilli had decided she wanted to learn how to cook and resolved to help her. It was wonderful having her home again. It seemed like a home again with her there. The sun began to burn through the fog, and the sand, pocked with clam-holes, glistened. *If I had a shovel and bucket*, Lilli thought, *I could dig some clams, and we could cook them later down on the beach*. But she had neither, so she decided to suggest a picnic lunch instead. Something fun; that darling roller coaster of a word, the meaning of which Lilli had nearly forgotten.

* * *

THE HOUSE MIGHT have shifted a bit, signaling Lilli's departure to the others. Something woke Charlotte, who put on her robe and slippers and scuffed downstairs to make coffee. She punched down the dough she'd made the night before for the hot cross buns, and rinsed and stacked the dinner dishes still sitting on the counter. Bea arrived in the kitchen, already dressed for church in a linen dress, her pageboy pulled back with a velvet band.

"You going to church, Char?" Bea said.

"I suppose. Coffee?"

Bea shook her head and filled the kettle for tea.

"Toast?"

Bea shrugged. She was not a morning person. "Is Lilli up?"

"Down on the beach, I think."

Bea snatched the singing kettle from the stove, silencing it, and poured water over the tea ball in her rose-patterned cup. Charlotte spread butter liberally on her toast, added a large spoonful of her beach plum jelly, took a bite, and smiled. Bea dunked the tea ball vigorously several times, pulled it from her cup, and placed it in the sink just as their mother appeared in the doorway, wearing an old silk kimono that hung so loosely on her gaunt frame it looked more draped than worn. Her eyes, enormous in her thin face, carried a vacant expression, making her seem as if she were perpetually poised to ask a question. Her daughters waited, expectant, but Blythe would simply stare through them, and then give a wan smile before turning away with a sorrowful look, as though she had asked her question and been disappointed by their answer.

Charlotte crossed the kitchen and gave her mother a hug—the tentative kind you might give a relative you hadn't seen in some time—and a peck on the cheek. "Coffee? I just made it."

Blythe looked bemused, and then became engrossed with a stray thread on her sleeve, worrying it with her fingers. Bea poured her a cup, set it down on the table, pulled out a chair, and guided her into it. Blythe smiled, said "Thank you," and then became fixated on the Easter lily that Bea had placed as the centerpiece. "How beautiful. Is it from the garden?" she asked.

"No, we bought it yesterday at Emerson's. You remember," Bea prompted.

Blythe gave a small nod, her expression indicating that she had no memory whatsoever of that event, and turned to stare at the ivy vines snaking their way up the wall. She ran her finger along one. "I promised Dori we'd finish these this week."

Bea and Charlotte exchanged concerned looks across the kitchen.

"Where's my Lilli?" Blythe then asked.

After a moment's confusion, Bea said, "Down on the beach, we think. Charlotte heard her go out earlier."

"Alone?" The alarm in their mother's voice, Bea and Charlotte would later agree, was the first emotion they'd heard there in some time.

"She'll be fine. She knows we're going to church. I'm sure she'll be right up. Shouldn't you be getting ready?" Bea sat down beside her mother and put a hand on her arm. So thin! It seemed as though she were vanishing before Bea's very eyes, despite all her efforts. Bea had instructed Mrs. Foley to put extra butter in her white sauces and to use half-and-half, rather than milk. She'd bought macaroons at Charnock's Bakery and kept the freezer stocked with strawberry ice cream, her mother's favorite. Bea's weekly menus included roast beef, pork chops, mashed potatoes with gravy, pot roast, green bean casserole, tuna casserole . . . She might just as well have served her mother the "crumpets" the girls used to offer their dolls at Blythe's tea parties—beach stones they would bring up and serve on Grandmother's best china—because Blythe barely touched a morsel.

She had merely poked and prodded last night's dessert—Charlotte's marshmallow, pineapple, and whipped cream concoction—finally spearing a pineapple chunk, which she'd brought halfway to her mouth, before her brow had furrowed, as though the effort of raising her fork the rest of the way were too much, and returned it to her plate. Bea decided to have Charlotte make a refrigerator cake. One way or another, she was determined to bring her mother around. "You could wear one of your pretty scarves. Comb your hair. Up," she added, not wanting to offend. "And wear that new lipstick I bought you."

Her mother nodded, but she was now staring intently at the ivy vines covering the wall. She stood and walked over to the sink. "These have no leaves," she said, pointing to the patch of unfinished vines under the cabinets to the left of the sink. "The ivy isn't growing."

Bea and Charlotte both stared at their mother, each searching, unsuccessfully, for a response to this statement. Blythe left her coffee untouched and wandered out of the kitchen, saying, "I must get the ivy to grow."

"Are you sure you wouldn't like to come? It's Easter. We could go to the cemetery after," Bea called. But her mother either didn't hear or chose not to answer. The back stairs barely creaked beneath her light tread. Bea banged her fist on the table. Blythe's coffee cup clattered in its saucer.

Charlotte checked the time. "Nine fifteen! Holy smokes, I better get dressed. Church will be packed. Call Lilli?" She popped the last of her toast into her mouth.

Bea nodded, but when Charlotte came back downstairs ten minutes later, Bea was waiting in the kitchen alone. "Where's Lilli?"

"Someone should stay here with Mother. I left her a note." Bea pointed to a slip of paper tucked beneath the Easter lily. "If she'd wanted to go she'd have come back by now." Bea shifted the plant so the note was more visible.

"Lilli doesn't wear a watch," Charlotte said.

"High time she started. In any event, there isn't time now for her to change." Moments later, with the windows rolled up in the Country Squire against the cool morning, neither one heard Lilli hail them as they rolled down the drive.

LILLI HAD CLIMBED far out onto the rocks that rimmed the cove in search of periwinkles, limpets, and hermit crabs in tidal pools, chatting all the while. "Look, Dori," she whispered, finding a starfish. She bent down to pick it up and, stroking its knobby surface, tucked herself behind a boulder as she stared out at Pequot Light, lost in dreams of the future: dreams of a life away from White Head, attending art school, traveling, opening a gallery, becoming a famous artist . . . A movement across the cove caught her eye: the Chapin family trooping out to their car. Church! Bea was always on Lilli for being late. She'd bought her a watch last fall, which Lilli rarely remembered either to wind or to wear. She clambered back along the rocks, raced across the beach, took the steps two at a time, and arrived just in time to catch sight, through the opening in the lilac hedge, of the Ford gliding down the drive.

Lilli was sure she'd seen her mother at the wheel, which helped offset her hurt and disappointment at being left behind, barely. Lilli didn't much care for church. She didn't mind missing that. She would sit in the pew and feel people's eyes on her, hear their nearly silent whispers that she was "the one who'd been with the little girl who'd drowned last summer." But Lilli did mind being left. To make herself feel better, she convinced herself that this trip to church, with Blythe driving, signaled the beginning of a welcome change in her mother—who seemed to have become more remote than ever in recent days. Soon all would be well. And so, lonely but resigned, she went onto the porch, still holding the starfish, and curled up on the glider. The sun was so warm that she soon drifted off to sleep.

BLYTHE CAME BACK downstairs shortly after Bea and Charlotte left. Unaware that Lilli was dozing on the porch, she went into the den, to the big rolltop desk. She took out a piece of paper, pale blue with her name embossed at the top, meaning to write a note, but instead she drew a leaf, and then another, and another, and soon had covered the entire page with leaves. She stared at the patchwork of leaves, and then went into the kitchen, where her now-cold cup of coffee still sat on the table. She emptied it down the drain, set the cup on the counter, and, using the same blue pen, drew leaves on the unfinished ivy vines under the cupboard to the left of the sink. These blue-ink ivy leaves were wobbly, and misshapen, some much too large, others too small. She stared at the leaves for a long while, before placing the pen on the counter and returning upstairs.

LILLI AWOKE WITH a start, unsure what had done it. Perhaps the house, once again, had shifted slightly, or a breeze had rattled a window frame. With sleepy eyes, she gazed for a moment through the glass of the sunporch, picturing a garden: phlox and daisies, stocks and peonies, lilies and asters. Perhaps today they could all rake off the leaves together, and her mother would identify the pale shoots that Lilli had seen pushing through the mulch. It amazed her to think about all that was hidden, waiting, inside those tiny tendrils: leaves, stems, brilliant blooms. A miracle. And all it took was sunlight, soil, and water. Maybe she could get her mother to plant a small cutting garden with her this summer. They could start the seeds in the greenhouse as her mother and Mr. Sylvia used to do.

She went upstairs to make her bed, and as she walked down the hall she heard a noise in the attic. She stopped and listened. The ship's clock in the living room bonged once, and somewhere downstairs, a door blew shut. Just the wind, she decided, and continued on. She propped the starfish on the mirror above her dressing table, read for a bit, and then, hungry, went down the back stairs to the kitchen for some of Charlotte's pineapple, marshmallow, and whipped cream from the night before. As she collected a spoonful of tiny marshmallows, she noticed Bea's note.

Lilli,

Charlotte and I waited but have gone on to church. Mother is here. Home before noon. Perhaps we can all have a picnic on the rocks.

Love, Bea

Delight was the first thing Lilli felt—a picnic!—then puzzled. Her mother here? Couldn't be. She was certain she'd seen her in the car. Lilli decided that Bea must have written the note just as Blythe had arrived in the kitchen, ready for church, and Bea—so surprised and pleased to see her mother up and dressed—had neglected to tear it up. She was positive her mother was driving. *Wasn't she?* Sudden doubt propelled her to the front stairs, where she called out, "Mother?" She went up, noting, as always, how the dark red cabbage roses on the wallpaper did not resemble any flower she'd ever seen. The canopy bed in her mother's room was empty and unmade. A number of outfits were draped over the wing chair by the window, and the top of her dressing table was littered with bracelets, necklaces, ring boxes, and several tubes of lipstick, their tops removed, the way they might have been if someone had dressed hurriedly and searched for just the right outfit and just the right shade to match. What's more, her mother's beautiful silk scarves, which usually hung neatly from the mirror frame, lay scattered about on the bench. Before Dori died, her mother had always worn one, a splash of color accenting her dress of navy, black, or gray. She must have worn one to church, Lilli decided. A very good sign. Lilli selected a lavender-and-pink scarf from the pile, draped it around her shoulders, and knotted it. Blythe and the girls, when they were little, would each tie a scarf around their necks like this and run about the lawn, pretending they were butterflies, scarf-wings fluttering.

It was as she was going back downstairs that Lilli noticed that the attic door was ajar, and she remembered the noise she'd heard. The attic contained only trunks of old clothes that the girls used to dress up in, boxes of *National Geographic* and *Life* magazine, Christmas decorations, some discarded furniture, and Dori's dollhouse. The dollhouse had stayed in the den after her death, trapped beneath the web of yarn that their mother had woven between slatted chair backs and around sailing trophies, over Grandmother's portrait, and wrapped around the brass fireplace poker and tongs, table legs, lamp bases, and spaniel-shaped doorstop. Someone, Lilli didn't know who, had finally untangled and rewound the yarn at the end of that long week and taken the dollhouse away. "Mom?" Lilli called up the stairs. "Mother?" she called again, louder, as she went up. The sound she'd heard earlier was probably just a family of mice who'd taken up residence inside one of the old bureaus pushed up against the wall. The girls often found stashes of seed in the toes of old boots. What reason would her mother have for coming up here?

Her question was answered when she reached the top of the stairs. Her mother, several of her colorful scarves knotted together to form a noose, dangled from a beam. Below her, an old kitchen chair lay tipped on its side. Lilli shrank against the wall, gasping, feeling half strangled herself, shaking and horrified. Blythe's eyes were open and they had the same inquisitive look that had become so familiar in the past months. But she looked oddly at peace, as though she'd finally found the answer to her unasked question.

When Lilli could finally move, she moved quickly. She went to her mother, wrapped her arms around her legs, and tried to lift her, thinking she could release the pressure on her neck. But Blythe's knees, which felt frail and knobby, only buckled. Lilli looked up and could see that the knot was tight around her mother's throat, and that she would need to loosen or untie it. She righted the overturned chair and climbed up onto it, bringing her face even with her mother's, which was flushed a shocking and unnatural shade. Lilli noted that her mother had chosen a dramatically dark red shade of lipstick and applied it carefully, and her hair was neatly combed, rolled, and pinned the way she used to wear it when she and George went out. Choking back sobs, Lilli wrapped one arm around Blythe's slender waist and picked at the knot, but was unable to see through her tears, and her hands shook badly. She needed to cut her down. *Of course. Why hadn't she thought of that?* Sobbing, hysterical, gulping for air, she jumped off the chair, knocking it over, ran to her grandmother's old sewing table, and pulled open a drawer so hard that it flew out of her hand, and a dozen spools of thread bounced out, unwinding themselves across the dusty floor. Dashing away tears so she could see, she grabbed a pair of pinking shears and ran back. She righted the chair, grasped her mother's body, and cut the scarf above her head. Blythe crumpled, and together they toppled off the chair and crashed to the floor.

Lilli heard the sound of running feet below, and soon Bea's and Charlotte's faces appeared in the stairwell. "Oh, my heavens, Lilli. What happened?" Bea said as she crossed the room and knelt beside Blythe, frantically picking at the knotted scarf. "Call Dr. Bartlett."

Lilli crab-walked backward, knowing it was too late for Dr. Bartlett. Charlotte, now also kneeling beside Blythe, reached a hand out to Lilli. But Lilli was sure she could see incomprehension on their faces. And something more. Doubt? Fear? Accusation? Lilli realized that she was still wearing the lavender-and-pink scarf around her shoulders. She stood and ran down the stairs to the telephone in the hallway, fumbling as she picked up the heavy receiver, searched the list taped to the wall for Dr. Bartlett's telephone number and, with shaking fingers, tried to dial.

NONE OF THEM referred to their mother's death as a suicide. She fell, is what they agreed to tell people. She'd been trying to reach something above the rafters in the attic—they were vague about what—and, in a freakish stroke of bad luck, had tumbled not only off the ladder but down the stairs. Her death was instantaneous. Thank God. The story was Bea's idea, and Charlotte had agreed at once that it was for the best. Lilli had said nothing. After she'd phoned Dr. Bartlett, she went downstairs to wait for him, the image of her mother's red lips, her eyelashes clumped with mascara, and her open, vacant brown eyes—like the doll Annabelle's—still fresh in her mind. By the time Dr. Bartlett arrived, the memory had already begun to soften, like a rocky ledge fading into fog. She could no longer recall the exact feel of her mother's flesh against her own, the bony kneecaps pressing against her stomach, the sickly sweet scent of her Tabu. Over the next few days, the images of her mother's face, the fragile feel of her bones, and the slackness of her body continued to be drawn away as though by some invisible force, like the bits of driftwood the girls would set sail from the beach when the tide and currents were right. By the time of the funeral, her mother's suicide had become like a dream to Lilli, the lie she and her sisters had agreed to tell simply a different kind of truth. Blythe *had* been reaching for something above the rafter: an escape from her pain, transcendence from this world, somewhere sturdy to secure the scarf. She had fallen. But even as time continued to pull Lilli's memory of the incident further and further away, blurring the details, she could never quite lose the feeling that she could have done something to prevent it: come in the kitchen door, say, instead of through the sunporch, thus seeing the note; or not fallen asleep on the glider; or not gone to the beach at all, or stayed longer. Then, at least, someone else would have found her.

None of them acknowledged that anyone who'd spoken with their mother—that number having grown smaller as Blythe had sequestered herself more and more after Dori's death, but still—would have sensed immediately that something was wrong and known the truth. But the citizens of White Head were as eager to accept the sisters' lie as the sisters were to tell it. And so when friends and neighbors stopped by and stood in the doorway with their casseroles and molded salads, expressing their sympathy and shock that such a tragic accident should happen to someone so young, so talented, and so pretty, Bea, Charlotte, or Lilli would simply accept the offered gift with thanks and shut the door.

Hammonds, Chapins, Pierces, and Halls filled the pews at the church and then rimmed the grave for Blythe's burial. Lilli stared at the three graves now lined up in a neat row, noting that the grass over Dori's still had not taken hold, nor had the ivy that their mother had planted (a cutting from the vines that wound around the base of George's stone).

She looked across the grave at Randall, who'd come up from the University of Maryland, where he was now a sophomore. She hadn't seen him since Dori's service. He smiled at her. She smiled back, startled by how unfamiliar a smile felt.

When the burial was over, the mourners gathered in the Niles dining room to sip punch and nibble crustless cucumber, egg, and tuna salad sandwiches that Charlotte had made, and tried to think of appropriate topics of conversation. Gardening and the weather were most popular, each guest no doubt calculating precisely what time they could depart without seeming rude. Lilli hoped they would be generous with their calculations and leave soon. Although Bea had set up creaky metal fans in the windows, they did little to stir the sticky air of that humid afternoon. "Hotter than tuffet," Bea had called it, sounding just like their grandmother. Randall laughed and said, "You want hot? Try Baltimore in September. Or College Park, for that matter." He was trying to liven things up, but people only nodded and mopped their foreheads and necks with handkerchiefs. Lilli thought College Park sounded very appealing, mostly because it wasn't White Head, wasn't this house, wasn't this room full of well-meaning people. The walls were closing in on her, pressing them all closer and closer together, and the voices were growing louder and louder. She needed air. Solitude. She eased away from the perspiring couples around the punch bowl and slipped out onto the sunporch, smiling at Mrs. Chapin and Mrs. Hallowell, who were using church bulletins to fan themselves. She went out the door to the yard, hesitated, waiting to see if she'd be called back—Bea would consider it a breach of good manners to leave. Hearing nothing, she walked, head down, between gardens still carpeted in leaves, past the battered remains of the crocuses. The daffodils had opened their brilliant yellow trumpets, and the leathery leaves of the tulips were pushing up through the mulch. How did flowers know when it was their time? How would Lilli know? There were risks in emerging too soon, like the crocus.

She was at the top of the steps to the beach; a few more paces and she'd be hidden from view, free. The tightness in her chest had loosened. She inhaled deeply, taking in the cool salty breeze off the water. Sunlight sparkled across the cove like jewels, or the "starfish" that Dori had loved. Lilli wanted to tuck herself into a crevice like a barnacle and wait, she wasn't sure for what. But as she started down the steps, she heard Randall call her name. She knew his voice, didn't need to turn, didn't want to stop, hoped he'd follow, felt certain he would. She went down one step, two, three, until she was out of sight of the house, and then stopped and turned. A moment later his face appeared. "I needed some air, some time alone," she said. He looked surprised, then nodded, and turned.

"No. Don't go. I didn't mean you." She watched as he came down the stairs toward her, his face, his hair, so much more stirring in person than how she'd recalled it from memory. She felt her eyes sting, and blinked. Tears rolled down her cheeks. Randall stood beside her, searched without success for a handkerchief, and blotted her tears with his thumb. Then he kissed her damp cheeks. Like a brother? Lilli didn't think so. She no longer felt flustered or tongue-tied. On the contrary, she felt strong and in control. He pulled back and they gazed at one another a moment, and then, without speaking, walked the rest of the way down, his hand light on Lilli's back, reminding her of their dance at the yacht club that night. She sat on the bottom step, and Randall tucked himself in beside her, his suit coat scratchy on her bare arm. She realized that it wasn't time alone she'd needed. Quite the opposite. It was human contact.

He covered her hands with his, and she studied the perfect pleating over his knuckles, the blue vein charting its way across the back of his hand and disappearing beneath the sleeve of his shirt. He was watching her. She traced the vein with her fingertip, longed to follow it up his forearm and into the soft hollow of his elbow. She envisioned its path along his upper arm, across his shoulder, to his neck. Saw, in the pulsing vein above his collar, his heart beating, fast. His neck was slick with sweat and Lilli imagined how it would feel against her lips: salty like the sea, but warm. She looked up to meet his gaze.

"Lilli—" he said, more a breath than a word.

Her own heart was pounding, too, her breath tight. A sudden panic rose in her. When those you hold closest leave you, the pain is sharp and deep and far worse than the dull, hollow ache of loneliness. "True love always comes with the potential for heartbreak," her mother had told her. *Is this love?* If so, Lilli wanted no part of it. She didn't think she could endure one more ounce of pain.

He studied her face a moment, and then, perhaps guessing her thoughts, took her hand and drew her back up the steps to the house.

LILLI woke up Tuesday morning a little past eight, joints aching, head throbbing. She would have stayed in bed longer, but Bea had agreed, after strawberry ice cream the night before—Lilli found three pints in her freezer—to meet at Beacon House at ten. Lilli scuffed into the bathroom and gazed into the mirror; she looked exhausted. Izzy had left a message on Lilli's cell phone that she was, indeed, coming to White Head, but neither mentioned the wedding nor offered a reason for why she hadn't told Lilli about this visit. Still, Lilli didn't mind. She was too pleased at the prospect of seeing her. There were a dozen reasons why it might have slipped Izzy's mind, she thought, as she turned on the shower. She would do what she could about moving Bea to Beacon House—she adjusted the temperature of the water—enjoy her visit with Izzy; talk her out of having her wedding at the house, which she didn't think would be hard once Izzy saw it; and leave for Boston as planned the following afternoon. If Charlotte called, then Lilli might extend her stay in the United States by a few days to help facilitate the move. Still, no matter what, she would soon be on a plane back to England to her cozy flat, her bright studio, and the lush and silent gardens hanging neatly in her gallery. She smiled and stepped into the shower.

Lilli was sitting in the Adirondack chair, cradling her empty coffee cup, wondering if she had time for a second, when she saw a white Mercedes bump into the parking lot. With a growing sense of foreboding, she watched Bea climb out, gaze around, and head toward the office. "Bea?" she called.

Bea turned at the sound of Lilli's voice and changed course.

"What are you doing here?"

"Picking you up so we can go to Beacon House. Don't tell me you forgot. You should write these things down, Lilli. I write everything down."

"We were going to meet *there*. At ten."

"Were we . . . ? Well, yes, but that seemed silly. Why take up two parking spots? I was up and figured I'd swing by." Bea took in the colorful Adirondack chairs above the stony beach and the quiet harbor, which Lilli had been so enjoying." Not much privacy here," she said.

Unable to think of a suitable response, Lilli excused herself, collected her jacket and purse from her room, and followed Bea to the car. As she climbed in, she noticed Randall's ashes on the backseat.

Bea pulled out into traffic and said, as though she'd just that moment thought of it, "I want to make one quick stop before we go over. You don't mind." She offered no further explanation, and Lilli rode along, gazing out the window, hoping that wherever it was they were headed served coffee. But they began a series of all-too-familiar turns, heading away from the center of town. "This is the way to the cemetery."

"Yes. I said to myself this morning, 'Why not just bury Randall's ashes?' It's not as though he cares. And then I thought, *Maybe Lilli would like to visit the cemetery.* So, I decided—"

"You might have called and asked me."

"So you don't want to visit Mother's and Daddy's graves? And Dori's? Is that what you're saying?" Bea turned to look at Lilli just as a gray squirrel loped across the road in front of them.

"Bea, look out!" Lilli shrilled.

Bea hit the brakes, and Lilli grabbed the dashboard. The driver behind them leaned on his horn.

"Good God, Lilli, are you trying to get us all killed? It was just a squirrel. They do that for sport, run across the road just as a car is coming. It's some sort of squirrel rite of passage." The Mercedes was moving again.

Lilli felt embarrassed and hurt by Bea's remark, which she thought was uncalled for and insensitive. "I'm saying you could have easily called and asked me," she snapped. She wanted to see the graves, but it was nearly nine thirty. "We don't have much time."

They rode in silence until Bea pulled into the cemetery, passing beneath the familiar iron archway suspended above the two stone pillars. "I'll just run you up the hill. Then I'll come back down and take care of this. . . ." She waved her hand in the direction of the backseat. "Won't take a minute."

She turned right on Hyacinth Path, left on Iris Way, left again on Daphne Drive, climbing steadily, and pulled over. Lilli stepped out and watched the white Mercedes make the reverse journey down the hill.

Beneath the big beech tree the grass was sparse and the soil damp and cool. The three stone markers stood in a row, ivy twining around their bases. Lilli plucked a few leaves from the wreath around Dori's. "I've missed you," she whispered, checking first to make sure no one was around. She read the inscription on the stone:

ISADORA B. NILES
SEPTEMBER 3, 1953 ~ SEPTEMBER 3, 1966

She touched her mother's and father's stones and sent each a silent prayer, as she did most nights: nothing specific, an acknowledgment and wish for their well-being, just in case there was something in the universe paying attention. She let her fingers linger a moment over the dates etched into her mother's stone: *June 21, 1920 ~ March 26, 1967*, and then walked over to sit on a nearby granite bench. It offered a good view of the Niles family plot, and beyond that the town of White Head, the harbor, and, in the distance, Sandy Cove. Above that, although not quite visible, was Lilli's old house.

Someone had planted purple, yellow, and white primroses before a nearby gravestone. Lilli remembered the purple, yellow, and white crocuses that had poked their way up too early through the thick thatch of leaves on Easter morning in 1967. They had lain battered and sodden from the six inches of late snow, which had already melted. *Timing is everything in life*, she thought.

Lilli stared out across the slope of the cemetery with its orderly flower beds planted with pansies, its pruned trees, and its lawn neatly bisected by narrow lanes. How little had changed there in forty years. The spreading beech with its glossy, new mahogany leaves still cast its shadow over the three Niles graves. Every year the nearby oak littered the ground with acorns, but no new oaks had been allowed to take root. And the maples—shaped like a child's drawing of a tree, Lilli always thought, with their straight trunks and nearly perfect halos of leaves—were taller and broader, but not different in any meaningful way. It was as though neither death nor the passage of time had been allowed to disrupt the landscape. How ironic, she thought, as there was nothing orderly about death, and time changed everything.

She realized that she'd been sitting on the cold stone bench a long time. She guessed it was well past ten o'clock and that they'd missed their appointment at Beacon House. She checked her watch: half past. She could see the white Mercedes snaking its way up the hill, and far above her a plane blazed a white path across the clear blue sky.

Izzy was standing beside her rental car with a cell phone pressed to her ear when the two sisters pulled up the drive. It had been a year since Lilli had seen her; she seemed taller, more beautiful, and positively radiant. Bea slid the Mercedes into the narrow bay of the garage and the two climbed out. "It's so good to see you both," Izzy said, snapping shut her phone and greeting them in the narrow space. "I don't know who to hug first! You, Auntie E. It's been much longer." Izzy bent down to hug Bea. "You're so tiny! How do you manage to stay so fit and trim?"

"Izzy, my goodness. I wouldn't have recognized you if I'd passed you on the street," Bea was saying. "How long has it been? You look like the Board of Health."

"That Christmas that Mom and I visited you and Uncle Randall." She paused. "I guess that's the last time. Fifteen years? No, more. Twenty? Is that possible? Of course I saw Aunt Lilli, what, a year ago in Chicago?" Izzy looked at Lilli across the top of the Mercedes.

"Oh?" Bea said, glancing at Lilli, eyebrows raised.

"I did the Monet exhibit at the Art Institute. Mom and Dad came. Poor Mom had to sit most of the time because of her knees. My brothers were both there, too." She backed out of the narrow space. "Aunt Lilli, amazingly, was in New York for an installation and flew out for a day. Wasn't that incredibly lucky?" Izzy wrapped her arms around Lilli and squeezed. "You look wonderful." Lilli hugged her back, tight.

"What time did you leave this morning?" Lilli asked, wanting to change the subject. "Must have been early."

"Indeed. Very lucky," Bea said, starting toward the house.

"Wait, Auntie E. I have something for you both." Izzy walked to her car, opened the back door, and handed each a small gift bag lined with tissue paper. "Open them," she commanded.

Bea unwrapped a ceramic periwinkle shell, Lilli a moon shell, whorled and iridescent. "Izzy. They're fantastic. Did you make them?"

"No, I make perfectly useless things, mostly out of metal. Too big. Too . . . well, ugly. I don't mean to say that *I* think they're ugly. Well, yes, I do, actually. You see, I intend them to be *real*. That is to say, not decorative. Not that there's anything wrong with decorative," she said in a rush, giving Lilli a worried glance. "Your paintings manage to be both very pleasing and representational. Real and not real at the same time? And still be something you'd want to hang in your living room. If you could afford one. Mine are, well, gritty, rusty, sharp, and mostly over six feet tall. Mom makes these. It's her new therapy." Izzy reached back into the car and hauled out a small suitcase. "I can't wait to see the house!" She linked her arm through Lilli's and the two trailed after Bea, who was halfway to the kitchen door.

Lilli watched for Izzy's reaction as they entered the kitchen, but Izzy said nothing about the peeling Formica counter, worn linoleum floor, outdated appliances, or faded curtains.

"My old room?"

"Yes. I'd offer to help," Bea added, "but my hips don't need any more trips up or down stairs than necessary."

Lilli considered mentioning that the unit at Beacon House was all on one level but decided against it. She didn't want to spoil her short time with Izzy. "I'll come up with you."

"Come right back downstairs, you two. I want to show Izzy the garden and discuss the wedding."

Lilli followed Izzy up the back stairs to what was once the room she'd shared with Dori. The younger woman looked around, smiling. "Just as I remember it. Not a thing has changed!" She sat down on Lilli's old bed and gave a little bounce. The bedsprings squeaked. "Gosh, I think this is even the same bed I slept on when I was little."

"Izzy, that's the same bed I slept on when *I* was little. I think that mattress is made of horsehair."

"Seriously?" Izzy laughed and flopped back. "Don't you wish more things in life could stay unchanged?"

Lilli sat on Dori's bed and glanced up at the familiar stains on the ceiling, along with a few new ones. The roof probably leaked. The Niles River had definitely lengthened and widened, or maybe it was just her different perspective. She was used to looking at it from her own childhood bed. The chick and elephant looked different as well, not as much like either shape. No wonder Dori could never quite see them, although she'd pretended she could. Lilli remembered how the ceiling had looked the night she lay, still shivering under the pile of camphory-smelling quilts and blankets, waiting for Dori, the shadow-branches dancing on the wall, that strange dream . . . How far back would she have to go to change the whole chain of events?

"Aunt Lilli?"

"Sorry, just looking at that crack in the ceiling. I used to think it looked like the Nile, and Dori thought I said Niles—that it had been named for us. Some change is good. Necessary. Healthy. Comes a time in everyone's life when they need to move on." *Or at least fix the roof and apply a new coat of plaster.* "Why do you want things to stay the same?"

Izzy rolled over to face Lilli, smiled, and said, picking at the chenille spread, "I guess this marriage thing has me a little spooked."

Before Lilli could decide which word in that sentence to question first, Izzy had rolled off the bed in one fluid motion and stepped over to the dressing table. "I don't believe it! See this?" She picked up a starfish propped up above the mirror. "I found that one day the last time we visited. It was winter, and Mom and I took a walk on the beach. Do you know Big-big?"

Lilli nodded.

"I wasn't sure if it was a name Mom made up for me. The tide was low, and we climbed up on Big-big and found this starfish. Maybe there'd been a storm or something. I don't know what it was doing up there, but Mom and I dried it, and I put it up here. I have a thing for starfish. I wear that starfish necklace you sent me all the time. See?" She pulled a pendant on a slim gold chain from inside the front of her blouse.

Lilli smiled. "I had no idea you were even thinking about getting married. Charlotte hadn't mentioned it."

"She doesn't know yet." Izzy looked sheepish. "It was rather . . . sudden." She dropped the pendant back inside her blouse.

Lilli felt a bit better—at least she wasn't the *last* to know— and decided to dig a little deeper. "And you really want to have it here? The garden . . . isn't what it once was. The last time you saw it was . . . when?"

Izzy twirled the starfish on the dresser top as she thought. "The garden? God, it must be . . . like, twenty-five years. I was about eleven. I spent a whole month here. I remember the big lawn, your mother's old sculptures, the beautiful view of the cove."

"Well, that's all changed quite a bit, Izzy. Gone, mostly. And wouldn't more of your friends come if you had the wedding in, say, Chicago?"

"I don't want a big wedding. Neither does Matumbé. I don't know, Auntie E suggested it, and I thought, *why not?*"

Lilli wondered if she'd heard correctly. "*Bea* suggested it?"

"Uh-huh. She called to tell me about Uncle Randall, and then started asking me a lot of questions—"

"What kind of questions?" Lilli interrupted.

"Oh, at first just about the weather and work, and then she asked about my love life. She's a hoot. So direct. I like that. Doesn't mince words. 'When are you getting married?' she says. The timing really was kind of amazing, actually, because Matumbé and I had just . . ." She hesitated, put the starfish back above the mirror and looked at her reflection. "Been tossing around the idea of possibly getting married . . ." Izzy glanced at Lilli in the mirror, "Soon. And she, right away, insists we have the wedding here. We were just going to go to a justice of the peace."

"You were *tossing around the idea* of *possibly* getting married? At a JP?" Lilli repeated.

"She said that wasn't a real wedding and that July was the perfect month for a garden ceremony. She made it all sound so . . . bride magazine. And she was so excited. I thought, with Uncle Randall dying and all—"

This was quite a different picture from the one that Bea had painted for her. "Izzy insisted," she had said. Lilli couldn't think *why* Bea would want to take this on. Could she really not see what the gardens and house looked like?

"I'm sure we would have gotten married. I think it's the right thing. No. It is. Definitely. It's the right thing. And this will be fine."

Fine. Lilli stood and smoothed the cheesecloth-thin chenille. "We should go back downstairs. Bea will be wondering what happened to us." Lilli followed Izzy out of the room. "Let's go look at the garden. You should decide for yourself, Izzy, if you want your wedding here. If not, just say so. It's your day. You do not have to settle for *fine.*"

But Izzy was already heading down the stairs, saying,

"Mom is always talking about this place, how great it was growing up here. She'll be crazy about the idea."

"CHARLOTTE'S WEDDING DAY was very like this," Bea was saying to Izzy when Lilli joined them in the crabbed and dispiriting yard. "Warmer, of course, since it was August. But sunny and breezy. It was a perfect day, wasn't it, Lilli?"

"Mmmm," Lilli said, watching Izzy, waiting for her reaction to the patchy lawn, the jumble of weeds, the blocked vista to the cove. But Izzy had closed her eyes and lifted her face to the sun, a Mona Lisa smile tugging at the corners of her mouth. "An extraordinary day," Lilli added.

"Your mother hasn't been east to see me in years. A sister should make some effort, don't you think?" Bea asked.

Izzy smiled and shrugged. "I've only got brothers," she said, and wandered over to sit on the wrought-iron bench beside the old sundial. She plucked a dead leaf from the azalea, tested the soil with her finger, and rotated the bare spot away from her.

Bea moved to the edge of the lawn and gestured through the tangle of bittersweet, to the listing, partially hidden arch. "Your father and his best man stood there, and we had chairs . . ." She hesitated, turning to indicate where, on Charlotte's wedding day, there'd been a lawn broad enough to accommodate seventy-five chairs in neat rows. "Well, now, how did we get all those chairs in here? We had over seventy guests."

Lilli turned to stare at a patch of lawn where she had planted a memorial cutting garden a few months after her mother's death, that long, hot summer of 1967, when life seemed suddenly like such a reckless and unpredictable pastime. Charlotte had stayed on in Boston, living with their Aunt Helen in the big house in Charles River Square and working at Massachusetts General Hospital, leaving Bea and Lilli alone together. Lilli had felt like someone recovering from a long illness. Afraid to move too fast or venture too far, she spent most of the summer on the sunporch or in the yard, sometimes drifting as far as the bottom of the steps leading down to the beach. She would lie in the hammock, her face turned toward the sun, and feel each cell's molecular transformation as it soaked up the energy. Or so it seemed. Her senses were so heightened that when the fog rolled in, she could feel each particle of mist tangle in her hair and each curl twining ever tighter. When a breeze lifted from the cove at low tide, the mud-flavored air seemed to press down on her chest, filling her with a dread she could neither examine nor name. She sensed each bud in the garden, well before the blossoms had opened, releasing their scent—well before the bumblebees and hummingbirds knew of them. One week, when the roses were in full bloom, the scent was so strong that Lilli had to spend the week indoors with the windows shut.

Standing there now, with Bea and Izzy, Lilli could almost make out the borders where her little memorial garden had been. She'd planted one in the same spot for two years. That first year, she had been preparing to transplant several flats of annuals, which she'd started in the greenhouse a few weeks before, tucking the seeds—some just bits of dried fluff, others more like grains of sand—into soil-filled eggshells in carefully labeled cartons. She had checked them daily, marveling as the tiny shoots had emerged and then differentiated into zinnias, stocks, hollyhocks, and petunias, although without the labels she would not have known which was which. "Remember to plant like-types together," Bea had said, so she carefully placed all the petunias in one section of the cutting garden, the zinnias in another, and so forth. Lilli liked the orderliness of the rows and the chiseled edges she'd created along all four sides of the bed. And she liked the feeling as she gently cracked each eggshell and tucked the fragile package with its delicate cargo securely into the ground. She felt comforted knowing that the plants would be there each time she returned.

"No, no, no, Lilli!" Bea had suddenly loomed over her, brow furrowed, gazing down with dismay at Lilli's little garden. She was wearing one of Blythe's large sunbonnets, an oversized shirt, and a stiff pair of gardening gloves, and Lilli had laughed and told her she'd make a very good scarecrow.

"You can't plant *all* the petunias together," Bea had said. "You must . . ." She made vague circular motions with her gloved hands. "Intersperse them. And what are the marigolds doing behind the hollyhocks? No one will see them. Take it all out and start over. And have you seen my clippers?"

"What are those in your hand?" Lilli asked.

"These are the old ones. Dull as mud. I bought a new pair last week. Red handles?"

"Did you check the greenhouse?"

"Well, of course I checked the greenhouse," Bea had said, clicking the old pruners several times in annoyance. "I suppose I could check again," she said, implying with her tone that she knew it would be an unnecessary trip.

Bea had marched off in search of the shears, and Lilli had carefully dug up the newly planted sprouts and rearranged them randomly, soon unsure which were hollyhocks and which petunias. She wasn't overly concerned with the garden itself. She was more interested in the flowers, which she planned to cut, arrange, and paint.

Bea reappeared a short while later, without the shears, just as Lilli was tucking the last plant into the only remaining empty space in the little garden, patting the damp loamy soil into place.

"Oh, heavens, Lillianne. You can't plant just one of each. It will look . . . messy. Go get a sheet of paper from the den, make a plan, and do it over." Muttering to herself, Bea had returned to her pruning with the dull shears.

Lilli had rocked back on her heels, wondering what had come over her sister, and studied the surrounding landscape, where wildflowers bloomed in riotous abandon, short and wide, thin and tall, pink, orange, and yellow. Mother Nature didn't use graph paper or color swatches and her gardens turned out all right. Lilli hadn't wanted to move the plants again; they'd looked weary from their repeated relocations and ready to set root. She felt responsible, having been the one to shake the seeds from the stiff paper packets where they'd been languishing in dry isolation and bring them to life. So she'd left them, and they'd done well enough, growing tall and straight and producing beautiful blossoms. Lilli had kept the little plot weed-free and watered it with manure tea, as her mother had done. But when it came time to cut the blooms, she found she couldn't, not until the zinnias were overblown and brown-tipped, the petunias sheer and limp as silk, and the hollyhocks studded with brown seed pods. Instead, Lilli had painted the little garden, which had changed almost daily, capturing each new permutation. She liked that part the best, but she had also liked bringing the plants to life and caring for them, hosting the bumblebees and butterflies and little chickadees that would perch precariously on the tips of the foxglove.

As she'd walked back to the house that long-ago day, she'd seen a shiny pair of red-handled pruning shears on the sundial beside the wrought-iron bench. She'd meant to tell Bea, but by the time she'd reached the house, the thought had completely slipped her mind.

"WHAT ARE YOU smiling at, Lilli?" Bea said, rousing Lilli from that June day, forty-plus years before.

"I'm sorry. Seventy guests? Yes, that's about right. The yard was a bit larger then."

"We always remember things from our childhood as bigger. Maybe it wasn't seventy. How many people were you planning to have, Izzy?"

"We hadn't really gotten that far." Izzy looked around, assessing, calculating. "Not many. Just family."

"Charlotte and her bridesmaids all walked down the center aisle," Bea said. "Uncle Parker gave Charlotte away. The groomsmen were up front by then." Bea turned to peer through the bittersweet as though a few ushers might be standing there still. "Of course we'll get all this cleaned up." Bea waved toward the jungle of weeds and vines.

Lilli didn't want to get into the ridiculousness of Bea's idea in front of Izzy, but neither did she want Bea to compromise Izzy's wedding day with her stubbornness and possibly delusional thinking.

"You were Mom's maid of honor, weren't you?" Izzy asked Bea.

"Matron, technically, although I've never liked that term. Sounds like a prison warden."

"Why weren't you and Uncle Randall married out here?"

"Winter wedding. Rather sudden. We had a small ceremony at the justice of the peace."

Izzy looked puzzled but said only, "I'd like to visit his grave, if there's time." He was so nice to me when I stayed here. Remember when he took me ice sailing?" She stood and began to pace the narrow yard.

Lilli glanced over at Bea. "What do you say, Bea, do you think there'll be time?" Bea frowned at Lilli. Randall's ashes were still on the backseat of the Mercedes.

Izzy completed her short survey, ending with a mock procession down the center, her hands clasped in front as though holding a bouquet, and then dropped back down on the bench, grinning. "I've seen pictures of Mom's wedding. Her dress was beautiful, but those bridesmaids' hats . . ." She rolled her eyes. "What were you all thinking?"

"We thought we were the last word in sophistication," Lilli said, with mock offense. "Poor Alice Bottomley looked like a toadstool."

"But your mother looked like a confection," Bea said.

" 'Like a meringue.' "

"Well, that's rather unkind," Bea said, eyeing Lilli.

"No, don't you remember? That's what Charlotte called herself. I'd said she looked good enough to eat."

"We'll string little white lights all over the yard. Dori loves sparkly things, don't you?" Bea said, turning to Izzy. "Have ever since you were little."

Izzy smiled and gave Bea a hug. "I do."

* * *

"I'll go grab a sweater," Izzy said to Lilli, and started up the stairs. Halfway, she turned and added, "It's so nice that you're back."

Izzy had suggested a walk on the beach after they returned from lunch, which she'd insisted on paying for. Bea did not complain about going out or about anything on the menu, and, Lilli noticed, she ate every morsel on her plate, including the garnish of radicchio and orange slice. Bea said she had some laundry to put away, leaving Izzy all to Lilli. They walked down the drive to the path above the Hammonds' and out onto the beach. The tide was in, so they trudged through the soft sand, warm from the sun, which charged the water's surface so it shone like Christmas lights. When they had traversed the beach and back again, they sat on the steps below the house.

Lilli could see Ned Chapin, out on the point, playing what looked like a cutthroat game of croquet with his children and grandchildren. "How is Charlotte?"

"Fine. I guess. I haven't been out to California for a while, so I haven't seen her. I'm just so busy with work, and flying is such a hassle these days." Izzy picked up a pebble and pitched it at a clamshell half-buried in the sand.

Lilli smiled, found another pebble, and tossed it, hitting the shell dead center.

"You're good!"

"Dori and I used to do this a lot."

"Dori," Izzy repeated and smiled. "Bea called me Dori. Did you hear?"

Lilli nodded, not sure if she should say anything about her concerns over Bea's condition. She decided to wait and see whether Izzy mentioned it. They pitched a few more pebbles.

"I think about her a lot. Do you? It must have been so incredibly sad, losing her like that. I can't imagine."

"Yes," Lilli said, looking at Izzy, who was searching for another pebble. "It was very sad."

"And then your mother dying like that. Mom said that you all found her? After church or something?"

The family lie had become a legend. "Yes," Lilli recited. "We'd just come back from church. Easter morning. Bottom of the attic stairs. We all found her. We've no idea what she was doing in the attic. Probably looking for something." Lilli shifted as she said this, the granite beneath her cold and unyielding. She didn't want to lie to Izzy, but the truth had been so long buried that she hardly remembered it herself anymore.

"I don't know what it's like to lose someone you love. I'm lucky that way, I guess. It must be very hard."

Lilli considered this. In one sense she'd lost Dori, but in another she'd kept her: untouched by time. Unlike some others she'd lost. They each pitched a few more pebbles at the shell, missing each time. Izzy reached forward and dug the sand away to make a bigger target. "I played with Dori's dollhouse one summer when I visited. Uncle Randall had fixed it up for me, made a few new pieces of furniture."

Lilli was taking aim as she said this. Her pebble went well wide of the target. "A few *new* pieces?"

"Yeah. They were amazing. There was this little tiny footstool and a—Why are you looking like that?"

"I . . . didn't realize he'd made *any* furniture. Didn't

realize, I guess, that anyone had ever played with that doll-house. Just hadn't thought about it."

"Oh! But he made *all* the pieces. He was so clever that way. Beds, tables, a rocking chair. There was even an ador-able painter's easel, if you can imagine such a thing, with an itsy-bitsy canvas." Izzy paused, smiled, and said, "Aunt Lilli, I believe I am quoting your grandmother when I say, 'Close your mouth. You're catching flies.'"

Lilli composed her face as she tried to picture what Izzy was describing, to understand what she was telling her. How had she not known this about Randall? "Where . . . ," she began. "Why . . . ," she tried. "What?" she finally concluded.

"You know that he made the dollhouse, right? He did say that it was a secret back then—he was only, like, nineteen or something and kind of embarrassed, I guess—but I assumed you knew. He worked on it all summer in his uncle's work shed, then set it up, and then . . . well, then, you know, Dori died, and no one ever played with it. So I did, a little, to make him feel better, although dollhouses were never my thing. I did like the furniture, though."

Lilli composed her expression as Izzy finished her story. Randall had made the dollhouse? "Did he say why he made it? Or . . ." Lilli suddenly felt like Alice, falling through the rabbit hole, everything suddenly wrong-sized and slightly askew. "I assume he made the new pieces . . . for you?"

Izzy nodded. "I guess so. I mean, he could have just liked making them."

"Was the easel one of the new pieces?" Lilli had never really seen the dollhouse up close. There had been just that one quick peek, through the den window. After Dori's death, someone had finally cleared away the yarn web, and Lilli had never known what became of the dollhouse. Maybe Randall had taken it back.

"That was definitely a new one."

Lilli nodded, wishing that, say, a Cheshire cat might materialize right about now and offer her a few insights about what to do with this new information and maybe a clue as to which direction to head.

"He brought it down from the attic and put it in the bedroom for me. Sometimes at night—don't think I'm crazy, Aunt Lilli—I felt Dori with me in the room."

Lilli had a sudden vision of her mother's late-night visits to that room, slipping in, silent and ghostlike, and doubted that Dori's was the only spirit roaming those hallways. She shivered, feeling the cold, rough surface of the rock through her thin slacks, and glanced out toward Big-big, cut off now from the mainland by the tide. "I don't think you're crazy. Dori was so present when she was alive, so fully alive, it wouldn't surprise me if she never made it completely across to the other side." Lilli pictured Dori climbing up on Big-big and jumping off, trying to touch the sky, then tumbling to the ground, her bottom all wet, laughing—

"She's doing pretty well, really," Izzy said.

Lilli looked at her, startled.

"Auntie E, I meant," Izzy said, laughing. "Aunt Lilli, you should see your expression! Still, it's good you're back. She shouldn't stay here in this house alone."

Lilli smiled and sighed with relief. "Well, I agree. I'm so glad you see it, too. It's nothing I can really put my finger on. I tried calling Charlotte—she is much better than I am at diagnosing things, obviously—but I haven't reached her yet. Even without Bea's . . . spaciness, there are the vision problems, hearing problems, arthritis . . . I could go on and on. I've been trying to persuade her to move to a retirement place in town. It has independent-living units. Very nice. Not having much luck, though—" Lilli broke off as Izzy looked puzzled.

"But now that you're here, why would she move?"

"Well, I'm only here a few days. In fact—"

"A few days? Auntie E said you were moving in with her."

"No, no, no." But even as she said this, things started to make sense to Lilli. Bea's unexpected and somewhat odd invitation to come for the service, Ned's surprise when Lilli told him her visit would be a short one, Jane Hunsicker's puzzling invitation to speak at the garden club. Lilli picked up another pebble, turned it over and over in her palm as she thought about Bea's resistance to visit Beacon House. Of course. She had her own plans. Had Izzy's wedding been part of this scheme? Undoubtedly. This made Lilli angry. She thought back to her conversation with Bea on the porch after the service. When had she called Izzy? Izzy was engraving a design in the sand with her toe. The unwashed dishes, the . . . feeblemindedness; were they part of the scheme, too? Lilli felt small even thinking such a thing, but couldn't stop herself. "Is that so?" she said, to fill what she feared was becoming an awkward silence. *"She'll do whatever it takes to win."* That was what Randall had said. Yes indeedy.

Izzy, etching the sand, seemed not to notice Lilli's silence or to suspect the emotions roiling inside her. And why would she? Lilli carefully composed her face, a half smile playing at her mouth. She was practiced at appearing in control, and in control she would be. *Family matters are private matters.* Izzy was family, but there were some things she couldn't know.

"Yes, of course Bea—your Auntie E—asked me to move in," Lilli said, hating the deception. "But, as soon as I arrived, I could see that it would be best, for Bea, to be somewhere else. A house that size requires a lot of work. And then there's the garden. The garden is, well . . . I'm sure you can see how much it would take to get it ready for a wedding. Your wedding! I decided to stay, to talk to you about that and . . . to help her . . . Auntie E, make plans to move elsewhere. Her idea makes no sense. For either of us. You can see that. Can't you?" But Izzy was still intent on her drawing, her mind elsewhere. Lilli suddenly felt hollow and exhausted and tired of the deception and the lies. She aimed the pebble at the clamshell and threw. It hit with such force the shell cracked.

Izzy looked up from her drawing, surprised, and smiled. "Bull's-eye."

Ten

THE roses were blooming again, and Lilli found that she could bear to be out in the yard with them this summer. Their fragrance no longer overwhelmed her, the breeze at low tide did nothing more than smell (as Charlotte was fond of saying) "like clam farts." Randall returned to White Head, strung the hammock between the birch trees, set up the badminton net, and changed the oil in the Country Squire. Although Lilli still refused to race, even to sail, she did go to the first dance at the yacht club, and she and Randall danced together nearly all night. At least ten dances, by Lilli's calculation. As the lyrics to "Turn Around, Look at Me" wound down, he'd kept his arms around her well after the music stopped.

The next day he took Lilli for a ride in his cousin's dark green Mustang convertible. He drove very fast along the ocean road with the top down, and Lilli perched on the back of the passenger seat, her hands braced against the windshield. Lilli's long convalescence seemed well and truly over.

One rainy Saturday in late July, Randall, Bea, and Lilli played a long game of Monopoly on the sunporch. When Bea started running out of money, Randall announced that anyone who landed on one of his properties—of which he had many—without sufficient funds could pay up in kisses. Bea had first frowned at Randall, and then issued a limp laugh and offered a sedate kiss. As play continued, she paid him quite a few more. Lilli had laughed right along with them each time, but didn't find it all that funny. She'd amassed a huge fortune.

"Anyone want anything?" Bea asked as she landed in jail. "I need food." She stood and made for the kitchen.

"Penury is hungry business. But so's philanthropy. One works up quite an appetite being rich and magnanimous. I'll take a beer," Randall said. "Thanks, lovey," he called as Bea headed out of the room. At this, she stopped and turned, seemed about to speak, and then her expression collapsed into one that Lilli didn't think she'd ever seen on her sister's face before: uncertainty.

"Why did you call her that?" Lilli asked, after Bea had disappeared, trying both to ignore and disguise the pinch of jealousy she felt.

Randall rattled the dice vigorously in his fist. "Just trying to get a rise out of her," he said, giving a half smile as he surveyed Bea's meager holdings. "This could be my only shot at not being the indebted one, my only shot at being in control of your older sister. Might as well make the most of it."

"I'm teaching myself how to cook," Lilli said, to change

the subject. "Can you stay for dinner? I'm making *Soufflé au Fromage* and charlotte chantilly. Charlotte's coming, too."

"Your French *est parfait, mademoiselle*. Did you know that I do a very good Julia Child imitation?"

"Well, it's good one of us does. My cooking is not that great."

THE FOUR OF them gathered later in the big kitchen, Lilli sporting a red beret that Randall had brought over. ("Sorry, they were fresh out of chef's toques at Simmons Department Store," he'd told her.) Randall was wearing one of Charlotte's ruffled aprons. He also brought a recording of Edith Piaf, who warbled away in the background as Lilli started cracking eggs.

"'The egg can be your best friend, if you just give it the right break,'" Randall said, channeling Julia Child. "'Be the big boss of the big cheese soufflé!'"

Lilli laughed and dropped an eggshell into the dish. "Shoot."

"Will you be using the charlotte mold for your chantilly this evening or for your soufflé?" Randall asked, examining the charlotte mold Lilli had bought. "Charlotte, your ears are simply darling, darling."

"Oh, heavens. I never thought of that. What am I going to cook the soufflé in?"

"Do not be concerned if you don't have a soufflé pan!" He was back to Julia. "One can always use . . ." He disappeared into the pantry and began searching through cupboards. "A Lilli pan!" he announced, returning with a flat-bottomed saucepan with straight sides.

Lilli giggled. "Stop. I'm going to lose my place in the recipe. For the roux, I need three tablespoons of butter—" She whacked off a hunk of butter and dropped it into a sauté pan, which sizzled and popped.

"Buttah. Buttah is bettah," proclaimed Randall. "Don't rue your roux."

"Three tablespoons of flour, and—oh, gosh," Lilli said, checking the cookbook. "I didn't boil the milk!"

"Right here," Charlotte said. "I knew you'd forget. You're very quiet this evening, Bea."

Lilli, who was separating eggs, glanced over to see Bea seated at the kitchen table, staring at the ivy stenciling.

"Too many cooks," she said. "You know what they say."

Lilli began beating egg whites.

"Beat those egg whites senseless, my dear," intoned Randall. "You want stiff peaks, remember. No, I think a little longer."

"My arm is going to fall off," Lilli complained.

"Here," Charlotte said, pulling out the electric mixer. "Pass me the Bea bowl."

Forty-five minutes later, having peeked in the oven only once, Lilli presented her creation. Charlotte had made a salad of iceberg wedges and French dressing and brought French bread from Boston. Lilli had also made *Choux Bruxelles à la Milanaise*, but she discovered that Brussels sprouts, even browned and with cheese, still taste like Brussels sprouts.

"Simmering them in cream doesn't help either," Charlotte noted.

"It's hard not to like their looks, though," Randall said. "Little little-bitty cabbages. Aren't they adorable, Bea?"

Bea looked up, startled. "I'm sorry. Who's adorable?"

"The *choux* . . . what did you call them? The miniature cabbages."

"These are Brussels sprouts," Bea said. "Not miniature cabbages."

"Yes, lovey, I know. But they look like—" He broke off. "To the chef! Bon appétit!"

"Bon appétit!" they chorused.

Lilli had neglected to thicken and chill the egg yolks for the *Charlotte Chantilly aux Fraises*, so it didn't fully set. She deemed it inedible and was about to dump it down the sink when Randall proclaimed that it deserved a more distinguished end. It deserved, he said, a burial at sea. "Down on the rocks," he declared. "Who's with me?"

Lilli immediately went to change her shoes. Charlotte said she needed to head back to Boston, and Bea gave Randall a hard look, before saying that she would stay behind and do the dishes.

There was no moon, so Randall took Lilli's hand as they made their way across the dark lawn and down the steps. Lilli felt the hairs on her neck rise a bit as she heard waves washing against the rocks in their ceaseless attempts to scrub away time. Although she felt better this summer, still the restless sea, with its endless cycle of tides, and the fogs that settled, amplifying sounds and veiling views, sometimes made her want to weep. From joy, from frustration, from anger, from sorrow, she didn't know. She only knew it often hurt to be here.

Randall pulled her down beside him on a rock and draped an arm across her shoulder. "I don't think it would want us to grieve," he said, staring down at the bowl of collapsed charlotte chantilly. "Do you?"

Lilli shook her head, not yet ready to trust her voice. She

would be fine. She'd felt this rising stew of confusing emotions before. "No. Perhaps just a few words about how much we cared. How hard we tried . . ."

"We did care. Deeply. I was really looking forward to this chantilly!" he blurted, and then resumed his mock-serious tone. "And I think it's important that we make clear that success, failure . . . these are all relative. While this chantilly might not have been as successful as a . . ." He trailed off.

"Molded dessert," Lilli supplied, starting to smile.

"Precisely that."

"It . . ." Lilli was unable to think of anything positive to say.

"It floats!" Randall exclaimed, upending the bowl and commending the pink substance to the deep. They watched as it bobbed among the waves, occasionally bumped up against the rocks, and finally disappeared into the dark. "You made a sensational *Ile Flottante*," Randall said.

"Floating Island," Lilli said.

"Floating Charlotte. We bid thee farewell."

Lilli started to laugh, and Randall tightened his hold on her shoulders. Lilli placed a light hand on his knee.

LATER, AS LILLI was getting ready for bed, still smiling over the image of the mound of pink Floating Charlotte drifting slowly out to sea, she went to pull the shade down and happened to glance out the window into the garden. Light from the living room spilled out onto the lawn, and she wondered, first, why Bea was still up and, second, whether she'd perhaps gone to bed and forgotten to turn out the light. She was about to go investigate when she caught sight of two figures, little more than shadows, really, beside the sundial. She squinted, trying to get a better look, wondering who, or what, would be on the lawn at this hour. She crossed the room to turn out the light, hoping to get a better view. By the time she'd returned, the figures were gone. A moment later, the living room light went out.

It was the end of August, nearly the end of summer. The landscape had dressed itself in yellow, and Lilli was in the yard, painting the flowers in her memorial garden. Bea was weeding nearby in her usual broad-brimmed hat and over-sized shirt.

Randall emerged from the copse of trees that separated the Niles house from his aunt and uncle's and strode across the lawn. "What a lovely domestic scene."

"I thought you were leaving," Bea said, glancing up.

"And good morning to you, too!" He tipped an imaginary hat to her and then plopped down beside Lilli. He handed her a tiny rowboat that he had whittled from a piece of driftwood.

"Randall! It's darling! What's it for?"

"For you. So you'll always think of me fondly."

As if she could ever think of him any other way. She turned the little boat over and over in her hands, marveling at the little plank seats. He'd even carved a pair of impossibly slender oars, hardly bigger than matchsticks.

He reached for her sketchpad and studied it a moment. "What color is that?" he asked, pointing to Lilli's palette.

"Quinacridone purple."

He frowned. "Good grief. Let's rename it. Impertinence. What's this one?"

"Burnt sienna."

"Poor sienna! Intrepid from now on. It will get more respect from the other colors. This one?"

"Cadmium red. No, that one's . . . Love?" Lilli ventured.

"Love," Randall repeated the word, and then pressed his lips together and shifted them side to side, like someone tasting wine. "Perhaps. But I think love is often a bit less . . . vibrant. What do you think, Miss Bea?"

Bea poked her head up from the garden. "What do I think about what? You missing your train? I think it very likely."

Randall raised his eyebrows at Lilli. "Someone has a bee in her bonnet this morning. Did you not get enough sleep last night, lovey?" Bea had returned to her weeding and did not respond. "That, Lilypad, I think, is Passion, not Love. What's this called?" he said, tapping a delphinium Lilli had painted.

"Cobalt violet, mostly. My favorite."

"That seems closer to Love. This?"

"Winsor blue."

"I will call that Eager Anticipation, or perhaps, Stick-to-it-iveness. I've always loved that word."

Bea exhaled so loudly that Lilli and Randall both turned her way in surprise. She unfolded herself from her place in the garden, dusted off her knees, and announced that she was going into the kitchen. With that, she marched off toward the house.

"And what will you do this year, Lilypad? Your senior year in high school. Hard to believe. I remember when you were toddling around in diapers."

"You do not!"

"I certainly do. You had very shapely legs, even then. And a very nice—"

"Stop!"

They moved over to the hammock and lay down together, Randall pushing them gently with his toe.

"Will you apply to college?"

Her shoulder felt warm where it touched his. If Lilli were to move the slightest bit to the right—which she did—her bare arm rested against his. Her pulse perked up to a trot. "I don't know. I guess so. Anything to get me out of White Head. What I really want to do is travel: Paris, Rome—I'm going to Florence right after Christmas vacation, did I tell you?" She turned her face to him and spied a tiny fleck of shaving cream behind his ear. She hesitated, then lifted her finger and blotted it away.

He turned. Their faces were very close. "I believe you did. At least once." He studied her face a moment before turning back to gaze up to the sky.

Lilli exhaled. "I'd really rather just paint."

"Why not go to art school?"

"You sound like Bea. She's been pestering me all week."

"Has she?" Randall sounded strangely pleased at this.

Lilli sighed. She wanted life, not college. She wanted life and Randall. She gave the hammock a firm nudge with her foot, and they swayed to and fro.

LATER, RANDALL SAID good-bye to Lilli and left, and everything good about White Head seemed to leave with him. She and Bea had a very quiet dinner, watched Ed Sullivan, and turned in early. The next day, Lilli went for a walk, trying to ease the dull ache that had lodged in her chest and throat. Something about this time of year, the end-of-summer smells, things drying and dying, made her uneasy and restless. She missed Randall. She didn't see how she would make it through this long year without him.

She was surprised and delighted, then, to see him when she returned from her walk, seated on the wrought-iron bench, talking with Bea. The two glanced up as Lilli called Randall's name. "You're here!" Had he come to say good-bye again? Was it possible he was staying? Couldn't bear to leave her? She trotted across the lawn toward him.

"Just leaving. Decided to stay one more day. Glad you caught me." He stood. "So, have a good fall, you two."

Lilli tried to hide her disappointment but could feel her smile sagging slightly. She glanced at Bea. But Bea was looking out across the cove, chewing the corner of her mouth, her eyebrows knit together.

AFTER RANDALL'S DEPARTURE, Lilli's life was all dark corners and doors shut on quiet, empty rooms. The house seemed to be waiting. The tables and sofas and lamps seemed to be waiting. Even the dust in the slanted shafts of sunlight that sliced through the windows seemed to be frozen in place, waiting. She hadn't the least idea what Bea was waiting for, nor how she spent her days after Lilli left each morning to catch the train to Boston for school. She didn't date, had no hobbies and no plans for the future, so far as Lilli knew. But Lilli was waiting for her life to begin, for an end to her senior year, and an end to her solitary life with Bea. She was waiting for the day when she could leave White Head forever and be with Randall.

When Lilli got home from school each day, she would find

Bea puttering somewhere in the house or yard. They seemed to have less and less to say to one another. When Bea did speak, she would often snap at Lilli for the least thing, then look at Lilli as though her burst of temper were somehow Lilli's fault. After muttering an apology, she would excuse herself from the room.

Lilli continued to work on her cooking. Although she had a flair for menu selection, she still lacked discipline, often leaving out an ingredient, mixing things in the wrong order, or forgetting to set the timer. Once, she forgot to read ahead to note that the marinade for a roast should be applied twelve hours before cooking. Still, she selected something new each night from *The Art of French Cooking* or from Charlotte's stained and dog-eared copy of *The Boston Cooking-School Cook Book*. Lilli envisioned holding impromptu gatherings as well as extravagant dinner parties at her home, which would be in Boston, or possibly New York, or even Paris. Not White Head, certainly. She would be an artist and would live abroad for a year to study painting in Florence—and return, filled with stories of her marvelous travels and adventures. She wrote to Randall about her dreams, unsure, at first, how he'd react—they were only dreams, after all, the sorts of things she could tell Charlotte, and could have shared with Dori, but not with Bea. She'd tried. Bea had listened and said, "If you want to study abroad, Lilli, I suggest you pay a little more attention to your studies here. You won't get anywhere with those grades."

Randall wrote back of squash matches and fraternity parties. He'd taken up long-distance running. Three miles a day, he said; she couldn't believe it, no one could run that far. He always asked about life in White Head. As far as Lilli was concerned, there was none worth reporting and she told him so.

Lilli would set the dining room table—all the extra panels removed—with the good rosebud china and heavy silver. ("If you use it you don't have to polish it as often," Grandmother, who'd never polished a stick of silver in her life, had always insisted.) Then she'd present her culinary creation to Bea, who would offer her opinion. *Filets de Poisson Pochés au Vin Blanc:* "A bit bland. Needs more *vin*." Chicken croquettes: "Maybe a tad chewy? Try less flour." Gratin dauphinois: "Much too rich for me." Bea would then compliment the centerpiece, or say she liked the way Lilli had arranged the food on the plate. Occasionally Lilli oversalted and overcooked items just to see if she could get a rise out of Bea. Anything to break the tedium of her life.

For her part, Bea would have oatmeal ready for Lilli before she set off for school. Lilli assumed that Bea thought she was doing Lilli a great favor in this act. She seemed quite proud of her one culinary effort. But Lilli hated the sludgy mound, beige and morose, that she would find nestled each morning on the bottom of a cream soup bowl. "Just add milk," Bea would instruct, regardless of whether the oatmeal was runny, stiff, or burned. Lilli didn't think it possible to ruin oatmeal in so many ways and wondered if it, too, was intentional. Was there a silent war being waged between sisters in the kitchen?

It was in October, as Lilli sat in the yard, painting the last of the hollyhocks, alyssum, and nicotiana in her cutting garden, that Bea appeared beside her, dangling the car keys. "Time you learned to drive, Lilli," she stated. They climbed into the old Ford, and Bea drove them down to Harbor Drive, where she pulled over and they changed seats. The day was warm, the water sun-spangled, the road straight and empty. Lilli shifted into gear and set slowly off. "Careful not to drift across the center line," Bea warned. Lilli corrected her steering, although she was certain she'd been well on her side. She glanced up at the Chapins' driveway as they passed. "Eyes forward, Lilli," Bea admonished. "You must always keep your eyes on the road. You can make occasional quick glances to each side, but then focus ahead."

Lilli steered the big car around the bend and down to the harbor, now nearly empty of boats. She savored the feeling of freedom and control. With her hands held tight to the wheel, she applied a light pressure to the accelerator with her foot, and the car surged forward. She released her foot, and it instantly slowed. Depress the brake pedal—not too quickly, she discovered—and they came to a stop. "Keep a steady pressure on the accelerator," Bea instructed. "Less wear and tear on the brakes." They passed the Wakemans', and Lilli glanced over to see if Nancy might be out on the front porch. She was, and Lilli waved.

"Eyes forward, Lilli, and hands on the wheel. Now there's an intersection up ahead. Be sure to allow plenty of room to slow down." Lilli nodded. She was well aware of the intersection—she had walked this route hundreds of times—and she was growing annoyed by Bea's constant commentary, which she felt was unnecessary. "Will you be quiet and let me drive?" Lilli judged that she had plenty of time, and turned to gaze again out to the harbor, to Brant Point, wishing Dori were in the backseat. She would have been bouncing up and down in excitement, urging Lilli to go faster. Lilli pictured her father beside her, praising her good driving and giving her encouragement. In Lilli's fantasy, Blythe was home, planning a special party to celebrate her achievement. And then she thought about Randall. Next summer, maybe he would let her drive the Mustang! Next summer, maybe—

"Stop! Stop!" Bea shrilled.

Lilli whipped around and punched the brakes. The car slammed to a stop, its front fender a few feet past the intersection. Bea slid partway off her seat, and Lilli banged her chin on the steering wheel.

"What are you trying to do, kill us?" Bea exploded.

Lilli was so startled by this she could only turn and stare, openmouthed, at her sister. There it was, exposed like some poor, dead thing washed up on the beach: the reason Bea had become so hard on Lilli, the reason she had become so unreachable, circling around Lilli in her own distant orbit. Bea blamed her. Lilli had suspected this the night she waited, alone, in her bedroom for Dori to come home. She had sensed it again, doubly so, when she'd seen her sister's expression, there in the attic, bent over their mother's lifeless body, taking in the scarf still knotted around Lilli's shoulders. Ever since then, there'd been tension building—especially noticeable this fall, but evident ever since the accident. It seemed to Lilli that nothing she did was ever quite right.

She put the car in park, climbed out, and shut the door firmly. Despite Bea's pleading question to tell her "what the devil was wrong now?" she turned and stalked away.

She didn't go directly home. She went, instead, into the little glade between Sandy Cove and the harbor, stopped in the clearing halfway in, and sat down, with her back against a cedar. She gazed up to the patchwork of blue created by the branches and thought about touching the sky.

* * *

AFTER THE DRIVING incident, the gulf between the two sisters seemed to grow wider each day, and Lilli set her sights more and more firmly beyond the bounds of White Head. Bea, it seemed, had a similar notion.

Lilli came home from school one afternoon a few days before Thanksgiving to find Bea in the kitchen, washing potatoes. "You know, Lilli. It's time we introduced you into society. You're turning eighteen this winter."

Lilli, who had an apple halfway to her mouth, raised an eyebrow. "Society? Are you joking?"

"No. I'm not. We need to find you a nice beau, a . . . future husband."

Lilli thought about Randall and said nothing.

"We could go into Boston and go shopping. For gowns. Charlotte knows . . ."

Bea continued prattling on, but Lilli had stopped listening. *Charlotte.* Lilli might have guessed. She'd told Charlotte about her plan to marry Randall. Charlotte hadn't been impressed. Would she have told Bea? Lilli didn't think so.

". . . to host a dance at the Ritz, or the Copley," Bea was saying. "We'll have to sign you up for some dance lessons, first, of course."

"Dance lessons. Bea, I am not one inch interested in debutante nonsense. I do not want to shop for gowns, take dance lessons, or have my nails done. Was this Charlotte's idea?"

Bea started slicing the potatoes. "How are you coming on your college applications?" she asked.

Lilli narrowed her eyes. What was going on? This was the

most Bea had spoken to her in weeks. Why this sudden interest in Lilli's future?

"Grandmother set aside money specifically so each of us could go to college," Bea said.

"You didn't go," Lilli countered.

"All the more reason you should," Bea shot back.

Lilli took a large bite of apple. "I'm thinking of applying to the Maryland Institute College of Art. For painting."

Bea looked up. "Maryland, you say?"

"I'm thinking of it."

"Why Maryland?"

"It's a good school. Besides, I've always wanted to see Maryland."

Bea gave Lilli a weak smile. "Yes," she said. "I've heard it's very nice."

And with that, she dropped the subject.

CHARLOTTE CAME HOME the week before Christmas, and she and Lilli baked up a storm. Lace cookies, haystacks, snickerdoodles, nut bars, Scottish fancies, and sand tarts. They streaked their hair, painted one another's toenails, paged through *Vogue* and *Mademoiselle*, and experimented with new shades of eye shadow and lipstick and painted Twiggy eyelashes on their lower lids. They put on the miniskirts and platform shoes that Charlotte had brought with her from Boston and gave a fashion show for Bea. She was in the den, eating popcorn and watching *The Virginian*. She pursed her lips as her two sisters pranced in, shook her head, and proclaimed that they looked like floozies.

"We knew you'd say that," Charlotte said, and they both pelted her with popcorn.

Lilli piled evergreens on the wide mantel in the living room and filled bowls with oranges tattooed with cloves. She couldn't remember ever having been as happy or ever being any happier, until she answered a knock at the back door on Sunday afternoon three days before Christmas to find Randall Marsh standing on the doorstep, a box of ribbon candy in hand. She stood, openmouthed, taking in the hank of hair falling across his forehead, the gray-green eyes, and the crooked grin. Oh, she would definitely marry him.

Forgetting not only that she wore turquoise eye shadow and false eyelashes, but that she was wearing a flour-covered apron and holding a chocolate-coated spoon, Lilli threw her arms around him and pressed her mouth to his. But he didn't seem to mind. He kissed her back, then laughed, and said, "Well, hello there. How's my Lilli?"

My Lilli!

Bea appeared in the hallway as Lilli pressed her lips to Randall's, and Randall released Lilli. He stepped slowly toward Bea, smiled, and leaned down to kiss her. She turned her face and offered him her cheek, which, Lilli noticed, was pink. Was she wearing rouge? Or blushing? Neither seemed likely. She did have on new shoes, Lilli noted, and her hair was newly cut and styled, as though she'd been expecting him.

"Man, it's good to be home."

"Home?" Lilli asked.

"Randall's staying with his aunt and uncle for Christmas," Bea said, unnecessarily. Where else would he be staying? Although Lilli did wonder how Bea knew this. And why hadn't anyone thought to tell *her*? Had Bea wanted to surprise her? Had Randall? Were they in this together? Lilli felt a stab of unexpected pleasure at this notion and gave them both a broad smile.

Next, Graham Bottomley, the Harvard medical student Charlotte had been dating, arrived, and they all drove out of town into a deep wooded area, cut down an eight-foot tree, and dragged it back to the car. They drove home with Randall standing on the tailgate, hugging the tree. Back at the house, they drank hot chocolate with tiny marshmallows and hung their wet woolens by the fire.

On Christmas Eve, Randall trimmed the tree under Bea's careful supervision. "The silver ball that says *Silent Night* goes in front, letters facing forward. Put the snowman down low, in case he falls. Not so much tinsel . . ." Lilli watched him carefully suspend each ornament as instructed, not seeming to mind her bossiness. He looked so at home. She pictured her mother sitting in her favorite chair, her father snugged in beside her, and Dori dancing around the tree, her eyes reflecting the light, glittering like tinsel.

Charlotte had baked gingerbread men to hang on the tree, and Lilli had decorated one for each of them: Bea's blond and smaller than the rest, Graham's with brown-rimmed spectacles. Randall's had green eyes and a wide grin. She'd draped a stethoscope on Charlotte's and given her own a mop of brown, curly hair. She added a silver dot to its left hand and nudged Charlotte, who grinned, and, with a wink, added one to her own cookie. Lilli's eyes widened and she gave her sister a hug. *Two weddings in one year! They could have a double wedding.* Randall hung Lilli's gingerbread cookie near the top and either didn't notice or chose not to comment on the shiny silver decoration.

On Christmas morning, Charlotte cooked bacon and shirred eggs, and Lilli attempted popovers, but, despite Charlotte's careful instruction, she added the milk all at once, so the batter was lumpy and they didn't rise fully. At midday they sat down to a turkey dinner with all the trimmings at a table expanded to accommodate Randall as well as his aunt and uncle. They lit candles, laughed, sang carols, mulled cider, traced their silhouettes, and played charades. *At last*, thought Lilli, as she drifted off to sleep that night, *my life is beginning*.

They drove into Boston for the dance at the Copley on New Year's Eve. The crowded ballroom was brightly lit and decorated with streamers, and Lilli danced at least a half dozen times with Randall. Of her other partners, when Charlotte later asked, Lilli could not recall a single name. They drank champagne and toasted to one another's health and prosperity. Graham and Charlotte sat in front on the way home, and Randall sat between Bea and Lilli in the back and held Lilli's hand the whole way.

It HAD BEEN cold enough for ice to form in the cove, so Charlotte suggested a skating party at the pond on New Year's Day. That morning, Lilli sat at her dressing table trying on hats. First, a stocking cap that made her look pixieish, then a balaclava that Bea had provided. But Lilli pulled it off immediately; it hid her hair, smelled of camphor, and looked like a binnacle cover. The last was the red beret Randall had brought over last summer when she'd made the cheese souf-flé. The hat would admittedly do little to keep her ears warm, but it looked very French and sophisticated. She added a touch of Peppermint Kiss to her lips, adjusted the hat down over one eye, studied the results in the mirror, and decided Randall would be unable to resist.

"I wish I could remember what Mother used to bring," Charlotte was saying as Lilli entered the kitchen. "I feel like I've forgotten something important." Charlotte was inspect-ing an army of bowls, tins, and Tupperware containers encamped on the kitchen table beside a large wicker hamper.

"Blankets and dry socks?" Lilli offered from the doorway.

Graham glanced up and whistled. "Lilli. Heavens. I feel underdressed."

"A skirt, Lilli? You'll freeze," Bea said. "Go put on pants."

"And dry mittens," Lilli said, ignoring her. "There used to be a basket of them in the attic."

"This is the picnic hamper, Lilli. That all went in the wool-ens hamper, which is in the basement. Be a lamb?"

"I'll help," Graham offered.

Graham and Lilli headed to the basement, Lilli intoning something about spiders as big as fists.

Bea shifted a few items on the table and popped the lid on a container of brownies. "What are you planning to do next year, Char, after you graduate?" she asked, casting a critical eye over the brownies. "Do you know?" Her tone was casual, as though she were only half-interested in the reply.

"Why?" Charlotte asked, suspicious, wondering whether Lilli had said something about her engagement. She hadn't yet told Bea. Graham said he wanted to ask her formally and hadn't yet found the right time.

Bea glanced up from her inspection of the brownies, "No reason. I was just asking." She put the brownies on the table and reached for a ceramic bowl covered with aluminum foil. "I was just wondering . . . if you were planning to move back here."

Charlotte sneaked a brownie, broke it in two, and ate half. "Mm . . ." she said, moving over to the sink and studying her reflection in the window. She could see her sister's as well. They looked like a photographic negative.

"I was . . ." Bea peeled back the aluminum foil and gazed into a bowl of potato salad. "I was thinking . . . maybe I'd sell this place and move into town."

Charlotte spun around. "Sell! You can't. This is . . . this is our home."

Bea carefully crimped the foil back over the potato salad and replaced the cover on the brownies and burped it. "Yes. It is. It's just—It's a bit lonely here at times, and a lot to take care of. Alone."

"We need to find someone for you to marry."

"Why do you say that?" Bea snapped.

Charlotte studied her sister a moment. "Because you're twenty-six and single? And you just said—"

Bea turned her back to Charlotte and continued her survey of the items on the table, lifting lids and peering under wrappers.

"I'm . . . moving to Chicago," Charlotte ventured, and pointed to the stethoscope on her gingerbread man, now lined up with the others above the bread box. "I was accepted at the University of Chicago Medical School." She was extremely proud of this achievement. Bea continued her silent inventory. Charlotte repeated, "I said—"

"Yes," Bea cut her off. "I'm sorry. Congratulations. That's wonderful. What will Graham do?"

"He'll go, too."

"Are you getting married? Or just going to . . . live together?" Bea said, practically spitting out the last two words.

Charlotte looked a bit startled. "Of course not," she said. "I mean, yes. We are getting married. This summer."

"Glad to hear it. That is the proper thing to do," Bea stated. "I'm very glad to hear it," she repeated. "All this 'free love' everyone's boasting about is . . . crazy. It's appalling." She addressed these last comments to the food as she tucked it all firmly into the hamper—containers of potato salad and cold chicken, rolls and brownies. "Daddy would have been shocked senseless at the very idea!" In went the thermos of hot chocolate.

"What are you talking about, Bea?" Charlotte asked, mystified.

Bea began to rearrange the containers in the basket. She was having difficulty fitting them all in neatly. "Nothing. I'm very happy for you. Very."

Charlotte started in on the other half of her brownie. "You don't really want to sell the house, do you? Isn't there anyone, any way?"

Bea grabbed the uneaten portion of brownie from Charlotte's hand and tossed it in the trash. "You really should watch what you eat." With that she unpacked the hamper, as only half of the items had fit. "Single women must be very careful. Appearances—" She shut the hamper lid with several bowls still on the table and began to buckle the leather straps. "And then there's Lilli." Bea was now speaking to the rejected picnic items. "She'll be here on school vacations . . ."

"I have no idea what you're talking about, Bea, but I wouldn't count on Lilli being here for vacations," Charlotte said, collecting the rejected items and returning some to the refrigerator.

"Why's that?" Bea asked.

Charlotte shook her head and started for the pantry. "You think the skirt's for Graham's benefit?" she said over her shoulder.

Lilli entered the kitchen just as Charlotte spoke and glared at her sister's retreating back. *What had she said?* Before she could pursue Charlotte into the pantry, Graham entered carrying a wicker laundry hamper. "What's for Graham's benefit?"

"The brownies, dear," Charlotte said, reemerging, taking the hamper from him and carrying it into the dining room.

"Where and when are you planning to get married?" Bea asked, following her.

Graham looked at Charlotte in surprise. "You told? I hadn't asked yet."

Charlotte set the basket on the dining room table. "Here, of course. Which is all the more reason you need to hang on to this house."

They dug through mothball-scented woolens, exclaiming over mittens and hats they hadn't seen in years, many of which Bea had knitted, most of which were far too small for anyone present.

WHAT THE NILES family had always called the skating "pond" was actually a rather large lake. They had gone there for picnics often when the girls' father was alive, their mother packing elaborate meals prepared by Mrs. Foley and bringing china plates from one of the many sets stacked in the tall cupboards in the pantry. George Niles taught each of his daughters to skate, propping them up behind an old kitchen chair where, on wobbly ankles and stiff legs, they would skitter along until steady enough to hold his arm. He was a graceful and fluid skater, and Lilli remembered feeling like a princess the first time she linked arms with him and glided out toward the middle of the lake. She was ten the winter he died and the skating parties stopped. Lilli took this day's outing as a sign of hope, something that had for many years been in rather short supply.

Randall had started a fire, which crackled and snapped, releasing sparks skyward—tiny rockets that soon fizzled in the cold air, turned to bits of black ash, and gusted away, to be replaced by another volley. He whistled when Lilli got out of the car. She leaned coquettishly against the fender, ignoring the cold air on her legs, and watched him stride up the rise from the campsite. Bea was struggling to pull the woolens hamper from the trunk, and Lilli knew she should offer to help, but Randall's eyes were on her, so she held her pose.

Then Randall noticed Bea struggling and called out, "Here, lovey, let me help you with that." Bea looked up, frowned, then thanked him, and handed him one side of the woolens hamper. Together, they toted the basket down the hill. Lilli had carried that basket out to the car all by herself, so she knew perfectly well that Randall, or even Bea, could have handled it alone. She puzzled over this as she grabbed the food hamper, which was much heavier, and hurried after them.

Ned Chapin, home for the holiday from Harvard, met her

halfway down. "Here, let me take that. How are you, Lilli? How's school?"

"Oh, thank you, Ned," Lilli said, handing him one side of the basket. She could see Bea, Charlotte, and Graham down at the campsite, setting out thermoses, spreading blankets, warming their hands. Randall was off to one side, lacing up his skates and talking with Mrs. McCallister, wife of the current yacht club commodore.

"That was a great dance at the Copley last night, wasn't it?"

"Were you there?"

"Yes," he said, stopping to look at her. "We danced . . . twice."

She felt rather small under his steady gaze. "Yes, of course. Sorry. Too much champagne, I guess." She laughed.

He smiled and said, "Happy New Year, Lilli," then leaned over and gave her a shy peck on the cheek, before taking the basket from her.

"Oh!" Lilli gave a nervous laugh. "Yes, same to you, Ned." She hoped Randall hadn't seen the kiss. She didn't want him to think there was anything between her and Ned. She gave a furtive glance down the hill, but Randall was already skating out to join the other men in a game of pond hockey. He hadn't seen a thing.

They continued down the hill, and Ned set the basket down on a log, touched the brim of his cap, and stepped away. Bea was still setting out picnic items, and Charlotte and Graham were sitting with their heads nearly touching, laughing together over something. Lilli stared out across the lake, wishing for her father's strong arm. She wasn't sure she'd even remember how to skate! She sat on a log near the edge of the lake, where she could see brown oak leaves trapped beneath the ice, and laced up.

The day was overcast, with occasional lazy snowflakes sifting down. The flakes would catch drafts and scoot sideways, and then spiral upward, as though undecided about where or whether to settle. Lilli tiptoed across the leaves and twigs frozen into the thin ice at the edge of the lake and pushed out. She wobbled, pushed again, wished once more for the strong arm of her father—or even a kitchen chair—to lean on, pushed again, and glided a bit until she found her balance. She pushed again, and again, curving back in a wide arc toward shore when she felt she had ventured too far, and curving again just before she reached the dark, thin ice at the lip of the lake. She retraced this wide circle, enjoying the scrape of her blades and the delicate ribbons of snow they carved up. Each time around, she grew steadier and braver and increased her speed. She had completed three nearly perfect circuits and was starting around again when she heard a familiar voice. "You're going in circles, you know." Randall skated up behind her and grabbed her waist. "You'll never get anywhere doing that."

Startled, Lilli lost her balance and nearly took them both down. He steadied her, spun around, took both her hands in his, and, skating backward, drew her around the circle one more time.

"Had enough?" he asked. Lilli, laughing, nodded, and he said, "Come on, then. There's something I want to show you." Arms around waists, they skated past the finger of land where their campfire was still spitting sparks into the cold, and then along the coved shore, smoke curling from the chimneys of the occasional cabin, to a section of the lake Lilli had never seen.

"Is that a boat?" Lilli stopped abruptly. Or tried to, nearly toppling them both. "A sailboat?" Lilli knew full well it was, but what was it doing here, now?

Randall grinned. "An ice boat. Want to go for a spin?"

Lilli hadn't been on any sort of boat since the *Whisper*. Though there was little chance of capsizing out here, she still hesitated.

"It'll be fine, Lilli," he said. "Trust me."

Lilli nodded and, hand in mittened hand, they skated over and were greeted by the boat's owner, whom Randall introduced as Scottie Miller, a fraternity brother.

"Lilli, you said? You have a sister, right?" He shook Lilli's hand. "Hi, how ya doin'?" Scottie looked at Randall. "You sly dog."

Randall seemed about to say something, but Scottie added, "And you're brave enough to go out with this guy?" He clapped Randall on the shoulder. "One of the craziest SOBs in our house. Stole the weather vane off a barn roof one time. He ever tell you that? Totally shitfaced—"

"That's enough, Miller."

Lilli shook her head, not sure if she was being teased. "No, he never mentioned it."

"Another time he drove six of us straight through to Fort Lauderdale for spring break. We drank a fifth of Wild Turkey every time we crossed a state line."

"Enough." Randall looked at Lilli. "Whadya say, Lilypad?"

"I'd say it's a good thing you weren't driving from Boston." Scottie laughed, clapped Randall on the shoulder, and said, "You lucky SOB."

What else could she say? She looked out across the uneven white surface of the lake, wondering if it was solid.

Wondering what they would do if the ice suddenly gave way. She pictured them trapped, like those oak leaves, able to make out the shapes of clouds and treetops and the horrified faces of friends peering down at them, unable to get free. She felt short of breath. Randall was watching, so she smiled and said, "Just don't expect me to set a spinnaker for you."

Randall laughed, and the two men pulled the boat out from the lee of the cove as Lilli skated along behind. When instructed, she climbed in, removed her skates, and sat in the center. Randall then turned the boat to catch the wind, hopped in the stern, trimmed the sail, and they were off. At first Lilli was too scared to do anything but hold on and grit her teeth, partly to keep them from chattering in the frigid air—her ears and legs were stinging—and partly from fear. Then she heard the scrape of the blades on ice, like the sound her own blades had made, but much louder. They skimmed along, picking up speed.

"Close your eyes," Randall shouted.

"What?"

"Close your eyes."

Lilli did, and soon sound and motion merged, and she felt weightless and free. She loosened her grip on the boat and turned to face forward, plucked off the beret (which was doing little good anyway), and tucked it beneath her knee so it wouldn't blow away. She held arms outstretched, feeling like a blade, carving the wind. She stayed this way until she felt the boat start to slow. She opened her eyes and saw that they'd sailed clear across the lake and were coming to a stop in the shelter of a small island near the opposite shore. Randall was looking at her with an odd expression that she could not read.

"Why are we stopping?" Lilli could have gone on like that for hours.

In one motion, he dropped the tiller, leaned forward, cupped her face in his hands, and kissed her. Not the brotherly, affectionate pecks he'd given her in the past, but one that was hard and insistent in a way that warmed Lilli and left her light-headed. She slipped her arms around his neck and pressed her body into his. She had imagined this moment so often she was worried her response might seem overrehearsed. If Randall noticed, he didn't complain. The kiss itself was both familiar and surprising, his mouth softer, his grip firmer than in her fantasies. Randall held her close and, his lips to her ear, said in a husky whisper, "Lilli, love."

Lilli was too startled to speak. She pressed her mouth to his again: that familiar mouth with its scar on the upper lip from an old hockey accident that left one of his teeth—knocked loose and which someone had the good sense to push back into place—slightly snaggled. He pulled back, his eyes drifting from Lilli's hair, to her eyes, and then her mouth, caressing without touching, and then he slid his hand down over her breast. She inhaled sharply and pulled away, blood pounding in her ears, hungering, barely breathing, waiting.

He said with a soft groan, "Oh, Lilli. Am I doing the right thing? God, I want you."

Lilli's eyes widened. "Randall—" She had thought about this moment for years, wanted it, planned it, even. Now it was here and she had no idea what to do. Should she say she loved him? Did she? *A life without one's true love,* her mother had told her that long-ago summer, *is no life at all.* Was that how she felt? That life without Randall would be no life at all? His breath warm on her ear, his beard rough against her cheek, and his startling scent—sweet and earthy—made her light up deep inside. Yes, she must love him.

She shifted forward to reach for him just as a gust of wind rose around them. It sang through the rigging and seized Lilli's red beret, no longer anchored by her knee, and sent it a few feet into the air, and then skittering across the ice. The note that the rigging strummed in the wind took her back instantly to the night she'd been in the *Whisper* with Dori, when the whole world became nothing more than that eerie sound and the sight of whitecaps furling in angry succession toward, and finally over, the boat, a world suddenly unstable and threatening to swallow her up. She remembered how tightly she'd clung to those oars, afraid to let go, afraid to reach her hand out to Dori. "No!" she cried, watching her beret dance away across the ice. And, just as though someone had started a movie reel, the emotions that had been stilled for more than two years began to unspool. The fear, the grief, the loss, the guilt. "No," she said again, to stop the memories, stop the feelings, stop the dread now coursing through her. She saw herself climbing the attic stairs that terrible day, which had started with such hope: daffodils ready to bloom, a starfish found on the rock. *"You don't wish on starfish, silly. I know but let's make a wish anyway."* She had. She had wished that her life would return to normal, that the people she was supposed to depend on would, once again, become solid and stable like the rocks in the cove, instead of ever-changing like the tides that slid in and out so one could never count on finding the beach the same two days in a row. She saw the overturned chair, the scarf knotted tight, the bruised-looking face, the careful makeup, her sisters rushing up the stairs— "No. Stop."

"Lilli? Are you okay?" Randall was looking at her with concern. "Talk to me."

"I can't," was all she could manage. She couldn't possibly explain, not with the icy cold waves washing over her, the heavy dress pulling her under. She did love him. That was the problem. The notion of binding herself to him seemed terribly risky, like rowing, blind, out into a dark harbor. You couldn't possibly know what lay out there: *"The great challenge is to be in love and not give in to the ever-present fear of losing it."*

"I want to go back," Lilli said, meaning back before the death of her mother, and Dori, and her father. Back to her childhood, when all the important decisions were made for you by grown-ups.

"Yeah. Sure. Right away. I didn't mean . . ."

"I can't," she said.

"I understand." Randall had climbed out of the boat and was tugging it out from the lee of the island.

He couldn't possibly, thought Lilli, still caught up in her own memories and feelings and thinking they were talking about the same thing. A cold sweat coated the nape of her neck. She hugged her arms to keep from shivering. "I'm so sorry," she said.

"No. God, no. Don't be sorry. I'm sorry. I shouldn't have—"

But Lilli was remembering how she'd known she shouldn't have rowed with Dori out into the harbor. Wondering if she'd known all along what it was she'd forgotten that night. She closed her eyes and shook her head, trying to block out the memories still unspooling themselves in her mind.

Randall set the sail, and the wind carried them back across the lake.

* * *

THAT NIGHT, LILLI told Charlotte how Randall had said he loved her, and how she'd seized up, been unable to speak, the awful memories squeezing all the air out of her.

"He said he loved you? Are you sure?"

"Yes, I'm sure." Lilli thought hard. "Pretty sure. Why is that so hard to believe?"

Charlotte tucked Lilli's hair behind her ear. "Have you ever considered cutting your hair? I think it would look terrific."

"He said *love* very clearly. And that he wanted to be with me. And then I freaked out."

Charlotte gave her a hug. "If he meant it, he'll tell you again."

"But I'm leaving tomorrow. He won't be able to call me."

"For two weeks! He'll wait. And don't seem too eager. Men like to pursue. Especially Italian men." Charlotte winked at Lilli. "Seriously, cut your hair in Italy. They'll all think you're a sexy Italian woman of about twenty-five."

Lilli stared glumly at herself in the mirror. "I'm such a dope."

"How about a fried-egg sandwich? It's the best antidote for dopiness."

CHARLOTTE AND GRAHAM bustled around the house the next day, getting ready to leave for Boston. They would take Lilli with them, dropping her off at Logan Airport for her flight to Rome. Bea helped Lilli finish her packing and, perhaps sensing that something was wrong, refrained from offering any last-minute travel tips. She'd tried the week before, and Lilli had archly pointed out that as Bea had never traveled to Europe, she might not be the best person to be doling out advice. She did make Lilli oatmeal for breakfast and even sprinkled raisins and brown sugar on top. It was actually not bad for once, Lilli had to admit, but she had no appetite. Bea gave her sisters and future brother-in-law quick, tight hugs as they trooped out to the car, and then she stood in the driveway waving as Graham's Camaro rolled down the drive.

Lilli spent the next two weeks feeling like a bit of flotsam adrift at the mercy of the seas. She was certain one day that she should call Randall and tell him she loved him, and equally certain the next that doing so would be a terrible mistake. She wondered what he was doing, why he didn't write, whether she should. Attaching herself to him filled her with terror. The thought of losing him forever filled her with despair.

Two weeks later, when Lilli straggled wrinkled, limp, and exhausted back up the jetway with her classmates and the other passengers returning from Italy, she was completely unprepared to see Randall waiting for her at the gate. She dropped her carry-on and lunged into his arms. He held her tight for a moment, then grabbed her bag, and they headed down to the carousel to retrieve her luggage.

"What are you doing here?" Lilli asked.

"Oh," Randall hesitated. "I decided not to finish the semester. Thought I might see what White Head is like in the winter."

Lilli gave him a smile intended to show that she understood and that he need not explain further. Not right now. There would be plenty of time for that later.

Lilli nattered nervously the entire way to White Head. Randall carried her bag in and deposited it in the kitchen, where Bea was standing, wearing an apron over her dress and an expression of anxious hope.

"No," he said to her. "Not yet."

"Not yet, what?" Lilli asked, not noticing Bea's expression sag from hope to exasperation. She was too busy opening her suitcase and digging out the gift she'd brought for Bea: a small ceramic pitcher, hand-painted with green and yellow fruit. "I didn't bring anything for you, Randall. I didn't . . ." She smiled at him shyly. "I didn't know you'd be here."

There followed an awkward pause until Randall said, "'Scuse me, ladies, I think I'll pop down to the basement." He turned to leave, but Bea caught his arm. "Hat and gloves in the basket. Could you at least do that?" she snapped.

Lilli, startled by Bea's tone, set the pitcher on the counter beside Randall's gloves and hat. "I'll do it." She grabbed them, walked to the back hall, pulled off her own hat and gloves, and tossed them all into the basket on the floor. She then removed her coat and went to hang it on her customary peg, but noticed several men's jackets there. *Odd*. She glanced down. A pair of large work boots stood beneath the jackets. She glanced around. A long fishing rod leaned against the wall in one corner beside, of all things, a double-barrel shotgun. Mystified, she returned to the kitchen and caught Bea and Randall whispering. They turned as she entered, wearing expressions that Lilli easily recognized as feigned innocence. It was a look she'd perfected in her youth and knew well. She crossed the kitchen to examine a stack of unfamiliar-looking books—one on boat building, another on duck hunting, and a third on fly fishing—perched on one corner of the table. A man's sweater drooped over the back of one chair.

A hazy picture was slowly forming in Lilli's mind. "Are you . . . staying here, Randall?"

"I'm just . . . I'll be in the basement," he said, and slipped past Lilli.

Lilli turned and stared at her sister.

"Lilli," Bea said, meeting her sister's gaze. "Randall and I are married."

LILLI WENT UPSTAIRS to her room, locked the door, and wept until she felt sick. Wept until she felt hollow inside. Wept in a way she never had before. Then she composed notes, a dozen at least, to Bea, detailing all the ways in which Bea had wronged her. What kind of sister would do such a thing? Surely Bea knew how much she loved Randall. True, she'd never told Bea, but Charlotte must have. She tore each one up in turn. She thought of going downstairs and confronting her, but the feelings roiled inside like hurricane winds, blowing this way and that, threatening and uncontrollable, and each time she reached for the door, the words she wanted to say lodged in her throat.

She resolved never to return to that house, never again to speak with Bea or Randall. How could they do this to her?

She called Charlotte and unloaded. Charlotte listened for a full fifteen minutes without speaking, and then said, "Are you sure you really loved him, Lilli?"

Which set Lilli off again. Of course she loved him! She had always loved him. She knew she should have tried to call him from Italy. "Charlotte, you told me he would wait," she raged.

"Lilli, if he wasn't willing to wait two weeks, maybe it's for the best. You're very young. There will be others, many others. You've got so much life ahead of you—"

"That, Charlotte," said Lilli quietly, "is precisely the problem." Lilli saw her life stretching before her, like some boundless body of water, both pointless and endless.

LILLI took Bea and Izzy out to dinner that night. Lilli watched Bea through enlightened eyes, wondering how she could have missed her manipulations to get her to move back to the house in White Head. A simply ridiculous idea! Whatever notion she'd had of clearing the air between them, of unburdening herself—whatever idealized image she'd had of reviving her relationship with Bea—had vanished, fading like morning mist, to reveal a familiar, rocky coastline beneath. Bea hadn't changed one whit in all those years. Lilli did not need her in her life.

Bea had squinted and frowned at the menu, gamely nibbled the sushi Lilli ordered for the table as an appetizer, and then looked so bewildered when her meal arrived that Lilli couldn't help smiling. Obviously she'd never seen anything like the tower of halibut and asparagus spears atop a mound of garlic mashed potatoes, crowned with frizzles of fried leek and a sprig of sage. Lilli concentrated on her lobster risotto, trying not to laugh.

Izzy had dropped Lilli off at the motel after dinner, and Lilli called Charlotte at her hotel in San Francisco.

"Lilli! How on earth did you find me here? Is everything okay?" Charlotte said.

"I need you to talk to Bea."

"Oh, Lilli." Charlotte sounded weary. She'd never liked being the shuttlecock, sailing back and forth between her two sisters, although she'd done it all her life. "I told you, we can't say anything. I knew you shouldn't have gone."

Lilli paced around her room, wondering how she'd ever found the wretched faux-wood furniture comforting. She thought of Izzy and Bea back at the house, perhaps chatting over cups of tea. "Not about that—although there is one quick thing. Izzy told me today—"

"Izzy? You talked with Izzy today?" Charlotte suddenly wary. "Why?"

"Izzy's here."

"Really." Charlotte's tone turned a shade cooler. "How did that come about?"

"It wasn't me. Bea invited her." Lilli remembered that Izzy hadn't told anyone about the wedding and now regretted bringing her up. It wouldn't do for Lilli to know before Charlotte. There was a certain protocol she had to respect. "She said that Bea intended for me to move in with her. That's why she invited me. Did you know?"

"What?" Charlotte's surprise was genuine, and her patience growing thin. Lilli could hear it in her voice. "Of course not, Lilli. Don't you think I would have said something to her? To you?"

"Yes. Sorry. But, listen, Char, we need to move Bea into independent, or maybe even assisted, living. You should see the house. See her. Her eyesight is bad, so's her hearing. Her hands shake. She forgets things, loses things, puts stuff in odd places—"

"So do I, Lilli. I'm sure Bea is fine. Yes, she has certain medical problems, but she's in no way ready for assisted living. At least, not so far as I'm aware. She's not senile, Lilli. She can make her own decision about this. I'm sorry she wasn't completely straight with you, but don't make this a grudge match."

"I'm not!" *Was she?*

"I've got to go. Graham's tapping his watch. We have a 'thing,' and I'm the honoree. It would be very bad form to miss it!"

After she hung up, Lilli sat awhile in the unfamiliar surroundings of her dimly lit room, feeling a bit like a newly transplanted seedling, unstable and vulnerable. She called Felicity and discussed, once again, the placement of her paintings for the exhibition.

WEDNESDAY MORNING, WITH her silk suit encased in dry cleaner's plastic and hanging in the back of her rental car, Lilli stood in Bea's driveway and wrapped Izzy in a tight embrace. Their time together had been so short. Izzy put her suitcase in her car and hugged Bea, thanking her for a wonderful visit. Bea patted Izzy's back and said, "You let me know when you and . . . your young man . . ."

"Matumbé," Izzy supplied.

"Ma-tum-bay," Bea said, "have picked a date. We'll take care of the rest."

"You know, we haven't completely decided that we want a big, fancy ceremony. What if we got married in Chicago? Did something very small, like you and Uncle Randall. Would you be very disappointed?"

Bea shot Lilli a suspicious glance. Lilli kept her gaze on Izzy, who was looking at Bea. "Indeed I would. Very. It doesn't have to be a lavish affair. We can have a nice intimate wedding out back. It's no trouble at all. I know how much this place means to you and . . ."

"Matumbé," Lilli said with no hint of humor. She couldn't wait to be settled into her five-star hotel in Boston, to be, once again, among people who appreciate art and fine food. "Have a safe trip, Izzy," Lilli said. "Enjoy your conference." She wrapped her in another hug and held her, eyes closed, and then whispered, "Remember, it's your day."

Izzy waved out the car window as she drove off, and Lilli followed Bea into the kitchen, where the darkness and stale air seemed even more settled than they had the day before. Bea lowered herself heavily into a kitchen chair. "The house seems so empty without Dori. She was here such a short time."

"Izzy," Lilli said, not bothering to soften her tone.

"What's that?"

"Izzy. You said Dori. You meant Izzy. That's the third time."

"No, I said Izzy. I'm sure of it."

"Yes, well, I need to get going. I've stayed longer than I should."

"You're leaving?"

"Yes. I'm leaving. I have the reception in Boston tonight, as you well know, and on Saturday I fly back to London. Where I live. Before I go—"

"You won't stay to help me plan Izzy's wedding?" Bea asked.

"No, Bea, I will have no part in your crazy scheme. I'm going to do my best to talk Izzy out of it, too. Besides, I have a life in London and I need to get back to it. You tricked me into coming here. The invitation to Randall's service wasn't a loving gesture. It was a totally selfish one. I could get past that, but not wrangling Izzy into having her wedding here when she doesn't want to, just so I would stay here longer and, as I now understand it, move in here with you."

"I don't know what you're talking about. You chose to come and you chose to stay. Izzy *wants* to have her wedding here. Always has. She told me so when she was little." Bea picked up a gardening catalog and leafed quickly through it.

"Izzy deserves to have a beautiful wedding. The wedding she wants. Where and when she wants it." Lilli paused, glanced out the window and down the drive. "Did you even *consider* asking me if I would move back here? No. It's all a game to you. You've always lived, Bea, as though life is one long round of competitions, and you just have to win. Well, you're not going to win this one. I will help you make arrangements to move—"

Bea slapped the catalog down on the table. "You do not have to make any 'arrangements.' I am staying right here, where I've lived for the past sixty-seven years. I had hoped that you might stay and help me with Do—Izzy's wedding, but if you won't, I'll do it myself. Perhaps you'll grace us with your presence on the big day?" Bea stood and walked to the sink, forcing Lilli to step aside.

She watched Bea fill the sink with soapy, lavender-scented water and put on a pair of blue rubber gloves. Then she looked around at the worn countertops, the archaic appliances, the stained walls. "I called Beacon House—"

Bea plunged plates into the water, sloshing suds on the floor. "Do not mention that place to me again. I am not going to be locked up in a home for the aged and infirm." She peeled off the gloves and tossed them on the counter. "Now if you'll excuse me, I'm going to go see about pulling some weeds. There's a great deal to be done before July." She headed toward the sunporch.

"Pull some weeds?" Lilli repeated, following. "Do you think you can do this by yourself? By hand? By July? You need a backhoe to clear this mess. It must have been ten years since anyone touched that garden."

"I will get Mr. Sylvia to come help."

"Mr. Sylvia! Oh, that's rich. Yes, why not call Mr. Sylvia. He's probably only eighty now. Listen to yourself, Bea. You cannot stay here."

Bea angled around to face her sister. "Nothing I've ever done has been quite right, quite good enough for you, has it, Lilli? I tried to watch out for you, and you've never been anything but critical, never done anything but run away. Never faced—" She stopped and turned back to face the garden. "I'd hoped . . . Well, never mind what I hoped. If you won't stay and help, then have the courtesy to leave me alone." With that she picked up a broad-brimmed hat and headed out the door.

Lilli followed her for a short distance, speaking to Bea's narrow, retreating back. "Watched out for me? Is that what you call it? You married Randall, with all the men you could have had, because you couldn't stand to see me win even once. You knew I loved him. What kind of sister does that? Well, there's something you don't know, Bea. . . ." Lilli trailed off as Bea slowly turned around, her blue eyes seeming to deepen a shade.

"Yes?" Bea's tone was challenging.

"Nothing."

Bea turned her back to Lilli. "You think I won that one?" she muttered. "Some prize."

"You were a stubborn young woman, Bea, and you've turned into a stubborn old one. No, on second thought, you were always a stubborn old woman. Well, I'm done playing games with you. Plan the wedding. Weed your garden. Live here as long as you like. You have my blessing. I'm leaving." With that Lilli marched out to her car, through the lilac hedge, where bees bobbed drunkenly among the fat purple panicles that sweetened the air as the leaves rustled softly in the breeze.

LILLI REPLAYED THE scene in her head for the entire forty-five-minute drive up to Boston. She turned in her rental car and took a cab to her hotel, chosen because it was a short walk across the Public Garden to the Grummage Gallery on Charles Street. She had just enough time for a nap. The events of the past few days, and that day in particular, had drained her more than she wished to acknowledge. There was one message—from Izzy—on her cell phone, saying how nice it had been to see them both and asking Lilli to please pass her thanks along to Auntie E, who hadn't answered Izzy's call. Lilli wasn't sure why, but she'd thought—hoped—the message might be from Bea, who hated voice mail and answering machines and was, no doubt, in a snit over Lilli's comments.

Except, Lilli knew, Bea wouldn't dream of being the one to break the silence and apologize, wouldn't admit she had anything to apologize for. Lilli was also unsure why she felt so discomfited by the way she'd left. Guilty, even. She'd said more than she intended, but it was all true and she'd meant every word. Still. Bea was her sister, recently widowed, seemingly failing, and that might well have been the last time Lilli would ever see her. Annoyed that her guilt and unease were casting such a long shadow over the evening's activities, she finally relented and called Bea. No answer. Well, Lilli thought, curling up between the four-hundred-count sheets and slipping on her eyeshades, she'd tried.

Bea stood in the garden for a long while after Lilli left, staring at the shoulder-high weeds, the unruly saplings, the overgrown beach roses. She'd done it all wrong. Again. The sky was cloudless, and the sun hot. She walked over to sit on the wrought-iron bench, picked up the azalea still resting on the sundial, and cradled it in her lap, frowning at the bare spot. She carried the plant over to the border of weeds, set it down, making sure the good side faced forward, and stepped back, a tired smile softening her face.

Then she picked up the plant, carried it into the house, and set it on the glass-topped coffee table. Her red-handled clippers lay on a shelf beneath. She bent to get them, wincing slightly, then took them back out into the garden and pruned a few branches from one of the beach roses, pausing now and again to stop and flex her fingers. She wiped beads of sweat from her forehead, squinted up into the sun, and returned to the house, setting the clippers on the sundial as she passed.

She walked into the kitchen, tried to open a window, and noticed the pill bottles on the counter. She checked her watch and frowned. After hesitating a moment, she tipped several tablets into her palm and swallowed them. She tied on an apron and started washing the dishes, leaning her elbows against the edge of the sink. The dishes finished, she plucked off the gloves, eased herself into one of the kitchen chairs, and then traced one of the ivy vines up the wall. She sighed and reached for the mail, which she sorted into neat stacks: bills, circulars, solicitations, magazines. She sat for a moment, staring at the piles, then pushed herself up from the table, removed her apron, and headed out the back door.

By EIGHT THIRTY that night the Grummage Gallery was crowded with couples dressed mostly in black who admired Lilli's paintings—hung on freshly painted, dark gray walls— as they sipped martinis and glasses of Cabernet and helped themselves to hors d'oeuvres. Lilli kept thinking about Bea. She couldn't help smiling, imagining Bea's reaction to Felicity's menu of squid ink tortellini and black capers on baby bok choy, petite fig and caramelized onion puffs, and miniature chicken liver flans with enoki mushrooms and chervil. She decided it would make a nice opener, an amusing topic of conversation, something they could laugh about together, before Lilli launched into the apology she had prepared. She slipped outside, stood under a streetlamp, and dialed. She pictured the gloomy house as Bea's phone rang and rang, Bea, no doubt, sound asleep in the den with the television so loud she couldn't have heard the phone anyway. She was annoyed, and slightly puzzled, to find that she felt, not triumph at being among the lively and sophisticated gathered in her honor at the gallery, but rather the sort of hollow sadness you feel when you realize that the item you'd hoped you'd simply misplaced was gone for good.

She tried Bea again later and still got no answer. Briefly she considered calling and asking Ned Chapin—or even the police—to drive over and check. But she was so certain that Bea was either ignoring the phone, intuiting that it was Lilli, or sound asleep in front of the television and couldn't hear it ringing, that she decided not to raise an alarm. Besides, she had to admit, she hated to involve outsiders in their business. She might have been gone for forty years, but she was still a Niles. Bea would be mortified to have Ned Chapin, or, worse yet, some uniformed stranger arrive at her front door inquiring after her, informing her that her sister has been trying reach her. "That so?" she'd say. "Well, as you can see, I'm perfectly fine. And if she was that concerned . . ." No, Lilli would try again in the morning. Eventually she'd catch Bea at an unguarded moment. She returned to the reception determined to make a go of it.

At ten the next morning, when Lilli still got no answer after several tries, she borrowed Felicity's car and set out for White Head. She easily navigated roads that just forty-eight hours earlier had seemed to start and end in the wrong places and experienced an unexpected feeling of homecoming as she passed the empty rocking chairs at Beacon House; the yacht club, quiet today; and the harbor, with the boats riding quiescent at their moorings. She passed the Chapins' driveway, followed the road along Sandy Cove, and turned up Bea's drive. The first thing she noted was the white Mercedes in the garage, at which point she nearly turned around. She'd

tried Bea's number several more times on her way up without success, yet Bea was evidently there. *Another ploy?* But
she'd come this far and thought she might as well apologize
in person. She practiced what she would say as she parked
the car. Something short, unemotional, focusing on behavior,
Bea's, and how it had affected Lilli, making amends for her
part—although she was still unclear what that was. Foisting an
unwanted solution on Bea? It was for her own good! Meddling
in her business? But Bea had made it Lilli's business, hadn't
she? Lilli had said some things she regretted. That was worth
an apology. But Bea should apologize, too, for making Lilli
drive all the way back up, if nothing else. She walked up to the
kitchen door and entered, rattling Patter's leash and calling out
Bea's name. The dishes were washed and stacked in the dish
drainer. The mail, unopened, was stacked in neat piles on the
table, at least. "Bea?" There was an unsettling stillness to the
house that Lilli tried her best to ignore but couldn't. There was
something uncomfortably familiar in the too-still silence.

She went into the den. Empty. The television was dark,
the packing material still scattered around the Footlights
shoe box. Wondering if Bea might be ill and unable to get
out of bed to answer the phone—Lilli didn't recall seeing
one in the bedroom—Lilli headed up the stairs, calling Bea's
name. The bedroom was empty, the canopy bed made. Did
she have plans to go away? Perhaps someone had picked her
up, Jane Hunsicker, maybe, and they'd gone into Boston to
a museum, or for some shopping. Lilli had a sudden image
of Bea walking, at that very moment, into the Grummage
Gallery and asking for her, having had the same feelings of
remorse and wish to apologize. She could have lost Lilli's cell
phone number. This image was so powerful that Lilli called

the gallery, where Felicity's assistant said that no one had been in asking for her, and then the hotel. Again, no one had stopped by. Had Lilli even told her which hotel she was staying at?

She listened deeply because the house seemed to be telling her something. "Bea?" Lilli called again and strained to hear what it might be saying. She imagined that she caught a faint whiff of Tabu and shivered, then inhaled deeply, allowing the phantom scent to fill her completely, until she felt light enough to sail away. She exhaled and reluctantly left the room, walked slowly down the hall, and paused before the attic door, her hand fingering the smooth porcelain knob. She turned it and eased open the door.

She could picture Blythe lying on the bottom step, her body crumpled and her neck broken, so convincing had the sisters' lie become after all these years. She stepped around this imagined place and climbed the stairs, first, second, third, fourth, avoiding the creaky fifth, she didn't know why, superstition, perhaps, or habit. She and Dori had played school here as they had on the steps leading up from the beach. Which hand held the marble? One had to guess correctly to advance, sixth, seventh, eighth . . . Dori always gave it away when it was her turn to be teacher, and Lilli would advance quickly. Lilli could hear the scurry of tiny paws as she stopped to catch her breath. The air seemed too thin here, as though she had climbed to a great altitude. Her eyes were level with the attic floor—she had not been up here since the day her mother died—and she could see an object in the center of the room, very near the spot where the chair had overturned beneath her mother's dangling body. She inhaled sharply and looked away, holding her breath, gripping the banister for support, her heart racing. She forced herself to look again. The object, she could now see, was large and rect-angular, a table, perhaps, and covered with one of the blankets they'd used at skating parties on the pond. She exhaled, steadied herself, and climbed the rest of the way.

She walked over to the blanket-draped object, knowing before she uncovered it what lay beneath: Dori's dollhouse. It was perfectly preserved, and why not? Izzy was the only one to have played with it in all these years. It was a nearly exact replica of the Niles house, minus the back wall, of course. And Randall had made it. He'd even finished painting the delicate green ivy vines on the kitchen walls, something Blythe had never managed to do downstairs. He truly must have loved this house. Lilli peered in one of the tiny windows, gazing in at the empty rooms.

A small box rested beside the dollhouse. Lilli opened it and began to remove its contents: two tables, three chairs, four beds, one desk, a footstool, several snippets of carpet, and a miniature painter's easel. She stood them on the floor beside her and began to place them in the house: one table in the kitchen and the other in the dining room, the desk and a chair in the den, the rest of the chairs in the living room, the beds in the rooms upstairs. The easel she placed in her pocket—there was no sign of the canvas that had gone with it. She sat back and admired her handiwork. "Where are you, Bea?" she whispered.

She stood to leave, but paused a moment in front of her grandmother's sewing table, still standing against one wall. It was coated with dust. She reached a tentative hand to the knob, then, darting an uneasy glance toward the rafter, changed her mind and returned quickly downstairs.

Lilli poked her head in the other bedrooms, one of which had obviously been Randall's. Here, she lingered a moment, fingering the tarnished silver brush set and the bowl of cuff links on his dresser. She opened the closet. The tweed jackets and gabardine slacks were not those of the young man Lilli had known. She retreated to the sunporch, where she found the pink azalea on the coffee table by the love seat. Bea had watered it. She could just make out something small and red in its place on the sundial and went out for a closer look. She found a pair of red-handled clippers and, on the wrought-iron bench beside the sundial, a pair of gloves. Lilli called out and peered into the brambly undergrowth encircling the yard, wondering if she might find Bea on her hands and knees, weeding, although the idea was preposterous. Holding Izzy's wedding here, Lilli was sure, had simply been a part of Bea's scheme to entice her to stay a few more weeks, hoping, by then, that Lilli would decide to move back. She wouldn't carry on with the notion now that Lilli was gone, and therefore would have no need to weed. She stood a moment, picturing a wedding, Charlotte's: the sun on the water, and then the sky turning pink as the sun set, the tiny lights in the trees, the music, the rows of white chairs, the tent . . .

Over by the neglected and overgrown path to the beach, Lilli spotted a small pile of beach rose trimmings. Lilli had to admire Bea's . . . fortitude, she'd call it if she were being charitable. Pigheadedness, if she weren't. It was a bold plan, Lilli had to admit, as she stared through the honeysuckle at the listing arch with its cargo of vines, trying to picture it liberated and garlanded with roses as it had been for Charlotte's wedding. Charlotte standing beside Graham, his eyes magnified by his thick lenses, and Randall . . . a sigh escaped as Lilli tried to square the memory of his firm, lithe body with the clothing upstairs. Was nothing sacred? He had looked so handsome that night in the greenhouse—

She knew at once. The knowledge hitting with the same satisfying yet frustrating certainty as when you remember, too late, that essential item you've forgotten to pack. She turned and, as though being borne along by a strong breeze, sailed through the opening in the lilac hedge and down the drive to the greenhouse. The door was ajar, and, although Lilli could see no movement through the milky glass, she could see that something was not right. She picked her way through the weeds and grapevines, trying to decide whether the path looked slightly more trampled than it had after her visit on Monday. She thought it did, a little. She tugged open the creaking door and stood, taking in the altered interior. The potting bench that George Niles had so lovingly but ineffectually constructed for Blythe lay in a heap, having given way under its too-heavy load of terra-cotta, soil, and gardening tools. Dirt, broken pottery, dried mums, and splintered wood now covered the floor. In the midst of this jumble, Lilli spotted one bright blue running shoe. At first she thought it must have come off Bea's foot, because its angle was so at odds with Bea's head, which was resting on the lowest riser, in a halo of dried blood. Her eyes were shut, and she looked almost as though she were taking a nap under a big comforter of dirt, broken terra-cotta, and rake handles. But her hairline was matted with blood, and Lilli realized, as she began to scoop soil away to uncover an ankle, that the shoe had not come off, but was still very much attached to Bea's foot and, somewhere beneath the rubble, to her leg, torso, shoulders, and head. Lilli bent down to check for a pulse as her fingers fumbled to find the tiny nine on her cell phone. Her knees gave way, and she crumpled onto the scattered debris as though she'd attempted to shoulder a too-heavy burden.

Twelve

AUGUST 1969

CHARLOTTE, in an ivory silk-taffeta gown, a circle of
ivy holding her veil, stood at the dressing table in her
mother's old bedroom, applying lipstick.

"You look sensational, Char," Lilli said, bending down so
their faces were even in the mirror. "Good enough to eat."

"Like a puffy meringue, you mean."

Lilli giggled and lowered her wide-brimmed hat so that it
covered one eye. Charlotte told her she looked just like Ingrid
Bergman in *Casablanca*.

"You are not fat," Bea said from across the room where
she was struggling to do up the buttons on Alice Bottomley's
dress.

"Just *large-boned*," Charlotte said. "Isn't that what Mother
used to call it? I am famished, though. Let's get on with this, so
I can eat. I've been dieting all summer and gained two pounds.
How do you two stay so trim? Honestly, Lilli, you're built like

a Greek goddess. And you, Bea, you're just no bigger than a minute. It's hard to believe, sometimes, that we're sisters."

Bea joined them at the mirror and tucked a few imaginary stray hairs under her hat, which she wore tipped back like Rebecca of Sunnybrook Farm. Dori gazed up at them from her silver-framed portrait on the dressing table. Lilli stepped away. She was still seething at Bea. It was awkward to be back in this house with her and Randall. The two of them carrying on like old married people.

"What do you think Dori would have looked like?" Charlotte asked. "I think tall like you, Lilli, and thin. And very pretty."

Lilli didn't reply. She was looking at Randall's silver brush set across the room on the bureau beside a bowl of his cuff links, and at the toes of his slippers peeking out from beneath the bed, as though he were under there, listening.

LILLI HAD LEFT White Head the morning after returning from Italy, the morning after learning that Randall and Bea had married. She'd moved into Boston to live with Aunt Helen and Charlotte in Charles River Square, refusing to stay in White Head, unwilling to face daily what might have been. Bea had tried to explain, but Lilli had given her a look of such searing anger, resentment, and accusation that she had completely silenced her. Lilli hadn't known she had such power. She'd been far too angry and hurt to talk, too fearful of what she might say, what she might do if she were to give words and action to her feelings; she knew what she was capable of. She had announced that she was leaving and would call a cab to take her to the train station.

She'd lingered a little while, in her room, sitting at her dressing table, recalling the night she'd sat on that same cane-seated bench while Dori pinned up her hair, and how they'd run to the yacht club through the moonlit foam at the edge of the water. What abrupt turns life can take if you're not paying attention. That day had ended so differently than it had begun: Blythe and her ridiculous pancake cake. How Lilli longed to go down the back stairs and find her mother, flour-dusted, cooking pancakes at the stove. She would fold Lilli in a floury hug and make things right. A wet snow that had fallen all night had softened the edges of the windowsill, and Lilli thought about the bird that had beat its wings against the glass that night, the voice of her father, *"No, not this one, the other one."* She stood and snapped the brass latches on her suitcase.

When it was time to leave, she'd bumped her suitcase down the stairs and found Randall waiting in the kitchen. He said that he wanted to drive her to the station, that he had sent the cab away. She'd pushed past him, dragging her suitcase through the snow to the car, refusing his offer of assistance. They'd ridden in silence, Lilli staring straight ahead into the onrush of snowflakes dancing before the windshield. She'd been torn between her desire to confront him and her desire not to prolong her misery, being there, so close beside him, knowing that he was lost to her forever in the way she'd wanted him for so long, knowing that he would drive back along snow-covered streets to the familiar house, her house, and to his wife. The snow was slowly filling the streets, muffling sounds and subtly altering the landscape, so that familiar landmarks were becoming unrecognizable. White Head was starting to take on a new shape, as though it were turning its back on her, even as she was doing the same to it. She got out at the station without having said one word. Randall carried her suitcase into the station and bent to kiss her cheek, but as he did, she turned her face, and their lips met and lingered there a moment longer than was quite proper. She didn't know why she'd done this, did not meet his eye after she stepped back, but simply murmured "Thank you" and walked to the ticket counter. It took her several tries to steady her fingers enough to extract the correct change.

"I WANT US each to wear something of Mother's," Charlotte was saying. She was holding a sapphire-and-diamond necklace out to Lilli. "This will look fabulous on you."

Startled, Lilli reached for the necklace. She put it on and looked in the mirror.

"Gosh, Lilli. You are starting to look more like Mother than she did."

"It's beautiful," Bea said, "but we don't want Lilli to outshine the bride."

"Oh, Bea," said Charlotte as Lilli reached for the clasp, "let her wear it. It's my wedding day. No arguments. *Please.* I'm about to marry the most perfect man in the world—"

"Perfect unless you've seen him in the altogether," Alice Bottomley said, joining the sisters at the mirror and adjusting the brim of her hat forward so it dipped over her eyes like Lilli's, which made stocky Alice seem to be peering out from under an awning.

"Alice!" Bea said.

"What? I'm his sister. Sisters see things. Graham is a wonderful guy, but naked he's all sort of—"

"Thank you, Alice," Bea cut her off. "I'm sure we've all

heard quite enough. Keep in mind that we have to stand up there facing Graham in fifteen—no, twelve minutes. I'm not sure we should have that image—"

"For your information, I've seen Graham in the altogether, and I think he's altogether perfect."

Bea looked shocked. "Charlotte!"

"Oh, Bea," Lilli said, assuming a greater degree of sophistication than she felt at Charlotte's announcement. She was enjoying Bea's discomfort, hoped to heighten it and, at the same time, to deflect attention away from herself. "They've been dating practically forever. Don't be such a prude." In fact, Lilli was as shocked as Bea but looked at Charlotte with a newfound admiration and gave her a smile in the mirror. The necklace really did look very nice.

"Here, let's find something for you, Bea," Charlotte said, returning Lilli's smile. "I'm wearing her pearls . . ." She reached for their mother's leather jewelry box on the dressing table, her initials in gold on the lid.

"I have something." Bea held up her left hand. "Mother's engagement ring."

Lilli thought it odd that Randall hadn't bought Bea her own ring, or at least given her one from his family. But, having just won the right to wear the necklace, she let it go. Alice announced from the window, "Your 'perfect groom' is wandering around outside, Charlotte, looking quite lost. It's hard for me to imagine someone quite that dopey being a surgeon. I hope I never—"

"Where's Randall?" Charlotte asked. "He was supposed to keep an eye on him."

"You asked Randall?" Bea, fluffing Charlotte's veil, sounded amused. "I'd check the bar."

An awkward hush fell over the room.

"What? That's where men go at weddings," Bea said. "At least mine does. Lilli, go tell the minister we're almost ready."

Lilli walked along the hall with her head down. She was still furious with Bea but wasn't sure how she felt about Randall. *Hurt? Disillusioned? Betrayed?* Since she'd been back for Charlotte's wedding, he'd tried to corner her several times, saying he wanted to talk. When he'd suggested a walk on the beach, Lilli invited Charlotte to join them. When he'd offered help with the dishes, she'd smiled, peeled off the rubber gloves, handed them to him, and left the kitchen. She did not want to be alone with him.

"Hello, Lilypad."

With her head down and hat brim covering her eyes, she hadn't seen Randall standing at the top of the stairs. She kept her head lowered and said, "Would you tell the minister we're almost ready?" She turned, adding softly, "And please don't call me that." She started back toward the bedroom, but he caught her arm.

"Lilli, talk to me. Please."

Lilli could feel the skin on her arm grow warm where he held it, and that warmth radiated up her arm to her face. She could feel it flush and kept it hidden beneath the brim of her hat.

"I miss you, Lilypad." He tightened his grip.

She wanted to pull away, but it was as if a current were flowing from his hand, into her arm, and through her body, soldering her feet to the floor.

"Can't we be friends?"

"Friends?" She looked up. That blunt little word shut off the current between them as abruptly as someone throwing a breaker. She pulled her arm free. Eventually, perhaps, she would forgive him, once she was clearer about what she felt and what she was forgiving him for. Eventually, perhaps, she might stop loving him. But be friends? That seemed unlikely. Frankly, she was offended that he'd suggested it. Lilli shook her head and started back toward the bedroom.

"At least let me explain," he said. Lilli kept walking. "Waltz with me?" he called just as she reached the bedroom door, and Bea stepped into the hall. There was a brief, awkward silence. Then Bea said, "Suppose we have the wedding first, and then, I'm sure she'd be delighted. Go get Graham, Randall. Charlotte's ready."

SEVENTY HEADS TURNED as Alice Bottomley appeared in the sunporch doorway, peered out from under her broad brim, and made her careful way down the steps and onto the grassy strip between the even rows of chairs. They'd set the lawn that morning with dozens of chairs and, inside the tent, covered the round tables with starched white cloths anchored with rocks so they wouldn't sail off in the breeze gusting up from the cove. They'd tied white ribbons to the rose-covered arch. The phlox, coneflowers, daisies, daylilies, hollyhocks, zinnias, sweet peas, morning glories, and picotee pinks were in full bloom. Three bridesmaids trailed after Alice, with Lilli, the tallest, last. She kept her face mostly hidden under her hat and matched her stride to the notes of the string quartet. She kept her gaze on the petal-strewn grass to avoid having to look at Randall, who was standing beside Graham to the right of the arch. She wouldn't, couldn't, allow herself to imagine, for even a moment, that the quartet was playing for her, that Randall was waiting for her, that this day was hers. But, in the end, she couldn't help herself, and her heart ached so that it was hard to breathe. She took her place across from him in the arch, turned, and smiled back at Charlotte, processing down the aisle on the arm of their Uncle Parker.

After the ceremony, the wedding party lined up for photographs, and Randall reached for Lilli's hand and held it, hidden behind the folds of her dress. She stiffened, wide-eyed, and forced a smile, not wanting to make a scene and ruin Charlotte's day. As soon as the photographer finished, Lilli broke away and, without looking at Randall, slipped into the group of gathered guests. She kept an eye on him throughout the cocktail hour. Knew, at all times, precisely where he was and put herself wherever he wasn't. At dinner, she sat between two of Graham's college chums, both very entertaining. Lilli had never had a martini before and decided after her second that she would never drink anything else. Randall was sitting beside Bea, but spent most of his time in conversation with Rita Lockwood, Lilli noted, a friend of Charlotte's from Radcliffe.

After dinner, Lilli danced with first one, and then the other of her dinner companions, as well as John Bradley, Jack Porter, Ned Chapin, and a host of other young men whose names she either didn't catch or quickly lost hold of. She prided herself on giving Randall barely a thought. She prided herself on this all through the evening, all the while keeping him securely at their center. Lilli surprised herself at how easy martinis made it to move from the moping, miserable girl she'd been for the past seven months to a chatty, laughing . . . happy girl, looking forward increasingly to the fall and the future—certainly if it included martinis, which had begun to dull even her fury at Bea. *She would not go to college. Bea be damned.* She would stay on in Boston and study painting at the Museum School. Why, yes, she told one young man, she would be pleased to attend that dance. Picnic along the Charles River? Absolutely, she said to another. A tailgate party before the Harvard-Yale football game? Most certainly, she assured a third. Why not? Her dreams of travel and fame, finally shared, timidly at first, and then more boldly as the gin flowed, were greeted with enthusiasm and excitement by her dance partners, with encouragement even, and, she thought, a little envy. One of her dinner companions attended Harvard Medical School; the other would be attending Harvard Law. She started to imagine a time when she might feel comfortable coming out to White Head for weekends, bringing along one of these two eligible men. Or maybe both! She would meet an artist, move to Paris, live in a garret, study art, and drink martinis for breakfast. Anything and everything seemed possible as the evening slid past.

Lilli was feeling quite content when, in an unguarded moment, Randall dropped into the empty chair beside her. *How long had it been empty?* It didn't matter. She was glad to see him! The band started playing "My Cherie Amour." He gestured toward the dance floor.

"My feet are tired. I've been dancing all night. Maybe I'll soak them in gin. They do that in Paris, you know. Take jaths in bin." Lilli giggled. "Ha! Baths in gin."

"Do they? I didn't know that. I believe they also dance in Paris."

"And they drink martinis for breakfast. Have you ever had a martini for breakfast?" she asked. "When I move to Paris, I am going to drink . . . martinisforbreakfast," she said all in a sigh. "They do that over there, too, you know. Did I just tell you that?"

"Twice. You seem to be quite an expert on Paris." He took her arm and attempted to tug her up and onto the dance floor. "For someone who's never been."

"Can't," she said, resisting. "Took them off." She pointed down at her unshod feet. "And lost them. Underthetable." She could see Bea handing out wedding cake, which Charlotte and Graham had cut a few minutes earlier. "Did you have cake?"

"Not yet."

"No. I meant at *your* wedding."

"A small one. Lilli, can we go somewhere and talk—"

"Small wedding. Small cake. Small bride. It all sounds rather . . . small." Lilli paused, liking the way she sounded: powerful and reckless, as though someone else was inside her talking. She knew it was the gin, and that she was going to suffer in the morning. And who was she fooling? The only person in the world she wanted to take gin baths in Paris with was Randall Marsh. Tears wet her eyelashes. *Damn. Her mascara would run.* She reached for her glass. Empty. *Double damn.* "We're already talking. Be a lamb and get me another?" She could hear Bea's voice in her head as she said this.

"Please?" Randall said, looking at her in a way that sent her heart galloping and her mind whirling. *Or was that also the gin?* "Down on the rocks?"

She chewed her lower lip, found it quite numb. "This dress, I'll have you know, is Italian silk. Very expensive. Not designed for climbing on rocks. And my shoes, wherever they are, aren't either." She lifted the tablecloth and peered underneath.

A young woman passed by then, tall, blond, and slender, wearing a floor-length gown, in a shade similar to the brides-maids'. A young man in a Nehru jacket was leading her out onto the dance floor. Dori would have been almost sixteen, a little younger than this girl, Lilli guessed, and then thought, *If Dori were here, what would she do?* She would not feel angry and betrayed. Yes, that was what Lilli felt most, betrayed. *What a waste of time*, she'd say, and then tell Lilli to forgive Randall, forgive Bea, accept what is, and move on to the next adventure. Lilli watched the young couple move awkwardly to the strains of "This Magic Moment." Randall had ducked under the table and soon reappeared holding Lilli's shoes. "The greenhouse? Ten minutes?"

TEN MINUTES LATER Lilli made her way a bit unsteadily through the lilac hedge and down the drive. The greenhouse stood in shadow, the moon, for the moment, hidden behind a cloud. The door creaked slightly when she opened it, and she paused, warmed by the scent of sun-baked wood and potting soil, brought back, for an instant, to her childhood. Her heart seemed to soften, and she sobered slightly. The big terra-cotta pots were lined up beneath the potting bench. Lilli supposed that Bea would fill them next month with mums, as Blythe had always done, and Mr. Sylvia, or Randall, would place them around the yard. An old gardening coat hung from a hook behind the door, and Lilli spread it over the lowest of the three narrow risers standing against the wall, where generations of seedlings had taken root and slowly unfurled, reaching toward the sun. She took a seat and waited, not sure why she'd come, not sure what Randall would say, not sure what she'd say, not sure how to move on and make the ache that seemed to be a permanent fixture in her heart go away. As she sat, listening to the music and laughter drift in from the reception and, closer, a chorus of crickets, she started to feel, for the first time in ever so long, safe and at peace.

She heard rustling, and then the door creaked, and Randall came in. The moon slid out from behind the cloud, and she could see him clearly. He was holding two champagne glasses in one hand and a candle in the other, and he had a bottle of champagne tucked under his arm. "I guess we don't need this." He blew out the candle and handed her a glass.

"I don't need this either," she said, taking it.

Randall was twisting the wire off the cork. "I'll try not to send it through the roof," he said, laughing as he eased it off. Champagne bubbled out, and he let it flow into her glass, poured one for himself, and set the bottle down on the potting bench. They sat in silence.

"I thought you wanted to talk," Lilli said finally. She took a slug of champagne for courage. "I thought I meant . . . something to you. That kiss. Out on the lake . . . You said—" She stopped, no longer exactly certain what he had said, out on the lake.

Randall took her hand and gently stroked it with his thumb. "You mean the world to me, Lilli. You always have."

She pulled her hand away—this was going to be harder than she'd imagined. "You married my sister." She sounded petulant. Couldn't help herself. She felt abandoned by Randall, as she had by Dori, by Blythe, by her father. They'd all left her. And now Charlotte would leave as well, move to Chicago with Graham. Lilli felt as groundless as a bit of dandelion fluff being borne along on a stiff breeze.

"That day on the lake, I thought we wanted the same thing. I'm sorry. I was out of line."

This was not what she wanted to hear. "We did," Lilli said. "We do. I'm sure of it."

Randall swallowed some champagne and loosened his tie. "But you got so . . . distant, angry almost. I decided I'd misread things. Badly." He rested his elbows on his knees and spoke toward the gravel floor. "We are in very different places in life. I wanted to settle down, here, and you are—barely out of high school, for God's sake." He took another swig and glanced her way. "Although you sure don't look it. And you have all your grand plans. All those places you want to see. This is all I want, Lilli. All I've ever wanted. This house, this town, sailing . . ." He trailed off. "You know how I got through the winters in Baltimore?" He hesitated, and then said, "Dreaming about this house, about White Head, about all of you, the yacht club, badminton on the lawn. Bea offered me that. And not just summers. I never meant to hurt you. I would never want to hurt you."

Lilli fingered the sapphire necklace as she searched for the words that might express even a fraction of what she was feeling. "Do you love her?" She didn't want to know but had to ask.

He thought a moment. "In a certain . . . cobalt violet sort of way."

She put down her empty glass. There was only one way to love someone: wholly, with all your heart and body. Lilli truly believed this. How could she make him see that a marriage of mere convenience was no marriage at all? *True love always comes with the potential for heartbreak,* her mother had told her. She was suddenly exhausted. The strain of the past few hours, days, months, maybe even years, had drained her the way the cove emptied when the tide ebbed and drew the water inexorably out to sea. She slipped her shoes off and rubbed her feet together, wanting now only to curl up on the bench and sleep.

"We make sense together," he said, removing his tie.

"Sense? What does sense have to do with love?" And with this, Lilli's words began to bubble up like the recently uncorked champagne. "Everything I ever wanted is in White Head now, too. I love you, Randall. I've loved you as long as I can remember. From since long before I knew what that word even meant. When I'm near you I can't think. When I'm not, I can't think of anything else. I don't want to be with anyone else." Once she'd said it she knew the truth of it. Maybe now she'd be free from the feelings that ran so swift and dangerous beneath the surface, like a riptide, threatening to drag her under. Lilli reached for her shoes, and, as she bent down, light-headed from champagne and martinis, she lost her balance. Randall caught her around the waist and held her, and she remembered how she'd felt, so long ago, dancing in his arms, sitting beside him after her mother's service. Safe. Protected. Home. She leaned against him and rested her head on his chest. She was so tired. He wrapped her in his arms and held her.

"Lilli . . ." It was just a whisper in her ear, but she lifted her face to his because the pull was as irresistible as the moon to the tides. They kissed, and he pulled her further inside that place she'd always known she was meant to be, and then he ran his lips along her cheek, found her ear. He was breathing hard, and Lilli began to burn with longing. She turned her head, needing his mouth again on hers. Their lips met, and she kissed him with all the passion that she'd held for so many years. She ran her hands up his neck and into his hair, wanting to touch places, so long cherished and off-limits. Wanted to know, with her fingertips, what she had explored so often with her eyes. Wanted to know him more intimately and not quite knowing how. His kiss became more insistent. She matched it, hoping to convey all that she felt, wanting him to know how it was to be wholly loved, with heart and body. Wanting to know, herself.

He pulled away, kissed her eyelids, her forehead. "Lilli. Love," she heard him breathe. She pressed herself to him. She needed him to know that there could be so much more between two people than "making sense together." He ran his hand down her back, igniting the skin beneath the thin silk, and then his hand was sliding up her belly, toward her breast. Afraid and excited, sensing she was losing control, not caring, unsure, she pressed against him, moved her arm down to block his hand.

"Lilli, my love," he murmured. "My darling girl."

"Yes." She raised her arms, hugged him around the neck.

His hand, now free, slid up over her breast. She wanted to pull back, and yet felt the urgency in his touch, and wanted to please him, wanted to match it with her own need, a need she did not fully understand and was uncertain how to satisfy. He was fumbling now with the buttons of her dress—there were dozens. His hands drifted down her sides, slid her dress up over her hips. His hands, warm, now kneading the skin of her thighs, his fingers exploring places she'd never been touched. She wanted him to stop. She did not want him to stop. She was dizzy, as dizzy as when she and Dori would join hands, look up into the sky, and spin around on the lawn.

When they stopped, they'd stumble around like drunks, laughing and falling, the world around them still whirling.

Randall's hands were now on her belly, sliding up, again, over her breasts, then behind her, unhooking her bra. Hands on flesh, her nipples tight beneath his fingers. She was burning, wet, yielding, still not quite willing to understand. *He loves me.* That was what he'd said. She felt him shrug out of his coat, his lips still pressed to hers. She was his. He was hers, as she had always known it should be.

LILLI WAS ON the ground, gazing up through the glass at the moon, the gardening coat spread out beneath her, partially protecting her from the dirt floor, and Randall was on top of her, his flesh warm and wet against her thighs. She wanted to stop, to sit up, but he was whispering her name over and over, saying that he needed her, or this, or wanted her, or this, she wasn't sure, couldn't quite make out the words. She felt pressure, pain, pumping. The moon slipped behind a cloud, and Lilli drifted back to the night that she and Dori had gone out in the *Whisper*, and the storm came up. Lilli wondered—as she so often had—whether she could have done something more when she heard Dori call her name. She'd never known. But now she realized that she hadn't needed to hold on to the oars to steady the boat, that she could have let go and reached for Dori. She had simply been afraid. And so she let go now and reached into the darkness.

Randall was stroking her cheek, wiping away tears, and Lilli stared past him, up through the glass ceiling at the moon, once again returned from behind a cloud. She slid her gaze back to Randall, tie dangling, hair mussed in an unfamiliar way, turning him into a stranger, discomfiting Lilli. She could feel the gardening coat beneath her, and the gravel, her dress hiked up and bunched around her waist. Her head throbbed, but she didn't care because her dreams were finally coming true. She combed her fingers through his hair, thrilling at the intimacy and happy to see, once again, her familiar friend. "I've dreamed of this moment so often, I feel like I'm still dreaming." In truth, Lilli felt too sick and hungover to have been dreaming. "How are we going to tell Bea?"

"Tell her?" He rolled to the side, hitched up his pants.

"We can't just run off. She's bound to notice. Bea notices things like that." Lilli straightened her dress, wondering what had become of her undergarments. "Let's live part of the year in Boston and part in Paris. We'll have martinis for breakfast here, and champagne over there. And make love before and after." She felt both shy and daring saying this, and adult now, although only eighteen.

But Randall wasn't looking at her. She wanted him to hold her again. To tell her again that he wanted her. She reached for his hand, but he was tucking in his shirt.

He pulled up his zipper. "Lilli . . ."

"On second thought, why not run off?" she said, sitting up and looking around for her panties. She wanted some more champagne, which she'd heard would cure a hangover. *How long had they been down here? What if Bea had been looking for them? What if Charlotte had thrown her bouquet?* Lilli spied a bit of lace draped over the top step, blushed, and reached for it. *When had Randall taken them off?*

"Lilli, I . . ." Randall was looking at her now, and not in a way that fit her notion of how a man should look at a woman at this intimate time. She'd read books. She'd seen movies.

"What, dearest?" How grown up she felt.

"We can't tell Bea."

"Can't tell her?" What was he suggesting?

"You're the most gorgeous creature I've ever laid eyes on. I adore you. Always have. But I can't leave Bea."

She felt as though she'd just landed hard on the ground— as she sometimes would after the girls' spinning game—the wind momentarily knocked out of her. "But all those things you said." Lilli couldn't remember exactly what they were, but promises were made, endearments uttered. He loved her.

"I meant them. All."

She stared dumbly at him. This made no sense.

"Lilli, I can't give you what you want. Can't be what you want. And you can't—"

"You are what I want," she managed.

"I'm not the man you think I am. I wish I were," he added, sounding like he truly meant it.

He reached out a hand to touch her hair. "Go to Paris, paint, drink champagne for breakfast, and take baths in gin, just like you said. Those are your dreams, Lilypad. Come and see us at holidays. I'll always be here, waiting for you."

It's difficult to know the precise moment that a tide turns and begins to ebb. One notes only that a little more of the beach is exposed, a little more of the barnacle-covered rocks visible. Lilli sensed that her life had turned in some significant way, although she didn't know how dramatic a turn. She knew only that she felt stranded, like a starfish high up on the beach, uncertain how she got there and unsure what to do next. Gathering what dignity she could, for she was certain that some parts of her wardrobe were still missing, she got to her feet.

"You will have a long wait, Randall" she said. With that she left and ran up the drive into the house through the back door, avoiding the kitchen, where she could see figures moving about inside.

Thirteen

LILLI felt very tired and very alone. Besides, she hated hospitals. Hated the antiseptic smell, the artificial light, the constant bustle. Bea had been breathing, barely, when Lilli found her in the greenhouse. An ambulance had arrived, and the medics soon determined that Bea was in shock and dehydrated and at the very least had a broken pelvis and probably a broken ankle. They stabilized her and asked if Lilli had the name of Bea's primary care physician (she didn't), whether Bea had a living will (Lilli didn't know), and whether Lilli was the next of kin (one of them, she told them), before racing off to Massachusetts General Hospital, sirens screaming. They wouldn't guarantee an outcome. Seated near Lilli in the waiting room were a young man and woman, holding hands. The woman blotted steady tears with a wad of balled-up tissues, and the man frequently fished a fresh one from his pocket to offer her. Across the room a mother and father sat slouched in adjoining chairs, reading deeply, while, at their feet, two children played quietly with a set of small action figures, giving Lilli the sense that they'd either done this before or been there a very long time, which depressed her even more. A group of three young women huddled in the corner. A fourth friend, Lilli couldn't help overhear, was having her stomach pumped. The girls discussed first why, and then how it happened, outcomes both good and bad. Then they would sit silent for a while, before one started in again, and they would repeat the process. They were trying to understand, Lilli knew, what role they had unwittingly played and whether some action they might have taken would have led to a different outcome. If so, perhaps they would not now be sitting in this ghastly room, their lives in temporary suspension.

Lilli knew just how they felt. She watched the girls sit silent for a time, busy fingers texting friends, updating them on this terrible occurrence. Lilli marveled at this new generation, always connecting with friends. What did they find to say? Lilli didn't have that many friends. Didn't have that much to say to the ones she did have. Soon one of the girls would launch into another series of questions, and they would, again, paddle the murky waters, struggling to see what lay below. Lilli wanted silence and wished they would stop talking, although she knew that the loudest voice was the one inside her head.

Others had left the waiting room during the four hours that she'd been there. Someone in surgical scrubs would enter, call out a name, and a hand would shoot up, and then the waiting party would gather his or her things and follow the one in scrubs through a set of automatic doors and down a tiled corridor that Lilli could glimpse each time the doors swung open. Lilli called Charlotte and recounted how she'd left White Head, called Bea several times, unsuccessfully, and then driven back and found her in the greenhouse.

"The greenhouse! What was she doing down there?" Charlotte asked.

"Have you talked with Dori?"

"Dori?"

"Izzy, sorry, I meant Izzy. Bea kept calling her Dori. Now she's got me doing it."

"No, she's at a conference. But you'd know that. You said you just saw her." Charlotte's voice held a slight edge. "Why?"

"Never mind. Bea thought she'd do some gardening."

"Gardening? I gathered she hadn't been doing much of that lately. Too tired keeping the house going, and her hips have been bothering her. I told her to see a doctor, get an MRI. She refused, of course. I also told her she should find someone to help her with the cleaning, but I guess money's a bit tight. Last time I called she answered all out of breath because she'd been washing the car. I ask you."

"I'd no idea." Bea hadn't mentioned financial difficulties. Lilli had attributed the condition of the house to Bea's age and poor health.

"Did she tell you how she does the laundry? Ties a dog leash on the laundry basket and pulls it down the basement stairs to the washer. Then bumps the clean laundry all the way back to the second floor. I told her she should get the machine moved to the first floor, she's got that big pantry—"

"No, I meant about the finances."

"What? Oh, well, I gather Randall squandered most of what was left her. Of course, Randall never worked a day after they married. Not really. Had a few schemes, all of which lost money. Vintage airplanes, importing latex gloves—"

"Hold on," Lilli said to Charlotte as a tired-looking woman in blue scrubs entered the waiting room. "Fernandez?"

A man in a bloodstained shirt, clutching a woman's purse in both hands, jumped up with a worried expression.

"I'll call you when I have any news," Lilli promised, too tired to continue the conversation. Charlotte gave her the likely name of Bea and Randall's physician, and they hung up.

Blue scrubs smiled, put a reassuring hand on the arm of the man in the bloodstained shirt, and led him past Lilli, through the magic doors, and down that tiled corridor, her sneakers making little squelching noises on the linoleum floor. Lilli recalled the soft soles of the nurse who had been so nice to her, so many years earlier in Chicago, as she sat, imprisoned and miserable, in that wheelchair, experiencing pain, grief, and shame in about equal portions. Her future was uncertain, but certainly not what she'd dreamed. Everyone who'd passed by seemed to sense Lilli's dark secret and to judge her for it. She'd wanted the pain to stop, not the physical pain so much but the emotional pain, because she didn't believe she could live through it. The nurse had padded up in her stout, sensible shoes, her opaque nylons making swishing sounds, and held Lilli's hand. Charlotte and Graham had gone off to attend to paperwork, and the nurse in her starched white uniform and perky cap, so young and vibrant with her bright red hair and green eyes, had smiled at Lilli, given her hand a squeeze, and said that everything was going to be fine, Lilli wouldn't feel a thing. Lilli had smiled back, wanting to believe it, and knowing it wasn't true.

She'd moved to Chicago in October 1969 and spent the next seven months in a rented room near Charlotte and

Graham, waiting. Lilli had told Bea that she was going out there to study at the Art Institute. She had, in fact, taken a watercolor class there that fall. She bought a small water-color set and little sketchpad, both of which she carried in her handbag. She did some still lifes in her room, and landscapes around the lake. Her instructor was very encouraging.

When the labor pains started, Lilli called Charlotte, and Graham had driven Lilli to the hospital. When the baby was born, they'd left Lilli alone with her for a little while, as they'd agreed. She was nineteen and unmarried and had known all along, of course, what she must do. But Lilli hadn't expected to feel such an attachment to someone she'd known such a short time. Although, really, when she looked into the tiny, scrunched face, it seemed to Lilli that she'd known her forever. Lilli took out her watercolor set, wet her brush in the water pitcher beside her bed, dabbed the brush in the square of red pigment, and then coated one of the pages in her sketchpad a watery pink. Quickly, she pressed the baby's tiny feet onto the damp page, and then carefully wiped clean the ten miniature toes and tiny soft pads, marveling at their perfection. The baby made only a small mewling sound, as though she were aware of the importance of this act to Lilli. Lilli had felt grief when she'd lost her father, her sister, her mother. What she felt giving up her infant daughter was an emotion so profound it defied naming, so awful it deserved to go unnamed.

Lilli still had that sketchpad on a shelf back home in Lon-don, but she had removed the page with the baby's footprints. That she'd carefully folded and carried always in her wallet.

"Lillianne Niles?"

Lilli snapped out of her reverie, or dream. Had she fallen

asleep? The family of four was gone, as were the three girls in the corner and the couple with the tissues, so she must have dozed. It was four o'clock. What day? Lilli panicked a moment, unable to recall. Oh, yes, Thursday. A young man, holding a clipboard, looking faintly annoyed and far too young to be a surgeon, was calling her name again, loudly, as though he were about to give up. "LILLIANNE NILES."

"Yes, here," Lilli said, her voice a croak. She was very thirsty, stiff, eyes burning.

"I'm Dr. Chang," he said, taking a seat beside Lilli. His green scrubs had flecks of something that looked like blood on them. Lilli tried not to stare. No magic swinging doors? No escort down the hall? This couldn't be good. Lilli knew she shouldn't have come back to White Head. Everything she touched, it seemed, ended badly. She braced herself for the news, images of Randall's recent service, the too-tidy funeral parlor spooling through her mind. Would she be family this time, or still guest?

"Ms. Niles?" Dr. Chang was looking at Lilli with concern. "Can I get you something? You look quite pale. Have you been sitting out here the whole time? Have you had anything to eat?"

How did I let this happen, again? Lilli closed her eyes. She tried to avoid too-close contact with people she cared about. She seemed to attract bad luck, or maybe carried it with her. She opened her eyes to find a nurse standing in front of her, more hospital magic, holding a cup of water in one hand and some saltines in the other. Lilli blinked. The nurse was still there. Dr. Chang was holding Lilli's wrist, checking her pulse. Images of her past coming at her now like waves. "Waves always come in three," Lilli said. Who had told her that? "The third is always the biggest." Dori, Blythe, Bea. Was this the third wave? Was it finally over? "I'm truly sorry. I should have left right after the service. But Izzy was coming." Lilli stopped, aware that she was babbling.

Dr. Chang and the nurse were looking at her with concerned, appraising eyes. The nurse opened the package of saltines and offered one to Lilli along with the cup of water.

Lilli, uneasy, veered her thoughts around to the safety of paperwork: autopsy, no; cremation, yes; obituary, Charlotte; find address book for phone numbers; service, perhaps she could use the same hymns and readings they'd used for Randall—*Good heavens, where did we leave Randall's ashes?* She resumed her planning: reception, at the Inn; flowers, big, blowsy bouquets of peonies and snapdragons. The young doctor was saying something, the nurse holding out another cup, this one with purple liquid, grape juice, probably. She tried to pay attention to the doctor's words, but she was suddenly picturing Dori with her little pewter trophy—the one Lilli now used to hold paintbrushes in her kitchen—sipping "wine" at supper that last night, the sparkly paper crown on her head, as Lilli hid behind her huge flower arrangement. Dr. Chang was still speaking, his voice very far away, and his words making no sense. She must pay closer attention. "When you're ready, you can go in," said Dr. Chang. "She's in the recovery room," he was saying. "I'm not sure she's quite awake enough yet to recognize you."

Had Lilli heard correctly? "She's alive?"

"Most definitely." He smiled. "Very much alive. We did a partial hip replacement. She might need a full one someday. There's quite a lot of bone loss. A good deal of arthritis, too. We pinned the ankle, and . . ." He rubbed the bridge of his nose under his glasses. "We'll see how she does over the next few days. Do you happen to know what meds she was taking? We have a list in her chart, but I'm not sure it's up-to-date. She's been prescribed some pretty powerful painkillers."

Lilli shook her head, recalling the brown bottles lined up on the kitchen counter.

"The fact that she's done this well is a good sign. She must be a fighter."

Lilli nodded again, numb, disoriented. Bea was alive. These were unfamiliar and uncharted waters for Lilli. "What happens next?"

"Well, a lot depends on your sister. As I said, there's extensive bone loss, and also pretty severe RA, rheumatoid arthritis, so how well she'll walk after this. . . . Let's just say she won't be doing any more break dancing." He grinned to signal that this was intended as a joke. Lilli managed a wan smile. "She'll be in recovery for another hour or so, then we'll move her to a room. When she's ready for discharge, she'll need two to four weeks of rehab, here or in a private facility. Then it's up to her. Does she live alone?"

Lilli nodded once again, wondered if she should be taking notes.

"Well, sixty-seven's not all that old these days. The sixties are the new forties, right? But you might want to look into some kind of assisted living, just in case. Our social worker can give you some names."

Lilli followed him through the doors, feeling on her back the envious eyes of those left behind in the waiting room, and down the tiled corridor, brightly lit and lined with beds and machines with tubes draped around them, to a curtained alcove of the recovery area. "She's disoriented from the anesthesia," said the nurse perched on a stool at the foot of Bea's bed. In the harsh, artificial light it took a moment for Lilli to recognize Bea. The figure lying there barely made a bulge in the bedclothes, with her thistledown hair in frizzled disarray on the pillowcase, her mouth open, and the blue veins visible beneath her nearly transparent skin. Lilli focused on a speck of dried blood on Bea's earlobe, relieved that she was asleep, as she looked uncharacteristically vulnerable, and Lilli would not have known how to speak to her or what to say.

WHEN LILLI GOT back to her hotel, she ordered a drink from room service. She needed something robust; a vodka tonic would not do. She started the water in the tub and called Geoffrey in London, completely forgetting that it was nearly ten P.M. there. After bringing him up to date on her delayed return to London, she then called Charlotte. She wasn't home, so Lilli left a brief message before she sank into the tub of scalding, scented water with the glass of Johnnie Walker by her side. She tried to silence the "If only Ida's" coursing through her mind. *If only Ida stayed. If only Ida stayed away . . .*

After refreshing the hot water twice, Lilli realized that her light-headedness and stomachache were probably hunger pains, given that she'd missed lunch, so she called room service again and ordered dinner, she didn't care what, "something light." A waiter arrived bearing a small carafe of white wine, grilled trout stuffed with crabmeat and wild mushrooms, a polenta cake, sautéed greens, and a fruit tart, which he set up with a candle, white linen tablecloth, and napkin by the window overlooking the Public Garden. Lilli sat down and, while she ate, watched the ebb and flow of traffic and pedestrians, bustling home from work or heading out to a restaurant or movie, all so purposeful. She pictured Bea asleep in her room, somewhere beyond the scattering of rooftops she could see across the Public Garden. "The trout is delicious, wouldn't you say?" Lilli whispered. She didn't need Bea's presence to know her caustic reply. It all tasted like so much sawdust.

THE NEXT DAY Lilli got a later start than she'd intended. She planned to drive back to White Head and look for the name of Bea's solicitor, collect her bank statements and tax documents, anything that might help her get a handle on Bea's finances, and to see what those pill bottles on the kitchen counter contained. She would stop first to visit Bea but would not mention her plan. Bea would undoubtedly have an issue with Lilli looking through her things, but Lilli was determined to make every possible effort to see Bea moved into Beacon House. She would pay, if necessary. She owed her that.

A beeping monitor above Bea's head provided the only reassurance that she was alive. Her cheeks were sunken, her color waxen. With her hair uncombed and in such uncharacteristic disarray—here and there a bit of dirt or dried foliage caught in it—and plastic tubing snaking into her arm, she looked like something from the underworld. On the table beside her bed was an untouched tray of food, a milk carton, a container of applesauce, and a plate with a heavy, gray plastic cover. Anyone could see that Bea could not sit up and eat it, but orders are orders in hospitals. A nurse was fiddling with the bag of fluid dripping into Bea's arm. Lilli paused in the doorway, holding a vase of irises, daffodils, and tulips. She would have simply left them and slipped away, but the nurse spotted her. "Oh! Aren't those lovely! You have a visitor, Mrs. Marsh," she said in the overloud voice and patronizing tone people tend to use with the sick. "Open your eyes, Mrs. Marsh, and look at the pretty flowers she brought!"

"Oh, don't wake her," Lilli said. "I'll just leave these and come back later."

"Oh, no, no. She's awake. Isn't she?" This she directed at Bea. "She'd love a little company, wouldn't you, Mrs. Marsh? OPEN YOUR EYES."

Bea's eyes startled open, and her gaze reminded Lilli of Blythe's in her final months, looking off into some other dimension—in Blythe's case, searching for the right time to cross over. What was Bea seeking? Family members who'd already made that final journey? Or was she just willing herself away from this loud nurse? Lilli couldn't tell, though it could as easily have been one as the other.

"Bea?"

"Mother?" Bea's voice sounded thin and reedy, as though she were calling into that higher astral plane. Then, again, Lilli thought, it could be the morphine.

"No, it's me, Lilli." She took a step closer to the bed, clutching the bouquet like a plate of armor. "How are you feeling?"

There was a long pause. "I've felt better."

"Are you the sister?" the nurse asked.

"The sister." Guilty as charged. Lilli nodded.

"Your sister here was the one to find you, Mrs. Marsh. Weren't you lucky she did?"

Bea closed her eyes, and Lilli steeled herself for the likely response: *Lucky? She's the one who put me here. Did you know . . . ?*

But Bea remained silent, and the nurse tried to fill the somewhat awkward silence. "I'll come back later and check her dressing," she said.

"No, please," Lilli said. "I just stopped in for a quick visit."

At which point Bea said, so softly the intonation was hard for Lilli to pick up, "Yes. Very lucky."

"I'll come back later, Bea. You get some rest." At this Bea's eyes flickered open and she fixed them on Lilli with a baleful gaze. No guesswork needed to interpret *that* look. *What other choice do I have, you ninny?* Lilli put the flowers on the bedside table, smiled at the nurse, and backed out of the room.

LILLI BEGAN HER search of Bea's medications in the kitchen. She found prednisone, oxycodone, tramadol (expired), and Evista, all with Bea's name on them, and a bottle of Diovan prescribed for Randall. She also found, in the cupboard, half-empty bottles of Motrin and Aleve, as well as fish oil, a multivitamin, and calcium, all unopened. She moved into the den, where she discovered a dozen unopened credit card bills in the top drawer of her father's old desk, and, below these, another dozen, opened, but unpaid. Tucked in a cubby beside several magazine renewal notices was a note from the garden club, politely reminding Bea that her annual membership fee was due. In the second drawer, Lilli found old scrapbooks and photo albums, their covers mildewed, their black pages brittle. She had difficulty opening the bottom drawer because of what turned out to be four jumbo plastic

Ziploc bags pregnant with letters, birthday cards, gradua-tion notices, wedding invitations, birth announcements, and thank-you notes for gifts Bea had sent. There were hundreds of them, dating back years. Many bore Charlotte's signature; one had Izzy's childish scrawl: *Please tell Uncle Randall thank you for the icebote ride. It was realy fun.* Lilli flipped through ten years' worth of Christmas cards, each year bound by a rubber band and an identifying scrap of paper with the year written in Bea's neat hand. An envelope containing strangers' obituaries nested beside a stack of postcards of Lilli's paint-ings, announcements for each of the exhibitions she'd had over the years in cities across the United States. *Where had Bea gotten them all? Why had she saved them?* On the back of one was written: *Our Lilli has done so well for herself!* But it was unsigned, and Lilli didn't recognize the handwriting.

She felt shame for Bea, and, by association, for herself, at all those unpaid bills. She wanted to believe that the accounts had been settled and the old bills left simply because the notion of shredding them was too monumental, a notion Lilli shared. She wanted to believe this so much that she resisted digging any further to see if it was true. Worse, though, than the shame was the pity she felt looking at an entire life zipped neatly into polyethylene and saved in the bottom drawer of a desk. As she gazed at the birth announcements and wedding invitations, at the postcards of her paintings, at a newspaper clipping about Graham's promotion to chair of the depart-ment of surgery, and invitations to Charlotte's numerous award ceremonies, it struck Lilli that it wasn't a retrospective of Bea's life she was viewing, but of the people in Bea's life. Of Bea's life, Lilli found nary a scrap.

After two hours, having unearthed nothing helpful and

grown thoroughly depressed, Lilli sought the sun. The house was cold and dark behind its barricade of foliage, matching her mood. She headed through the living room to a sunny spot in the yard. The red-handled clippers still rested on the sundial, and she briefly considered trimming around the windows to let in more light. But the clippers were no match for the pachyderm-sized junipers and the heavy mantle of wisteria winding its way up to the roof. She could just make out, below the house, between the bittersweet and beach roses, a sliver of the cove and the white triangle of a sail that appeared to be painted on the horizon.

Back inside she left a message for Charlotte to call if she could think of anywhere Bea and Randall might have kept their personal papers, and then, thinking that Bea might like a few items with her in the hospital, went upstairs. The sun shone through the western window, depositing a dappled rectangle of yellow on the faded wallpaper and highlighting a thin film of dust on the mirror over the dressing table. Lilli opened the door of Bea's closet, one that ran deep under the eaves and had offered an ideal spot for hide-and-seek. It was packed with clothes, crushed so closely together that Lilli doubted there was room for even one more item. On the shelf above, a stack of hatboxes stood beside two opaque storage bags, the objects inside pressing shadowy shapes onto the yellowed plastic. A jumble of sneakers with holes in the toes and worn slippers lined the closet floor. A dozen pairs of pumps nested in quilted pockets on the door.

Lilli managed to extract a garment from the jammed rack, lifted the dry cleaner's plastic, and found a fuchsia silk spaghetti-strapped dress, cocktail length, that would have looked smashing on Bea thirty-five years earlier. She was certain that Bea would never wear it again, couldn't imagine why she'd hung on to it, and so she put it on the bed, thinking she'd start a pile of clothes to take to Goodwill, or perhaps a vintage consignment shop, if Bea's finances were as grim as Charlotte suggested. She pawed through, as best she could, the rest of the clothes, finding floor-length gowns, tailored tweed blazers circa 1975, frilly blouses, and skirts in various styles, lengths, and fabrics. Was nothing current? She scanned the shoes. Most were also years out of style. One pair, dyed fuchsia, she placed on the floor below the dress, and then, in a fit of bizarre whimsy that she found hard to explain, decided to search for a suitable hat. She found a close-fitting number of black feathers and jet beads with a short veil in one of the boxes. One of Blythe's; Lilli remembered it well. *Certainly we must have gloves.* She returned to the closet and pulled down one of the storage bags.

The plastic was brittle with age, and the zipper, somewhat corroded, resisted at first, but then stuttered open to reveal twelve tightly rolled balls of yarn in blue, yellow, red, green, white, pink, and brown. Lilli recognized it instantly. Dori's spiderweb. Too curious to resist, Lilli pulled out the second zippered storage bag and opened it. A girl's green shorts, neatly folded, a few blouses, a beige sweater, and a red dress with white piping that Lilli remembered Dori getting for school at Simmons Department Store the September she died. Bea had bought Lilli an identical one in navy. Farther down she found Dori's favorite flowered pajamas, worn and washed so often the flannel was little more than gauze. Lilli lowered herself to sit among the sneakers and slippers on the closet floor, held the soft bundle to her face, and inhaled. Mothballs, yes, but also, faintly, the Tabu perfume their mother wore and, under that, salt air, freshly cut grass, and lilac bubble bath. They would often sneak outside after bath time to spy on the grown-ups having cookouts on the rocks.

No one had spoken of Dori's death after it happened. Not to Lilli, at least. There were a few questions from the police, at first, about the accident, and then . . . silence. That silence was harder to endure than questions, many of which Lilli couldn't have answered but would have liked to try. She could have borne, would have welcomed tears, rage, accusations. What she couldn't bear was the ghastly silence. Because her family hadn't spoken of it, neither had she. She'd tucked the memories away in the recesses of her mind, tucked them, as Bea—or maybe Blythe—had done with Dori's clothes, waiting, waiting. For what?

Compelled by a force she did not understand, she walked down the hall to her old bedroom and opened the closet door. The rack was hung with dresses, slacks, blouses. She didn't need to look through them to know that most were hers. She opened the drawers in the little painted bureau. Some were empty—cleared, perhaps for Izzy's visit, or even Lilli's return. One contained spare pillowcases. But in one drawer, neatly folded, were shirts Lilli had left when she packed her suitcase after learning of Bea and Randall's marriage, and then again the night of Charlotte's wedding, half-crazed with grief (and still a little drunk) and swearing she'd never be back. She hadn't, at eighteen, dreamed how long never is. She lifted out a pink-striped camp shirt, a white halter top, a navy blue sweater with a rolled collar that Bea had knit for her. She'd loved that sweater but had left it out of spite. Now she sat down on the narrow twin bed, holding it. Although it was only late afternoon she was tired, so she stretched out on the chenille spread and slept.

SHE AWOKE SEVERAL hours later, stiff and disoriented, and lay for a moment, gazing up at the widened Niles River snaking its way across the ceiling, trying to decide what to do. She felt drawn by the sort of morbid curiosity of an onlooker at a roadside accident to see what else was hiding in the shadowy corners of this house, lurking deep in closets far under the eaves, or waiting behind closed doors. Only a few days earlier, she had been reluctant even to walk into the strangely familiar kitchen; now she wanted to turn the house inside out, exposing it all to daylight.

She called the hospital and rattled off the list of medications she'd found, including Randall's. Was it possible, Lilli had asked the doctor, that Bea had taken too many pills, or the wrong ones, given her failing eyesight? The doctor said it was certainly possible and informed Lilli that Bea had resisted all attempts at physical therapy. "If that continues," the doctor warned, "she'll go downhill, fast." Lilli wasn't sure what to say, or how, or even whether she could help. She pictured her sister languishing in a slow demise of bedsores, as her ligaments and tendons slowly broke down, her bones dissolved, and her muscles atrophied, her mind becoming more addled each day from the drugs.

Lilli gave herself a pinch. This house seemed to bring out a dark side she didn't care for. She pulled an old jacket from the front hall closet, certain that it still held the faint smell of Uncle Parker's pipe tobacco, and headed out to her car. It was almost seven and still light, the sky tinted pink and orange.

She drove into town, noticing more of the houses that used to belong to old friends, their names forgotten. She picked up some smoked salmon, crackers, and a bottle of San Pellegrino at S.S. Pierce, as she was now calling it, and headed down to the yacht club. Ned Chapin, as she'd guessed he would be, was leaning against the railing, with a small wicker basket by his side. He was eating an ice cream cone.

"Is that dinner or dessert?" Lilli asked.

He turned, startled, and then beamed. "I thought you were leaving us."

Lilli told him about Bea.

"I'm so sorry. I hadn't heard. That's unusual for this town."

They leaned against the railing, gazing out across the harbor, the sky coloring more intensely by the minute.

"Watching a sunset looking east," Lilli noted, "is like watching a play from backstage."

Ned chuckled. "I like being behind the scenes. Always have. My wife and I used to vacation in Naples, Florida. Sunsets are quite an event there. One of the men in our building played taps on his bugle from his balcony, and we'd gather around the pool with our drinks and toast the last bit of sun as it slipped into the gulf. Tell you the truth, that always seemed rather sad to me. Here, I can watch the sky grow from pink to coral to deep, deep red, and never know the precise moment when day becomes night. But sunrises, now those are something to celebrate, and we have the perfect spot from our point. But, then, so did you."

"I'm famished," Lilli blurted out.

Ned reached into his basket and pulled out a wedge of Brie, a pear, some grapes, and a box of wafers. "The ice cream was dessert. Sometimes . . ." He trailed off. "I hope I remembered a knife." He rummaged further and pulled out a cheese knife, along with a folded bit of newspaper, yellowed and worn. "Here, I found this in an old scrapbook. I didn't know . . ." He handed it to Lilli.

She unfolded it and below a photograph of a smiling Bea Niles and Randall Marsh, read the caption, *"Sailing Couple Tie the Knot."* She'd seen it, of course, but not for many years.

"My wife tended to save things. I thought Bea might like to have it."

"Thank you," Lilli said, thinking both of Randall's ashes, still on the backseat of Bea's car, and the cubic yards of memorabilia in Bea's desk drawers. "I'm sure she'll treasure it."

"Please stop me if I'm crossing the line ahead of the starting gun, but why did you leave so suddenly and not come back? Was it this?" He gestured to the newspaper clipping. "You went to Chicago, wasn't it?"

Lilli topped a cracker with some cheese and popped it in her mouth, to avoid answering right away. "Yes, briefly. Charlotte and Graham were there, the Art Institute . . ." She trailed off, hoping this would be sufficient. There were many reasons she'd left: Dori's and Blythe's deaths, Randall and Bea's marriage, the night in the greenhouse at Charlotte's wedding . . . it was difficult to separate them, each connected to the next; impossible to know, as with the waves washing around the yacht club pilings beneath them, where one ended and the next began.

Each, in itself, had been reason enough to leave. But the baby had been the reason she'd stayed away. She'd hoped that with Randall gone, she could come back and tell Bea, put things right. She still wasn't sure how she would have done that, what it would have taken, or what "right" might even have looked like. She only knew that she'd carried a tremendous burden around with her all these years and that even the terrible price she'd paid hadn't been high enough to release her from it. Coming back, she'd hoped she could start over, the way she'd begin a new oil painting on a fresh canvas. She'd found, though, that the canvas in this case was an old one, gessoed over, and the colors beneath had begun to bleed through. As she stood in the waning light, trying to decide how or whether to respond more fully to Ned, thinking over her findings of the afternoon, she could see not only patches of color emerging on this imaginary canvas, but a whole picture. A landscape she hadn't cared for, the colors too dark, the proportion all wrong, and all of it too far gone to fix. She reached for another cracker and gestured toward the horizon. "Quite a show we put on tonight, wouldn't you say?"

Ned studied her a moment, seemed about to speak, but then turned to admire the deep red afterglow. "I'd say we outdid ourselves."

THEY LINGERED ON the deck outside the yacht club until the color had faded and the sky turned a pearly gray. They'd finished the Brie, the crackers, the salmon, and the fruit and swapped stories from their youth. Lilli noted with embarrassment that Ned was often missing in her retelling of events at which he had obviously been present; in many cases, he'd even spoken to or danced with her. In spite of that, by the time they said good night, Lilli had achieved a feeling of contentment, which lasted until she pulled up Bea's drive and saw the dark windows of the house and the old Mercedes in the garage. She'd come back to lock up and pick up a few items for Bea before driving to Boston, where she looked forward to sinking into the marble tub in her hotel bathroom and savoring the square of dark chocolate that would be waiting for her on the pillow of her turned-down bed. She hoisted herself from the car, crunched across the gravel drive, and retrieved Randall's ashes from the backseat of the Mercedes, intending to put them somewhere inside for now. God knew what she ought to do with them for eternity. One more thing to settle.

But when she opened the kitchen door, setting the dog leash jangling, noticing, again, but from a different point of view, the plastic laundry basket lined with Randall's socks that sat beneath the coats in the back hall, she sensed something beckoning her, something seeking her attention, something she'd left undone. She carried Randall's ashes through the kitchen and into the den and set them on the desk. She lingered a moment, her hand resting on the box, their first intimate moment since 1969. *Was that it? The thing she'd left undone?* She listened. No, the house was pulling her farther in. She wasn't finished yet.

Lilli closed her eyes. She heard the hum of electricity, the mechanical ticktock of a clock (an hour slow, she'd noted earlier), the scurry of tiny feet in the wall, a creak as the house contracted with the dampening air. *Perhaps the house is tired*, Lilli thought. Perhaps it wanted to be done, wanted to allow the wisteria to take charge, as the determined vine seemed likely to do if left unchecked. She listened. No, the house was conveying something else. Lilli heard another creak, the rat-tat-tat of a branch against a windowpane, smelled the musty odor of old books, the faint fragrance of Uncle Parker's pipe tobacco emanating from the jacket she wore, and then—was she imagining it?—the sweet, buttery smell of pancakes. *Is that it?* Was the house longing to be filled again with the sound of children's laughter as they made their way around its interior, clambering over tables, chairs, and mantels to avoid touching the floor; hungering for the robust smell of roasting turkey and simmering cranberries; wanting once more the warmth and crackle of fires on its cold hearths; asking to be caressed?

She opened her eyes and ran her hand along a bookshelf, finding it surprisingly dust-free; straightened a few volumes, plumped the cushions in the sagging armchair, trailed her fingers along the wall as she went through the living room, turning on more lights. She was smiling now. She climbed the stairs, sweeping her palm along the wallpaper, coarse and dry beneath her fingertips. The faded cabbage roses seemed to perk up a bit beneath her touch. As she walked down the hall, she opened doors, turned on lights, tugged open windows stiff with disuse.

She ran hot water into the tub, watching steam rise into the air, found bath salts, and poured them in so the room filled with the scent of lily of the valley. As she perched on the edge of the tub, stirring the fragrant water with her hand, she pictured two red-faced girls who'd stayed too long at the beach, soaking in this very tub, shrieking with startled pain and delight, and Bea, calling through the door. "Are you girls all right in there?" She turned off the water and polished the steam away with a washcloth embroidered with her initials. And as she stared at her reflection, she wondered where that innocent, red-cheeked girl had gone.

She walked down the hall, pressing a hand against the wall on either side—she and Dori used to inch along that way: hand-foot, hand-foot, adventurers scaling Mt. Everest. She felt a spasm of joy rise and bubble into laughter. In Bea's bedroom, moonlight streamed in, replacing the earlier shaft of sun. She flicked on the bedside light. The bright fuchsia dress lay across the bed, the jaunty feathered hat above it, and the matching shoes beneath, as though someone young and vibrant, full of hope and eager anticipation, had been getting ready for an evening out. Lilli understood at once that this was what she'd left undone, this was what the house had beckoned her to complete. She moved to the dressing table.

"Pearl studs or gold hoops?" she asked aloud, sifting through a jumble of earrings in a white cardboard box on the dressing table. She found a pair of gold love knots that would look perfect. She set them on the bed near the hat. Still not finished.

"A necklace?" She slid open the top drawer, finding a battalion of small velvet, leather, and cardboard boxes. She selected one of gray velvet and released its catch. The top sprang open to reveal . . . baby teeth. This discovery made Lilli somewhat less eager to open the next. *It's late, Lilli*, she thought to herself, *go back to Boston*. But she reached for the red leather box, opened it, found locks of hair: blond and dark, each secured with a rusted hair clip. Her playful mood now becalmed, she wished only to be away from this house, safe in the marble sanctity of her hotel. She tried to shut the drawer, but it caught on something at the back. She slid the layer of small boxes aside and peered in, spied a brown leather jewelry case. She cleared a path and slid it out, set it on the dressing table, and lifted the lid.

On top, a tray held rings set with onyx, moonstone, and topaz; enamel clip-on earrings; and a bangle bracelet in pink gold that was so small Lilli couldn't get it past her knuckles. Brooches and cameos dangled loosely from the lid's worn satin lining. Lilli remembered her mother wearing some of these items when she appeared, unexpectedly, in an evening gown at the dinner table. Occasionally she would anchor one of her scarves with a brooch.

Lilli lifted the velvet-covered tray with its cargo of rings and bracelets and there, coiled into a tight circle, lay the sapphire-and-diamond necklace that Lilli had worn at Charlotte's wedding. It had come off in the greenhouse that night with Randall, but she hadn't noticed until she was in her room, gazing at her tear-stained face in the mirror, wondering what she'd done and what she would do next. She'd always wondered what had become of it. She fingered it a moment before carrying it over to the bed and arranging it above the neckline of the silk fuchsia dress. Who had found it? Bea? Why keep it hidden here? Or did it only seem to be hiding?

She hurried back down the hall, turning off lights and closing windows and doors, feeling no longer liberator but intruder, needing to put things back right and escape. The voices that had beckoned her into the house now seemed to whisper accusations, the dust-filled corners and dark recesses of closets no longer harboring innocent childhood memories but old skeletons, pointing long accusatory fingers. In the bathroom, she released the now-cool water from the tub, turned, and caught her reflection in the mirror, half-expecting to see the tear-stained face of an eighteen-year-old girl gazing back. But no, she saw only her own tired, grown-up self. She stared. The face in the mirror smiled. Lilli blinked. The voices in the house had stilled. Lilli gazed deep into those eyes gazing back at her from the mirror, hoping for revelation. "I can't stay," she said.

"You think you can stay away?" the woman in the mirror replied.

A new toothbrush stood in a tarnished silver cup on the sink rim. Lilli brushed her teeth, keeping her eyes fixed on those in the mirror, liberator or prisoner, she still wasn't sure. Then she washed her face with the worn, monogrammed washcloth and dried it with an equally worn, but clean and neatly folded towel—no doubt both recently humped up stairs in the laundry basket—and went to her old room. There she undressed and slipped between cool sheets on the stiff, lumpy mattress, certain she would get no sleep. "Good night, Dori," she whispered, and wondered if Blythe would visit in the night.

THE following morning, after a restless night, Lilli made a pot of strong coffee, filtered through a square of decorative paper towel. She considered making a bowl of commemorative oatmeal, but, as there was no milk, she settled for toast and jam. Charlotte had left a message on her cell phone, saying that she recalled an old file cabinet in the basement where Lilli might find some of Bea's papers.

The shiny washer and dryer stood at the bottom of the basement stairs like hostages in a junk shop. Against a far wall, barricaded behind bicycles, golf clubs, and wooden skis, was the metal file cabinet. Lilli made her slow way through the broken lamps and appliances, three-legged chairs, slow cookers, aluminum ice trays, stained linen, broken-handled mops, sleds, skates, and rakes with missing tines. She felt like a condemned woman on her final walk, forced to review the rummage of her life. A brownish-yellow glow emanated from the crusty window wells where every spring Dori and Lilli used to find and liberate tiny frogs from thickets of damp leaves. Dust-blanketed cobwebs sagged from the ceiling.

The file cabinet, once she reached it, offered only five-year-old bank statements, Dori's and Bea's birth certificates, her parents' death certificates, Randall's draft card, Bea and Randall's marriage license, their old passports, and an expired term life insurance policy. Lilli began to worry that Bea and Randall had done no estate planning, and that Charlotte's dour assessment of Bea's financial situation might not be dour enough. Just what this meant, Lilli wasn't sure. She perched on a vinyl-upholstered stool beside the file cabinet and tried to think what to do. Nothing came. She took a sip of coffee and lifted the lid on a water-stained cardboard box: mildewed *National Geographic*s.

As she started making her way back through this residue of her childhood, she spied three wicker hampers set on top of each other. She rested her coffee cup on a rusty chest freezer and opened the uppermost one. There, beneath a cloud of camphor, lay old scarves, socks, mittens, and hats, including her balaclava, her stocking cap, and the red beret. This she put on, sneezed, and promptly removed. She placed the top hamper on a nearby steamer trunk that had once belonged to their grandmother and opened the second hamper to find several moth-eaten cloth napkins, a few pieces of tarnished flatware, and two metal tins containing dry brownie crumbs and a few scraps of wax paper. She didn't open the third hamper, only moved it aside, knowing already that it contained picnic blankets. She wanted what lay beneath: the green-paint-splotched enamel table that her mother had used for a palette when painting the ivy on the kitchen walls.

Lilli ran her fingers over the stippled, uneven surface, remembering how she'd watched with fascination as her mother squeezed out the yellow and blue worms of paint from the crinkly metal tubes onto this table, which had stood under the north-facing kitchen window. She would mash the colors with a small palette knife and dab the resulting green goo onto the wall with her brush, adjusting the color to make one leaf more yellow, another, darker green. Blythe would let Lilli mix her own bit of paint on a corner of the table and make tiny leaves—just as she had, on occasion, let the girls dip teaspoons into the pancake batter and cook their own miniature pancakes in the shape of Mickey Mouse. Lilli allowed herself a moment to grieve, something she hadn't done in the days, weeks, months, and then years following her mother's death. Although Blythe had died suddenly, she had left them slowly, the distance between her and her children growing for months, almost imperceptibly, like a boat sailing directly away. Only when the gulf between is very wide do you realize in which direction the boat has been moving.

On the basement floor, beneath the table, was a stout wooden box. Her mother's old paints. Lilli carried it upstairs, thinking she might clean and oil it and take it back with her to London. The mere thought of London brought her great cheer. Having exhumed more of her childhood than she'd intended or cared to, and having found nothing of help regarding Bea's finances, Lilli decided to head to Boston after stopping at the hospital on the way. Perhaps Bea would be awake, lucid, and agreeable enough to provide Lilli with some information. She retrieved the small overnight bag that she'd packed for Bea, grabbed her purse and keys, and left, stopping at S.S. Pierce on the way to buy a turkey sandwich without mayonnaise.

* * *

BEA'S EYES WERE closed when Lilli arrived, and she looked wan and lifeless. The monitor above the bed displayed her temperature and pulse and occasionally beeped out her blood pressure. "Bea?" she ventured softly. Bea's eyes fluttered open, and Lilli could see that her focus was even more distant than it had been the day before. She seemed now to be looking right through that dividing veil, deep into the world on the other side. Lilli longed to know who she saw there. "It's Lilli. How are you?"

Bea didn't respond, and Lilli opened her mouth to repeat her question, when Bea said, "I wish people would stop asking me that. How do you suppose I am?" She shifted and uttered a light moan. "What time is it?"

Lilli set the overnight bag on the chair and sat at the end of the bed. "About noon. On Saturday."

Bea's eyes landed on the vase of flowers Lilli had brought the day before. "Mother was here. She brought me those."

Lilli thought that between the painkillers and the head injury, it was very likely that Bea had seen Blythe, and let it pass. "Are you hungry?" She unwrapped the turkey sandwich, put it on the tray table, and rolled it closer to Bea. She went to raise the head of the bed when she noticed that Bea's hands were tied with strips of gauze to the bed rail. Blinking back unexpected tears, Lilli fumbled as she untied the knots, noting that Bea's skin was heavily bruised and as delicate as tissue. "There, that better?" Lilli offered her half a sandwich.

"Not hungry." Bea turned her head away. "When can I go home?"

"You need to eat. It's from S.S. Pierce." Lilli took a seat in the chair next to the bed. "They tell me you're not doing your physical therapy."

Bea sniffed. "Incompetents." She glanced at the sandwich. "What kind?"

"Turkey. With no mayo."

Bea hesitated. "Maybe just one bite." She bit off one corner. "Today I would have preferred mayonnaise. They practically starve you in here." She shifted to get a better angle and winced. "Don't know what's happened to my hips. Must be a front moving in."

"Do you remember falling?"

"Falling?" Bea's focus shifted, and Lilli pictured Bea's mind fighting its way down internal corridors, befuddled by painkillers, searching for the lost memory. "Well, of course I remember. A person doesn't forget a thing like that." Her expression, a mixture of childlike helplessness, fear, and false bravado, made it clear to Lilli that she had no memory of it at all. "I was . . ."

"In the greenhouse," Lilli prompted gently. Bea's trademark pride now seemed as brittle as the delicate rose-patterned china, her memory as porous as her bones.

"Yes. Yes," The second *yes* was more forceful, as some interior vista cleared and a memory popped into view. "Some damn fool—probably Randall—put all the pots up on the bench. Sometimes that boy just doesn't use his head. I have a sister like that." Bea chewed for a moment, swallowed. "When was that?"

"A few days ago. Wednesday, probably. Maybe Thursday morning."

"Well, which was it?"

"We're not quite sure."

"'*We're* not,' eh? Well, how do you expect *me* to be?" She took another bite of her sandwich, chewed meditatively, swallowed loudly. "This is Saturday, you say?"

Lilli nodded, not trusting herself to speak.

"Where have you been all this time? Why didn't you come see us?"

Lilli wasn't sure what "time" Bea was referring to, or who "us" was, so she opened the overnight bag and said, "At the house. I did come. Yesterday. And brought you those." She pointed to the flowers.

Bea wiped her mouth with the bedsheet. "Ah, so now you're staying there. I wondered what it would take." She squinted as she reached for the second half of her sandwich. "Are they from the garden?"

"I thought you might like these." Lilli held out a pair of glasses.

"I suppose you brought all my mail, too."

"Just a few gardening catalogs." Lilli slipped the glasses onto Bea's nose, balancing them on the oxygen tubing draped over her ears.

"Did you make this? It's quite good." Bea indicated her remaining bit of sandwich. "I don't suppose you happened to remember anything to drink?"

Lilli took a can of ginger ale from the grocery bag, opened it, inserted a straw, and handed it to Bea. "Are you warm enough?"

"I'm fine." Bea shrugged. "Well, maybe a little cold." She pointed to a cotton blanket at the foot of the bed. "But leave my arms free."

Lilli pulled the blanket up over Bea's lap, then sat back down in the chair and took the small cardboard box from the overnight bag, weighing when, whether, what, and how to say all that hung between them. She wondered if the time for repair had passed. If Bea remained inactive, her mind could recede permanently, and the next time Lilli came to visit she would be a complete stranger. Or Bea could die suddenly in the night of a blood clot. The doctor had said that was possible.

Lilli lifted the sapphire-and-diamond necklace from its nest of cotton batting, slid the tray table to one side, and draped the necklace on Bea's blanketed knee. It flashed and gleamed in the harsh light.

Bea hesitated for a moment before picking it up and examining it, as if there were some question about whose sapphire-and-diamond necklace it was. She set it back down. The room was silent except for the slight whir above Bea's bed as the machine took her blood pressure: slightly elevated now. "A bit formal for this outfit, don't you think?" Bea kept her eyes lowered. Her expression revealed nothing about what she might be thinking or feeling. "I found it in the greenhouse. Years ago."

"Any idea how it got there?" Lilli prompted, both wanting and not wanting to know what Bea knew. She felt as if she were back in that dinghy with Dori, hearing the swish of surf, knowing that one wrong stroke of the oar could send the boat onto the rocks, but unable to stop rowing.

"I suspect Izzy dropped it."

"Izzy?" This caught Lilli off guard. She shipped her oars and waited.

Bea lifted her gaze from the necklace to Lilli, who was reminded how quickly the color of her sister's eyes could shift from cornflower to that blue of the innermost, hottest part of a flame. "Charlotte brought her to visit one summer when she was little. About ten years old, I should think. It was a shame that you couldn't join us." Her tone was even, but her gaze seemed to challenge Lilli, to dare her to speak. Lilli remained silent, watchful. "You might recall that I invited you?" Bea dropped her focus to the necklace, the contest over. "Izzy would dig around in my closet and dresser and come clomping down the stairs in a pair of my—usually favorite— shoes." She sneaked a glance at Lilli and then fingered the necklace. "What is it about little girls that makes them want to borrow other people's things?"

Lilli assumed this was rhetorical and didn't respond.

"She'd be wearing one of my old evening gowns, swathed in scarves and dripping with beads, gloves on her hands, and an old hat, feathered and veiled, perched on her head. She likely had this necklace on once and never realized that she dropped it. Probably had no idea how valuable it was—what she'd lost." Bea looked up as though to say, *Your move.*

Lilli's heart was pounding as it had when she'd climbed into that leaky dinghy with Bea several days earlier for their failed attempt to sprinkle Randall's ashes. *If they hooked me up to that monitor, it would probably explode.* She waited a moment to steady her voice. "Maybe she knew, but was afraid to tell you."

"Could be." Bea was nodding, her gaze still on Lilli. "Very likely. Which would be a shame, really. It's not healthy to keep secrets. They're not like wishes, you know. If you tell wishes they often don't come true, but it's best to share secrets. When they're your own, of course. Not when they're someone else's."

Bea closed her eyes, and Lilli took it as a signal that the conversation was over. She didn't entirely believe Bea, and there was more Lilli wanted to discuss. More, she was certain, that Bea knew. But Bea looked pale and defeated in her faded hospital gown, in that sterile room, with tubes and wires connecting her to high-tech equipment—this sister who didn't own, and disliked even speaking into, an answering machine and whose appliances were at least thirty years old. So Lilli stayed silent.

Was it cowardice or compassion? Lilli knew well that "saying nothing" was illusory, just as leaving a place was not the same as never having been there. Silence was a position. Silent or not, one was equally complicit in the outcome. She took the necklace from Bea's blanketed knee and put it back in the box, closed the lid, and slipped it into her purse. "I'll just put it back in your dressing table, shall I?"

With her eyes still closed, Bea said, "Do what you want. It never suited me, and I certainly have nowhere to wear it now." Soon her breathing assumed the uneven, burbly sounds of someone sleeping—reminding Lilli that she and Dori had fooled no one with their perfect pretend sleep.

Lilli left the hospital—after mentioning to the nurse that Mrs. Marsh had eaten a sandwich and would probably eat a bowl of strawberry ice cream, remembering the three pints in Bea's freezer, if someone brought her one. This elicited raised eyebrows and a comment that one should never underestimate the power of a sister's love, to which Lilli could only give a wry smile and agree that that was certainly something one should never do. Then she walked over to the Grummage Gallery, where she learned that Felicity had sold two of her paintings. She promised to have Geoffrey ship over several more.

Lilli decided to postpone her return to London until Bea was in rehabilitation. Geoffrey had the London gallery well in hand and, she reasoned, it would give her a chance to learn more about the Grummage Gallery. She would return to White Head the next day, she decided, and see what other secrets might lie moldering within the decaying detritus of her childhood. Besides, she needed to begin readying the house for sale, as it now seemed certain that Bea would never go home.

She made a circuit of the gallery, studying her work, which all seemed a bit flat to her, static and safe. She decided to paint the house and gardens in White Head as they had been in her childhood, to capture and hold them before the house was sold and lost to her forever. An oil painting, she decided, a medium she rarely worked in. Oil paintings required too much commitment. Once you were in one you had to stay in. Watercolors that go wrong are more easily discarded. Lilli would take the painting home to London, or perhaps Bea might like it in her new home. Felicity directed Lilli to an art supply store, where she ordered a pad, a canvas, paints, brushes, and an easel before returning to her room at the hotel. It had been only about twenty-four hours since she was last there, but it felt like weeks. She was seized with nostalgia at the sight of her nightgown hanging on the back of the bathroom door, her papers on the desk, her book on the bedside table. Like encountering old friends at an unexpected time and place. Lilli lowered the shades. She would visit Bea again in the afternoon, but now she needed a little time to recover from the jet lag of moving too quickly between decades.

THE SUN WAS shining the next day as Lilli pulled into the drive, and the house seemed . . . happy to see her. In the back hall, she grabbed the laundry basket and carried it upstairs to Randall's bedroom, which had once been Charlotte's. She opened the top drawer of his dresser and found the little rowboat that he had carved for her, nestled among the socks. Lilli removed it and sat on the edge of his bed, holding it in her palm as she gazed around—at the comb and brush on the dresser, the striped tie slung over the back of a chair, the stack of books beside the bed. A quahog shell, holding a dollar or so of loose change, stood on the dresser beside a few photographs, including one of Lilli. She couldn't have been more than sixteen or seventeen. Her face was lit with laughter, and she was pointing to something beyond the range of the camera. She stood and gently placed the little rowboat beside it, and then left the room, closing the door behind her.

FIVE DAYS LATER, Bea was discharged to the South Shore Rehabilitation Hospital for two to four weeks of physical therapy. From there, according to the rheumatologist, she could either go home with someone to look after her—pending a visit from Sterling Vista Home Care, who would determine what modifications the house needed—or to an independent or assisted-living facility, depending on how much progress she made and her condition at discharge. Lilli wouldn't bother asking Sterling Vista to make a house call. Bea would not tolerate a stranger in her home, "peeking in closets, and putting things away so I can't find them." She'd made this clear when the rheumatologist had offered her prognosis. Lilli resisted, barely, reminding Bea that she couldn't find things now. The doctor had also informed Lilli that Bea had dangerously high levels of oxycodone in her blood, which probably had given rise to some of her symptoms, such as dizziness,

memory lapses, tinnitus, and confusion. She also had cataracts and might want to consider surgery for those. The doctor recommended tapering her off the prednisone and trying
a different drug. Bea's nutrition needed attention, too.

Lilli began moving items from the house, shifting them
from hall closet to hallway, from basement to garage, and
from garage to a strangely weed-free and perfectly rectangu-
lar space behind it. During her first week she made multiple
sketches for her painting but did not apply even one dab of oil
to canvas. She brought up the white enameled table to use as
her palette, stationed it under the north-facing window in the
kitchen, and deposited blobs of carmine, vermilion, ochre,
and burnt umber on the once-perfect sea of cobalt and virid-
ian. She mashed them together and still she couldn't begin.
She felt as though she were in irons, headed directly into the
wind, sails snapping, and sheets flopping about on deck. All
sound and motion, and none of it forward-moving.

Lilli visited Bea daily, even though she disliked the low
brick building that housed the rehabilitation hospital. It
looked unloved and unsuited for its purpose. Reminded her
of an elementary school when all the children were on vacation. Someone had made a halfhearted attempt to create a
homelike atmosphere inside, with a hooked rug in the waiting area and crocheted afghans lining the backs of the sofa
and chairs. Lilli wondered if the inmates—for this is how
Bea referred to them—had made them in occupational therapy. The whole place smelled like fresh bandages and tapi-
oca. Often, while Lilli was there, one of the inmates would
make her way down the corridor behind a walker: two tiny
steps and a small, uneven lurch of the walker, two more tentative steps and another feeble push, a health care worker or

family member idling alongside, trying to look encouraging, a phony smile pasted on her face, her eyes telling the real story. She would glance at Lilli, seeking an ally. Lilli always looked away. She vowed that she would never make that long trek to nowhere at Bea's side. That was unlikely, in any event; the nurse had told Lilli that Bea, in her first week, had balked at physical therapy and barely touched her food. If this continued, she could end up bedridden in a nursing home.

Lilli usually brought a book to read aloud, something to focus on besides Bea's nearly translucent skin and vacant stare and her gnarled knuckles as she pleated and unpleated her white cotton blanket. One day they played bingo on cards provided by a volunteer, a voice calling out the numbers over the intercom.

"Fourteen, Bea," Lilli said. "You have a fourteen. Mark it off. That's bingo." Bea's card lay untouched on her lap. She looked up, startled, and stared at Lilli—or through her, Lilli still was never quite sure who or what Bea was seeing—but she made no mark on her card with the fat crayon, also provided by the pink-smocked volunteer. "Don't you want to win, Bea?"

Bea spoke little these days. She smiled at appropriate moments to convey that she was paying attention, her genteel upbringing not allowing her to do otherwise, but she never initiated conversation. She dropped her gaze to the number-covered square of paper in her lap. Watching her, Lilli suddenly saw how pathetic her situation was. Perhaps she could get Bea a little window garden, or a color-by-numbers set; she had no idea what Bea had done for relaxation before the accident, besides watch television.

"Life's a journey, Lilli, not a race." Bea's voice was low, as though she had said this many times before and was tired of repeating it. Lilli looked down at her own bingo card, definitely not a winner, and then back at Bea. This sister who had made everything in life a competition was giving up.

BACK AT THE house that afternoon, the telephone rang as Lilli was sorting through papers at the desk, mostly just shifting them from one pile to another, not making any real headway. Lilli had few callers, fewer still on the landline, and the loud jangling startled her.

"Aunt Lilli?" came the voice on the other end. "Mom wants me to have it in California, and Dad's being no help. Could you talk with her?"

"Izzy?" The poor thing sounded distraught.

"Yes. Sorry. It makes no sense for anyone. Except her, I suppose."

"Who?" Lilli was trying to make sense out of what Izzy was saying. "Are you talking about the wedding?" Lilli had put it completely out of her mind, assuming that it had been postponed, as her life has been. It was startling to think that the world had been churning along out there beyond the borders of White Head and the South Shore Rehabilitation Hospital, projects being completed, tasks on lists getting checked off. "And you want a small ceremony in Chicago?"

"Yyyeeessss," Izzy replied, dragging out the word, suggesting that was not in the least what she wanted. "Ah. I did. I was thinking, wondering, if we could still do the wedding in White Head. At the White Head Inn," she added quickly. "Once Auntie E is . . . more mobile. She seemed so much to want to be involved. I'd hate to have it somewhere where she couldn't even attend."

Lilli doodled on the blotter, which was marbled with coffee rings, undecipherable half-messages—*Belknap's 6 pm, Bartlett on vacation 8/15–8/22, call Franny*—and faded telephone numbers that she'd been tempted all week to call just to see if anyone would answer. "What about Charlotte's knees? Wouldn't coming all this way be hard for her?"

"Oh, don't you start, Aunt Lilli. You're my only hope. Everyone thinks this is crazy, but I thought maybe it would give Auntie E something to push for. Mom told me that you said she wasn't doing well. Maybe she just needs a good reason to get up and get better. Mom's knees will be fine, by the way. She says she'll be playing tennis again by fall. What do you say? Mom loves White Head. She'll come around."

Lilli stared around the den at the hundreds of old books lining the shelves, having not yet found the strength or time to box them up and ship them off to the library or a used-book store. It unsettled her to think of someone doing that to *her* books, her cookware and paint supplies, while she languished in a hospital. Her gaze landed on the black box containing Randall's ashes, still nestled between the complete set of *Arabian Nights* and a book on antique airplanes.

"You wouldn't have to do any work. I know you've got your hands full with the house and Auntie E and the new gallery. You haven't sold it yet, have you?"

"The gallery?"

"The house."

"Good heavens, Isadora, it's only been two weeks!"

"Right. I'll do all the arrangements and come east a week

or so before the wedding. Mom, too. Maybe we could even help you some, you know . . . clean stuff out?"

"Hm." Lilli didn't know why she was stalling. She would not refuse Izzy. Or miss spending time with her. Lilli now understood that even with Randall gone, nothing could change between them. Certainly not the past. She'd agreed to surrender her completely. It was best for Izzy. Charlotte had insisted. For Lilli, it had been, all these years, like skating across an interminable, uneven, and uncertain surface of a frozen lake, and that would continue. She wrote *Izzy's wedding* on the blotter. But she was being offered an opportunity to be part of this important event. Bea had also offered her this, she realized, but she hadn't recognized it for what it was. "I could call the inn for you and see—"

"No. You don't have to do a thing. I already called, you know, just to see if this was even possible? And they had a cancellation for the first Saturday in August."

"August." Lilli had hoped to see Bea rehabilitated and installed somewhere—she still hoped Beacon House, but Bea would have to be able to get out of bed unassisted and walk a bit by herself—by mid-June, the first of July at the latest, and herself back in London shortly thereafter. Perhaps this would give Bea the incentive Lilli had been unable to provide. "I thought you and Matumbé were thinking of sooner than that."

"Before I forget, I'd like to wear Mom's wedding dress. She wonders if it's still in a trunk in the attic. Could you check? It's the *only* favor I'll ask. I *promise*."

If the dress wasn't there, it would be the only thing Bea had not saved in the past sixty years, Lilli thought. "It might not be in very good shape. We have mice. And you'd have to take it in quite a bit. Charlotte was . . . large-boned."

"Mm," Izzy said.

THE NEXT DAY, as Lilli was in her old room, tucking some newly purchased items from Saks and Ann Taylor into the drawers beside her old camp shirts and halter tops, Ned Chapin called and invited her over for lunch. The day was sunny, with a warm gentle breeze, so Lilli decided to walk.

The Chapins lived in White Head's oldest house. It was said to have been built by a shipwright; the gray clapboard was perched out on the point like a ship that had fetched up on the rocks. Ned greeted Lilli at the door and led her through low-ceilinged, compact rooms with fresh paint on plaster walls and cheerful upholstery on antique chairs. Everything seemed perfectly proportioned but slightly miniaturized, the illusion heightened as both she and Ned were tall. A portrait of the Chapin family hung above the living room couch: four boys with hair ranging from auburn to strawberry blond.

They stood in the living room, before a broad window, gazing out at Ned's rose garden. She told him of Bea's seeming indifference about her future and her own frustration at Bea's lack of effort. "Bea has an opportunity for a very comfortable life at Beacon House," she told him. "And she's throwing it away, doing absolutely nothing to help herself get it. I've done everything I can."

He gave Lilli a sideways, somewhat assessing, look, and then said, "Come with me. I'd like to show you something." He led her along a path through the rose garden, bees weaving drunkenly among the fragrant blossoms, to the point where a Herreshoff tugged at its mooring just offshore. Lilli, wondering if this could possibly be what he wanted to show her—Herreshoffs here were as common as gulls—smiled politely and said, "Your third?"

"You recognize her?"

Lilli frowned, shaded her eyes, and squinted out at the boat, as though that would make a difference. "Should I?"

"It's the *Loon*."

"Our *Loon*!" Lilli studied the little white boat, bobbing in the sunshine. *Could be.*

"I found her . . . in a boatyard a few years ago. She was in pretty rough shape."

"Amazing. Why did you buy her?"

He squinted out toward the boat. "We share a history. I couldn't just leave her there. Some things are worth a little effort."

Lilli looked out across the sun-dazzled water.

"Look at the water. It's starfish."

"That's not starfish, silly. It's phosphorescence."

"It should be called starfish. Let's make a wish for good luck."

"You wish on stars, Dori . . ." "Not starfish." Lilli finished her thought aloud, and Ned glanced at her, puzzled. Then he nodded and walked over to the rose garden, pulled a pair of small scissors from his pocket, and snipped off a few fading blooms.

Lilli watched him before shifting her gaze back to the *Loon*. She pictured that perfect rectangle, conveniently weed-free, behind the garage. It was just the size and shape of a boat in a cradle. "Bea and Randall were having financial difficulties. Did you know that?" she asked.

Ned silently studied the spent roses in his hand.

"You didn't find the *Loon* in a boatyard, did you?"

He snipped a fresh rose and began trimming the thorns from the stem. "She'd been dry-docked behind the house for years. I thought she deserved a better end. It's a hobby of mine."

"Rescuing old friends?"

"Restoring old boats." He snipped a few more blooms from the rosebushes. "Didn't take too much to bring her back. She'd been cared for very lovingly in her day. Makes all the difference." Ned handed Lilli the bouquet of roses. "You missed my talk at the garden club. The ladies were enthralled."

Lilli gazed down at the blossoms, each unfolding in layered perfection. "These are beautiful." Then she added, "I've never had much luck growing things. Anyway, I prefer painting them. It's more predictable. My gardens always look exactly as I want. The right balance, symmetry, intensity. If there's too much blue, I add a little red and, voilà, the flower becomes violet." *Impertinence*, Lilli suddenly thought, remembering that long-ago day in the garden with Randall when he'd renamed all the colors. Indeed.

"If perfection's what you're after . . ." Ned chuckled and returned the scissors to his pocket. "Don't take up gardening. Even if you manage to get it 'perfect' one year, the next year the lilies are too big, or the irises bloom a week early, or the rain knocks down the poppies and peonies right at their peak."

"So your garden's never finished. I paint a garden until it's just the way I want it, then I stop and put it in a frame. The lilies will always bloom with the foxglove. Peonies are always at their peak."

"I like a little uncertainty. Things change, but that's life, isn't it? We do what we can and leave the rest to Mother Nature. Honestly, I like the process every bit as much as the product."

Lilli pointed to the spent roses in Ned's hand. "My roses never fade."

Ned smiled and took her arm, and they walked back to the house. "So, in Lilli's garden, nothing ever dies. That's a very special gift."

She thought about this as she followed him into the kitchen, where he'd set a small table with a cloth spangled with violets, matching napkins, bone-china plates, gleaming silverware, and crystal glasses. She was about to respond but was silenced by the sight of one of her paintings—delphinium, pale yellow coreopsis, and splashes of red poppy against gray fieldstone, a sliver of water and a single white sail in the background. She felt a bit uncomfortable, as though discovering that she and Ned had a mutual close friend and wondering what that friend might have revealed about her. She understood, as she studied the painting, why switching to oils had been so challenging. Watercolors have a dreamy quality, inviting reflection as though they were painted, and meant to be viewed, in the past tense. Oils are much more present, demanding the immediate engagement of artist and viewer. She also understood, as she stared, that her gardens never died because they were never alive. This jogged a dim memory, faint and fleeting, like the distant slamming of an upstairs door.

"It brings me great joy, especially in the winter," Ned was saying, following her gaze. He filled a vase with water, added the roses he'd cut, and placed them in the center of the table. "Just until you leave. They don't like to be out of water too long. Not like your flowers." Lilli glanced at him to see if he was teasing, wondering if he had somehow read her mind, prepared to defend herself. But he was looking at her painting, not at her, and his expression was one of pure admiration.

After lobster salad, croissants, and fresh strawberries from his greenhouse, Ned wrapped Lilli's roses in a dampened paper towel and sealed them in a plastic bag for her, and she set off for home. She wanted to return his luncheon invitation, but as she walked down his long drive, bordered by glistening hostas and rhododendron covered in showy purple flowers, not a weed in sight, she couldn't picture entertaining him in the gloomy dining room or on the faded, unreliable wicker of the sunporch, gazing through grimy windows to the weed-choked yard. She decided instead to invite him out to lunch.

Lilli had been waiting for the right time to talk with Bea about her finances, which seemed every bit as dire as Charlotte foretold. But the right time hadn't occurred. Lilli thought it very generous of Ned to help out Bea and Randall, and in such an unobtrusive way. But perhaps a conversation would not be necessary, as the money from the sale of the house would pay for someone to care for Bea during her stay in the nursing home, if that was where she ended up, which now seemed likely. "Her stay"—the euphemism seemed as obvious as the old stump in your yard that you tell yourself you can make into something useful and lovely. It was obvious that Bea's stay was permanent and would be followed only by her death and a six-foot hole beside the others in the cemetery, marked by a matching marble headstone and more choking ivy.

Lilli sighed, determined to put these thoughts from her mind and enjoy the still-warm afternoon and the scent of fresh-cut grass that filled the air at the foot of the Chapins' drive. She turned the corner and came upon a young man loading a lawn mower onto a utility trailer hitched to a truck. *Sylvia's Landscaping & Nursery* was painted in bold red-and-green letters on its door. Lilli stared at the youth with his curly dark hair. He looked up, caught Lilli staring, and said, "Anne Morrow Lindbergh, isn't it?"

"Excuse me?"

"The roses. Mr. Chapin's prize-winners?"

"Is this your truck?"

He gave the strap a final tug. "Yes, ma'am. You need your lawn mowed?"

"Are . . . are you Mr. Sylvia?"

His grin widened. "Technically. But most everybody calls me Joey."

Lilli recalled her conversation with Bea before she'd left in a huff for Boston and Bea had made her fateful trip to the greenhouse. "Call Mr. Sylvia," Lilli had mimicked, thinking of Giuseppe from her childhood. Lilli hadn't considered the possibility of another Mr. Sylvia. "I knew a Giuseppe Sylvia years ago."

"My grandpa. He used to work for some families around here. Then he started a nursery in the late sixties. My Dad, Ernie, still runs it. I started the landscaping business about ten years ago. Kinda went full circle, I guess." He grinned, and Lilli could see clearly the man with the halting English who'd marked his place in *Little Women* with a seed pod, kept the shrubs around the house trimmed to a manageable size, and placed potted mums around their yard in the fall, before tucking the big pots carefully *under* the potting bench for winter. "You live around here?" he asked.

"No. My sister does. Bea Marsh?"

"Sure, nice lady. Lives across the cove." He shook his head. "Used to do some work for them. They kinda let the place go the past few years." He looked away, fiddled with something on the trailer.

"We're selling it, Joey. I need someone to sort of neaten the place up. You know, prune the lilacs, take down the trees that are blocking the view . . ." Lilli hesitated. What would one call what the gardens needed? "Overhaul the gardens?"

"Oh, that's a real shame. Beautiful property, that one. Wish I could afford it." He gave a self-deprecating laugh at the preposterousness of such an idea. "I'm pretty busy, but I'll see if I can fit you in. I always liked Mrs. Marsh. Always spoke her mind and knew a thing or two about gardens."

"Do you have a card?"

He pulled a stack from his breast pocket and handed her one, a dirty fingerprint stamping the corner. "Sorry about that."

"No, it's fine. It was very nice meeting you, Joey."

"Likewise."

Lilli continued along the road and across the cove, where the sun winked like starfish on the water, and children with plastic pails made castles in the sand. She listened for her mother's voice calling to her from an upstairs window.

Fifteen

ANOTHER week went by and the little card with its dirty thumbprint sat on the edge of the desk by the phone, untouched. Lilli made no further progress in the house. There was so little time, she told herself, between her gallery duties and visits to Bea, who now seemed more likely than ever to qualify for nothing beyond life in a nursing home. Lilli did, however, complete her painting.

The day after she finished, she stopped by the center and found Bea sitting in a wheelchair in her small, sparsely furnished room. The television was on with the sound off. On-screen an audience of mainly women cheered wildly but silently as Ellen DeGeneres interviewed a guest.

"I brought you something." Lilli held out the painting of the house and gardens as they'd looked in the 1950s. She'd used a picture from one of the old photo albums in the desk, its black pages so brittle that bits broke off whenever she handled them and sifted like autumn leaves onto the carpet. Many photographs were missing, leaving only the small paper triangles that had once secured them, bracketing empty spaces, names written carefully beneath, as though the missing subjects—who'd perhaps wandered off somewhere together—might one day return.

In the painting, the house trim gleamed white, and the wisteria dotted the gray shingles in a brilliant periwinkle. All around, gardens bloomed in lemon, ultramarine, magenta, rose, and deep green. Lilli set the painting on the floor, leaning against the dresser.

Bea studied it a long moment. "You've painted every flower blooming all at once."

Lilli had made no effort at realism. She'd wanted to evoke the vitality she recalled from her early childhood, which the house now seemed to lack and to long for. She hadn't achieved exactly what she'd wanted, but had been pleased with the results, as she'd so rarely worked in oil. "Some people might say thank you," she snapped. She hadn't been sleeping well, and her fuse had grown short. "I painted it because I thought it would give you something nice to look at here and"—she took a breath to calm the emotions roiling inside her, threatening to breach—"at Beacon House."

"Beacon House." Bea swiveled around to face Lilli.

"Yes, if you'll make a little effort. Otherwise, a nursing home." *Might as well be blunt.*

Bea considered this as she turned to look once more at the painting. "'Make a little effort?' Why? I don't want to go to Beacon House. Never did." Bea shifted her focus to the silent, animated television screen. "Why did you stay, Lilli? I thought you were due back in London. You couldn't wait to leave when you first arrived. Why is it suddenly so important to you, after all these years, how I'm doing, where I live?"

Lilli studied the painting. *Something was . . . off. Missing. What?*

"What do you want, Lilli?" Bea asked softly.

Want? Lilli considered a moment. She had no idea. Didn't think there were words to describe what could fill up the hollow place inside her that had been there as long as she could remember. She was tired. Tired of drifting through life with no more purpose than a silky tuft of milkweed without its seed, floating, lighter than air. "Release," she said. The word hung between them. As she waited for Bea's response, Lilli felt horribly exposed and wished she could take it back, roll it up like one of Bea's balls of yarn, put it safely in plastic, and store it in the back of a deep closet.

"Release," Bea repeated, and then said it again. "Release?" As if to confirm that she'd heard right. She then appeared to give this word the studied concentration of someone choosing a name for her new baby. "I'd have guessed something closer to revenge."

Lilli hesitated. "It seems a bit late for that now."

"Release from what?"

This conversation, Lilli thought. But she'd come this far, might as well keep going. "Guilt."

Bea stared at her sister, hard. "How can I possibly give you that?" Bea turned to the television. Ellen danced on stage, laughing.

Lilli nodded, relieved, disappointed, and not at all surprised. She picked up the painting and propped it up on the dresser. "Well, then, there's not much else to say, is there?"

"Oh, I think there's a great deal else to say." Bea swiveled back to face Lilli. "It's not that I don't want to 'release' you. It's that I can't. You're the only one who can do that."

Lilli did not wish to be held in Bea's steady blue gaze, so she studied the painting, still wondering what was missing. Out of the corner of her eye she could see Ellen walking through the audience interviewing people. Everyone was laughing, waving, wanting to be chosen.

"You resent me, Lilli. I thought you might have outgrown it, but I saw it in your eyes the very first moment you arrived, as you stood there, assessing the condition of the house, judging me for how I live. By now, I'm sure, you've dug through every inch of the house and found quite a few things that surprised, maybe even shocked you. I've hung on to things because I always believed that someday . . ." She paused a moment, shrugged, and continued, aware, perhaps, that time was limited. ". . . that someday our family would be together again. A silly notion, I guess. But, Lilli, I haven't clung to the past, even though I've kept much of it. I put all the keepsakes away and face forward. You, though, you *act* as though you left everything behind when you moved to Boston, and then Chicago, and New York, and finally England. You crossed an entire ocean to get far, far away from me, White Head, Randall, and . . ." She frowned and took a long breath. "All the unwanted memories. But you brought them all with you, didn't you? I'll bet not a single day goes by that you don't relive the night Dori died, the morning you found Mother. My dear, it's not healthy to dwell too much on what's past. We can't change it. It's all right to glance back, Lilli, but don't stare."

Lilli was now staring at Bea, shocked as much by her candor as by her words, which hit Lilli like the low, bellowing horn that sounded from Pequot Light when the fog rolled in and buried the coast in a dense blanket of white. And then Lilli got angry, angrier than she could ever remember being, her feelings and memories appearing as though they'd been exposed by a receding tide. "That's easy for you. You were the good one. Older. Always right. Always the victor." Lilli ran her fingers along the painting, liking the feel of the uneven surface, perhaps hoping for inspiration. *What was missing?* "And you've won again. You're right, again. I've relived that evening with Dori probably a thousand times over the years." And suddenly Lilli felt as though a talk show host were holding out her microphone to her, and she were about to confess her sins to a television audience of millions. Her voice dropped to a whisper. "It would have been so easy to say, 'No, Dori, it's too late for a row. Let's go home and look for Russian subs . . .'" She paused. "Russian subs. Jesus." She took a breath and continued, "'. . . from the rocks below the house.' And we'd go home and—" Lilli stopped.

"And what?" Bea said. "Dori lives, so Mother doesn't kill herself, and you marry Randall and—?" She broke off here, staring at Lilli, challenging. *Your move.*

Lilli had the sense that she'd somehow gotten distracted, and the conversation had taken an unintended turn. She wanted to turn it back, but the television audience seemed to be waiting, hungry for the big reveal. "And . . . ?" Lilli prompted, wanting Bea to finish her sentence so Lilli wouldn't have to.

"And live happily ever after," Bea finished, clearly disappointed in Lilli. She glanced at the television, picked up the remote, and shut it off.

"Live happily ever after?" Lilli pressed, the now-dark

screen of the television making her feel very alone. Her chest was tight, and a light sweat had broken out on her upper lip. She wondered if she was having a heart attack, briefly amused by the irony if she and Bea were to end up here together.

Bea looked annoyed. "With Izzy. There, I said it. That's the guilt you want me to release you from. What you want my forgiveness for, isn't it? The reason you came back?"

Lilli had been desiring, dreading, avoiding, and planning this moment for nearly forty years. Now it was here. "How long have you known?"

Bea turned her chair to look out the window. The view wasn't much: parking lot, a thin strip of lawn where someone had planted pansies. The flowers, with their silly, smiling faces, looked as though they were trying to make the most of a bad situation. "Lilli, you never gave me much credit in the brains department, but this really didn't take a genius to unravel. You follow Charlotte and Graham to Chicago and, nine months after their wedding, with Charlotte in medical school and having told me in no uncertain terms that they were going to wait—they have a baby. Well, I know these things sometimes happen. But I saw you run up the drive the night of Charlotte's wedding, tears streaming down your face, and then Randall, looking like he'd just won the club championship, leave the greenhouse. It was rather obvious. Even so, I didn't *know* until I saw Izzy. Sturdy Charlotte and flat-footed, myopic Graham could simply never have produced that child. Look at their twins! R. J. and David are charming, but one could hardly call them handsome. No, my dear, Izzy, with her long legs, her dark complexion, her thick hair—Gypsies, isn't that what Mother used to say about the two of you?—is your spitting image. Except her eyes. Those are the exact color of Randall's. When she visited us, it was like having you home again, Lilli. Like you, she was always galloping about, so busy chasing her dreams that she missed some of the best things along the way." Bea turned her chair so she could see the painting. "Besides, Charlotte is a terrible liar. So unlike the two of us."

For a moment Lilli couldn't speak. Then, "Why didn't you say anything?" she whispered.

"Me? It wasn't mine to tell. I told you it's best to share secrets, but only if they're yours. I don't know whether Randall ever knew. I certainly wasn't going to tell him. He wasn't the most observant of men. Not where family was concerned. He had an eye for the women, make no mistake, but in this case he was blind. I suppose we all are when there's something right in front of us that we simply can't bear to see." She fixed her gaze on Lilli. "And why didn't *you* say anything?"

"Like what? I made love with your husband, am carrying his child, and now I want him?"

Bea considered this. "Depending on the day and my mood, I might have said he's all yours."

"Not funny." Lilli stared at the painting. *Why had she made it so cheerful?* "I was devastated when you married him, Bea. How could you? You must have known how I felt about him."

"You think I married him to spite you, or to win some sort of contest that you seem determined to think I was always waging between us. Well, if that was the case then I'd say I got exactly what I deserved. Here's the truth, Lilli, plain and simple. I . . . needed to hang on to the house—to my family, our family, what was left of it. There was a time when I thought about selling, moving into Boston, having—" She folded her arms. "This house was my duty. This family was my duty. You had your painting, dreams, ambitions. Talent. Charlotte had Graham, her medical career. I had . . ." Bea sighed, unfolded her arms, and stared at her hands. "You are right about one thing, I cannot maintain that house alone. Couldn't then, can't now. Randall wanted to live there. He wanted us to just *live together.* I was shocked!" She smiled, mocking her own innocence. "I finally agreed. But only if we got married. I always thought Charlotte and Graham would come back east after medical school. But they never did. And I figured that you'd be in Boston or New York and would come up to visit, eventually marry and have children—Why didn't you?"

"I thought it would be unfaithful."

Bea snorted. "To Randall? That's setting the bar rather low."

"No, unfaithful to Izzy. I had to give her up but I didn't have to replace her. Couldn't. It was the same with Randall, in a way. Although, after that night, I never felt quite the same about him. The safe place he'd always seemed to offer was gone."

Bea sighed and shook her head. "I knew you . . . cared for Randall. But I also knew what sort of man he was and that you didn't. I loved him, too, in my way. We made a good team. I figured I'd let him do what he wanted—drink and chase women—and he'd help me maintain the house. I thought he'd change, of course. But, he didn't. Even so, I kept my end of the bargain. For a while, I honestly thought we could make a go of it. Don't thank me, Lilli, but I did you a favor marrying him. I don't suppose you want to hear that."

Lilli raised an eyebrow.

"No, I didn't think so. Well, I could apologize—I do apologize—but consider this: On the second night of our honeymoon, Randall told me he was going out for cigarettes. Two hours later I get a phone call from the bartender of the place next door. Randall, drunk, thought he was in the hotel, and had racked up quite a bill, which he was trying to charge to our room. I had to go down and bail him out. Which is pretty much what I did for the next forty years. Or not. Sometimes I let him figure it out for himself. Or let his *amour du jour* pay. You weren't his first and certainly not his last. Randall had certain . . . appetites, which I did not share. Did you notice how many more women there were at his funeral than men?"

Bea rolled her chair closer to the dresser and studied the painting. "Well, you make your bed, you lie in it. What I hoped for never happened and seems unlikely to now. Maybe you do know best. Go ahead and sell the house. That's what you're planning, isn't it?"

Lilli remained silent.

"You know what else I was waiting for all this time? This seems to be my day to unburden myself. A secret *I've* never shared. I've been waiting all these years for my childhood to start." She glanced at Lilli, her blue eyes carrying an expression that Lilli had so rarely seen there before: uncertainty. "You look surprised. You're always so quick to remind me that I'm only nine years older than you. But I'm not. I'm much, much older. Have been right from the beginning. I was the one to take your hand crossing the street and to make sure you and Dori didn't boil yourselves alive in the tub. Give you some structure and rules. I always felt responsible for you. Mother and Daddy, God bless them, Daddy was a perpetual child thanks to Grandmother. And Mother, well, her 'artistic temperament' . . . Always up for a dance in Boston, a party on the rocks, and you two little ones up to who knows what. Out late spying on them. You think I didn't know? Anything could have happened to you. Did, of course, finally, to Dori."

"Your worst fear, and it was my fault."

"Wrong again." Bea knit her arthritic fingers together. "That wasn't my worst fear. And I never blamed you, Lilli. It was my fault. I should have known that you wouldn't be able to resist going to that dance. No one could resist Randall. I was the one who persuaded Mother not to let you. I knew Randall had his eye on you. He was so terribly charming and handsome, and you were growing up so fast and becoming so beautiful. There I was, small and bony and pinched. Why would he have chosen me? It all seems so silly and pointless now.

"I needed him. And I did think, for a while after we married, that we'd have a life together. Maybe, once you moved to London, we'd go visit you, since you didn't seem inclined to visit us." Again her eyes assumed a vulnerable look that seemed to Lilli terribly misplaced. "You know I've never been in an airplane?" She turned back to the painting, wheeled herself a bit closer and appeared to study it, but Lilli saw her swipe a tear from her cheek. She didn't remember ever having seen Bea cry. Lilli tried to think of all the accusations she'd wanted to hurl at Bea over the years and couldn't come up with one.

They sat in silence for a while, until Bea spoke again. "No, my worst fear was that you'd both be lost. And then, of course, you were." She reached out and ran her hand over the surface of the painting, perhaps wondering what Lilli had felt there, what she'd been searching for.

Lilli felt drained. The way she sometimes felt when she'd labored over a painting for weeks only to have it turn out all wrong. *Small, bony, pinched? Never blamed me? Waiting for her childhood to begin?* Lilli sat down in a nearby chair, not trusting herself to speak but knowing that she must. "It wasn't just Randall, or Izzy, or Dori, or Mother. They're not the only reasons I didn't come home. You thought you were taking care of us, Bea, and maybe you were, but I felt like I spent my whole childhood standing in your shadow. I had to go that far away to get out of it. To find some sunlight."

Bea turned once again to face Lilli, the steel back in her eyes. "Oh, there you go again, Lilli. Did you find the sunlight?"

Lilli could now feel tears prickling her own eyes. She shook her head and looked down.

"Of course not. That wasn't my shadow you were standing in. It was yours. Turn around, Lilli, the shadow will disappear." Bea looked back at the painting. "It's funny that this is how you remember it. I don't recall it nearly so bright and colorful."

"I'm sorry, Bea," Lilli whispered before walking out.

On the drive home it came to her what the painting was missing. People.

WHEN LILLI ARRIVED at the house she was surprised to see the Sylvia's Landscaping & Nursery truck parked in the driveway. The forsythia by the kitchen door had been pruned, as had the evergreens that barricaded the back of the house. They'd reduced the lilac hedge by half. She walked through the widened opening and was stunned by the sight of Ned Chapin's house on the opposite shore, people picnicking below on the beach, waves lapping Big-big, and, in the distance, a small fleet of white sails. A man was brush-hogging the last of the tangle of bittersweet, honeysuckle, grapevine, and spindly maples and poplars that had once been their mother's garden and had lined up several of her sculptures, buried for years and now huddled at one end of the yard, like refugees seeking asylum.

The man with the brush hog spotted her, waved, killed the engine, and walked over with his hand extended. "Ms. Niles?"

He, too, had Giuseppe Sylvia's curly hair and engaging smile.

"Tony Sylvia. Hope you don't mind we got started. Joey had a pretty good idea what you wanted from what you told him, and we had a cancellation. Seize the moment, you know? Once we get the brush cleared, you want us to rototill some flower beds, or just reseed the whole thing to lawn? We got a lot a good stock at the nursery." He seemed both eager and uncertain, perhaps thrown by Lilli's damp face and teary eyes.

Lilli glanced to the far end of the yard, where the tilting garden arch had collapsed. The old rose vines, it seemed, were all that had held it up. A fresh salty breeze rose from the cove, where the sun sparkled on the water like starfish.

"Do you sell garden arches?" she asked.

L ILLI pulled the old white Mercedes up to the curb in front of Beacon House, checked her hair in the rear-view mirror, and hurried up a path bordered by petunias and impatiens, now leggy in the August heat. As she clattered up the steps and crossed the porch she heard a familiar voice call out, "Yoo-hoo! Looking for someone?" Bea was sitting in a rocker, her purse clutched in her lap, a walker by her side. Lilli was surprised to see her out there. She'd been at Beacon House for several weeks, but this was the first time she'd graced the porch.

"I'm sorry, I'm a bit late."

Bea checked her watch. "I still don't see why we have to get there so early. It's not as though we're the ones getting married." She reached for her walker.

"Are you sure you wouldn't be more comfortable in a wheelchair, Bea?"

"I probably would. But I simply refuse to be wheeled about like a tray of hors d'oeuvres at your daughter's wedding."

"Bea, we talked about that. Izzy cannot know—"

"I know, I know. Put that thing here in front of me."

Lilli did not want to argue about this, or anything else, today, so she positioned the walker in front of her sister, helped her out of her chair, and shuffled alongside, trying to hide her impatience as Bea made her slow passage along the length of the porch toward the ramp. "What if we just use a wheelchair to get you to the car?" Lilli suggested.

Bea never broke stride. "I need to make a little effort, I've been told, if I ever want to be free of this thing."

Lilli bit her lip.

"The wedding is not for another two hours, Lilli. I'm sure I can get there by then."

"Yes, but there's a little something I want to do before the wedding." Lilli had thought two hours would be plenty of time. Suddenly she wasn't so sure. Then again, once they got to the car—*if* they got to the car; three minutes had passed and they were only halfway down the ramp—the rest wouldn't require much walking.

Bea paused and looked at Lilli. "What would that be?" she asked, her tone suspicious.

Lilli pretended she hadn't heard and walked ahead to open the car door. With some shuffling and fumbling, they installed Bea in the front seat and her walker in the back. "I'm going to drive again one day, you know," Bea said.

"Are you now?" Lilli pulled away from the curb, did a U-turn, and headed for the harbor.

"This is not the way to the White Head Inn, Lillianne."

"I know."

Bea stared ahead, her brow pinched in concern. They approached the yacht club. "I saw the damnedest thing just before you arrived." Bea scanned the harbor. "There."

A seaplane was making its way between the boats as they pulled into the parking lot. "Wait here," Lilli commanded, and walked over to the top of the gangway and watched as the plane completed its taxi to the dock. A young man opened the door, jumped down, and secured the plane. Dexter Parmenter greeted him, and the two shook hands. Dexter turned and spotted Lilli, waved, and bounded up the gangway. She pointed back to the car, where they could see Bea peering through the windshield. Dexter headed over, opened the door, helped her out, and then swept her into his arms and carried her down to the float.

"What's all this?" she demanded, but her tone held an edge of excitement that she couldn't quite disguise.

"We have some unfinished business," Lilli said.

Dexter handed Bea up to the pilot, now inside the plane, and then helped Lilli aboard.

Bea sat, wide-eyed and, for once, silent as the plane taxied slowly back out through the harbor and into open water. The pilot pushed the throttle, and the plane surged forward, sending out big plumes of salt spray. Bea clutched the armrests and said nothing, but her eyes were bright with tears.

The plane lifted and made a wide circle over the Harbor View Motel, with its row of Adirondack chairs facing the harbor and the stony beach. They flew over boats in the channel, those on deck craning to watch this unusual spectacle. The plane headed up the coast, over Ned Chapin's house and the *Loon*, anchored off the point and strung with signal flags in a colorful salute to this journey for an old friend. They passed over Sandy Cove, where bright striped towels dotted the beach. Bea had her face pressed to the glass, looking down at the white-topped tables on the newly sodded lawn surrounding her house, the freshly planted gardens, the rose-covered arch. Caterers in black and white moved among the tables, setting places and anchoring the tablecloths with rocks. Nearby, two wide columns of chairs stood in neat rows. Someone, it looked to Lilli like one of the twins, was tying on blue ribbons. He looked up at the sound of the plane's engine overhead, turned, and called to the others, and soon Charlotte, Izzy, Matumbé, and Graham had joined him on the wide green lawn, all waving madly.

"Oh, Lilli," Bea breathed. "What have you done?"

"Joey and Tony Sylvia did most of it," Lilli said casually.

Bea turned and looked at her. "You called Mr. Sylvia, eh?"

"You let me know when," the pilot shouted over the noise of the engine. Lilli pointed to Pequot Light, rising straight and solemn-looking from the Atlantic. He nodded, and the plane banked away from shore, circling the lighthouse, decreasing in altitude, until it skimmed just above the surface of the water. He leaned over and opened the door, and Lilli removed a shoe box from a handled shopping bag, and lifted the top. "Would you like to do the honors, or shall I?"

"Be my guest," Bea said.

Lilli upended the box. The ashes caught in the backwash of the propellers and swirled into the air before falling to the sea.

"Not sure he deserved all this," Bea said, watching them fall.

"No, but we did."

Bea turned her head back to the window, but not before Lilli caught her smile.

* * *

When they arrived at the house, Izzy rushed out to greet them with Matumbé in tow. Bea frowned her disapproval. "The groom is not supposed to see the bride before the—" She stopped abruptly at the sight of her niece in Charlotte's dress, which didn't have to be taken in as much as Lilli had thought, given that Izzy was now five months pregnant with the future Niles Bottomley Ojukwu. "Well," was all Bea said. "Well, well."

Izzy gave her a big hug. "We saw you up there. Did you see us waving? Was it fun? Not the sprinkling, I imagine that was rather gruesome, but the flight? Oh! What do you think?" She gestured around at the house and yard. "Do you like your new gardens? Come see what Aunt Lilli's done inside." She shot off toward the kitchen door.

"Can't someone give the child a Valium?" Bea whispered. "Oh, I suppose not in her condition. Pity." Charlotte, who had joined them in the driveway, took Bea's arm, and they walked to the ramp leading to the kitchen door, wide enough now for a wheelchair. Lilli followed with the walker.

The kitchen was still being renovated, but Lilli had stenciled ivy on three of the newly painted walls. On the fourth she'd painted a mural of a garden. They walked through widened doorways into the dining room, the living room, and den, converted now to a bedroom. Gone were the desk, sagging armchair, stacks of magazines, and metal television tables. The Sylvias had pruned the lilacs, and Lilli had had the room painted buttercup yellow, and put Indian shutters in the windows. Light streamed onto the canopy bed, the dollhouse now standing on the dresser, and a portrait Lilli had painted from the photograph of the four sisters seated on the overturned rowboat. A door connected the bedroom to a full bath, where the old powder room once stood. Bea was silent during the entire tour.

"I haven't quite finished the upstairs," Lilli said. "It will be another month or so."

Bea nodded, blinking rapidly.

A string quartet began to play outside. "Oh, heavens," said Izzy. "They're starting."

"Not without us, they're not," said Bea, finding her voice. "Would someone be kind enough to escort me to my seat?"

Charlotte and Lilli each took an arm, and the three walked back through the living room to the sunporch—where the repotted azalea was putting on a brilliant, if somewhat lopsided show—down the short ramp and onto the soft green lawn, rimmed by beds of lilies, zinnias, cleome, and foxglove, inside whose bell-shaped flowers bumblebees rumbled drunkenly as they gathered pollen. Daisies nodded in the breeze, as though keeping time to the music. The three women proceeded down the aisle and took their seats in the front row, beside Graham, R. J., and David, and across the aisle sat a dozen of Matumbé's relatives, many in colorful dashikis. A minister stood before a new arch covered with climbing yellow roses, thanks to Ned, who'd smiled at Lilli from the second row as she passed by and took her seat. The quartet began the wedding march, and Izzy appeared, arms linked with Matumbé. Bea whispered, as Lilli helped her to her feet, "Really, Lillianne. Yellow roses? The red look much better."

Lilli just smiled, as she turned and watched Izzy walk down the aisle.

Her Sister's Shadow

Discussion Questions

1. What did you think of Lilli when she was first introduced? Did your opinion of her change as the novel progressed?

2. What was your reaction when Lilli and Bea reunited after forty years? Did you anticipate a more emotional reunion? How would you have reacted in that situation if you were Lilli? If you were Bea?

3. On page 74 Lilli purchases an azalea for Bea—something that would brighten up the house and cheer her up. Bea doesn't seem to appreciate the gesture and informs Lilli that they usually purchase their plants at another store. What was your reaction to Bea's dismissiveness? What do you think was underlying Bea's reaction?

4. Discuss the differences between Lilli and Dori's relationship, Lilli and Charlotte's relationship, and Lilli and Bea's relationship. How do each of these relationships differ? Why do you think they differ so significantly?

5. "Adults could stay up past midnight, drinking and singing

at clambakes on the beach. Adults could take the train into Boston whenever they wished and spend the day chatting in smoke-filled rooms and riding on trolley cars. Ladies could wear gowns, lipstick, and high heels, put their hair up, and waltz at the yacht club with Randall Marsh. Adults could make their own decisions. How could anyone think childhood was idyllic with all this waiting? Lilli wished her childhood well past" (page 96). What causes her to feel this way? While growing up, did you ever share Lilli's attitude toward childhood? Do you ever wish you could be a child again?

6. What was your reaction to Blythe's suicide? What was her mental state before Dori's death? Why do the daughters decide never to refer to their mother's death as a suicide?

7. Lilli recalls her mother telling her that "true love always comes with the potential for heartbreak" (page 123). Do you agree with this statement? Does the statement ring true for Lilli?

8. In Chapter Ten Bea announces that she and Randall have married. What was your reaction to this? Do you think Lilli really loved Randall? What do you think are his reasons for marrying Bea?

9. "'Life's a journey, Lilli, not a race.' Bea's voice was low, as though she had said this many times before and was tired of repeating it. . . . This sister who had made everything in life a competition was giving up" (pages 313–314). Is this a philosophy you agree with? Do you think Lilli lived by this

creed? Did Bea? What are some ways a person can appreciate the journey of life every day?

10. The novel begins with Randall's funeral and fills in details of his life as the story progresses. How do you feel about Randall in the end? Do you think his feelings for Bea and Lilli were genuine?

11. Throughout the novel, the story moves between the past and the present. Why does the author do this? What knowledge do you gain by the story being told in this format? Did you find that this style provides you with a better understanding of the characters?

12. Imagine Lilli's life after the novel. How do you think it unfolds? What role does her past play in that life?

13. Discuss the title of this novel. Who is it referring to?